HARMONIA

A.L. HAWKE

PHANTOM HEART, LLC

ISBN: 978-1-953919-44-1 (ebook)

ISBN: 978-1-953919-47-2 (paperback)

ISBN: 978-1-953919-53-3 (hardback)

Library of Congress Control Number: 2023945400

This is a work of fiction. It comes directly from the author's imagination. The book also includes fictitious names, characters, places, and incidents. Any public names are used solely for creative purposes. Any resemblance to actual people, living or dead, or to companies, institutions, or locales is entirely coincidental or accidental.

Line edited by Stephanie Marshall Ward

Proofread by Alexa B., alexabooks.wixsite.com/authors

Cover, Ancestry Chart & Map © 2023 by Sean Counley

Published by Phantom Heart, LLC

27702 Crown Valley Pkwy D-4, #201

Ladera Ranch, CA 92694, USA

Printed and bound in the United States of America

First printing September, 2023

Learn more about A.L. Hawke at www.alhawke.com

Correspondence: contact@alhawke.com

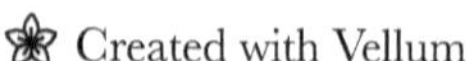 Created with Vellum

THE AMBROSIA DYNASTY

The Amazon nymphs of Azure Blue lived longer life spans than humans.
Legend claims Queen Danaë lived for over three centuries. This family tree spans over half a millennium.

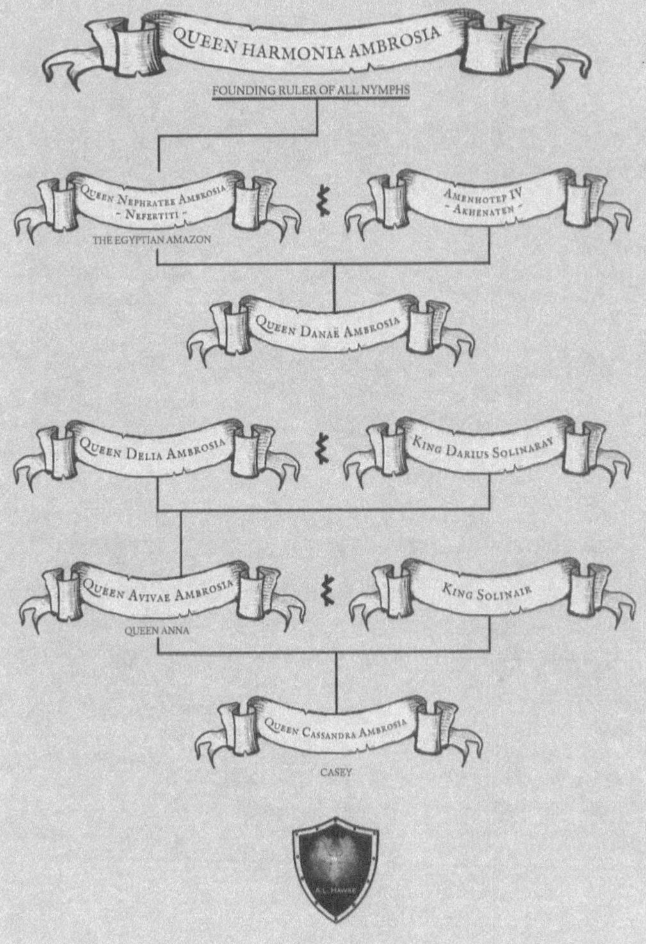

ARBITUS PYRAMID
NAPEA
Azurea
Hellena
SHADOW FOREST
AZBRANTH
CRYSTAL LAKE
LOGENCI
THE CONTINENT OF ATAIA
1350BC
Str

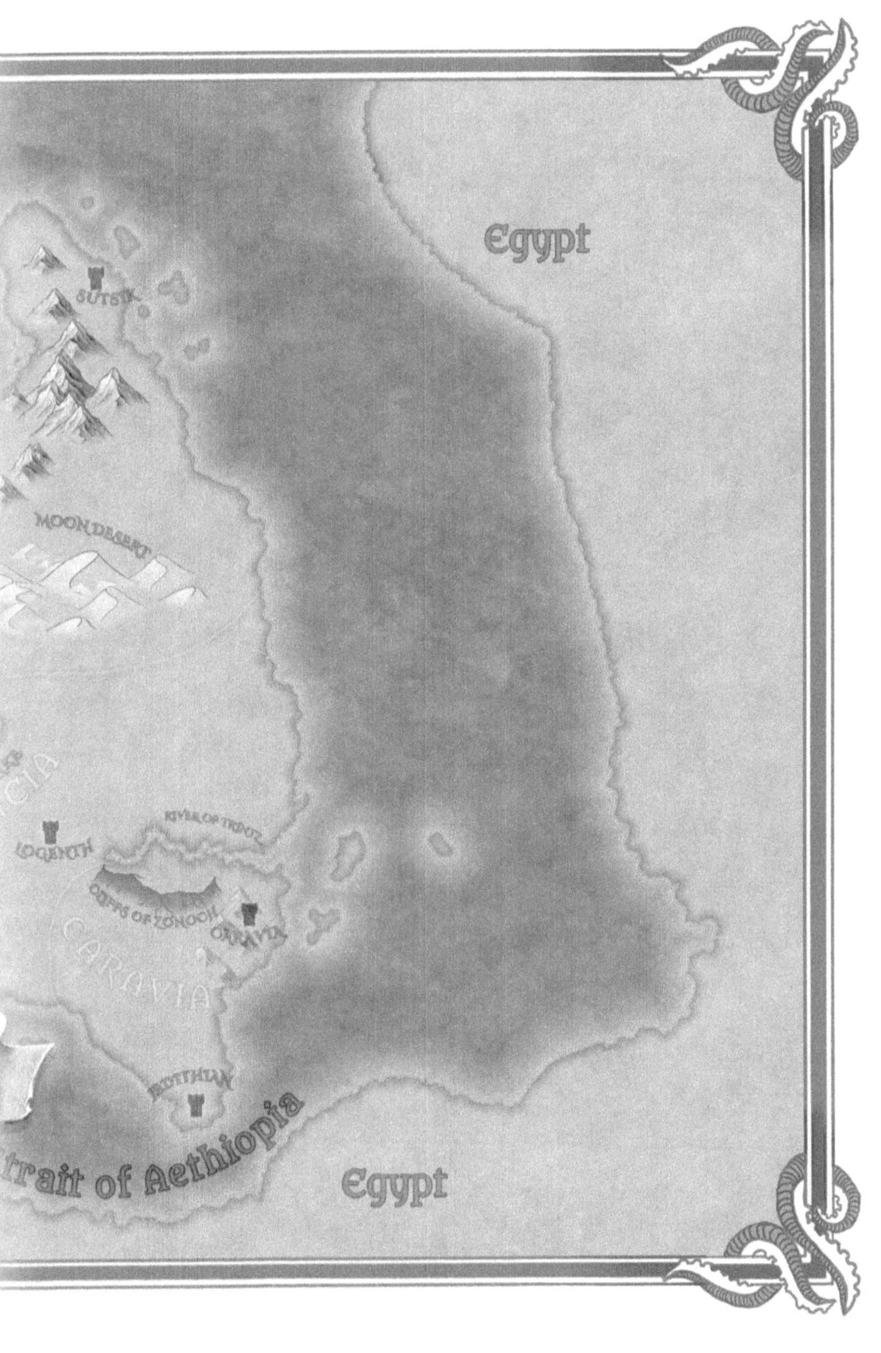

SUTSIX
MOON DESERT
RIVER OF TROTZ
LOGENIH
OPPS OF ZONOOH
OKAVIX
CARAVIA
KOITHIAN
Strait of Aethiopia
Egypt
Egypt

1

TEMERITY

Harmonia could not take her eyes off the shiny red ruby held in her blue palm. She brought it up to her nose, smelled its sweet wine aroma, and ran a blue finger over the red leaves. It was more wonderful than anything she had ever imagined. She brought the hard skin up to her lips, kissed it, then pulled the flesh with her teeth, licking and sucking the juices as they dripped down her chin and trickled down her neck. Her tongue ran along all the perfect tiny rubies inside, biting the piquant seeds. Then she dug around the red-stained white meat, sweeping inside with her blue fingers to get out the rest of the treasure. As the juices dripped down her naked chest, it was only then that she thought of her predicament.

Rays of turquoise crept under the great Ambitus Pyramid of Azure Blue. Still in a crouched position, snapping her head left and right, she searched for intruders. She pulled out her knife from a sheath on the animal hide around her waist. She would be less visible in the shadow of night, but still discoverable. She'd have to act fast.

Was the fruit so wonderful because it was forbidden? The sea god, Poseidon, had forbidden nymphs to cross beyond the Blue River. So it wasn't just that the myrle berry was fresh and sweet. That's not what made the berry special. It was impermissible.

When she didn't see an intruder, she sheathed her knife and bit into more of the flesh of the fruit, savoring the red juice and making more of a mess on her body. She didn't rise from a squatting position in the myrle berry grove until she had completely devoured her delicious ruby. Finally, when she had had her fill, she stood over the blue brush.

Running her fingers through her long black hair, pulling it back from her eyes, she gazed back toward the setting green sun. The gilded Ambitus Pyramid towered above her home. The structure was so large that it looked like a solid wall touching the clouds. She watched as the turquoise sun fell below the wall of gold.

A calm breeze blew. As the green rays completely faded, it became cold and dark and she yearned for the shelter of her tree canopy.

That's when she heard footsteps. Twigs snapped and leaves stirred. She fell back in a squatting position under the leaves.

Four little people, dwarfs known as Mandrigel, trotted small white horses through the trees. They dragged a cart with a fallen deer. A spear jutted out of their kill. The dwarfs wore drab gray tunics with long beards and bald heads. Their skin was a darker blue than hers, almost purple, but they had the same bright azure blue eyes she had. There was no time to run.

"Aieee!" Harmonia cried, jumping from the bushes. "*Biltrie belew negotraie! Aieee! Aieee!*"

"What have you done?" cried one, looking up at her. "You trespass on our grounds?"

"*Bachee. Bachee.*"

"You can explain yourself to the king!" said another, brandishing his dagger. But if she surrendered, their king would kill her. According to their edict, to avoid repeating the battle that had taken place a century ago, justice for her violation would be execution.

"Aieee!" she cried again, shaking her head and swinging her knife.

She charged them. The closest Mandrigel tried to step back, but her blade cut his flesh deeply. He cried out and blood flowed from his arm. She used her knife to strike again at his belly. He fell. Then she aimed at the face of another but missed. She tripped. One of the dwarfs pounced on her, rolling with her over the ground. Being bigger, she easily pinned him down and drew the knife across his throat.

Another dwarf grabbed the long metal spear that was jutting from the fallen blue deer. He lunged at her, and the spear chafed her left arm. She squinted wickedly. The dwarf put his hand up with bulging eyes. That's when the last dwarf jumped her from behind; then he was hanging from her neck. She pinned the bulging-eyed dwarf under her and quickly sliced his throat. Then she stood tall with the last dwarf still hanging on her back, shaking and choking her. She tried to throw him off, but he clung tightly. One more throw and he fell.

She and the last remaining dwarf stared at the spear lying on the ground only a few yards away. She scrambled through the mud and blue-green leaves for it. After grabbing it, she hurled it in the air, caught it, and thrust the long blade into the chest of her last victim. Then she hunched over her kill with her hands on her knees, panting.

She searched the orchard. Everything had turned quiet so fast. But the moon was bright, and the stars were getting brighter.

She heard whimpering. It wasn't a stranger, it was her. Looking down at the four small fallen bodies filled her with disgust. She had never killed a dwarf. But she hadn't tasted the myrle berry either. She would be hunted. Now they would execute her and hurt her people.

2

HUNGER

Accompanying the rising green sun of Azure Blue, the sound of a salpinx echoed along the valley, a sound that had not been heard for hundreds of years. But it did not come from the dwarfs. Harmonia saw the dwarfs stabbing and wrestling her sisters by their great Blue River. The sound came from above. A gilded chariot rushed down from the golden wall of Ambitus Pyramid. Then it stopped and floated for a moment in the mist and descended slowly onto the battlefield. The chariot was led by four large flying black steeds with fiery eyes and smoke blowing from their nostrils. The charioteer was a giant god, bald, with massive arms, tanned skin, and his shirtless chest displaying a strong physique. Behind him sat two others. The strong male god was Hades. Sitting behind him was a lady with long flowing blond hair and pale skin wearing an elegant white peplos. She was Sara, or Demeter, the grain goddess. The blond girl beside Sara looked like her mother, wearing a smaller version of Sara's dress. She was Cora, the goddess Persephone.

The Olympian gods hovered over the melee along the river, shouting at the two opposing sides to stop fighting.

"Stand aside!" shouted Hades. "Make way!"

Hades jumped off his chariot midair. Then he gestured toward one of the grass clearings beside the river.

"You remain by the trees," Hades said to the dwarfs. "Nymphs, gather in line by the river."

The chariot landed. Sara stepped off with her daughter gracefully, walking—no, gliding—over the blue-green grass in gilded shoes. The pair stepped over dead bodies—both dwarfs and nymphs. Sara held her hand out as if expecting someone to assist her. Cora quickly grabbed her mother's hand, stepping around the bloody bodies beneath them.

All the nymphs were bare-breasted, wearing only animal skins around their waists. Their blue-tinged skin, athletic with rippling muscles, was muddied and bloodied from battle. Many of her enemies wore simple gray or brown tunics. But some of the Mandrigel dwarfs wore shiny white breastplates and pteruges—their ancient armor from the mythical nymph war.

Harmonia stood crouched over a slain dwarf. Her crime with the myrle berry would be discovered. She was finished. But she didn't care so much for herself. She'd die for her family. And she felt pride that her family had fought and died by her side.

Hades' bright azure eyes wandered about and fell upon Harmonia. For a moment, it seemed the king of gods gazed only at her. But then he broke the spell by grabbing a wounded nymph beside him and pushing her in line.

"Line up!" Hades cried. "Everyone arrange yourselves in one line by the river."

After the line formed, Sara approached them, holding her daughter's hand. She gazed at each blue body covered in dirt and blood. Many were so wounded that it pained them to stand.

"Disgusting," Sara muttered, wrinkling her nose. "Smelly. Absolutely disgusting. Witness, Cora, the filth that lies beneath our home."

"Yes, Mother."

Sara approached one of the nymphs beside Harmonia. Her long blond hair was bloodstained, and blood oozed from a terrible wound in her chest. She struggled to breathe. Sara pressed her finger deep into her chest wound, and the nymph collapsed.

"Stand in line!" cried Hades.

Sara laughed and kicked the nymph, who was still lying on the ground. Then she kneeled on the ground and lifted the nymph's head by grasping a fistful of her dark hair. "Let us see your mouth," Sara said with a fake smile. "Come, come. Open." The nymph tried to oblige, but she seemed too weak. Sara grabbed her jaw hard and opened her mouth.

"She'll be dead by nightfall," Hades said, gazing down in pity.

"Dreadful, disgusting, filthy animals." Sara shook her head and dropped the nymph's head on the ground.

"Should Kore help them?" Hades asked.

"I won't!" cried Cora, shaking her head violently. "You can't let Uncle do that, Mother."

"Of course not, child," Sara said calmly. "Calm yourself." She looked down at the fallen nymph, too sick to stand. "Let Moira decide their fate."

"I won't do it, Uncle," Cora cried.

Everything around Harmonia blurred through her tears. The wounded nymph that had been manhandled by the goddess, now lying lifeless during the child's tantrum, was one of her sisters.

"Don't worry, child," Sara said, chuckling. "There will be no healing filthy naiads."

Sara glided away from Harmonia. She methodically checked each mouth. "Open." She had to stand on her toes, for the nymphs were a tall race.

The green sun now shone over the glowing Blue River. There by the shiny water, the dwarfs picked up their dead, even gathering slain nymphs. After checking every mouth, Sara and Cora approached Harmonia again.

"Open," Sara said to Harmonia. "Go ahead, now open your mouth."

Harmonia opened her mouth slightly, showing her teeth. Sara pressed her cheeks hard. It felt like the clutch of the strongest warrior's hands. Sara smiled as she reached in and said, "Now, if you bite, I shall remove your tongue." Sara reached in and swept a finger along her tongue. Then she smelled her finger.

"This is not the smell of blood." Sara squinted at Harmonia with a sly smile. "Not blood at all." Then her smile grew wider, a wicked grin.

"Is this the one, Mother?" Cora asked.

"Yes, child. This is the one."

"Boy, you're gonna get it."

"Is curiosity worth starting a war?" Sara asked Harmonia. Sara gestured to the battlefield. "Was it worth this bloodshed, all for a pomegranate?" She squinted at Harmonia, but Harmonia did not even know what a pomegranate was. "A *myrle berry*, you stupid blue ape." She turned to her brother Hades and clapped her hands. "Bind her. Imada has its source."

Hades came from behind and twisted her hands behind her back. Then he threw a rope around her neck. Some of the nymphs beside her began to cry. Harmonia didn't. She was resigned to her fate.

"Stand tall," Sara ordered, raising a finger. Hades forced her body erect. "Now be careful how you answer me, wood nymph, for if you say the wrong thing..." Harmonia removed a curved knife from its sheath. "I shall cut out your tongue. Do you understand?"

Harmonia nodded.

"Tell me, child, how is it that you have the stains of myrle berries in your mouth? Did one of the little men come and visit you with a gift? Or did you...pick them?"

Harmonia met the goddess's gaze. But she didn't answer. And her silence made Sara's eyes flicker red.

"Hmm!" Sara grabbed her chin hard. "*Speak!*"

"I ate one."

"So then you are to blame for this bloody battle?"

Harmonia shook her head.

"She didn't know!" lied one of the other nymphs. It was Harmonia's older sister, Guila. "She had wandered—"

With incredible speed, Sara ran to Guila. Harmonia had never seen someone move so fast. Then, with a quick turn, Sara broke her sister's neck. Guila fell lifeless to the ground. Harmonia screamed in horror. Many of the other nymphs were sobbing.

All the nymphs stirred. Some further down the line even dared to assume a fighting stance before the gods.

"Stand in line!" thundered Hades. "All of you! Or we shall slay each and every one of you!"

"*It is because of you that your immortal die, is it not?*" cried Sara, standing before Harmonia. "*How many in your immortal family will never open their eyes after this transgression? How selfish. All for the theft of a fruit! A myrle berry. A pomegranate! Do you deny the charge?*"

But Harmonia was staring at her fallen sister, Guila, with tears flowing down her face.

"Hmm?" Sara bent down to meet her eyes. "Are you... crying? Do I see tears? You're fortunate that I don't run a sword through everyone in your clan. Imada forbade you to cross the fields. What is your name, offender?"

"Harmonia."

"Tell Imada why you did it, Harmonia."

But Harmonia wasn't listening. She was staring down at Guila again.

"Answer me!"

Harmonia shook her head.

"Answer your gods, Theoi, Harmonia," echoed Hades gently.

Harmonia finally glanced back at Sara. Then her eyes narrowed. "I was hungry."

Someone gasped. It was the witch-girl goddess. The little girl had her hand over her mouth, staring at Harmonia, snapping her head back and forth between her mother and Hades. Then Sara's eyes burned so red that they flashed Harmonia's face with red light. And then…

Hades burst out laughing. Cora laughed too.

Sara struck Harmonia with her palm. Such a slap from a mortal would just be a hit, but it threw Harmonia out of Hades' tight grasp and to the floor. Then Sara snatched the rope circling Harmonia's neck and dragged her across the mud.

"It's because of you that over a hundred of Cronos's slaves lie dead! It is your actions that led a hundred of your people to lose their lives. All for hunger!? Did you or did you not eat the myrle berry? Admit your guilt again before Lord Cronos and Imada!"

"I already… have," Harmonia said, gasping for air, "Yes. I ate it."

"Yet you don't accept blame?" And Sara tugged the rope hard, forcing Harmonia to gasp again as she dragged her. "Why?"

"Let her speak, Sister," said Hades wearily, walking beside Sara.

Sara released her and Harmonia fell to the ground.

"I ate the fruit." Harmonia looked up, panting. Her neck burned terribly. It felt as if her head had been severed off. "Yes… I did. But no, I do not accept blame. Olympus made that edict. We never agreed. My people never accepted the boundary."

"Imada's law is the law of the world, maiden," replied Hades. "Disobeying Imada is rebellion against Cronos. Rebellion against Cronos is rebellion against everything."

"My people are hungry," Harmonia objected, still choking on the ground. "The small land given to us, on this side of the Blue River, is not enough to sustain us. Not only am I hungry, Lord Hades, we all are."

Many of her sisters murmured in agreement, but it seemed that no one dared speak aloud.

"Liar," Hades said, looking down at her. "You have enough food."

"Why even speak to her!" Sara yanked Harmonia's rope again, pulling her to her knees. Then the goddess dragged her once more, forcing her to claw on the dirt to keep up with her. *"Disturb my peace? All because you were hungry!"* Sara pointed at the dwarfs by the river. More dwarfs had arrived, crossing the river, and they were gathering the dead, stacking the bodies of dwarfs and nymphs. Sara approached a gray-haired dwarf with a long beard, his white armor adorned with necklaces of gold and rubies. His white breast plate and pteruges were splashed crimson. His bearded face was covered in mud and grime. The old man bowed deeply. Then all the other dwarfs, even those by the river, fell to their knees.

"King Pangrin," Sara said, "this Napean nymph has been caught stealing myrle berries from your lands. The deaths of your friends are because of her trespass. All because she said she was *hungry*. What say you? What punishment does this thief deserve?"

Harmonia stared up at the old man. Then she was shocked to see him consider the question.

"Banish her," the dwarf said.

"Banish her, Pangrin?" said Hades with a laugh. "How droll. She's responsible for all this death."

"Yes, Lord Hades. But if I am to choose her fate, I ask for banishment."

"But why?"

"Because she came for the myrle berry, but we chased her. She is not the only one to blame for the bloodshed. My men should have tried to capture her with her clan. We should have let her escape and then asked her clan to surrender her for trial. The nymphs are primitive and disorderly, but this one is loved by them. Let her suffer by taking her away from the family that she loves. For a Napean nymph that values family over all else, banishment is far worse than death."

"You fear a martyr?" asked Hades.

"No. I ask for justice. Banishment is just, Orcus."

"One day, Pangrin, you shall die for clemency over ambrosia," said the little witch-girl. The words were inhuman, as if coming from a grown woman. Hades stared at Cora.

When there was more murmuring from the dwarfs, Hades raised his hand.

"Perhaps this solution is acceptable, Sister," Hades said. "Zeus can watch her. And as Pangrin says, their family is their greatest value. Banishment is a hard punishment for a Napean wood nymph."

Sara gazed at her brother in shock. Then she squinted and examined his face. But then...she smiled. And that evil grin made even Hades back up and squirm.

"Cora, child," Sara said, grinning, "return to the chariot. Mother will be with you soon, dear."

Cora looked up, confused, but obeyed. Sara watched her daughter until she sat inside the chariot.

"So it shall be, Brother," Sara replied to Hades. "So it shall be. But her punishment shall remain proper justice for Imada." She jerked up the rope around Harmonia's neck, making her fall to the ground. Harmonia clamored in the mud again before rising to her knees. "It appears this is the only way to get the ingrate to bow." Sara laughed. "Do not rejoice in my decision to let you live, offender. Banishment is not justice in my eyes. But I know what will make this justice.

"Go with her, Brother, back to her family. Bind the nymph's mouth and eyes. Then watch her people. Discover the ones that love her dearly. The first ones to rejoice after hearing of your clemency. Watch those that are happiest with the news of her return. Then take her own curved knife, grab each and every one, and slice their throats. Only the happiest. Will that suit her selfish philautia?"

"No!" Harmonia said, shaking her head desperately. "Kill me!" She looked up at the god known as Hades, meeting his gaze. He furrowed his brow. "Kill me, please. Please. I am to blame. God, please take my life!"

"Kill them by my own hand, Sister?" Hades asked Sara, gazing down at Harmonia.

Sara whirled around and glared at Hades. "This sentence is given by Imada. Their fate was given to me this dawn by our father, Lord Cronos supreme. And Lord Zeus. They will be pleased by my order. Do you question it?"

"No. I question *you*."

"Take me and strike me down!" cried Harmonia. "Please, I would rather die than live through such a disgrace!"

"Now be smart about it, Brother," Sara said to Hades, with a chuckle, glancing down at Harmonia. "She shall feign coldness. Watch those that run to her. Only the ones that love her the most. Then kill them."

Harmonia tried to tackle the goddess. Harmonia punched and kicked Demeter. Sara merely laughed, snatched her wrist, and hurled her to the ground again. "You shall learn submission, nymph, or you will awaken in my brother's depths."

"But that's all I desire, Thesmophoros! Please, sentence me to death, no one else! I tasted the berry, not them! I deserve execution, not them!"

"Unbind her wrists but cover those infernal lips," Sara said, cocking her head back at her brother. "Remember, watch her closely, Orcus. Watch and see who embraces her. See who loves her the most. Then provide them Imada justice. The Mandrigel king suggested it, after all."

And she shoved her at Hades' feet.

"Deisa," Hades said under his breath.

"Please." Harmonia clasped her hands on her knees

before Hades. "Please! Kill me! It is my fault. I ate the fruit. I did it. They did nothing! Please, Lord Hades, take my life!"

"But no, rejoice, my child," Sara said with a smirk. "The Mandrigel king saved you. Thank King Pangrin. One day, decades from now, you may return. That is, if your people will ever forgive you and take you back." Sara cackled wickedly.

Hades gently helped Harmonia to her feet and guided her back toward her people. But when Hades dropped her knife and refused to cover the nymph's lips, Sara impatiently rushed over, hoisted up Harmonia, tore a piece of her white dress, and tied it over her mouth.

After Harmonia was hugged and cheered by her closest friends, Sara bound Harmonia's eyes. But not her ears. And just before her eyes were completely covered, she saw Hades' chariot fly off as Sara brandished her knife. Then came a curtain of darkness.

Then came the screams.

3

A NEW FRIEND

Harmonia built shelters for many moons along the yellow sandy beaches of man. She was on foreign land, but she had seen this yellow and brown world before. She used to see the strange colors across the sea when climbing the pyramid by her Blue River. At first, her eyes had burned for the lack of blue. And her body had felt weighed down by thick air. But in time, she had become acclimated to this strange world.

She lived. That was all. For she felt dread every day over her plight. And she heard the screams of her sisters every night. The dwarf king had been right, banishment was the cruelest torture for a Napean nymph.

One day, like any other, as she bathed in a stream among the trees, running her long dark hair under the flowing waterfall, she heard footsteps in the bushes. She had grown accustomed to this weird world where the squirrels and deer were brown, but as she gazed through the green leaves, she saw such a strange animal. It was so white that it seemed to reflect the yellow sunlight. A pearl white horse, like the large horses men rode during the games, but this one had a brilliant horn on its head that shone multicolored under sunlight. And wings along its sides.

Harmonia walked barefoot over wet leaves. Strangely, the animal didn't stir. It stood regal. Then she gently touched the white feathered wings. They were like a bird's feathers. She ran her blue palm along the horse's soft mane. But as her palm touched the horn, the unicorn backed up.

"Shh, it's okay, girl. It's all right. Where did you come from? Hmm? How come you're here?"

The unicorn slowly crept closer and bent its head down before her.

"So beautiful. You are so beautiful."

The horse neighed and nodded.

"Where are you from? Hmm? I've never seen an animal like you. Except the flying beasts of Hades, but you're different. Beautiful. Hmm? You have such a lovely horn. Hmm? What is your name? I will call you…Antilus. Yes, I call you Antilus after your horn." Harmonia kissed the animal's head. Even the fur along Antilus's head was soft. "But you should find better company than me. I'm just a miserable wood nymph."

Harmonia was surprised to see the animal shake her head.

By twilight, Harmonia was running along the yellow sandy shore beside her new companion. The unicorn followed her everywhere. Then, by a large open, grassy field, the nymph caressed the horse's head in her arms again. But then, late at night by the fire, while embracing the unicorn's head, Harmonia wept. Were they tears of joy or tears of sorrow? She didn't know. Whichever it was, for some reason, she cried all night in the company of her new friend, as hard as she had wept the night after the battle on the Blue River.

IT TOOK A DAY, only a day, before Harmonia drummed up enough courage to mount the flying unicorn. First she clutched the unicorn's neck tightly as she rode along the sands. Then she gasped in wonder as Antilus took off into the air.

Harmonia soared so high that she could clearly see her beloved blue world from across the sea. She saw the giant gilded pyramid and, even from here, the gold seemed to shine over a quarter of the isle. The other isle was like a shining sky-blue gemstone. And as she dared to fly a little farther, she could even make out the purple shore, like an amethyst jewel.

When she returned and bathed again under her waterfall, she had thoughts of flying over the strait and returning home. Yes, she could do it. She could fly home! But the gods. No. The Olympian gods would stop her. Demeter's sentence was a human lifetime. But one day, one day she would fly over the strait.

Footsteps on leaves in the surrounding foliage made her open her eyes wide. Antilus? No, it wasn't her new friend. Between leaves and branches, she saw a tall man wearing a long black cloak. His eyes stared from under a hood. Harmonia quickly covered her body as best she could under the waterfall. Then her embarrassment turned to rage.

"*Aieee!*" she cried. "*Aieee! Biltrie. Biltrie!*"

The man removed the black hood from his head. Still behind branches, she clearly saw his rippling chest, huge arms, and stomach over simple dark pants. He was bald with a short beard. She recognized him as Hades, the one who had tied her beside her sisters by the river. But before she could lunge at him, the god turned and walked off.

She covered her waist with a leather wrap and quickly followed.

Hades stood beside Antilus, petting her white flying unicorn under a large oak tree. Antilus laid her head in his arms. Harmonia approached him and assumed a fighting stance. "*Biltrie!*"

"I am a god, Harmonia," he said, with his back still turned to her. He ran his fingers along the unicorn's soft feathered wings. "Speak the language of Imada, not that primitive tongue, if you wish to address me."

"Away beast! Away! You are the beast who killed my family!"

"That's better." He sighed and turned to her. "But I've come to make amends. To see how you are faring on the beaches in your banishment."

"How can there be amends for what you've done to me!"

She whistled. Hades furrowed his brow. Antilus flapped her great wings before Hades and struck the god in the face, throwing him to the ground. Hades lay on the grass, stunned. Then he sat up and burst into laughter. Harmonia was still crouched in a fighting stance. He raised a hand. "Stop. Let me explain."

She didn't. She whistled again. This time, the horse flapped its great wings and hovered in the air. Harmonia mounted her unicorn and flew off.

"Wait, I wish to speak with you!"

"Biltrie! Biltrie! You murdered my family!"

As the red sun dipped over the horizon and she flew through clouds, she didn't steer the unicorn in any direction. She only wanted to fly away from the beast. Antilus flew away from Azure Blue and across the sea. That was how intelligent this unicorn was; Antilus had learned how much Harmonia loathed the view of her home world.

As the red sun shone over the horizon, Harmonia gazed at the leagues of green forests before her. To her left, she saw mountains. There were so many yellow and brown lands—this realm was so much bigger than Azure Blue. To her right a sandy beach seemed to pass forever. She flew on until the sun dipped below the horizon and changed the blue sky to orange red. But she never gazed in the direction of home, for the great pyramid was large enough to reflect sun and moonlight.

That only reminded of her banishment. Slowly she descended to her hovel, praying that infernal god had left.

Her home was simple. She used branches and twigs as shelter on grass not far from the shore. Fortunately, it was warm outside, but already it was getting cold at night. Soon it would be winter, and she would long for the animal fur coats her people wore to keep warm in the snow.

She built a simple fire. Then she leaned back against Antilus, who had lain down beside her. She picked up some leftover meat, skewered on a stick. It was a tree mouse she had caught in the morning. She roasted it for a quick bite. Then she sucked on the stick. Dear Maina's cinnamon spice and sharp herbs were gone. No delicacies like home here.

"It seems you're enjoying my gift."

The dark-hooded god stood over her. At least now Harmonia had clothes covering her below the waist.

"She's from you?" Harmonia asked, chewing on meat by the fire.

"Yes, my queen," he said with a short bow. Then he stroked his beard in thought. "Consider it… an apology."

"My family's dead."

"I didn't give the order."

"You killed them."

"The butchering was from my sister. You live because of me. I spoke to King Pangrin before Sara did." He laughed. "Do you believe that a king who had been forced into battle and watched the deaths of a hundred of his brothers would spare you? No, you were the cause of the battle by the Blue River. Your hubris caused the deaths of hundreds. Don't blame me for your banishment."

"And now I am here alive, far from home. More miserable than if I had been slain. Leave me. Away with you."

"No."

She turned and squinted. *"Come here to gloat over my misery then?"*

"Captivating." He kneeled close to her. She moved back in revulsion. "Fascinating. But my sister was right to be angry with you. For such hubris, you deserved far worse than a life cooking rats. You deserved to be taken to my realm."

"Is that why you've come? To bury me? Fine. This is no life for a Napean nymph, over brown and yellow sands. Take me to the ferryman and be done with me."

"King Pangrin did what he had to do to survive. Just as you shall do as queen of the Amazon. You will survive, and if you act right, you can live. You may live very well, Queen Harmonia."

"Why are you calling me *queen*?" she asked, chuckling. "Is this more mockery?" But then she smiled. She didn't know why, but there was something about this god, this man, that made her smile. He was handsome. His muscular physique was pleasing to her eyes. He was stronger and mightier than anyone she had seen in the games. And his azure eyes, like her own, seemed oddly tranquil. Such a strange juxtaposition to his hard face.

"Do I look like a queen to you?" Harmonia asked, chewing again. "Hmm? Or is it my bare chest you desire? My tits?" And she hit her chest. "I hear human women cover them? Is that why you've come? To ravish me? I warn you, I'll fight you to my very last breath."

Hades laughed again. Then he shook his head and turned serious. "Perhaps."

She glared at him. Then she leaped up and pushed her unicorn toward him. Antilus scrambled to keep the fire from singeing her hoofs. "Take her! I don't want her! Here! Take your gift back. I want nothing from you! *I hate you!*"

Then she ran.

When she got to the shore, she kept running along the sand. As her blue feet met a receding wave under the full moon, she stopped and stared across the strait, accidentally looking homeward. The shadow of a gilded pyramid rose to the clouds in the moonlight under the starry sky. It was breathtaking. And absolutely horrible. She hated it. Like the pomegranate, now that isle, her very home, was forbidden.

She ran her hand down her disheveled black tresses. She felt grimy. Somehow the salty sea had twisted and tangled her hair.

Hades had followed. He was walking slowly with Antilus down a sandy hill toward her.

Tears streamed down her face. The tears mixed with the salt water from an incoming wave. How much crying would be enough?

"What do you want from me!"

"You."

"What?"

"Oh yes," Hades said, "You were right. I desire you." He was so tall, towering over her, staring down into her eyes. "I desire you. But I am not a beast, Harmonia. I am a god."

Her heart quickened. His gaze shifted to her chest, and he gently ran a finger along her curves and along her side. Then a few fingers circled over the contours of one of her breasts. He leaned down and kissed her cheek and lips ever so gently. Tenderly. So soft. So oddly soft for such a strong brute.

"Don't," she breathed.

He ran his other hand down her back and traced the contours of her lower back down to the crack of her butt and along the leather cloth around her waist.

"Don't."

He lightly kissed her lips again and pulled her into an embrace..

"*DON'T!*" She pushed away from him. "I... I give you nothing! I won't bow to you. And I won't ever let you touch me! Rape me, kill me, if that is your way. But I am a nymph. Not a woman to be led around like a dog. I know that is the way men do things in these yellow lands. But know this, god, I shall never bow to anyone again, not even you! I've sworn this since the fight with the dwarfs."

"Even if I were to promise you anything you desire, Harmonia?"

"No." Then she turned from him. "No. No, not even then."

"Anything?" He ran his fingers through her long dark hair. "For you?"

"No," she said, swatting his hand like a fly.

He laughed.

"No! No!"

He sat down on a stone on the shore. He picked up a stick and played with the sand in the moonlight, staring, across the strait, at her home. If she left him there and returned to her hovel, he'd probably continue brooding on her beach.

"You're a liar," she said. "It was by your hand. I heard what Sara ordered you to do."

"That was Sara. But Sara is led by Imada. Had I disobeyed, Cronos would have imprisoned me in the depths. Believe me, Harmonia, I wanted no part of that despicable act. I would have taken far more pleasure in cutting down the dwarfs. You see—" The brute smiled again at her. "You were right to take the fruit. Indeed, it's yours. You have every right to it." He opened his arms wide. "The whole world is yours. Well, it could be. If you let me help you. I'm not your enemy."

She shook her head violently. Had there still been hope of hurting him, she would have had the unicorn lunge at him again. But Antilus was roaming along the waves now.

He stood up and wagged a finger. "You need a name." Then he slapped his leg and looked away, rubbing his beard in thought. "Something your people can call you and your kin when you go into battle. Your spirit will help you win. Your people are fighters. Amazons are meant for war. Your heart is fierce. With great ease, you can subdue the Mandrigel. And with Napea as a base, you can make your way into Gaia and, one day, take Argos."

"It is not our way to have family names," Harmonia said, shaking her head. "Nor do nymphs wish to take the world. War is man's trade."

"But it could be *your* trade."

She looked at him rebelliously, but then she looked down. "I am nothing."

He approached and gently lifted her chin. He touched her cheek. "You are everything. More than any mortal in Gaia. But your family needs a name."

"I said don't," she snatched his wrist. "Don't touch me."

"Such spirit. Fearless before a god. Aidoneus shall call you Ambrosia. To your people, you shall be known as Harmonia Ambrosia. For your kin shall be like the bread of the gods. Eternal. A force that shall rebel against my brother forever. As for your first name…" He chuckled. "That's a lie. There is nothing peaceful about you, Harmony. You do not hold peace, you offer order. As known in the time of Sargon, and even the ancient Ubaid people before, I shall teach you to line up your nymphs with shields and spears. But, my dear Azure queen, you will never provide peace, I suspect, not even to me."

"I don't care what you call me," she said. Then she dared meet his gaze. "You took everything. No… not you, Hades… you… You seem to have given me the only thing I care for now. Antilus."

"You accept my gift?"

She nodded.

"Do you believe me when I tell you your people were not slain by my hand?"

"Yes."

He nodded. Then he raised his fist under the full moon. She gazed at his hand as if it were a weapon. "What you will do with Antilus, Queen of the Amazon, shall be glorious. You will give birth to Ambrosia, a family that—like the food of the gods—shall live eternally. The Ambrosias will seed destruction of my father, sister, and brothers. You don't hate me, Harmonia." He laughed and sat back down on the stone. "You hate subjugation. That was the source of your rebellion. You took the berry because you wanted to be free. I can make those seeds grow. I can teach you. For man, I gave Prometheus and Pandora. For the nymphs, it shall be you. But the price will be hard. Yet I have no doubt that out of everyone I've ever known, you have the strength for it. You and I shall be friends as we seed our revenge on my family."

"Theoi killed my family. Your family."

"Aye. And for your first lesson, nymph, tell me why?"

"Punishment."

"No. Think, Harmony. Why? Why would Sara give such a terrible order? As powerful as my family are, Olympus fears you. I spared you because of that fear. Zeus thundered for days after your rebellion. The price was to take your friends and family, which satisfied their thirst for blood just long enough to permit my request for banishment. My niece, the child grain goddess, prophesizes that one day you shall become a powerful queen. You shall rule an empire. The only way for you to be queen is to be loved by your people. So what does my sister do? She orders the death of everyone who cares for you. She executes your family. But it's futile. Her daughter never errs in prophecy. You are queen.

"Ask yourself, do you hate me or subjugation, Harmonia? Theoi serves their family just as nymphs serve theirs. That is why I did not fight Sara's order. But if you help me, we shall take our revenge. If you help me, Harmony, I will champion you. All I ask in return is that you do what you did in that field outside your home every day you breathe for the rest of your days. Take everything in this world that is rightfully yours."

"What is mine?" she asked with a smirk. Then she dared run her palm along the hairs of his beard.

He closed his eyes and inhaled deeply. "Everything."

Harmonia burst into laughter. "I am nothing. If I am something to you, then you are the stupidest of all gods."

"Accept my gift. Fly Antilus deep south beyond Shadow Forest. Leave the shore and don't turn back. The banishment holds only for Napea, not Atala. Head into the first settlements of man. Learn. Unlike a human, you have decades. Use your banishment to learn from men. They outnumber you, but you were made stronger. Then, when you are ready, return to your people and teach them. Teach the Amazon to create and use swords, shields, and spears so that they can conquer all that Theoi love. Then you and I shall take our revenge."

"But I am a simple wood nymph."

"No." He looked down at her as if in rapture again and slowly shook his head. That excited her. Then he embraced her. He ran his hand down her body once more. Then he whispered in her ear: "You are a great many things, but not nothing. Look how you fought me. A god. I've never met anyone who stands without fear before a god."

"Very well," she said gently, pushing him from her arms. "I accept your gifts, god."

He laughed.

"But I warn you." She looked deep into his eyes and raised a finger. "Never deceive me. Never lie to me, or I shall plan vengeance on *you*." But somehow she found herself in his arms again. "Perhaps there are good gods out there."

She let go of him and turned away with every intention of returning to her camp alone, but he yanked her wrist back hard.

"Not yet…"

He spun her around and pulled her close into his arms again. His embrace was steel. She had never felt such strength from anyone. He kissed her hard on the lips. But her helplessness in his embrace infuriated her. She lurched back and slapped him across the face. And yet, part of her desired him.

She wanted him to take her. To ravish her. And her slap only seemed to make him hungrier.

He rubbed his cheek. Then he smiled.

She found herself on the wet sand wrestling him. But when he got on his knees in the sand, crouching close to kiss her on the lips again, she slugged him across the face with both fists, as hard as she could.

"*Biltrie!*" she cried again. "*Biltrie!*"

"Savage witch!" He wiped a drop of crimson from his lips.

Then she shocked him, and herself, by leaping on top of him. She straddled him and raised his hands to caress her naked breasts. She leaned down and kissed him on the lips hard. He laughed between kisses as she explored his mouth. Then he laughed more as she pulled down his pants. But then, even with her heart pounding in desire, the moment he was naked on the sand under her, she leaped off him and ran to Antilus.

She jumped on her unicorn's back. Antilus flapped her white feathered wings.

Hades stared up from the sand in shock as she hovered over him.

"I shall consider your offer," Harmonia said. "But know this, Aidoneus, I shall never bow. And if I do as you say, if I travel and conquer man's lands, let it be known that my future shall be by my hands. Let it be known that all my conquests shall be by Harmonia."

"Rightfully so," he said, with a nod, still sitting on the sand.

4

———

THE STRANGER

Harmonia flew Antilus over unfathomable stretches of trees. She had already flown nearly two times the distance of her entire Isle of Napea. Even as trees became sparse among vast wheat fields, the continent seemed to continue to stretch out forever. After a break in the dark woods, she explored dirt roads lined by thatched-roof cottages amid long wood fences penning sheep, goats, and cattle. She trotted Antilus along these roads, through sparse villages. And it was here, by an olive orchard, where Harmonia met her first human woman.

Only men were permitted by the gods to sail across the strait during the Olympiad games. But this young girl was carrying a wicker basket full of fruit. Her long white robe was fastened at the shoulder by a brooch. The peplos draped down to the woman's sandals, and her long wavy dark hair was tied back. She had a beaded necklace of stones of multiple colors. She reminded Harmonia of the female Mandrigel dwarfs… no, lovelier—more like the goddesses. When the girl spotted Harmonia, she dropped her basket. Then she stared. Harmonia made it worse when, out of habit, she pulled out her dagger and stood in a warrior stance.

"Bentri fors Holeei? Holeei? Holeei?"

"What do you want?" cried the stranger, shaking. Her words were in the language of the gods. Then the woman gazed at Harmonia's naked chest.

Another woman, farther down the road, gasped. She, too, wore an elegant long dress covering her chest.

"You are a nymph?" asked the lady, wide-eyed. "A wood nymph?"

Harmonia came close to the woman's face, her blade an inch from the woman's neck. She could slay her with one sweep of her blade. It'd be easy. But instead, she bent down, still brandishing her knife, and grabbed a red apple that had dropped to the ground. Then she bit into it right in front of the woman's face.

"You!" cried a man's voice. "You there!"

The stranger wore a bronze breastplate with pteruges. Harmonia hadn't seen such clothes on any person, except the gods.

Harmonia leaped on her unicorn and flew off.

Moons passed. Perhaps years? Time lost all meaning. Harmonia learned to live, just as her champion, Hades, had instructed her to do. Most of the time she hid watching the women tilling their fields, cooking, or picking fruit from the trees. Then she learned to steal. She was good at stealing. She could hunt deer and fowl, but it became far easier to just take things. Her alien presence usually sufficed. Or, when particularly brazen, she entered their homes. And most of the men and women in these parts didn't know how to fight.

She protected herself by acting dumb. She knew their language, the Atalan language of the gods, but she feigned ignorance and spoke Napean. She knew her best protection was her ability to surprise, attack, and then flee.

But out of all that fascinated her, the most endearing was the sight of battle. She witnessed terrible fights to the death between large groups of men. First, armies would stand in line facing each other with flags waving. Most wore long thick fur coats; only the leaders wore metal. They'd shout at each other and wave their weapons. Then they'd charge, brandishing axes, some on horseback, and collide with one another. It was like the games, but this was a sport to the death. And she loved it.

When winter came, she stole thick wool coats from many of these soldiers to keep warm. When the weather turned temperate again, she stole dresses from passersby, like the first lady she met on the road. She learned to ape females' mannerisms and, as the years passed, she knew she succeeded when she spoke to wandering townsfolk and they no longer ran.

She finally ended her long migration by a beautiful lake. Here, where surrounding trees seemed to wrap their arms around her, sheltering her from the sun's golden rays and frigid wind, she found the most beautiful gem in the entire continent. Streams cascaded into waterfalls, and these fell to smaller falls—she used the smallest to bathe. And she swam in the lake, recollecting her wood nymphs' joy when swimming in the waters of her Blue River in Azure.

She learned that this body of water was named Crystal Lake in the land of Logencia. She was told Logencia stretched all the way from the thick forests to the lake, and westward to the sea. Then she was told that one king in the city of Logenth ruled it all. His name was King Karthra. And when she learned of the king, she left her home to meet him.

Far south of Crystal Lake, after passing stinking bogs and ugly marshes, Harmonia came across a large stone gate guarding an entrance. And yet, as Harmonia stood by this gate, it seemed the lands inside did not look much different from those without. The only thing the wall seemed to protect was more grasslands and a city center with a huge tented structure. Here a couple of dirt roads converged. She would have headed to the tent structure had not two guards detained her by the gate.

The guards ordered her to stand aside. She obeyed, until a guard groped her body. When he touched her, asking her to relinquish her weapons, she slew them with her dagger.

She was shocked to discover how easy it was to kill these two men. Even in elegant bronze metal pteruges, the guards could not match her speed with her simple dagger. She had been trained to avoid the arteries in the neck and eyes in the games. But now, in battle, she aimed for these precious spots.

Then she gazed down at her kill. She was in trouble again. This was confirmed as a wave of soldiers in bronze metal armor came rushing toward her.

Guards apprehended her, roped her hands behind her, and led her through dirty walkways and alleys, past more farmland and thatched-roof cottages, to the large central tent. It had a stone foundation but was covered with a huge linen top. She was told this was the royal hall.

About a hundred people filled the torchlit hall. At the far end was a wooden stage. And on the stage a king sat upon a wooden dais. Many of this warlord's subjects, men and women, lay on the floor before the stage, eating and drinking. Some were naked, roaring with laughter and acting like silly children. Seeing bare-breasted women in public with men was very strange, indeed. Other girls wore transparent clothes, like those her nymphs wore in the games. Moving to the music of cymbals and a lyre, they danced beside the stage.

She was escorted before the king's throne between the two guards. Her dark peplos, pilfered many moons ago from a woman traveling on a dark path in the woods, looked like rags compared to the dresses many elegant women wore. She saw some violet peplos and lovely gold and silver jewelry. The ladies wore makeup on their faces and gold about their necks and ears. So lovely, she wished she could wear such beautiful clothes.

"Bow before your king!" one of the guards shouted.

Ah, so this was the king of Logenth. She would finally meet him. But she wouldn't bow. She would never bow again.

"Bow!" A guard struck her legs, and that made her fall to her knees.

"Aieee! Aieee!" she snapped, whirling back.

Everyone in the hall turned to her when they heard her strange language. Even the king, who had a woman on his lap, squinted down.

"What pleasure do you bring me?" asked the king with a grin.

"A habiru loitering by the gate, sire. She killed five guards and wounded a sixth."

"A habiru woman killed my guards?" asked King Karthra with a laugh, sitting straighter.

Harmonia scowled at him.

The large, short man had a long bushy beard and wore a thick animal hide draped over his shoulder. Gold rings and necklaces abounded over his animal hide. The hide was filthy, as were his greasy cheeks and beard. This was the king of Logencia? He seemed like a beastly man.

"Who are you?" the king asked. "The color of your face is…blue."

"I am Queen Harmonia," Harmonia said. More subjects turned as she spoke perfect Atalan. "I am the queen of Argos. Ruler of North Atala. I come from the Isle of Napea."

"I know no queen of Argos." King Karthra pushed the young girl off his lap. Then he stood up and turned to two men. One was old with a long gray beard. The other was very handsome, dressed differently from anyone else in the Court. His armor was painted light blue, and strange black paint circled his eyes.

"Ruler of the North, Azerius?" the king asked the handsome stranger. "Have you heard of such a thing?"

Azerius shook his head. Unlike the king, Azerius was tall with broad shoulders, strong, and athletic. His prowess was like Hades'. He seemed overconfident, but his eyes looked about curiously with intelligence. He was what she had imagined the great king of Logencia would be. Azerius wore black paint along his eyes. She had never seen this before. And he was a beardless man, something she had not seen in her travels. His hair was dark brown and curly and flowed down his shoulders. His cheekbones were hard, and his nose was sharp. He had a large forehead.

"We know of no queen ruling Argos, my lord," Azerius said with a look of amusement, watching her. "Mycenae is ruled by kings under Olympus. And the Isle of Napea is ruled by no one. It is said that there is only a colony of wood nymphs and dwarfs in Napea, under the great Olympus Pyramid, the home of the gods. They're a primitive race. There is no queen in Argos. And no one in Napea rules a thing." He smiled at Harmonia, furrowing his brow. "But I do know of the crystal witch by the lake. She is known to be a blue nymph, sire. Legend says a blue witch there takes weary travelers to bed only to kill and pilfer from them."

"Well, Caravian, a habiru stands before you claiming to be not a witch but a queen of Argos," said the king with a laugh. And with that, the whole tent burst into laughter. "How droll! Perhaps she's mad? Are you stricken by madness, wood nymph? Hmm? You attack my guards? Kill five. Why? Well, Queen of Argos, King Karthra welcomes a Mycenean queen to Logenth. Now she shall be put to death. Your sentence shall be having your royal body thrown in the pit tomorrow morning. What say you to that, *Queen*?" He stomped his foot, still laughing. "Take her away. But… Be kind. Be nice. Take the poor mad woman's life quickly. Why, she provides amusement."

Harmonia yanked her arms from the two guards pulling her. "I was sent by Lord Hades." That sent gasps throughout the hall. Some made strange hand signals.

"Wait," cried the king, raising his palm. He looked at Azerius again. Azerius shrugged. King Karthra walked slowly from his stage and approached her. The guards by her sides held her more tightly. He turned to one of them. "How did she slay five guards by the gate?"

"With this, sire," said a guard, handing the king a dagger.

The king examined the knife.

"Crude," he said. "It could snap in battle." Karthra held the blade to her neck, forcing her to lift her head. "Fierce woman, you are," he said, running the blade along her cheek. Then he said quietly, "Hades? The God of Darkness is your champion? Is this another lie?"

"I came here by the will of Hades. I swear it. He has asked me to observe man. That man—" She gestured to Azerius with a nod. "Is correct. I am a Napean nymph. But I am their queen. This is truth. And it has been foretold that I shall one day rule Napea, so says the goddess Persephone, the young grain goddess. And one day, it is truth, one day I shall take Argos from the Myceneans. Just as one day I shall take Logenth from you."

He guffawed in her face, and the stench from his mouth made her reel back. Then came laughter all over the Court.

"How droll! How droll!" He slapped his fat leg and laughed some more. "A queen? Indeed! Very well, *Queen.*" He threw her knife on the stage. "Now you threaten the king of Logencia? So be it. I sentence the queen of Argos to die in the pit tomorrow. It's too bad that all of your subjects in Hellena shall miss the fall of their revered ruler." He turned to the guards. "Take this habiru away. Forget my former order. Forget kindness. Make her suffer for wasting my time."

5

THE CRYSTAL WITCH

HARMONIA WAS NOT PUT TO DEATH. SHE ESCAPED, USING THE ancient magic of her unicorn, Antilus. The unicorn came to her in the night. It materialized inside her cell. Then as Harmonia mounted Antilus, crouching under the low ceiling, its horn emitted bright multicolored light, and Harmonia found herself outside, free.

As she flew from Logenth, a hundred of the king's guards pursued her. In nearby villages, she hid behind thickets and trees as they hunted her. Then she came up from behind and slew them. She stole a bow from one of them and flung arrows at those that were left. She knew not only how to hunt fowl, but how to hunt man too. She killed every single one of her pursuers.

Except one. That man in Court that fascinated her. Azerius. The handsome man wearing shiny blue armor with black paint over his eyes. This man followed her too. He chased her all the way back to her favorite lake.

What sort of a man are you? Your hair is long and curly and you're clean shaven. And your eyes, there's dark paint around them. Are you from the fabled far lands of Aethiopia? Egypt?

He fascinated her, but her fascination turned to rage when

he started climbing down the cliffside near her shelter. He climbed down the rocks carrying a sword on his back, a beautiful silvery blade. It was something rare in these parts, something she hadn't seen since the swords of the dwarfs.

She climbed up around him and snuck up from behind.

"You there. Stop!" Harmonia cried. "What do you want?" She drew an arrow from the quiver on her back and armed her bow. "I have the higher ground. Tell me why I should not shoot you down!"

"Wait!" he cried, raising a hand. "Wait." He looked down nervously. Then he gazed up searching for her, but the yellow sun blinded his eyes. They were at least two hundred feet up. The drop would be just as perilous as her arrow.

She fired a warning shot a few feet from him.

"Wait!"

"This is my home," she said. "Tell me why I shouldn't slay you now."

"I've been meaning to talk to you."

"Talk?" she swayed a bit with a sudden fear of falling. Still, she forced herself to stand on a very narrow ledge. "Talk? About what?" She laughed. "You've been hunting me since Logenth. You're as bad as the rest of them."

"Look..." He tried to steady himself while shielding his eyes from the sun's rays with one hand. He kept his other hand out trying to calm her. Then he climbed another step closer to her. He was only a few feet away. He swayed as he struggled to balance. "I heard you at the palace. I... I just need to know if all that you said was true. Are you truly a queen?"

"Yes." She brushed her long black hair away from her eyes. "It's true. You are in the presence of a queen. Why wouldn't I be?"

"And Hades sent you? And you're Napean? Or you're from Mycenae?"

"I told you already. Why should I tell you anything more?"

"Because I've never met a woman like you."

And she had never met a man like him. Unlike the other men she had seen in her travels, he seemed to exude great confidence and courage. She laughed. "Perhaps I should be asking the questions, sir." She pointed an arrow at his head again. "Who are you? You don't look like the men from the Hinterlands."

"I am General Azerius, serving under King Tolen II of Caravia." He looked like he would have bowed, had he had room to stand. "I am Caravian."

"Car-a-v-ian? What is that?"

He laughed. "You really don't know much, do you?"

She stared, swaying a little, barely balancing on the ledge. "What is a Car-a-v-ian? Tell me before I slay you."

"Perhaps it would be better if we make our way down first, my lady. It's a lot more comfortable conversing at normal heights."

"What is a Car-a-v-ian?" she asked, shaking her head. "Tell me now!"

"Caravia," he replied with a quick nervous glance over his shoulder. "Caravia is a kingdom far south of Logencia. It is the greatest kingdom in the world."

"Hmm. Perhaps you should take me there."

"Take you there?"

"Yeah." She looked up at the sun then peered down at him. "Take me. I shall allow you to live for that, General. Speak to your king. Perhaps he can help me and my people. Instead of that sarding stupid stinking King Karthra."

"You wish me to grant you an audience with the king of Caravia?" he asked snidely.

"Queen Harmonia permits it."

"After you killed five guards and wounded a sixth at the gates of Logenth? Logencia and Caravia are not brothers, but I hardly desire to witness the same fate in my beloved city."

"They attacked me. They asked for my knife."

He squinted at her in confusion. "You believe a foreigner is permitted to gain entrance to a major city carrying weapons without a writ by the king? Such is not our code of justice."

"What is a code of justice?"

"What is a *code of justice?*" he repeated in bewilderment.

She didn't like his tone. So she made the bow tauter. Shade fell over them from a cloud overhead. That permitted him to stop shielding his eyes and stare up at her. He did not appear afraid, he seemed fascinated.

"Wait! I'm merely repeating your words to understand. Please, let's talk down at the bottom where it's safer."

She debated whether to just launch the arrow. It'd be easier. One arrow through his head and he'd fall and die. Then she could have her dinner and perhaps lie in the moonlight in peace. It would be a warm, pleasant evening by her lake tonight. She had been tracking the stars, and this time of year was temperate. One quick arrow between his eyes would penetrate his head. He would tumble down the rocks off the ledge, and she'd be done with him. Then she could descend and perhaps have a swim.

"My duty was to watch the barbarians of Logenth in Logencia upon orders of my king, King Tolen," said Azerius. "I did this in order to report back any threats to my kingdom. You represented a threat when you said you were a queen from Argos. But now that I've met you, I hardly find you a threat. Or a queen, for that matter." And he laughed.

"Then you're an idiot to insult me so!" she shouted. "I have an arrow pointed at your head, fool! You are a spy, then?"

"No, wait. Wait!" He shook his head and looked down. "Forget that. The more you speak, the more wonder you give me. Please… Put the weapon down. There's a lot more to you than meets the eye, isn't there, Queen Harmonia? I'm beginning to believe you really were sent by a god."

"I don't care what you believe. I have thousands of

subjects in Napea that will one day overrun these feeble settlements. It shall all be under my rule. One day, I shall be queen, not only of the nymphs but of you."

"I've heard stories of a witch in these parts," he said, shaking his head. "You're no queen. You're the crystal witch of the lake. You lie in wait by this lake killing weary travelers and taking to bed young boys. Everyone's heard of you. You are a troll under a bridge. Or, even worse, a bear, wild, untamed, dangerous. But you're not a queen."

"*Watch this queen kill you!*"

And she leaped at him. It was suicide, but her intent was quite serious. This was an honorable man, and she would not kill him with an arrow. She would wrestle and throw him.

She dropped her bow and arrow, letting them fall down the rocks below. Then she lashed at him with her newest pilfered knife. They wrestled and they both nearly fell over. In shock, he managed to stand in a fighting position on a narrow rock. She cut him, ripping the leather on his shoulder as he struggled to balance, dodging the blade. This Azerius was a very skilled fighter, perhaps the best she had ever fought. He was far better than the guards in Logenth. On these narrow stones, Harmonia had, perhaps, finally met her match. Good. She would die today with honor at the hand of a general.

He parried her thrusts and somehow disarmed her. Then he flipped her and she fell under him on the gray boulders. She thought she would fall two hundred feet to her death, but he had pushed her onto a larger rock below. He leaped over her and pointed her own fallen dagger at her throat.

As he threatened to kill her, she burst into laughter. He opened his eyes in shock.

"Do it," she said under him. "Please. Kill me. Kill me now, Caravian general."

"What's the matter with you? You wish to die?"

"Kill me. Or let me live, coward. Slice the crystal witch's throat. I dare you."

He threw her blade down in disgust. But he still pinned her to the ground. He stared at her. His face was so close that she could smell his sweat and feel his panting breath. And his eyes searched hers. She had called him a coward playfully. This was the bravest man she had ever known.

"I'm going to get up very slowly, *Queen*. I only ask that you get up slowly too. We don't have a lot of room on this ledge. I see that you don't value your life. But I value mine."

"Such value makes you weak, General."

He squinted. Then she laughed in his face again.

Rays of sunlight burst around the clouds again, making her squint at him. He shook his head slowly as he hesitantly released her, and he stood as close to the edge of the cliff as he could without falling off the rocks. She saw his ankles quake. As they both struggled to catch their breath, he finally spoke. "I think you should know…I'm afraid of heights."

That made her laugh even more.

Carefully placing his feet on the stones, he began to descend the cliff. As she rose to her knees and brushed the dirt from her clothes, she watched him climb down.

"Come to the bottom where we can talk without risking our lives, Queen," he said, carefully climbing down. At times, he turned and stuck out his hand, but she was a stubborn nymph and refused, still standing at the top of the cliff watching. When he reached the bottom, he turned with his arms folded and waited by a tall oak tree.

She was amused by the reaction on his face as she descended. She did not show any reticence as she leaped from stone to stone, making it to the bottom in half the time it had taken him.

They walked together. Crystal Lake was huge. Beautiful. And abandoned. Her private treasure, kept more private by her exploits as the "crystal witch." Yes, she had killed weary travelers—even lain with some men. But it was because she valued her private lands and would give them to no other. She loved living here in solitude and punished anyone who broke her silence. Until now... Now she found herself walking silently with a stranger around her lake.

At first, she let him walk ahead of her. He said nothing but kept looking back with an amused smile as he led the way on the edge of the lake. After a short trek, she walked by him and took the lead. It was like a game, and she loved it. One followed the other, and then they switched. They walked all afternoon like this, circling the lake at least twice. But anytime he said a word, she ignored him.

She finally stopped at the water's edge, picked up a rock on the shore, and skipped it along the water. It was such a beautiful day. The lake reflected the yellow sun, and it was warm with a clear breeze. She turned and saw him close beside her.

"What is it you want from me, General?" she snapped. "Be grateful I spared your life. I show little clemency to people who cross into my territory. Most perish by Harmonia. Now, she will allow you to return to your army. If you wish, you may go in peace."

"*You* spared my life?"

"Yes. That's what I did."

"I just want to talk."

"I have nothing to say."

"Are you really from the North? Do you really have other people with blue skin like yours? I thought nymphs were a fantasy. I have never seen a lady so beautiful…but so blue."

"I am a Napean nymph," she said with a shrug, brushing hair back from her eyes. "We are called Amazon by the Myceneans of Hellena. I'm a favorite of my god. Of Hades. He is my lord and lover. I am his and his alone. And I *am* queen of my people. But I have been banished. Now I live by this lake. But I am no *witch*."

He nodded.

"I am a queen."

"I don't doubt it."

He knelt before her. She rolled her eyes. Then the sight of him kneeling with his head down made her burst into laughter again.

"My queen," he said, reaching for her hand. She gave it to him, and he stared at her blue palm. It was a lighter shade of blue than her body. Then he gently kissed the back of her hand.

"General Azerius. Now that I've spared you, you will take me to your king, King Tolen?"

He smiled as he looked up and he chuckled too. "I see no house. Where does the nymph of Crystal Lake sleep?"

"My home is under Ambitus Pyramid, on the Blue River of Azure Blue."

He stood up beside her and grabbed her hand, lightly turning her to face him. Then he looked deep into her eyes. They gazed at each other in silence for a moment. Then he ran his hand through her hair. At first, she snatched it, but then she let him. She looked into his eyes and felt entranced.

"Where is your home *here*, beautiful nymph?"

"Are you planning an invasion? The lake is my home. I sleep by it. It's as simple as that."

He took her extended hand gently and played with her fingers under the bright sunlight. Her blue fingers seemed to glisten in the rays of yellow light. Then he gently kissed her hand again.

"I wasn't completely straight with you, Harmonia. I did not follow you only because of your words about Argos. I followed you because you bewitched me. When you came to the Hall, I could not take my eyes off you. I still can't."

She shook her head. "You should know, Azerius, if your desire is to bed me, I kill every man who desires me. I will ruin you." But her heart quickened and she breathed harder looking into his eyes. Then she felt wicked. "I've allowed boys who pass here, even without such flowery words, to have my body. Then I slay them.”

“The crystal witch.”

“Harmonia Ambrosia,” she said, shaking her head.

“Slay me, Queen.”

“What?”

He thumped the polished blue brass on his chest. “Kill me if that’s your wish, Queen. It’s a fair trade.”

“But you, you’re worse than those men because you’ve hunted me. You took me, and...” He came close and did what she had been waiting for him to do all afternoon. He gently touched his soft lips to hers. They stood together beside the water as it gently lapped by her feet. “All men who hunt me, I kill,” she breathed. “And now you—” Their lips met again. He held her tightly in his strong arms. And they just kissed. “I… kill those who bed me. Is that your desire, Azerius?”

“Yes. If I could have just one night with you.”

“I will not slay you, General Azerius,” she said, pulling away. “Leave me. Go before it’s too late. People I love always die.”

“No,” he said, coming closer again.

He ran his hands down her wool coat, reached inside, and cupped her breasts. She felt herself shake her head. Then she reached slowly down into his pants leg for his dagger. As he touched her cheek and held her chin close for another kiss, she cut his thigh with his own knife. Then she ran. He didn’t cry out. Nor did he give chase.

She ran until she reached the forest trees. Finally, among the thick brush and shadows, she turned back. Azerius still stood by the lake edge, staring out at the falling sun, searching the lake. He didn’t run away. He didn’t even bother to nurse his fresh wound. He just kept looking for her.

6

THE COTTAGE

Days passed. And the stubborn general set up camp beside her lake, refusing to leave. On the third day, she walked to the shore. Standing only a handful of yards from the general, she stripped off her clothes and jumped into the water. He had been roasting deer meat upon a stick. She felt his gaze on her as she swam. Then she got out of the water, dripping, and wrung out her long hair. She patted her hands along her wet body. Then she returned to the woods without a word.

The next day, she loudly sang the songs of her people. He left his post and walked to the cliffside where they had met. Here at the bottom, under the beautiful falls, stood Harmonia in the nude, bathing. He walked close to her. She sang some more, turning her back on him.

Azerius did nothing. But he also didn't leave.

After a fortnight, when the general was still camped in the same spot on the river's edge, eating meat or fowl and lighting fires by evening, she had had enough.

"Go! Leave! No man is allowed here! Why are you still here? I live alone."

He was sitting on a log by the fire. He was out of his

armor, wearing only brown linen pants, displaying rippling muscles along his chest and arms. He looked up, amused, then stared back at the fire. He was stirring the flames with a stick and seemed to be absent-mindedly staring at the small campfire.

"Why stay here?" she asked. "Why don't you go…go back to your Car-av-a."

He shrugged. He crouched over the fire picking at charred meat.

"There's some left," he said. "Would you like some food?"

She looked down at his hands. He held a piece of flesh cooked over the fire. She looked at his eyes, then got angry at his snarky expression.

"I can fend for myself."

"I don't doubt it…but you can have some of my meat. It's wild boar. Please, it's fresh."

"No."

He responded with a shrug and laid the cooked meat on leaves beside him. He stared back at the fire. Then he turned and looked out over the lake. He picked his teeth.

"Don't you have some army to command? Are you…are you not a general? Don't you…don't you need to report back to your king? What sort of a general are you?"

"Why do you care?" He shrugged.

"I care a lot about armies," she said proudly, kneeling near him. "I admire them. I admire man's ability to command soldiers. I've watched them gather about the Hinterlands and march. I watched their order. I study and love them. I want to create the same order for my people one day."

"The Hinterlands are barbaric and disorderly. The men here don't know the difference between a stick and a sword."

She reached down and snatched the meat from the leaves. Then she crouched across from him and just stared at him while chewing on his meat.

"Yes," she said with her mouth full. "I know. I want to see your army. And you can introduce me to your king."

The food was fresh and tasted good. Soon she turned toward the lake and stared out for a while as the sun's golden rays reflected off the quiet waves. Then, after she had eaten her fill, she looked at him. He seemed to be studying her.

"Why are you here?" she cried with her mouth still full. "Don't lie to me. Why not return home? I am no threat to your people. Just leave. I don't want you in my home anymore."

"I can return, Harmony. If you'd like, I can return home with *you*."

"With me?" she asked with a laugh. Then she ate around the last bone. "With me? What makes you think I would want to go with you?"

"I can show you a real army. The way men practice fighting, since it interests you so much. I can teach you. I am a general, the head general of a kingdom."

"Humph."

"And I can show you manners." He said it as if this insult were a simple fact.

"*Go home!*" She stood up and threw the last piece of meat at him. "What do you think I am? An animal?"

"You lack manners, Harmonia," he said, jumping up.

"Manners taught by Zeus?" She whirled around. "I don't need manners. Manners are created by man. I worship Hades."

"If you want to know how we live, how we fight, you have to learn our ways. You'll have to learn to live like us. You have to learn to live like men."

"Go waste more time sitting alone by a lake."

And she walked off.

But as she approached some trees, she hid and looked back. For she knew now that he had not left because of her.

She desired him. And now she knew he desired her. She

watched him looking for her again. She had watched him every day since he first came to her home. She had watched him bathe, so she had seen him naked too. He was so handsome. His muscles were so hard and strong. He fascinated her. She knew he wouldn't leave. She knew he was there for her alone.

She wondered if he would stay here waiting for her forever. It would not be so bad for her eyes.

But she stopped tempting him with her body. She kept her distance. But she still watched him.

A few days later, it started to rain. The torrential rain was so terrible that Azerius ran toward the trees, not to find his beautiful maiden, but simply to find shelter. She watched him as he struggled through the dense thicket and shrubs beside the lake. The forest canopy slowed down the pelting water. He searched for warmth, then he began digging under some bushes for cover. As the water drenched him, he worked hard to set up a clearing to shield him from the pouring rain. She crept up behind him and tapped him on the shoulder. With quick reflexes, he spun around and was ready to throw her.

"Follow me, General," she said sternly, standing over him.

She, too, was drenched with her hair flat over her forehead and shoulders. Her beige clothes were saturated to the point of being dark brown.

She took him by the hand and led him farther into the deep woods. She felt him play with her fingers. At one point, he tried to stop to speak, but she wouldn't let him. She tugged him toward shelter.

They crisscrossed natural trails between thickets and foliage. Then they climbed a short incline. He slipped a few times in the mud, and she caught him, helping him up.

Then they finally reached a clearing. There, in the midst of the dense forest, far from the lake, was a cottage. It was built of wood and stood among grass. She had built it here so that she could still see the edge of her beloved lake between the trees, but they were deep in the forest. It was the perfect location to look over the lake and yet remain hidden. She had watched him from here too.

She opened her wooden door. Then she smiled at his reaction. It was a one-room cottage with weapons lining the walls —swords, lances, shields, and axes. One side had a hole that served as a window looking out upon the lake. A yellow curtain waved back and forth in the wind and rain. And there was a bed on the ground made of animal hide.

"Where did you find this?" he asked, astonished.

"I didn't find it, General," she said with a giggle. "I built it. This is my home. You think I am an animal, eh? You think a lady goes about sleeping in leaves and mud? I hate you for that."

He looked at her, dumbfounded.

"You think me wild? Your witch of Crystal Lake. I hate all men for such thoughts. I told you, I am the Azure queen. I can do anything a man can do, in fact, far better."

He shook his head as he continued staring around the room. He picked up a long broadsword from the wall and ran his hand over a silver chainmail breastplate.

"And these?"

"Mementos. Battle trophies. For all the fools who tried to slay the crystal witch. I've killed all of them. I told you, I kill all men who visit me."

He nodded, running his fingers along the silver sword. "Will you kill me now then?"

"You're wet." She touched his olive-skinned chest and ran her fingers down each arm. He had ripples showing strongly developed abdominal and pectoral muscles too. He was perfectly fit. And perfectly hard. She untied her wet dress and let it fall before him. He touched her naked breasts, but she stopped him. She ran her fingers through his chest hair. Then she ran a hand along his face. When she had first seen him, his skin was shaven. Now he was growing a beard. Man's hair grew fast. She touched those hairs in wonder. He just stood still staring into her eyes.

"Beautiful," he stammered.

"No. You are beautiful," she said, waving her hand over his skin. Then she gazed deep into his eyes. She chuckled. "I copied my home from Logencia. I... I watched them as they worked and learned how they built their cottages. Then I made mine."

"It must have taken so long."

"I've been here for years, human," she said with a shrug. "If I'm uninjured, I can live forever. It is another curse of the gods."

He touched his lips to hers gently. She felt him run his hand along her wet body until it landed on her naked butt and ran along the crack. He pulled her close to him, and their tongues danced. And they kissed like this, their wet, naked skin touching, in the warmth of her cottage for the longest time. The rain and wind raged against her home. But she felt safe in this man's arms. And she wished the night could last forever.

"You may bed me tonight," she said. "I owe you for the breakfast you gave me. And for all your time waiting."

"And after, Harmony? Then you will slay me?"

"I've collected food for the rainy season. If it is too wet tomorrow, you can be inside with me through the storm."

She finally stopped touching him. But her eyes looked up into his again.

"And after?" he breathed.

"Some general," she said quietly with a chuckle. "You would rather spend the winter by the lake than with your army? What are you doing here, Azerius? Why haven't you gone home?"

"I think I've fallen in love." He ran his hand along her cheek. She nodded and closed her eyes, kissing him. Then she opened them and traced the dark paint around his eyes with a finger.

"Why do you darken your eyes?"

"My people are from the lands of the sun. Caravians come from across the Strait of Aegyptus. Long ago, we were with our Egyptian brethren."

"Can you teach me how to do this?"

"Yes."

They kissed again. Then, between more caresses and touching of lips, "Take me with you back to your lands, Azerius. Teach me to fight with your sword. Can you do that? If you do that, I... I... The queen shall exchange...love with you."

7

LOVE

HARMONIA SLEPT IN AZERIUS'S ARMS MANY TIMES BEFORE they reached Caravia. She had not felt such happiness since she had lived with her family in Azurea. She had thought she would never experience such joy again. When they reached the Shryer Valley of Trialga, under the Cliffs of Zonoch, she spent her evenings with him alone by candlelight in his villa. And as she stared into his eyes in the flickering yellow candlelight, it felt as if there was only one soul in the whole universe. Azerius and Harmonia.

One evening, as she watched him across a wooden table quietly savoring the taste of well-cooked mutton, arugula, carrots, and cabbage while sipping red wine, she turned to the window. Even the glass was a great wonder on this continent. She had never seen glass until Caravia. She had heard that the Mandrigel had stone masons and were experts in crystal, but here it was embedded in the wall of Azerius's home. He told her with pride that even across the Strait of Aethiopia, the Egyptians had not mastered such arts.

Through the window she gazed at the great Cliffs of Zonoch. He had told her that above, at its highest height, was a great stone wall. And behind the wall shone a blue castle—like the blue of his armor. On a very clear day, she could occasionally see a blue sparkle under sunlight, like lapis lazuli, but she and Azerius had yet to pass through the gates.

"Perhaps one day you can take me to Azurea, Harmony," Azerius said.

"Oh, you must see Azure one day, Azerius. It's more beautiful than any land in Gaia. The pyramid glows gold across the whole island. And the birds and squirrels and all the furry beasts are more colorful and vibrant than here. Everything is blue. Everything."

"So you've said," he said, sipping from his glass. "Truly, I believe it as I gaze at you. Blue like you."

"But it's far. Now I'd much rather visit your city, General, up the mountain. When can we go to Caravia?"

He forked some mutton then looked through the window, nodding absent-mindedly.

"You look beautiful in your dress, Harmony. And I see you've colored your eyes."

"Kyus helped," she said with a laugh.

Kyus was a boy, maybe sixteen years of age, with curly black hair. He wore kohl like his master. He had told her he had been brought as a slave from the East. He was a cautious, fearful boy and was often mistreated by his master, Azerius. But not by Harmonia. Harmonia liked him. She learned everything she could from the slave. For his master, Azerius, was far more mysterious. As much as she loved him, he seemed to hide things all the time.

"The city, Azerius," she said, forking a carrot into her mouth. "You promised. The city. You must show me the castle you've spoken so much about. We have to go up the cliffside and see it. Oh, when can we do that, darling?"

"Soon." He bit into more mutton. Then he said, with his mouth full, "And one day, I'll return with you to Crystal Lake. And from there, we can pass the great barrier of Shadow

Forest in the north, past the desert and beyond, to *your* amazing lands."

"Yes," she said with a nod. "I'd like that." Then she giggled like a little girl.

He smiled. "What is it?" he asked.

"You."

"Me? You are so different from anyone I've ever met, Harmony. Almost simple. You're lively, pretty, bounding with energy. So smart. But lately you seem sweet, not dangerous as you did when we first met. I think I've tamed you, darling."

She didn't like that. For a flash, it made her angry. Had she let down her guard? Did he intend to do something terrible to her when she least expected it? He could now. Perhaps she had grown too soft?

She released his hand. His eyes opened wide in surprise, and then he laughed even more.

"Oh Harmony, but you're still fierce, aren't you?"

"No more than you, my love. No more than you. We're merely what the Greeks call us in the games. Amazons. Strong, brave. As you are as a soldier."

"But I know no other woman with so much strength," he said with a nod. "Perhaps…no man?"

She nodded. Then he laughed and she joined him, laughing again. They raised their wooden mugs of sweet mead.

Oh, but she was happy. So happy. Even happier than she had been living in Azure Blue. For years after her banishment she had wandered the world without meaning; now, with this man, she felt purpose again. Life. Simply living with this man meant everything to her. Every morning in Caravia, she'd open her eyes early, excited to live a new day. The happiness was so foreign to her.

If only she had not transgressed with the myrle berry. That idiotic act of rebellion with the dwarfs had cost her this joy. Even if she had at least waited a year or more, the games would have arrived. And with the games would have come a man like Azerius. Then she could have had a baby and raised her in Napea. And perhaps she never would have left Azurea?

Was this happiness? Did she finally have everything she had ever wanted?

"What are you thinking, Harmony? You're always thinking so much."

She took his hand again. "How much I love you, Azerius."

8

SURPRISE

"I HAVE TO LEAVE IN A FORTNIGHT," AZERIUS SAID BRISKLY BY
the entrance to the study. She was looking at something from
his library. A papyrus. She had spent a few moons now trying
to decipher symbols. It was in Akkadian, and Azerius had
permitted an elder man in the village to satisfy her curiosity.
Akkadian was the universal written language in all lands of
Gaia. She had learned that there was another language,
written by the sea people. But even the Egyptians used Akkadian. "After I go to the castle to meet my brother, I'll return,
and I thought I could take you far south to Jedithian. If we go
before winter, the tide will be just right to walk along the
shore, like you dreamed."

She had only caught glimpses of the sea from the Cliffs of
Zonoch as she had looked down from the magnificent valley
of Trialga on Antilus. She had not told him that she had flown
far beyond Caravia, all the way across the strait to Egypt, and
seen the Nile years before.

"I would love to go, Azerius. I'd love to see these lands for
the first time."

"Then it shall be, my love. Then it shall be."

He jumped up and kneeled before her. Then he ran a hand over her straight black hair and light-blue cheeks.

"I've never known anyone more beautiful."

"Yes, well…" She giggled. She shook out her long hair and pressed a finger against his chest. "You promised to take me to Caravia, not Jedithian. To present me your regiment. I want to see the lines of your army. You promised me you would show me your men. You know how much I love that."

"I've shown you enough. You mastered my sword in a day."

"No, your army," she snapped. Their heads were so close as to practically be touching. And she considered kissing him. Instead, she rebuked him by wagging a finger. "You promised to show me the castle. Perhaps take me to meet your brother tomorrow? You promised. It's been so long, Azerius."

"When I return—" He bent down and finally did what her lips desired. "You can watch but…"

"What?"

"From a distance."

Her eyes narrowed. He laughed nervously. Then he ran his hand along her neck gently, and she closed her eyes with a smile.

"Are you ashamed of your *crystal witch*?"

"Don't say that," he said, not stopping his wandering hands. He turned serious. "I'm not ashamed. Never. I'm *afraid* of her."

She laughed.

He was gazing at her breasts. She was wearing a long dress made of white and red linen from the city of Nineveh. He had brought her a few of these from the Far East. It was a gift from the empire beyond Canaan, said to be worn by noble women. And she wore kohl every day now, at his request, like all the citizenry of Caravia. She fit in well and was beautiful, if it wasn't for her blue skin.

Was he ashamed of her blue? The villa was a mansion

with beautiful grounds. There was a garden, a stable, and a huge kitchen, all occupied by the general's slaves. But it seemed no one left the estate. It was like all the assistants in his home were in prison with her. She even asked Kyus if he had gone to the city. He told her he hadn't been to the city in years.

Azerius's hands wandered up her legs. She let him. Then he explored her mouth, running his tongue along hers. She closed her eyes and felt tingles along her back from his touch. Then she drew him closer and removed his simple tunic, her blue fingers wandering along his strong arms and hard stomach. She laughed as she felt him lift her long dress over her arms. The weather was temperate this time of year, and she was naked underneath, but not cold. He explored her breasts and her firm nipples with one hand as he ran the other along her perfect athletic body, down her arms and over her hips, and then between her legs.

"I thought you had to leave," she said.

"In a fortnight, Harmony. That's many days. You are the most beautiful—"

He threw her on the rug and laid his heavy naked body over hers. Then, in rapture, he kissed her again on the neck and along her arms.

"The king," she insisted, even as he continued to touch and stroke her. "You will show me him. And your army. It's time Queen Harmonia meets King Tolen."

"You are persistent, aren't you? Perhaps I should show you something else?"

"When you return…show me your army. Show me… Yes, show me… I love you, Azerius. I love you so much."

SHE AWOKE EARLY the next day, discovering herself naked in her large, soft bed and in a wonderful mood, having slept better than she could remember. She stretched out her arms, put her dress back on, and made her way into the kitchen, where Kyus absent-mindedly and sleepily handed her a metal plate of eggs. Harmonia looked around and asked the boy if he knew where Azerius had gone. Kyus pointed at the front door and shrugged. "He just went out with his men."

"I thought he was heading to the castle?"

"Maybe after his men," he said with another shrug and yawn. "The sun just rose, Harmony. Why are you up so early?"

She seemed to wake up early every day now.

Today she would follow him. Yes, she would watch him. If he wouldn't show her the army willingly, she'd sneak around and see him organize his regiment herself. *It's time.* She was a seasoned enough hunter to follow his tracks stealthily so that he didn't notice her. He wasn't so hard to track.

She followed his footprints to smoke forming behind a hill. There she smelled cooked meat, it smelled like wild boar, and she could hear laughter and men shouting. As she got closer and walked around the hillside, she realized it was a military camp, only about a mile from their home.

She walked stealthily toward the tents. When she saw men walking in light-blue armor toward the edge of camp, she hid behind some trees. Many carried light-blue flags, the same flags hoisted on poles by tents surrounding the campgrounds. The Caravian flags. And the men wore the light-blue armor of Caravia, the metal glistening in the sunlight. She had never seen so much metal.

Then she caught him. The general riding tall and proud, in polished blue, atop his brown stallion before his lines of men. They held spears and shields and stood perfectly still. He seemed at home among his men. And with his confidence and prowess, she loved him even more. She understood that his army was *his* family. These soldiers were his brothers. He gathered a hundred men in a line in perfect harmony. These were the best fighters, according to Azerius, in the known world. He had told her he trained this special elite guard to defend the borders from Egypt. And even the far northern lands she had recently learned of: Hatti, Alashiya, Arzawa and Mitanni.

Another cavalry, with hundreds of foot soldiers, stood together in a perfect line—erect and at attention while General Azerius trotted before them. He inspected their spears, shields, shoulder pads, breastplates, helms, and shoes. He even checked the sharpness of their swords. They were punished for the slightest imperfection. And yet all of them knew Azerius and smiled—when permitted. She was mesmerized by everything. It was their comradery and closeness, just like her nymph family, that she loved. This was so much like her Amazon sisters back home.

She sat all day behind the bushes watching. Then she was startled as she saw him, over fifty yards away, cock his head back to the bushes she hid behind. Had he seen her? Of course he had. She considered that he might have known she was there all along.

He smiled.

Then she ran home.

9

HER CONFIDENCE

"I HAVE TO GO FOR A FEW DAYS TO THE CASTLE, HARMONIA. I told you I have to visit the king."

She watched him all afternoon, packing and preparing for his journey—the journey she wanted to join him in. She had fought with him the whole day, explaining why she should accompany him. Now, in late afternoon, he was stuffing his last tunics inside a bag as she lay on her side just watching him. He walked to an adjoining room, and she heard him put on his armor. Then the sound of the clanging metal of his pteruges. Kyus had polished it the day before. Just as she had prepared her perfect dresses—clothes she would be wearing for no one.

She jumped up and walked into the adjoining room. There Azerius stood staring into a large mirror.

"Take me," she insisted, putting her arms around him from behind. "Please."

He sighed deeply. "Must we fight again?"

"Not fight. Just take me."

She twirled stupidly behind him like a little girl, wearing a long scarlet dress. She performed the nymph dance of the games. She had on simple linen, translucent like a nightgown and certainly not something that she could wear outside the home. He laughed. When she finished her dance, she leaned against the wall with her arms folded, pouting.

"You can't leave without me," she admonished him, wagging a finger. "You said that the next time you'd leave, you'd be taking me to the shore. You never did that either."

"But I can't take you now, my love. We've been through this a thousand times."

She yanked at his arm and pulled him close, shaking her head. She looked up into his eyes and ran a hand through his curly hair.

"You're so beautiful, Harmony," he said. "So lovely. But winter's coming. And there are a lot of troubles along the eastern shore with Amurru. Amurru is not controlled by Egypt. They want to make excursions into the continent through Sutsik. And if they're assisted by Mitanni and Assyria, I smell war. You'll have to stay with Kyus for a long while if that happens."

She pulled away from him. "I was not a good girl, you know." She was surprised to hear her voice breaking. "I did terrible things. You once said so yourself. The crystal witch as you called me..." Sudden tears fell. "The crystal witch never deserved you, Azerius, but you've tamed her. Yes, you have. Only you. So now you should take your witch to the city. I'm ready to be a good girl for you and only you. I'm ready to meet your brother."

"You act like I'm leaving for good."

She shook her head. Then she touched his sparkling metal breastplate. "Of all the things you've shown me of your world, I think I like this best. It is what makes your brothers know who their true family is. You all look alike. No one hurts anybody by mistake, because they are family. It is the sharpest diamond."

"Harmony..." He lifted her chin. "I never showed you that. You came uninvited to my camp."

She frowned and he couldn't help but laugh. He tied a bag on the floor and frowned, looking at her. He ran his hand along her cheek. "Come on. What is it? I've left before. You've been acting crazy today."

"When you ride up to your castle again, they will all look like you," she said with a shrug. "They will all wear the same clothes. The same dress. I remember the last time, you had practically forgotten me when you returned. It's as if they all wear this armor. They are your brothers and sisters. Caravians. But I never will be Caravian. Even with my eye makeup. My speech. My imitation of your accent and movements. None of your women have my skin color. You wear your blue metal when you fight in battle, but I wear blue on my skin forever. No one up there looks like me. And I believe that is why you will never take me there."

"They don't look like you," he replied matter-of-factly. Then he looked impatiently at a pile of his clothes. "But I gave you makeup to hide your color."

"It's for my face," she said with a shrug. "It doesn't cover everything."

"Then don't complain if I don't show you around town," he said with a sigh.

"You'll leave me one day."

She turned from him, feeling suddenly very sad. Terribly depressed because, somehow, she was sure that was true. Then she brushed another tear from her eyes. She looked out the window near the adjacent dining room toward the valley. This window faced the cliffs under the blue castle. That is where he would leave her.

"Oh, Harmony!" he ran to her and embraced her. "You're being ridiculous."

"Am I?"

"I'll be back soon, okay?" he said, brushing her hair back from her eyes. "Stop worrying."

"I love you."

"I know. And I love you. I shall return soon. I promise."

"All right."

He removed the armor and laid it down with some of his bags. He would travel in a simple tunic. Then he picked up a small bag and left the armor on the floor. Kyus would take it later.

He packed everything into a chariot outside. He walked to the front door. He would have walked out had Harmony not stopped him. She tapped on the back of his neck.

He turned. She smiled wide.

"Azerius…"

"Hmm? Yes? What is it?"

"I'm pregnant."

"What?"

"I'm pregnant."

He searched her face.

"I just know it. Nymphs know when it's time. And I haven't had my time with the moon in the longest time. And…" She pointed to her stomach with a large grin. "I'm growing in my belly. I'm pregnant, Azerius. That was the other reason I wanted to go with you. I'm going to have your baby."

He stood frozen at the threshold. His eyes opened wide. Then his mouth seemed to drop open. He turned pale. Peaked.

There was complete silence. He dropped his bag and stared at her, looking as if he would strike her. Harmonia's heart was racing in anticipation, having waited so long to tell him. She had to tell him now because with his talk of war, he might not be back till after she delivered. She had excitedly waited for just the right moment. Now she felt like she had picked the wrong one.

His anger left him and he laughed, shaking his head.

"A joke. You can be so cruel, Harmony. You told me you were barren. You said your people come from the pyramid.

You said you can't have a child unless it is part of the games and with the blessings of Olympus."

She simply shook her head and touched her belly. "Nephrea will be born in six moons, my love. I feel it and I know it. And if she is as beautiful as you, she will be the prettiest girl in the entire world. So I shall name her Nephrea, which means beauty. Nephratee in Napea. Nefertiti in Caravian and Egyptian. Nefer. Beauty, Azerius, beauty. Isn't this wonderful?"

He only stared, searching her eyes. And she did too, for she wondered how he was taking the news.

"Are you… sad?"

He said nothing.

"I just know it," she continued, practically giddy. Then she started spinning around the room, dancing again in her red dress. "I've been sick too. My stomach is starting to bulge. See."

She showed him her belly again. Azerius returned inside and stared at the ground.

"I didn't believe it either, Azerius. But it's true. I see all the signs. Just look at my stomach. I'm so happy. I'm so happy! You made me so happy. And wait for Nephrea! She'll be beautiful, I just know she will. I mean, she'll have to be a girl. I don't think nymphs can have boys. But I've never known a nymph to deliver outside of Azurea either, so…I don't know. She'll be wonderful. Coming from you, you're so handsome, she will be so very pretty. I can't wait to have my very own baby. She will be so beautiful. I just know it, Azerius. I know she will."

He ran a hand through his curly hair and fell on a chair by the door. Then he just sat there, frozen. Harmonia's joy was deflated. It looked as though she had killed his favorite horse or burned down the house.

"I'm sorry. You *are* sad."

"Harmonia!" he shouted. "I have a wife!"

"A wife? Oh …" She knelt by him and took his hand. Then she looked into his eyes with a comforting smile. "Then you can tell her too."

He stared at her in shock. his eyes bulging. She ran a hand over his shoulder, but he batted it away. He stared back at the floor, and then he put his head in both his hands.

"What have I done?" he asked, running his hand through his hair again. "What have I done? What will I do?"

"What's the matter?"

"A child?" he asked, as if hearing it for the first time. Harmonia seemed to be making it worse by simply nodding. "And you've *named* her?" His face filled with disgust. "You must get rid of her!"

"What?"

"You can't have a child." He shook his head like crazy. "It won't be permitted. The king won't allow it."

"I'd rather die than kill this child, Azerius. I will never do that."

He squinted at her and jumped up. "You have to."

"No."

"I… I must go, Harmonia. Sard it all, I'm running late. We'll talk about this when I return. Somehow it will work out. I'll return in a quarter moon."

He ran out of the room and rushed to his chariot. He didn't even look back. It was bad enough that he was leaving without a hug, now he wouldn't even look at her.

She touched her belly and felt fear for the first time. She had never trusted anyone in her life. Was she stupid to have trusted him?

She walked to the glass window and saw Kyus walking Antilus slowly over wild grass by a wooden fence. Then she saw her lover shouting at Kyus and barking orders to him, now in the foulest mood. She had never seen him so angry. Why was he angry? In her Isle of Napea, many men from the games bedded with nymphs all the time. And it was a common practice to have multiple suitors. And even if they never saw their daughters again, they felt no anger or hatred toward the nymphs. They felt joy for their lovers, for their future children. Why was it so different here in Caravia?

She leaned her head on the warm glass. Then she shook her head.

Nephrea, wait and see, you will be so beautiful. Don't worry. And your father will love you.

CAPTAIN HADRIAN

AZERIUS HAD PLANNED FOR WEEKS TO ENTERTAIN A POWERFUL guest. Every day he watched his young servant Kyus and the other slaves busy themselves about his property tending trees and sweeping the road, repainting the entry gate, rearranging the indoor furniture, and cleaning the stables, all to make everything perfect for his guest. And now, in his villa at sunset, he sat with Captain Hadrian on his outdoor patio overlooking the backyard orchard and fields while being entertained, unintentionally, by the swordplay of his lover.

Harmonia jumped and parried, slicing the air at an invisible enemy over a patch of wild grass surrounded by trees. Her motion was skilled, even alluring, as it was perfectly smooth and agile like a dancer, yet no opponent would want to be her sparring partner. The sweat dripped from Harmonia's blue forehead as she moved about in tightly roped saffron linen. Even when facing his aged childhood friend, he could hear the wind pierced by her blade.

Hadrian watched too, squinting. He reclined on an outdoor carpet. A fire had already been made between them for after sunset.

The old man had long, unkempt gray hair with a long

brown leather coat but retained light-blue leather guards for his shins and forearms. It was an informal uniform that he wore on the battlefield. Hadrian had always been the sort of man who looked uncomfortable in civilian clothes. The captain sipped beer from a silver cup, furrowing his brow, seemingly scrutinizing Harmonia's ballet.

"I met her at Crystal Lake," said Azerius. "Well, she actually showed up in King Karthra's Court. You should have seen her. Such pride. Such bravery. She claims to be a queen and I believe her. She stood tall before the crowd as the barbarians pronounced her sentence. She's strong and cunning, but ignorant. Not stupid, you see, just very ignorant of the world."

"Who taught her to move like that?"

"She taught herself. I showed her some of our ways, and she showed me a thing or two from the wild. She claims that the wood nymphs back home learn to dance with blades too. In a day or two, she learned our sword arts and can now fight as well as I can."

"I see," Hadrian said, nodding slowly. Hadrian turned from her dance and looked into Azerius's eyes. "Son, you told me you met her only a couple moons ago."

"No. Far longer. I've hidden her, I suppose." He chuckled uncomfortably. "I'm sorry. I couldn't tell anyone."

Hadrian just drank more beer from the goblet.

Kyus walked over and bowed before Hadrian. "Would you like something to eat before supper, sire? We have dry mutton. I'm afraid it's going to take a little longer than I expected for the rest of it. I was detained tending to the lady's horse."

Hadrian's eyes widened. Azerius figured it was the comment "lady's horse." No woman owned anything in Caravia.

"No, no," Hadrian replied.

Azerius cocked his head back, watching his lover dance. He hadn't spoken to Harmonia for two weeks after finding out about the baby, but now, after enough time had passed, he accepted the pregnancy and was back to loving her. Before her audience, Harmonia kept jumping and slicing the air seemingly with even more fervor.

"What do you think?" asked Azerius, sipping beer and staring.

"She's dangerous."

Azerius couldn't help but laugh.

"You told me what lies in her belly," Hadrian added. "I tell you, she is dangerous, son."

Azerius shrugged and slouched back on his elbow.

"It is a simple matter, Azerius, and you needn't have asked for my counsel."

Azerius nodded, rose, and walked over to a table to pour himself some more beer from a wooden pitcher. Then he sipped it and stared again at the sword show with his friend. She did not stop her terrible display. It seemed his lover's energy was boundless.

"What can you tell me about Karthra?" the captain asked, changing the subject. "Have things changed? Is the fool still planning an attack in the North? Is he moving beyond his stinking bogs? Is he threatening Iselborn in Azerbanith? Or King Milus?"

"I'd rather kill myself," he answered, staring at his lover.

"Hmm?"

"I'd rather kill myself than lose her."

"General, what do you think of King Karthra of Logencia?"

"Hmm? Karthra is a fat, stupid, lazy fool. Logenth is no threat. We have no foreign threats within the continent. And you should never have suggested the trip to the king. It was a complete waste of time. Except for—" He gestured at her with the hand holding the cup. "Her."

"She is why you summoned me?"

"I'm lost." He nodded. "I don't know what to do."

"Oh, come on, Azerius!" Hadrian said, slapping his leg.

"She's just a woman. Take care of her. There is no confusion in the matter of women."

"She's not just a woman. She's greater than any woman I've ever known."

"Don't be an imbecile." Hadrian covered his ears. Then he pointed at him, admonishing him like a child, just like he had done when Azerius was a young boy. "You are the chief general of Caravia, Azerius. You're married to Lady Ila, and you have four beautiful children. Go to them. Your royal family. And you will remain royal. After you kill this nymph. You don't need counsel, you need someone to whack you over the head."

"Need I remind you, I'm your superior."

"Oh, stop!" The old man wearily rubbed his eyes. "May I remind *you* that I helped raise you when you were still wetting yourself. If you don't want to kill her, kill the child then. Fetch some Pennyroyal tea and have her drink it, or send a viper to visit her at night. Or…pound on her sarding belly! Maybe if you're lucky, her dancing around today will do it for you. Just don't tell me you don't know what to do. If you don't, be assured your brother will know what to do. The king loves you, General, but he knows how to keep the peace in Caravia. I warn you the king knows well what's going on here. Rumors abound in the city, and he isn't pleased." The old man sighed and sank back on his elbow. He grabbed a vine of grapes, still watching Azerius from the corner of his eye. Then he shook his head. "This is beneath you. A child is woman's talk. Take care of it and make sure the abomination is never born. Your baby will not even be human. I've protected your reputation as best I can in Court, but a sarding blue nymph baby is not going to bode well. It will ruin you."

Azerius nervously looked over at Harmonia, wondering if she had heard them. She seemed none the wiser, still slashing the air with her sword.

"Tell my brother that nothing has changed since my travels," Azerius said. "He should concentrate on the surrounding empires, not Atala. King Karthra holds an untrained barbaric army. My nymph maiden alone could conquer his undisciplined and savage kingdom. We do not have problems in the North. The East and South across the sea, now that is another matter."

Hadrian seemed relieved at the change in discourse and nodded.

"Hmm. Nothing's changed. The water protects us, Azerius. But King Tolen differs in opinion. Your brother worries over this fool of a king of yours, not because of Karthra's strength, but because of his location. He has stretched further than any king before, and he rules the center of the continent. If he and the other lords were to band together further, they could—"

"They will never band together, Hadrian," Azerius said. Then he looked over at Harmonia again. At times she looked over, seemingly knowing they were watching her. "Never. We have order, they do not." He pulled the rope securing his thin brown robe and reclined even more.

Yes, by the gods, even my wood nymph maiden holds more order than these barbarians.

"The sea and cliffs guard us from the North," Azerius added. "Caravia is protected. We are safe. Tell my brother."

"Tell him yourself."

Then his guest watched Harmonia twirl in circles, flipping around like a monkey. No, she did not fight like his men —she fought like a dancer. That was nothing he had taught her.

"I'm not really worried about Karthra," Hadrian said, shaking his head. Then he reached forward and discreetly pointed at her. He spoke softly: "If she is with child, either get rid of her or get rid of the child. You cannot have both. At least do that, my friend. The king might allow an affair to continue. He already has up to now. I can see what I can do for it to continue. *If* you compromise and kill the child. You cannot have both, I tell you."

Azerius sighed deeply. Then he shook his head. "She won't allow it."

"Oh, by the gods!" Hadrian ran his hand over his face. Then he lowered his head and rubbed his eyes again. "She? Who sarding cares what she won't allow! Has the lack of war warped your mind? Or is it camping alone outside the city with a nymph? Are you an idiot?"

"She can continue to live here under the castle with the baby," Azerius said, equally quietly.

"With a blue baby?" Hadrian snapped in a hushed whisper. "A bloody blue nymph baby! What do you think the king will say? Or the people? More importantly, my dear friend, what will your *wife* say at the birth of a nymph child?"

"She doesn't have to know."

"Don't be stupid. She already knows. No one has any sense of privacy here, you know that. I've done my best to protect you, lad. Ila let you bed this witch because it makes you happy. She deserves bounds of love for that. But—" He pointed at him as if he would slap him in the face with his finger. "I warn you, a child is a disgrace to Lady Ila and our royal family. A *nymph* child is abhorrent. She will not stand for the damage to her reputation, and neither will your brother. And…neither will I."

"I love her."

"Who cares. You can have any woman in the palace. Is this lady of the lake that good in bed?"

"Don't speak of it anymore," Azerius replied.

"You came to me."

Azerius nodded, but he turned from his friend.

Then, after both sat silent, still mesmerized by the dancing nymph, he jumped up to get more beer.

Hadrian's smile vanished as Harmonia came, swaying her hips, over to the patio. But not only was there fear in his old friend's expression, there was awe. It seemed every time a stranger met her, they were transfixed by her presence.

"Kyus," Harmonia hollered over to him as she approached the two friends. The slave was washing a dish by a nearby fountain. "Get me a towel! And be quick. It's so hot."

Kyus bowed to the nymph.

"I saw you watching me," Harmonia said with a grin. "Am I doing well with the blade, sir?"

But Hadrian didn't answer.

"Beautifully, Harmony," said Azerius. "Absolutely beautifully. This is my dear friend Captain Hadrian. He is a soldier of our army too. Hadrian, meet Harmonia."

She walked over to Hadrian and nodded. He glanced at her oddly, surprised at the lack of respect. She did not bow her head nor kneel before him, as was customary for a lady when meeting a man.

Hadrian cleared his throat. "Azerius tells me you are a queen? A nymph queen from the mystical Isle of Napea, the land of Olympus?"

"Yes. I am the Azure Nymph Queen. I am Amazon."

"He said your world is blue. Like your hands and skin. And that the sun is green?"

"Yes."

"Incredible."

"It is an isle blessed by the gods, General. By Lord Hades."

"Blessed by Lord Hades?" asked Hadrian, sitting up straighter. He flashed a look at Azerius. "Sounds like hubris. Blessed by the god of death?"

"Hades blesses Napea," she said with a shrug.

Then she wiped some more sweat off her forehead. The slave finally handed her a towel, and she wiped her face, chest, arms, and slightly protruding belly.

"Hades prefers my race," Harmonia said. "He looks down upon Cronos's lands and humans. He wants all of the continent of Atala to be part of his domain, not his father's or brother's."

"Sounds like hubris to speak of Zeus like that," repeated Hadrian.

"I am under Hades' care, not Zeus's. I care nothing for Zeus. Zeus only concerns himself with man. Blessed Hades is for my people, the Amazon."

Then she carelessly tossed the sword that she held under one of her arms toward a tree. Had this been a haphazard throw, it would have been ignored, but it landed perfectly erect beside a tree trunk. It was as if it was the finale to her show.

"Why don't you go inside and wash up, my love," said Azerius. "Kyus can attend to you. Supper will be ready soon."

She kissed him slowly on the cheek. Then she gave Hadrian an inkling of the bow he had been waiting for, although it was more of a quick dip of her head.

Azerius turned to Hadrian. He was surprised by the expression on his old mentor's face. This was a general who had once fought off Egyptians in battle on the beaches of Caravia when outnumbered five-fold, scaled to the unreachable heights of Zonoch to defend the kingdom from Hinterland barbarians, and fought in the East, in the land of Canaan. This brave, powerful man had a look Azerius had never seen on his face—fear.

"Get rid of her. Get rid of her now, Azerius."

11

MY GOD

"Oh Antilus, you shall be Nephrea's too, girl."

Antilus neighed as if understanding.

"Why, the princess shall ride you like I have, into the clouds and one day under the green sun over the land that shall be hers."

Kyus walked over carrying a pile of logs in his arms. "Harmony, I can tend Antilus for you."

"You'd like to, wouldn't you?" Harmonia asked with a giggle.

The baby stirred. She lay wrapped in a blanket beside a tree.

"Oh Nephrea, perhaps…"

Kyus ran to the baby.

"No, Kyus, you tend Antilus and I will tend Nephrea."

"That's what I said," he said with a laugh.

The slave put the logs down and gently grabbed Antilus's head. The white unicorn snuggled into his arms and Harmonia giggled again. Then Harmonia carried her baby into the house. Nephrea would not stop crying in her arms.

Harmonia sat down on pillows beside the dining room table, allowing the baby to suckle her breast. It was dimly lit inside the house, almost like evening, even though it was a clear day outside. And the smell of eggs and meat lingered. She would have preferred the outdoors, but the baby always seemed quieter in the darkness of the indoors.

There was a knock at the door, and Harmonia assumed it was Kyus. But Kyus would have simply walked in. This visitor kept knocking.

"Come in. The door's open."

A very tall man in a long black robe with a hood walked in. He lowered his hood and looked at her and the baby. Then Harmonia did her best to jump up while nursing her.

"Queen Harmonia," Hades said. "My lovely Harmony. It's been too long. How are you, my dear queen?"

"Lord Hades." She moved the baby away and covered herself with her peplos. Nephrea started crying again. "But… what brings you here now?"

Hades grabbed a red apple off a table and bit into it, then walked over to a nearby wooden bench. He sat down and looked with disdain at the baby.

"Sit, Harmonia," he said, "Sit back down. I see your princess is born. Happy birthday."

"She is my beautiful Nephree."

"Nephratee. A fitting Napean name. Beautiful because she is your daughter, of course, my lovely flower. I didn't even need Kore to predict she would be beautiful."

"Thank you, Lord Hades."

Kyus barged through the door stammering, "Do you know this man? He ignored the guards by the gates."

Hades cocked his head back, looking amused.

"Yes, leave us, Kyus," Harmonia said. "He is a friend."

"He barged in."

"No, *you* just barged in, slave," Hades said, finally looking at him and wagging a finger. "Now get out."

"Very well…madam," he stammered with a cough. "Do

you want me to take Nephrea? Or…would you like me to get your guest some mutton or figs? Or perhaps mead?"

"Never mind, Kyus. Just go."

Hades chuckled, shaking his head. Then he took another large bite of his apple.

When the slave was gone and the door was shut, Hades turned back and said, "I wish my visit could be more pleasant. I've come to warn you. You're in danger. I instructed you to learn, and you have done my bidding well for many years. Now it has been long enough to have served your banishment. I can petition and convince my brother Zeus and sister Sara that you may return to Azurea. They will permit this for me. But you must leave Caravia now. I never wished you to live with Caravians. I fear you are forgetting your quest."

"I never knew I was on a quest."

"All lives are on a quest. Yours has become muddled. Now I am trying to return harmony to you, Harmonia."

She adjusted her dress, exposing her breast, and resumed breastfeeding the baby in front of him.

"Your family, Harmonia, do you remember them? Your family? The nymphs of Napea? Your closest sisters, who were murdered by mine. You crossed the strait to learn to fight to avenge their deaths? Don't you remember?"

"Of course I do!" Harmonia snapped. And she was surprised at the sudden bite in her tone. She had been so used to joy that she had almost forgotten bitterness.

"And you've endured, Queen. You've learned. But now you are about to make a grave error in your disregard for your people." He leaned forward. "Are you holidaying here, Amazon? Enjoying rest and relaxation in an enemy's lands? Is this to be your fate? An incubator for a maggot in an illegitimate union with a man who cares little for you?"

"Perhaps Kyus is right. Maybe you should leave."

Hades wagged a finger before her. "You don't belong here.

Not only that, you're getting weak. If I had said those words a year ago, you wouldn't have suggested I leave, you would have gotten up and struck me in the face. I warn you, if you stay in Caravia, you will experience more misery than you can possibly imagine."

"I'm happy here."

Then she smiled and stared down at her baby as Nephrea suckled. The small, fat baby responded to her, clutching her more tightly.

"I see how you've darkened your eyes," he said with a hint of disgust. "Not that I totally mind. Foreign customs shall be yet another affront to Zeus and Hera."

"Why not?" she asked with a raised eyebrow. "I am Caravian. I repeat, great Hades, what can I do for you? Why are you here? What can I do for my god? Would shouting at you be better?"

"If it was genuine, yes." He took a deep breath and shook his head. "Don't ask me to get out of here. *You* get out of here. Return to your people and avenge your family. Take the nymphs and take Gaia. Don't live under man; force man to live under you. That little worm in your arms will thank you later."

"For the first time in my life, I'm happy—overjoyed with this little *maggot and worm*, as you call her, in my company."

"If you remain here, they will poison you, strangle you, or cut you down with an axe for the crystal witch that they believe you are. You will die happily. You and your baby shall die in absolute bliss."

That got her attention. She trembled. "Is that a prophecy? Did the witch goddess predict that?"

He shook his head. "It is a conclusion that even a child could reach." Then he bit into his apple again.

"Just go. Azerius loves me."

"Yes. And he will kill you."

"He loves me."

"And after he kills you, he will kill that little darling in your arms."

She pulled her baby closer. Another shiver ran down her back, because seeing the god's expression, she believed him. Or at least she thought he believed it.

"I can protect her," Hades said. "Give me the child and return to Azure Blue. While you build your famed Amazon nation, I shall guard her. You cannot have both. If you do not meet your destiny, you will fail in your usefulness to me. I will abandon you and take the treasures I've given you, and you will suffer. You will fall. Not by my wish, but by your own. I warn you, Harmonia, because unlike this idiotic general, I love you. Not him. I do."

"Is that it? Are you jealous of him?"

"*Do not toy with a god, Harmonia!*" he thundered, jumping up. He towered over her, and his shadow cast over her and the baby made Nephrea begin to cry. Harmonia shook too in response to his fury. "Your happiness is fleeting! You cannot escape this fate. You are *my* seed, which will eventually destroy Zeus! You are *MY flower, not his! Not a Caravian's. You are mine! My seed. NOT HIS!* Do you understand? You ask if I am jealous. *YES!* Now leave him!"

She jumped up and ran out of the room taking Nephrea. She heard him follow her down the walkway.

"Get away from me!" she said, spinning around. "Do not ever speak to me like that again! I never wanted your help! You came to me. I don't want to hear any more of this. You and Sara banished me. You didn't have the courage to stop her. How should I expect you to help me now? You're just like the rest of your family. You say you love me? Well, I don't love you. All right? Go away!"

He grabbed her shoulder and raised his palm to strike her but, instead, he fumbled for something in his robe. He pulled out a golden rod studded with diamonds and rubies. She thought he was about to use it as a weapon to strike her, so she covered her head, but instead he raised it and it lengthened before her eyes. It glistened even in the dim light of twilight.

"Behold my scepter," he said, pushing the staff against her chest. "This is the scepter of the gods. More beautiful, I say, than even Zeus's thunderbolt or Poseidon's trident. Take my staff and wave it over a flower in your garden. Choose one that is withering, like you. Do it. Any of them that is dying. And you will see why I choose you and your people above all else. After this spectacle, after you see it with your own eyes, I will leave."

She looked down at her baby, who was restless and crying in her arms. Then she looked up and shook her head.

"Forget the baby! Do as I say. Use the staff and save a dying flower."

She looked up at the god, confused. He gestured impatiently to her flower garden beside the house.

Kyus dropped a bucket of water beside Antilus and headed across the grass field toward her. He must have heard their fight.

Harmonia laid Nephrea down gently even as the baby still cried.

"Try it," he said. "Quickly. After you see, I promise I will go."

She resolved to obey him, primarily so he'd leave. She walked over to some withered white lilies.

"Now wave the staff over a dead one. Choose the one that has been dead longest. Go ahead."

She wrinkled her brow but obeyed. She waved it over a flower. Then her eyes bulged as the white flower became whole again.

"What sort of magic is this?"

"Magic?" he said with a smile. "Not magic. You. Behold the power of Ambrosia. It is the power of the queen of all nymphs. Yours. Only a nymph queen could wield my scepter so. Because only a nymph queen is favored by me. A part of *my* family. Even I cannot do what you have just done. My love wills this power for your people. My love for you, Harmonia. I have chosen you. You have the power to revive your people. Not I."

She pulled the white lily from the bush and stared at it in her blue palm. The petals were perfectly whole, without a blemish.

"But I did nothing."

"You are my flower," he said, shaking his head and running his hand down her azure cheek, as Azerius often did. "Only Ambrosia will be the instrument to bring life to lifelessness. Light in my darkness. By Hades. I am a dark god, but with you by my side, we may raise life. With you as my weapon, we shall bring life to Atala, like your child. Then we shall move on to the entire world. Forget Nephrea. Forget Caravia. Rule this world as you were meant to do. With me by your side. Aidoneus and Harmonia."

And he leaned down and kissed her gently on her cheek.

"Unhand her, sir!" Kyus ran right up to the god's face in fury. "This is General Azerius's home! He would not look kindly upon you touching his lady."

"*His lady?* His lady indeed, slave." Then Hades turned to Harmonia and bowed before her. "My queen, I take my leave as promised. Your company is becoming irksome. I came to warn you. Just as Kyus's family was killed by Assyrians in the land of Hontfur, I see terrible things for you if you remain here. Other bad omens have been, in fact, prophesied by my niece. You are certainly not Azerius's *lady*. Azerius has a wife. You are mine."

"How did you know about Hontfur, sir?" asked the slave. He was so shocked that he seemed to have forgotten all about Harmonia. Hades threw his black hood over his head and walked toward the door of the villa.

"You don't belong here," Hades said without turning around. "My offer still stands. I can protect the child. When

Azerius returns, ask for me in the stars and, by the power of Astraios, I shall help the young princess survive. Not that I care for her, I only care for your lineage. For Ambrosia. I will guard her in exchange for your reunion with your people. Simply look toward the stars with your prayers. Even after you have forsaken me tonight, I will still hear your prayer. That is how strong my love is for you. But you shall be punished for your lack of faith. So also warns Kore, the goddess Persephone."

"Goodbye sir," said Kyus, still in shock.

Hades rushed off toward the grassy fields. Harmonia watched until he reached under a tree and vanished before their eyes.

"Who was that man?" asked Kyus.

"He is my god."

12

GATHERING KINDLING

AZERIUS DID NOT RETURN ALONE TO THE VILLA. Accompanying him was a unit of a hundred blue-metal-clad soldiers rushing by horseback down the cliffs from Caravia, trailing light-blue flags. She had spotted them while practicing sword play again in the orchard, as she jumped about, dancing and slicing the air. Kyus had been tending nearby plum trees when he turned toward the sound of their hoofs. The army wore the blue armor of Caravia. It was twilight and already some of the soldiers carried torches whose flame and smoke stirred behind them like smoky tails.

Harmonia stopped and stared. She thought that perhaps there was a disturbance among the citizenry to elicit such a great show of force. Then, from the corner of her eye, she caught Kyus running to her in a panic.

"Harmony! Harmony!"

Harmonia stood erect, staring with a big grin at the approaching army.

"Harmonia?"

"Yes Kyus, what is it?"

"You must go!"

"Go? Go where? Why? Azerius has returned."

"Leave. Go! Get out of here. You're in danger. I've heard rumors. Now I see it to be true. Master never rides with his men from the city. He returns alone. Their approaching his villa is terrible. Either they intend to battle a fierce army in Trialga, or they came to battle *you*. Imprison or kill you!"

She looked back and chuckled nervously. "Don't be silly." He started tugging wildly at her arm. Finally, she batted him away. "Stop it, Kyus!"

"You must go! Hide or get out of here!"

"I won't," she said, shaking her head. But she searched her slave's face. He was so worried.

"Harmonia," he continued in a panic, "master is returning with an army. He means to hurt or imprison you. Even if he loves you, he won't have the power to stop the king. He could simply be following his brother's orders to gather up his men and take you to the dungeon!"

The approaching torches brightened the grassy courtyard in front of the villa. She looked back at Kyus and searched his eyes. Then she heaved a sigh. "I can't believe…but…very well, release Antilus, Kyus, from the stable. Let my monokera roam free."

"Release Antilus? Why? You must run."

"I won't abandon Azerius. But you can release Antilus from the stable."

"Harmonia. No. You must go!"

"Obey me, Kyus. Release Antilus. Say nothing more. I greet his army with honor."

Kyus hesitated for a moment. He kept shaking his head, staring at the line of men and torches.

"Release her!" she shouted to Kyus. *"Obey me, Kyus!"* The shout knocked sense into her slave. He tipped his head and ran.

It didn't take long for the horses to arrive at the front gates. They rode down and circled the villa. Harmonia simply stood by the entrance, waiting for their approach. When she saw Azerius, she smiled and waved.

"Azerius! Azerius!"

He didn't return the greeting. He looked down from atop his horse, seeming miserable. His face was drawn and he stared at the ground. Then he clenched a fist as his other hand shook.

"Are you the crystal witch of the lake?" asked a soldier beside him.

"I am not a witch."

The leader wore a blue helmet and had a short gray beard. He wore the same light-blue armor as her lover. The man turned to Azerius. Azerius slowly nodded.

Before Harmonia could say another word, a heavy roped net was thrown over her. As she fell under its weight, she felt them search her body and remove her sword or, rather, Azerius's sword, and some knives hidden in her leather boots and belt.

"What's the meaning of this!" asked Harmonia. "Azerius? I am the lady of this house. Stop this!"

But Azerius was still atop his horse, staring at the ground.

"Azerius! Azerius!"

A soldier crouched down and touched her ears. Then he touched her hand.

"She's blue, all right. This is the habiru witch. We have her."

"I'm no witch!"

"Bring her to a tree," said Azerius quietly. He spoke coldly, without emotion, but each word was said slowly, as if it pained him. "By order of the king."

"And the child?"

"Build a pyre by the tree for both mother and child."

"Aye, sire."

"Azerius, my lord!" cried Kyus, running to his horse. He

tugged at his leg. "Let her go! This is Harmony! Let Harmony go! This is your Harmony!"

"Away," Azerius cried and he kicked Kyus. "Get out of here, slave!"

Kyus stood over the net looking down at Harmonia. Tears formed in his eyes.

When she saw a soldier grab Nephrea from the house, Harmonia lost all reason. That broke all her stoicism. It drove her to madness.

She yelled and screamed and kicked under the net. She shouted to the clouds and cursed the sky. She didn't care if anyone answered. She looked at Azerius in disbelief. He still sat atop his horse with no emotion, no words, stupidly staring down at nothing. His betrayal was more painful than the sharpest sword.

They dragged her along the grass like an animal.

Azerius dismounted and walked beside her as they dragged her to the largest oak tree near the orchard beside his villa. They brought sticks, leaves, and tinder and lit the base of the tree on fire.

"At least save our child!" Harmonia cried to Azerius. "Please, by the gods, Azerius, please! Do whatever you want to me, but please save Nephrea! Save your daughter! I beg you!"

He said nothing. He merely walked beside her.

"You're her father! Answer me! Can you no longer speak? Are you that much of a coward! You're her father! You can't do this to our baby!"

She was pulled over rocks, flipping her onto her back, and slid further across muddy grass.

"What's wrong with you! Speak to me!"

"I am not the father of a nymph child," he said quietly.

She left him then. She closed her eyes and left him. She left everything…

SHE FOUND herself standing in line back along the Blue River. And her sisters, her family, stood with her as the goddess Demeter, the one they called Sara, and her wretched witch daughter, Cora, also known as the goddess Persephone, walked by each of her sisters, opening their mouths like animals, seeking the culprit. She tasted the forbidden myrle berry still on her tongue. And she watched as the gods shoved, slapped, and stabbed her sisters.

A tall man in a black cloak walked beside Sara. But he gazed at only one person. One nymph in the line. Her. Right into her eyes. He looked at her with curiosity. Or awe…or…

"Is curiosity worth starting a war, nymph?" asked Sara. Sara gestured to the battlefield, the river full of dead bodies. "Hmm? Was it worth this bloodshed? How many in your immortal family will never open their eyes after this transgression? You're to blame. How selfish. All for the theft of a fruit? A myrle berry. A *pomegranate*. Tell me. Why did you do it?"

"I was hungry."

"FORGIVE ME." Azerius said quietly, crouching beside her. Tears fell from his eyes. "Please forgive me, Harmony. You don't understand what's happening. This is the king's order. Your child and you will completely ruin me. I can't stop this."

She no longer cried. If death was her fate, she would do it honorably. Even if it meant the death of her child. But if there was any hope for Nephrea…

The ropes of the net were cut, and one of the large fiends grabbed her arm and pulled her to her feet. Azerius pushed the guard to the ground and shouted at him. Apparently, he didn't like the way he was handling her—a stupid thing, for the brute was about to burn her. Then Azerius led her to the burning tree.

"I will make this fast, my love. Don't worry," he said

quietly, removing his sword from the scabbard, "I will cut you. All right? I know how to do it so that you pass *before* the flames. Forgive me. Please. I know you…will not…cannot. But I know how to make this fast and painless…then I will do the same to that nymph baby."

"You will do nothing to my child! And every step you take that hurts me, one day, I shall hurt you many times more!"

Her hatred for this fool, this *man*, gave her the strength to finally whistle. The first time she whistled it was almost too hard for her lips to make the sound. But the second one was shrill. And as Azerius grabbed her arm again, she no longer fought, but she wouldn't stop whistling and gazing up to the dark, cloudy sky.

As they reached the fiery tree, Azerius unsheathed his sword.

But then he fell to the ground wailing in despair. With a sick, twisted irony, Harmonia helped him up before the oak tree. A fire now raged over the trunk of the largest tree at the villa.

It was then that the guards surrounding them stared and pointed up at the sky. Many signaled to Azerius in a panic, crying out to him, but the general was too distraught to notice. A few feet above hovered her winged white unicorn Antilus. The men took out their bows and began shooting at the unicorn. That made Azerius finally look up. The unicorn flew away to avoid the arrows but did not stray far.

Harmonia dropped all of her weight on Azerius's thick arm, the one that held his sword. Then she flipped her body with enough speed and torque to throw him. As he fell, she grabbed the fallen sword from his hand. The blade cut her arm and she bled, but the pain didn't stop her. Before the general could say another word, she plunged his own sword into his stomach. And she did not just stab him once. No, she thrust the sword repeatedly, again and again, penetrating his blue armor, spraying blood all over her face and hands.

"May Aidoneus have his way with you upon your death!"

As the guards ran to him, she spat on him.

Then she ran. She sprinted through the large open field. Her arm burned in sharp pain. So did her heart. She kept seeing Azerius's eyes widen in shock as she thrusted the sword into him. And now his blood burned her eyes.

She whistled again as arrows began to whistle past her. One penetrated the leather on her right calf, making her fall. When she looked back, she saw the whole army, all hundred men, running after her. Some held torches lighting their way. In the distance, she even caught Kyus staring.

Antilus hovered over her. A few arrows hit the white unicorn, and blood stained its white feathers. But Antilus would not leave her. Finally, when she got close enough, she leaped upon the unicorn, jumping from her one good leg. This was a remarkable feat in itself. She climbed up atop the horse, straightened, and then shot straight up into the sky.

Then she strafed back to the villa and faced the soldiers. Raising their general's sword she let out the battle cry of the Napeans.

"Aieee! Aieee!"

Her eyes stung from her lover's blood. Her bloody face must really have made her look like the witch or banshee they thought she was.

She searched the grounds for her baby, but she could not find her. She passed over the villa a few times, then across the stables and gardens and orchards in the back. She searched everywhere, amid javelins and arrows, but the soldiers must have taken her.

Then, when she was ready to dismount and fight the entire army if she must to find Nephrea, she heard the voice of her god, *"Fly to the highest summit atop Zonoch. Go now! I shall protect your daughter, Nephratee. I swear it, Harmonia. Run! Fly now!"*

She obeyed. She flew up the cliffs to the highest peaks,

even higher than the kingdom of Caravia, higher than any man could climb.

The night sky was now pitch black. The light of the stars and the moon shimmered faintly through clouds above.

She landed at the peak and stood with her white unicorn, looking down into the valley. There, far below, hundreds of bright yellow dots, torches, still lit the villa. His army would not abandon their fallen general. With luck, her Aidoneus would not only save her child but would send Azerius to Charon the ferryman.

She stood panting for the longest time, worrying over Nephrea. Or was she weeping? She was so disturbed that she didn't know. Her mind was fitful, her thoughts spinning in a disorderly fashion. At times, she returned to the Blue River and was fighting the dwarfs. Or facing Demeter.

She walked alongside a tranquil stream. In the moonlight, she saw the reflection of her yellow shirt and pants stained red and blood still flowing from her right arm and left calf. Upon her face was a mask—a crimson-stained mask of blood. She reached shaky, bloody fingers into the pool to wash away the blood, but instead, as if struck by madness, she leaped up, staring at the stars, and laughed. Her reaction surprised her. She roared with laughter. Fools! Their hunt for a "witch"?! She had twisted their vendetta into the death and mockery of their general. How dare they! She gazed up at the night sky and laughed and laughed. But when she had had her fill of her mirth, all turned quiet. Then she gazed down at her hands, still stained with a film of blood.

She fell to her knees and squinted her burning eyes, staring up at the dark clouds.

"Great Aidoneus…if you can hear me, save my child. Please. If you save Nephratee and care for her, as promised, I swear I will do anything you ask. I will do your bidding. I will be your flower. For the rest of my life, I shall devote myself to you."

There was silence and she felt foolish. But he had promised to protect her. Hadn't he?

Then she felt terror. What if he hadn't? Had she been so distraught, so confused, that she had imagined the god spoke to her? Had she abandoned her daughter?

But then she heard a voice through the wind, "I hear your prayer, my flower. Be at ease. I have taken the princess into my protection. Nephratee is safe. But now that you have sworn your allegiance to me, I ask that you go to Azure Blue without her. Build your Amazon army. Subdue the Mandrigel and build your kingdom. Then fulfill your destiny and the will of your champion. Take vengeance on my brother and sister. Take your revenge on man. When all is accomplished in Azurea, I shall return your child. I swear it. Go now. You will have your daughter, your princess, and you shall have far more. This I bequeath to you upon the will and love of your Aidoneus. And one day, by the words of the grain goddess, Atala shall all be yours as emperor and sovereign ruler. After my will be done."

She nodded and cupped her head in her hands. She could smell the iron and filth on her fingertips. She felt so weak.

And then she wept. After being happy for such a long time, she now felt completely alone, perhaps more alone than she had ever before. Hades had been right. She had let her guard down. She would never let her guard down again. Her arms and legs ached, her open gashes burned, but no pain was greater than the despair remaining in her heart. She wept thinking of her lost daughter and even…even the man now lost that she had once loved.

She would not return to her home by the lake. And Caravia and the villa, she would never go back there again. Her deepest love was now her bitterest hatred. She had complete hatred for not only Azerius but all men. For they had mocked and hurt her. Now she would hurt them. Liars and deceivers. Never again would she trust any of them. She would do her master's bidding and take vengeance on them all.

If Hades lived up to his bargain and saved her daughter, she would never tell Nephrea the true identity of her father. She would erase the coward from her life as he had tried to erase hers. Now she felt shame. She was embarrassed that she had ever trusted him. Or any man.

"I do your bidding, Aidoneus."

"After this final, terrible lesson, your eyes are open. And now all eyes behold you."

13

THE STRATOS

THIRTY HAND-PICKED NYMPHS, WHO WERE THE MOST proficient with bow and arrow and the most loyal, followed their Amazon nymph queen to the Mandrigelian border near the river. Harmonia called this new elite force of nymphs Imada. That was an honor, the only honor, given to the gods above—really an honor for her champion god, Hades, who had told her that he had created the Imada force on Olympus in their dealings with man. Of course, her Imada had no idea of her intentions. She had learned to be secretive. Some nymphs simply believed she was searching for a new water hole or hunting ground for their home. But others were far more suspicious, watching Harmonia as she sharpened their knives and inspected their arrows.

Her elite force was instructed to dress alike. Not armor, for they didn't have the means to forge bronze, but matching leather uniforms fashioned for comfort. They were adapted from the clothes used for the games, lightweight but strong enough to protect them from blades. And, for the first time, she decreed that they would cover their chests, for she knew her sisters would one day move south. The "armor" ran from shoulder to knee and was held by rope. Nothing so fancy as what was seen in Caravia, but much tighter and lighter than the long, thick brown coats they wore in the winter. Their dark hair was long, not always tied back. And she did not order them to darken their eyes as in the South. But she darkened her eyes. She reasoned that the kohl around her eyes would mark her status above all others, even the elders in her clan. Each and every Imada soldier carried a bag of quills on her back and small bronze knives stowed in her boots and belt. Some carried sharp spears with forged bronze tips. One day, when she found the means, she would arm them with swords.

And now, after years of preparation, her elite force crouched under the blue and green foliage near a clearing by their glowing Blue River. She chuckled and shook her head at the irony. Four dwarfs, exactly four as before, walked through their myrle berry orchards towing a carriage with a slain animal and carrying grain on their backs. All four wore short, simple white chitons.

Harmonia whispered to her favorite, a young nymph perhaps better with the bow than she was, named Jaida. "Ready your bow, Jaida. Order the others."

Jaida was only seventeen years old but had been trained since the age of fourteen, when Harmonia returned to Azure. She was the youngest but fiercest of her Imada.

"What are you planning, Harmony?" Jaida asked.

She gave Jaida a big smile. This made Jaida even more excited.

Harmonia signaled for the other archers to duck down. Then she addressed all of them quietly.

"Hades watches us. He guards us from the infernal gods who are our enemies. I require cover. Ready your arrows. Protect your queen from danger."

"By our very lives," replied another nymph.

Harmonia nodded slowly. A few murmured to each other nervously. But as Harmonia looked at them, they quickly bowed their heads before her and quieted.

Harmonia jumped up and whistled. It was her special whistle, shrill enough to startle the four Mandrigel dwarfs. They whirled around, but it was doubtful they spotted the other Amazons crouched in the thicket.

"Keep me covered," she snapped, cocking her head back.

And she ran. She ran like the wind, faster than any man.

Antilus swooped down and scooped her up on her back. Within seconds Harmonia rose high above the dwarfs, circled a few times overhead, and landed directly in front of the four of them.

The dwarfs backed up in shock. Two of them dropped their bags. Another just stood frozen with his mouth gaping open.

"Where is your king?" Harmonia asked, sitting tall atop her unicorn.

They looked at each other bewildered.

"Where is the king of the Mandrigel?" she said more slowly. Then she drew her sword. The sight of a fully clothed Napean nymph landing on a flying horse was likely bizarre enough for the dwarfs. Now, as she wielded Azerius's sword, reflecting green in the turquoise sunlight, the dwarfs were so shocked that they stood dumbstruck.

"The queen shall ask one last time. Where is the king of the Mandrigel? Where is King Pangrin?"

"Who are you?" snapped one, finally brandishing a knife. She figured he was the leader. He had graying dark hair and was stubbier than the other three. He finally came to his senses and became angry. "You're forbidden to cross the river, nymph. This orchard lies in Mandrigel territory."

"You speak with Harmonia Ambrosia, the Amazon queen of Napea, reigning sovereign over Azure Blue. And this is the last thing I shall ever say to you. Now answer me."

She looked around the fields and waited for a moment. But when they persisted in silence, she leaped from her unicorn and stood before them with her sword drawn. They stepped back further. One fell to the ground.

"I have decided," Harmonia said, gesturing to the orchard with her sword, "that the land from the Stratos River up to this orchard is ours. My people will be allowed up to this point so that they may partake in the myrle berry. Your people will not. And every week that passes without hearing from your king, I will take a little more. So if he wishes not to be heard, tell him I shall take more and more of this island. Tell him that the nymphs are in need of land. We are hungry. But if he dares show the Amazon queen disrespect, inform him that I shall move in and take everything from Ambitus Pyramid to his fortress, all the way to the very borders of the sea."

The leader ran his hand angrily down his beard, stomped his feet, and snorted. The snort made Harmonia wrinkle her nose in disgust. Then the purple on his face shone a bright violet under the green sun. After she had lived so many years in Atala, away from these strange men, they looked somehow more perverse and alien to her than before. Then Harmonia caught fear in the elder's eyes. Her bravado was working. Her heart quickened at the thought of simply slaying him. And then, as if answering her desire, the eldest gray-haired man foolishly charged her with his dagger.

Like many he had been trained in the ancient war with the nymphs centuries ago. He knew how to maneuver around Harmonia's sword. But Harmonia was trained too. She was trained by the chief general of Caravia.

With the finesse she had practiced for years, she spun around until she saw an opening in the fool's stance. Then she filleted him with her sword.

She spun around to the other three. The death of their friend had come so quickly that they stared in shock. She smiled and wiped the fresh red blood off his shaking body. Another two charged. She raised her sword but was unable to strike. Each one fell to the ground following a whistle of arrows. As arrows rained down, Harmonia grabbed the last one, the littlest and youngest dwarf, the only unarmed one, and drew him into her embrace. She used her own body to shield him from the arrows of her Imada. Then she signaled her people, hiding in the bushes and trees, to hold their fire.

The last Mandrigel shook in her embrace. She whispered: "Go find Pangrin, little one. Tell him everything that transpired today in the orchard by the lake. Tell him that Queen Harmonia Ambrosia of Azure Blue has returned from her banishment and now requests an audience. And reparations."

And the last dwarf hobbled away and ran.

Her Imada held their heads low, and their eyes moved fitfully as they returned to their people by the river. The nymphs stopped their work and glanced up from what they were doing, as if they sensed something was wrong. Harmonia didn't say a word, but her sisters had already told them. She hadn't ordered them not to.

Krythra, one of the elders, brazenly rushed up to Harmonia.

"How dare you!"

Krythra had long, disheveled curly hair. Her dark hair was turning gray. She was far older than Harmonia, nearly as old as Harmonia's nanna, beloved Maina. And she was one of many nymphs that hadn't welcomed Harmonia home from Caravia. Harmonia loathed Krythra.

"How dare I what?" snapped Harmonia. "We're tired, Krythra. There was a disturbance while we went picking fruit in one of the orchards."

Jaida and the rest of her travelers stopped and stared at Krythra, whose cheeks turned violet in rage. No one ever challenged Harmonia, but Krythra was furious. And she had four other elders by her side—elders who had also never approved of Harmonia's actions.

"You did it again, didn't you?" Krythra seethed. "Ever since you've been back, you've stirred up trouble, skipping over every edict in Azure. Even naming. You propose our very river be renamed the Stratos? Even that is a term for war. Your clothes—" She touched Harmonia's shoulder. "You're turning us all into soldiers. For what? Maybe we want peace. Why stir things up with the dwarfs? We've had enough. Everything is up to you and no one else can say a thing."

"It sounds like you've just said enough."

"They'll be coming any minute, fool!" Krythra replied in a panic. "You broke our treaty and the Mandrigel will fight us. Again! This is why you were banished decades ago. Why would you do this again? Theoi will come and kill all of us! Is this what all this training was for?"

"I never signed a treaty. Did you sign a treaty, elder?"

"We should never have taken you back. It is for this same reason that the gods banished you."

All the crowds no longer greeted their sisters or spoke of their fight. Now the whole village stared at Harmonia and Krythra.

Old hag. How dare you speak to me like this in front of the village.

Harmonia glared. The old lady backed up. Harmonia considered cutting the woman down with her sword right here before the village, but that would be... improper. The stupid woman could become a martyr. And that would distract the other nymphs from the upcoming battle.

"My dear Krythra, the gods didn't banish me." She stuck her index finger into the old woman's chest. "You did. It was suggested by the gods and the dwarfs, but sanctioned by your council. You and your elders made the agreement in the name of subjugation. Just as you subjugated us to live by this infertile, stale, and boring river two centuries ago. And now, as I've returned—as you have so kindly pointed out—I find that my sisters are starving. I find that they live day to day without food. So I think it's time to expand. Perhaps take a delicious berry or two more from our neighbor."

"Not without council!"

"Go speak with your council about the incoming invasion," Harmonia snapped back. "Go talk while my soldiers prepare for battle." She turned her back on the woman, but then she whirled around one last time and added, "Or perhaps, Krythra, *you* can protect us. Perhaps I should order my Imada to stand down?"

That threw the entire village into a panic. It manifested all the tension from the news of their crime. There was so much shouting that Harmonia couldn't hear her own thoughts.

After gnashing her teeth and running her hand angrily through her hair, Harmonia cried, *"Ektaxis!"* All her Imada stood at attention. "Quiet them," she muttered, raising her fist into the air.

All her Imada brandished their knives before the crowd. At first there were gasps. Then the village turned silent.

Harmonia turned to the source, her newest enemy, Krythra. She walked right up to her and spoke loudly enough for all to hear. "We are at war, sister. But don't worry. Despite your disrespect, I will protect you." And with this, Harmonia dropped her fist and all her Imada fell at ease.

"Rest, my beloved Amazons," Harmonia said to the village with a smile. "Our ancient enemy is coming. But we are prepared. And I have been assured personally that, this time, the infernal gods will not interfere. This battle shall be won swiftly and fairly." She smiled at Jaida and the young girl smiled back. "They don't know what they're up against."

Then she turned her back on her people and walked with her entourage of guards back to her cottage—the largest cottage, the only cottage, beside the Blue River, which she had ordered her people to refer to as the Stratos.

By the time the dwarfs were close enough to the border, Harmonia heard the nervous yells of her people. Some rapped on her door and shouted in panic. Others screamed in horror. She ignored all of them, fanning her anger at Krythra and the elder council. But after letting their cries fester long enough, she finally stepped out.

Even still, she did not walk to the edge of the river, where the enemy was approaching. She mounted Antilus and flew off into the sky as she heard more cries under her. But she didn't order her Imada to stand down. They readied their bows and arrows.

She watched the battle from the green sky. And when the dwarfs were close enough to her people, indeed, they were surprised. This would not be like the battle that had ruined her. Most of the dwarfs would not live to cross the water. A volley of arrows rained down on them. She had trained her Imada with the bow for many moons, and few missed. A handful of dwarfs wore lovely white battle armor and helms with well-constructed enchanted swords. Only those knights were not injured by the arrows, for the arrows were made of wood with bronze tips. But so many others without this protection fell, bloodying the river. Within a moment, nearly half of the dwarf army that had invaded lay dead in the water. The remaining armor-clad soldiers were swimming or wading in the river.

Then a bloody battle, hand to hand, ensued. Some dwarfs jumped on the nymphs with daggers of their own. Others held swords and shields. But most were speared with staffs. The nymphs had been skilled with staffs and javelins ever since the games, and Harmonia had the spears constructed in the way of the Hinterlands, with bronze tips. It was not the strongest, but it was sharp and stronger than their primitive sticks.

Harmonia had intended to not join the fight. But then her eyes opened wide in disgust. She caught a handful of nymphs fighting on the side of the dwarfs.

Such betrayal was intolerable. Nymph would never battle nymph! And so, armed with her quiver on her back, in the clouds, she threw arrow after arrow at the traitors.

The fight was over before it began. Harmonia had known it would be, but she had wanted her people to witness it. And she had wanted them to know that it would be won by their hands, not hers. The only remaining soldiers were a handful of prisoners wearing their enchanted white Mandrigelian armor.

She landed Antilus by the river, and her people rushed her, cheering and embracing her.

"Did we do good, my queen?" asked Jaida. That was the first time a nymph had called her by her title. Harmonia embraced Jaida tightly and laughed joyfully.

"You're so young, Jaida, born before my first battle. But you hold the queen's greatest trust and allegiance. I shall call you chief general of the Amazon."

"A great honor, Harmony!"

Only a handful of nymphs died that day. But the dwarfs' bodies littered the sides of the river. One of the dead bodies was Krythra. The cause of Krythra's death was a mystery. It was said that she died by an arrow through the back of her head.

14

A NEEDLE AND THREAD

HARMONIA BUSIED HERSELF WITH A NEEDLE AND THREAD OVER a small pleated Egyptian kalisiris. Outside the linen cloth of her two-room war tent, she could hear the murmuring of her people and, if she listened closely enough, the sounds of the dwarfs murmuring behind their fortress walls too. She hummed a tune Maina had often hummed about the Stratos as the tent walls lightly fluttered in the wind and rain. She could smell the moisture beneath the remaining wafts of ginger and turmeric from her evening supper. But the snow had ended. Her champion god had promised it so.

After another failure with her thread, she picked up the dress from her lap and angrily tossed it at a chair. It just wasn't right, and she wasn't even sure of the length. How tall would her daughter be now?

To her left was a workroom strewn with oil lamps, vases. Pilfered treasures from the dwarfs, like gold vases, necklaces, bracelets, and silver goblets, were piled on the dirty blue floor. But most celebrated was the Mandrigelian armor—a collection of white painted shields, spears, daggers, and swords that lined the walls as mementos. They were similar to what she had displayed in her cottage at Crystal Lake. To her right lay her bedroom with a bed, dresser, and mirror.

Draped along walls and on the floor were brightly colored tapestries. These pieces of art had been woven as a tribute, depicting victory in her recent battles. Ten years of fighting had passed, but she was confident that after she captured the fortress the Napean war would be over.

One large tapestry hanging on the tent wall was of a nymph flying a white unicorn through a great snowy tempest over the wall of the Mandrigel fortress. That nymph was the queen of Azure Blue herself, Harmonia. For when all had seemed lost—as Sara infernally threw flurries at her army, protecting the dwarf city in ice—it had taken Harmonia's stone will to fly over the city walls with Antilus, through the storm, to show her people that the wall could be breached. Another rug depicted a terrible battle with nymphs wielding swords against dwarfs on dangerous precipices along the great heights in the northeast cliffs.

But it was a third piece that she treasured most now. This one was of the city of the Mandrigel, a mural modeled after a map created based on her personal recollection of the inner workings of the city after she executed her daring flyover. She had told cartographers of streets arranged neatly in stone, buildings stacked in perfect order, and merchants walking with carriages, selling to the citizenry, ignorant of the war outside. The artists who had created this tapestry had used the authentic map but embellished it. Her memory of that aerial view was from so long ago she wasn't sure if it was still accurate. Anyway, very soon she would use the map drawn on papyrus of this very mural to assist her army when they got past the walls.

Her great Amazon artists sewed history, while Harmonia was attempting to sew a dress for her daughter.

She threw her legs up on a small wooden table and grumbled.

Oh, Nephrea! How am I to sew an Egyptian dress for you? Fancy, I am the great queen of Azure, but can't send a proper dress from your mother.

She stared at her wooden door. All she had to do was walk through the door to see the drawbridges. She had besieged them. Two thousand of her Azure Amazon had camped around the fields of long blue-green grass for weeks threatening them. Would she put the rats to death? And when would be the best time for her to ceremonially enter through the gates?

She yawned. Then she smiled in victory.

Amazon, we shall take the fortress come Fall Harvest. Then I can eat mutton and cakes while we roast the little sarding rats by spikes along their fields. She laughed at her wicked thoughts. *But, Sara, I will be merciful. Oh, don't worry. I won't kill all of them. Only the ones that love you the most.*

She was disturbed by a knock at her wooden door.

She jumped and looked down at her clothes. Despite the rain, it was hot outside and she wore only a thin white linen gown from her shoulders to her ankles, held by a large silver brooch at the shoulder. It was translucent, showing the blue contours of her bosoms and her nipples.

"Hold on," she barked. "What is it? I asked for no visitors."

"A *man*, my lord," said a shaky, husky voice. It was her subject Milda.

"A *man*?" Harmonia asked. Then she laughed and looked down at her outfit. "Oh, have him come in then."

"It's Hades," she added in a very frightened voice.

Of course it was. What other man would dare cross the strait and visit her? Hades walked in, crouching to fit through the doorway, wearing his black cloak.

"Queen Harmonia," he said with a deep bow, removing his hood.

She looked into his eyes and smiled. He ran his hand

along her cheek. She let him. Then, as he looked down, she remembered the gown and her smile became sly.

"Can I get anything for you?" asked Milda.

"*Get out, Mildew!*" cried Harmonia. Milda stumbled out, shutting the door.

Harmonia took a deep breath and straightened her clothes. Then, as she had once watched the goddess Demeter do, she did not walk but glided gracefully across her tent. She lifted a glass pitcher of red myrle berry wine and poured it into two crystal glasses on the large wooden dining table. She felt his stare.

I am Amazon. The Queen of Azure. So? Go ahead and look. Even if my chest is naked, what of it? A man can greet a woman without a shirt. So shall I.

She smiled at him as she handed him a crystal glass. Then they both turned oddly quiet. Her hand ran lightly over his large forearm. He gazed at her even more hungrily as he sat on a wooden chair, and she lay on her side on a couch across from him.

"My eyes are up here, Lord Hades."

"Forgive me," he sputtered quickly, lifting his eyes with a chuckle. "I am helpless before you. You're lovelier than I remembered."

"My breasts are beautiful?"

"No." He shook his head. "I mean, yes, Harmonia." He gazed into her eyes. She could never forget those eyes. Amid his hard cheekbones and forehead and sharp nose, his blue eyes seemed, oddly, so tender and sweet. "*Everything* about you is beautiful, my flower."

"I didn't expect company now."

"Perhaps you should change?"

"You remember when we walked naked by the river," she said with a shrug.

"Always a pleasure to see you, Amazon queen," he said

with a chuckle. "How do you fare? I see you've camped by their gates?"

"It's been too long," she replied, becoming serious. "How is *she*?"

"How is who?"

"*She*." Harmonia merely raised her brow.

He shook his head, confused. "Who?"

"My Nephratee?"

"Ah, the princess. Don't concern yourself about her. Nefertiti is in good hands with Hustaph in Giza. She is safe and running about in Egypt by the Nile. Safe as promised."

"Did you send her my gifts?"

"Of course I did." Hades stretched his arms, leaned back in his wooden chair, and uttered a yawn.

"Has she asked about me? Does she remember me?"

"Oh, Harmony, you last saw her when she was four years old. Do you recall when you were four? Why should you care for children? You've banned the games. Enough small talk. When are you going to sack the fortress?"

"You and your infernal family have willed this to be a ten-year war."

"To grow the stables, my dear. To grow your army and Imada. We've spoken of this many times before. Your foes are men in Atala who've trained for thousands of years. Ten years is not so long. And look outside your tent. I finally cleared the ice for you."

"The dwarfs surprise me too, Hades. The little twits have brains, don't they? I think you and I underestimated them. I think they fight as well as men. We take ground and they steal it back. Even without the interference of your infernal family. This back and forth grows tiresome. Very tiresome. They are brave. But I've finally cornered them—"

"Yes, yes. You've followed my advice and starved them in siege. But now the weather is temperate. Some can run and forage for food and escape in the woods. And their fortress wall is one of the mightiest in all of Gaia. You must move forward. When is your final advance?"

She picked up her cup of sweet red myrle wine and drank slowly from it. Then she lay back, yawned, and said, "Whenever it pleases the Amazon queen. The Amazon queen does not really care for them, their small wives, their litters of offspring, or anyone else other than my Amazon in these lands. If the rats don't accept my terms, I shall simply raid the fortress and burn every one of them on a stick to roast for an evening meal. I am looking outside Napea, Aidoneus. Just as planned."

"And you've trained Imada splendidly, my love. Your army is great. The speed at which you built it is admirable. But ..." He looked up as if coming up with an idea. She knew it was phony: he was about to tell her something he had planned before he even entered her tent. "I suggest," he continued, sipping wine, "you keep the dwarfs as slaves. Don't roast them. Use them, as Poseidon and Hermes did, to make the fortress a great palace for the nymphs and their queen. The dwarfs are known for their skills in bronze, iron, silver, gold, and crystal. Let them transform their ancient home into a home of your own. Build it in crystal so that it may reflect the blue beauty of Olympus. Let this new home shine like Crystal Lake, as a crystal for you, dear Azure queen, my love. Then, to prepare to move on to Caravia, make them forge weapons and armor. After all this is done, *then* you can roast them for dinner if you'd like, though I doubt they'll make a tasty meal."

She looked at the mural of their city on the wall. Then she imagined all those buildings and roads being hers. Amazons'.

"Yes, if this is the wish of my god."

"No," he said, shaking his head with a chuckle. "Do whatever you'd like. You're the sovereign queen of Azure Blue. Roast them, eat them if you wish."

"I don't want to eat them, Hades," she said, turning from

him and chuckling. "Or even enslave them. But they will not rule over any of my blue soil."

"Well, sometimes that's what worries me. As much of a witch as you are—and you can be a nasty one—sometimes I fear you're turning soft."

"Soft?" she snapped with a smirk. "Me? You think I'm soft?"

He didn't reply. He just stared at her smugly, sipping wine.

"You shall see when the time is right." She drank the rest of the cup and jumped up to pour another. Even now, as she refilled their cups, Hades' eyes did not stop staring at her face and body, almost as if in a trance. He remained silent until Harmonia returned to her seat and smiled at him, reclining again comfortably. She knew her looks pleased him.

"Do not doubt your flower, Hades. I do your bidding, as long as you fulfill your promise with my Nephree. It serves me both ways. Vengeance with love. You said that after the island is taken, you can bring my daughter to me."

He heaved a sigh and nodded. "When I have arranged Olympus for less interference, then yes, it will be safe enough to bring her here. Alas, I swear I thought Azure would be yours in a year. Not a decade. We needed this preparation, but you're right. Perhaps it's my fault."

"Yes, it is."

He stared at her. Her lips curled in a larger smile.

"Even if I summon her, all may not be well in Egypt," he said. "General Azerius is looking for your daughter. I saw him send scouts to territories along the Egyptian coast. Even further down, into Aethiopia." He stopped for a moment as if to determine whether to tell her more. Her face burned. Then her whole body trembled in rage. It was the name of that infernal man. Azerius. More so, it was the thought that he would touch her daughter. She had to put her wine down to avoid spilling it with her shaky hand. "There is a tale of a blue

Atalan girl living in Egypt, and it has spread south of the Aethiopian Strait. Tale of a nymph girl."

"Why would that imbecile chase a rumor?" she snapped.

"Because some other imbecile named her. And that same imbecile didn't properly kill her father with his sword. When Azerius heard of a blue Nefertiti, *Nephrea*, in Busiri, he asked for leave from King Tolen II and went with a group of men to Waset. Your old lover spent two moons along the Nile looking for the blue Nefertiti."

"Why didn't he find her?"

Looking smug, he ran his palm along the edge of the crystal glass. Then he gulped it all down. "Perhaps you've waited too long to take their fortress," he replied, wagging a finger. "I've stilled Demeter's cold fingers for a moon now. The weather is perfect."

"Why didn't Azerius find her?"

"Why do you think?" he asked pompously, pointing at himself. Then he took a deep breath and sighed. "After wasting his time searching in Southern Egypt, he returned, very likely passing the home of Hustaph in Aneb-Hetch on his way back home to the Strait of Aethiopia."

"I don't understand. How could she evade him?"

"I led him off the track. I made him think she was over twenty leagues east of her true home. There was no way for her to reunite with him."

"I don't want to talk about that man," she said, looking away and shaking her head. "If you love your flower, you will sneak up behind Azerius and slice his throat for me. Never mention him again. You're no less upset he lived than I am."

"I would have thought a thank you would have been nicer, my sweet, over your daughter, but you're too much of a witch for that, aren't you?" He walked to her couch and kneeled before her. He stroked her hair but she batted his hand away.

"You promised to protect her!" she snapped, pointing a finger at his face. "You...promised. This rumor of yours could have cost my daughter her life. Then I would hate you more than I hate Cronos."

A flicker of red appeared in Hades' eyes. He squinted at her. But he didn't get up. And she didn't turn away, glaring at him.

"I do your bidding, if you do mine," Harmonia said. "Protect my daughter. Keep her from seeing me and my business in this war on the isle. That was the plan. Fine. Why change it? Only when the Napean lands are at peace under nymphs, then and only then may you return her to me. That is the agreement. Do you understand?"

"Yes, my love," he said with a sweet smile. "That's what I've been saying." Then he burst into laughter. He reached out and touched her neck, but she batted him away again.

"Don't touch me! I'm as impatient to see my daughter as to end this war."

He got up and stood over her.

"Disrespectful wench," he said. But as she turned her back on him, he laughed. "I came here to tell you of this because time is running out. As fast as you've built your army—and you've done splendidly, Harmony—you will lose it all if you don't act quickly and take the fortress. I can hold off Demeter for only so long. For *our* daughter's sake, take the castle now—"

"The queen has decided to take it at the time of the Fall Harvest," she said, raising a finger with her back turned to him. Then she walked over to the table and poured herself another glass of wine. "In a fortnight. Then and only then. Of course, as a lowly nymph, I am under your power. Do you order me? You are that much of a brute, are you not?"

"I wouldn't dare order you to do anything."

She laughed in spite of herself. "The Amazon queen shall take the fortress upon Fall Harvest. Then she shall have the rats build a beautiful crystal palace in its place. A splendid idea, yes? When the crystal castle is built, you may send for my daughter. That way she can finally see her mother in her full splendor."

"A wonderful plan."

"And I have another. The Mandrigel will forge me swords, spears, and armor." She pointed to her collection on the wall. "And we will forge ships like in the lands of Tyre. We will build a fleet and sail across the sea to Caravia like the Phoenicians. There I will meet the general and make him pay for man's betrayal. And then, even if it takes a hundred years, I will return to Azure and sail to Mycenae, taking Argos as another spoil for our people. Man shall be under the rule of the Azure queen. But we will build temples, as we have in Azure, to pray to you in your honor."

"As it should be, my love. Splendid. Only…you cannot wage war by ship."

"Why?"

"That was another thing I needed to speak with you about."

He sat back down and drank more from his cup. And then he oddly looked nervous. For a god to look nervous was almost amusing. At first, he wagged his finger, but he couldn't get himself to say whatever was on his mind. She was amused and wondered if the god, *a god*, actually feared telling her anything.

"In order to protect the princess and your Isle of Napea from my brother, and end Demeter's protection of the Mandrigel, Poseidon and I have signed an edict forbidding your people to ever sail again by sea."

She shook and blushed in anger again. "What?"

"You will not be able to travel by sea. Poseidon will see to that. You can, of course, fly over the strait by unicorn, with the monokera that have now been cultivated by Imada. Then you can invade by land."

Harmonia jumped up and stared at him. "What of my

ships? Our plan was to fight by sea! Caravia? What of the maps, the galleys, the navy we planned?"

"No."

"The galleys? Your superior weaponry, rivaling Phoenicia, promised by Hephaistos?"

"No." He shook his head.

"Was it all a waste?"

"No nymph will be permitted to travel by water. That edict was signed on Olympus with Zeus and Poseidon. My brother will sink any ship sailed by a nymph over his waters."

"Then how will we get to Caravia! How will I take vengeance on the man who tried to kill your flower!"

"By foot. By air. But not by sea."

"The unicorns can't fly ninety leagues south! I want Caravia, not a barren desert or Karthra's primitive stinking bog!"

"Harmonia," he said, running a hand over his bald head, "while you battled the Mandrigel, I battled my father. The tremors you've felt beneath you and the thunder from atop the pyramid on Olympus were war with the remaining Titans. We fought Cronos. Together, we battled him. Demeter drugged him, Poseidon drowned him, then my brother Zeus took his thunderbolt and bound his hands and feet. My father, the source of Imada's order—which killed your family—is imprisoned in the depths now. I dragged Cronos deep down into the depths of the pyramid, into the land of the Underworld, and shackled him deep in the fiery city of Tartarus. He is imprisoned in stone to live the rest of eternity bound under Gaia." He paused for a moment and gave her a faint smile. "It was justified. If you knew Cronos you would know that he once wished the destruction of your people and even of my brother and me. If you hate any god, it should be him."

But she wasn't listening. The idea had been to use her home in Napea as a base to launch a naval assault on

Southern Atala. From there, they could sail to Mycenae and perhaps the Egyptian empire. Now how was she to do it? By land? The distance from the northern tip of Atala to Egypt was days by horseback. No monokera could fly all the way down in a day, certainly not an army. Even the trip to the Isle of Minoa, on the eastern border of Hellena, was over twenty leagues across water—this could barely be done by the best of monokera, except maybe Antilus. Finally, when he began describing his taming of one of the creatures from Tartarus, a three-headed dog with the tail of a serpent and the body of a lion, Harmonia lost all reason.

"Are you an idiot!"

"What? What did you say?"

"Are you a complete fool? You knew our plans. How could you let your family get in the way of them? Unless you're trying to sabotage me. Perhaps you are as weak as they are? Perhaps not only do I fight dwarfs and Sara, I fight you too!"

He stood up. Then he smiled. It was not a kind smile. It was the sort of smile she imagined the god gave to foes before tearing them in half with his bare hands.

"I am trying to explain to you why this happened, my love. While I chained my father, Cronos, Zeus took control of Olympus. I was given full reign in the depths, as God of the Underworld—"

"Then you were given the greatest piece of shit in the world! You were banished into a cave! Don't lie to me. You think I'm stupid? This is why you look so worn, so defeated. You must think I'm dumb if you think I don't see through your failures! And now that failure extends to my Amazons and all hope of sailing by sea!"

"Enough! How dare you speak to a god like this!"

He raised his hand as if to hit her. His lips fluttered and his tanned skin turned redder. Then she saw something she had never seen before—his eyes glowed bright red.

But she smiled. She absolutely adored the fact that she had gotten under his skin and affected him so much.

"Strike me," she said, moving closer to his fist. "Do it. Go ahead. Strike me down and kill me, if that is why you came to my bedroom tonight. Hit me. I want you to. Especially as you spoiled our only way to fight. Your flower is no longer of any use to you."

He was breathing hard, struggling to control his infamous rage. But she only became more obstinate as she faced those glowing red eyes.

"You know how few of us there are here," she continued quietly. "I needed every advantage I could get in order to fight an army much larger than my own. Now, with your surrender of this naval advantage, the sea, there will be no element of surprise. I may as well announce my arrival in Logencia, great God of the Underworld."

Great God of the Underworld. His eyes burned so red that her face and blue chest glowed. And his eyes opened wider. It was said matter-of-factly, but, indeed, she had said "*GREAT God of the Underworld*" as a way to mock him. He raised a hand to strike her again, but instead…he shoved her. She could not dodge the speed of his hands. She fell beside the dining room table. It was powerful and violent but, apparently, not meant to be. He rushed down to help her, seeming to regret it as soon as she fell.

She leaped up, grabbed the glass pitcher, and swung it hard at his head, shattering it and splashing the remains of the red wine all over his face and chest. He was so surprised that he stood stupidly before her.

"There! You hit me! Now I hit you! Now get out of my tent, you sarding turd! OUT! Either kill me or leave, but get your beastly presence away from me! I don't want to see you ever again! You've ruined me! Taken me down, just as you've taken yourself down to the depths of Gaia! All the while, you act like it's some sort of pleasant news that you've become the biggest loser in all of Olympus."

The blow certainly didn't cripple him. Neither did her words, now even more blasphemous. Instead, it burned out the red flame in his eyes. He sat back down on her couch and shook his head, rubbing his forehead. Harmonia's heart raced. Whereas before she had felt it beat out of desire for him, now she wanted to kill him.

"Perhaps it's the myrle berry wine," he said quietly. "I'm sorry."

"*GET OUT!*"

"Even if I wish to stay?" he asked quietly with a sly smile. "Even if by a god's decree, I order you to take me into bed?"

"You…you can do as you wish to me as a god," she said, looking away, "of course, I am powerless before you. But you should have some small sense of honor and decency as a *man*, if you are one."

He burst into laughter. "Ah, but you're not a woman, Harmonia. And that insult is nugatory knowing how much you despise all men. No woman breaks a bowl over a man's head. Certainly not a god's."

"I was upset," she said, still looking away. "I… I didn't mean to quarrel, but you should have pushed your sister and brothers, not me, and never agreed to that edict. Or to ceding your rights to your father's kingdoms."

"We didn't quarrel, Harmony. A mortal wouldn't dare fight a god." Then he looked up. "How peculiar, it seems Dionysus has sent ampullas of the myrle berry wine in honor of your victory. It is falling from your ceiling now, dear queen."

She chuckled in spite of herself. "The edict is unfair. Is there any way it can be reversed?"

"No."

She walked to her bedside and pulled a white sheet off the mattress. Then she filled her cup with water from a stone container near the foot of the bed.

"I shall take the fortress before Fall Harvest. Is that fast enough, Orcus, god of death? Lord of...the Underworld. For Imada?"

"Yes, that will do splendidly, Amazon queen."

"After I take the fortress..." She dipped the white sheet in the cup and gently wiped his face and head. "You can bring me my Nephree. She is almost a woman now. It is fitting that she is with me when we begin our battle with man. Fighting insignificant rats is not something our daughter should see. But fighting man is."

"I cannot promise her safety yet."

"I don't care anymore. The princess must be by the queen's side."

Then she used her tongue instead of the sheet to clean some of the red juices from his neck. She licked him. She sent kisses along his neck. She felt dizzy from wine and wondered if, indeed, it had been the drink that had made her dare fight a god.

"Now that Nephree shall be initiated as a lady," Harmonia said gently, pushing him away for a moment to explain, "she may return to me. As an adult. You see, Hades, I am not fit to mother a baby or a child. You knew this when you took her from me. But a daughter who can battle with me against man and be my heir, that is something that must be witnessed by the people. I would give my very life for that."

He nodded and ran his hand gently over her cheek. And then down over her breasts. The linen was so thin that he fingered her nipples.

"I'm sorry, my love. I won't push you ever again."

"Humph," she said, moving her lips back to his. "You didn't. You were just doing what all men do, trying to keep a lady in line. Isn't that what men do?"

"Not you, Harmony. No one can do that."

"And why is that?" She slowly pulled off his soiled black cloak. Then she untied his pants and pulled them off his legs. He wore no shirt, and she ran her hand along his chest. Then she ran it between his legs. And while she moved her hand, she bent down kissing his chest, then licked the curves of his fully developed pecs and abs.

He closed his eyes.

"Because you're not a lady."

She jumped off him, irate again. Then he burst out laughing.

"Oh, Harmony! I've never found anyone more splendid than you." And he grabbed her tightly. "It's been too long!"

"Unhand me, brute!" she shouted, but she couldn't help but smile. "Unhand me! You have no right!"

"I have every right."

He grabbed his cup of wine from beside the chair and spilled it over her white nightgown.

"Look, it seems Dionysus rains the fruit of the vine again in your honor. Here, I'll help you change."

And he tore her gown open with both hands, exposing her nude body.

"Oh! There's never been more vulgar a man than you! So strong and handsome, and yet so vile!" She mounted him. "Make love to me, Hades."

He kissed her cheek hard and ran his hand under her gown, over her breasts, and down between her legs. At first, she moved away, but then she leaned into him. She laughed as his grip bound her. She truly felt helpless in his arms. Her heart raced again, this time in desire for him.

"Am I the only one who can hold you, Azure queen? A god?"

"Shh. Make love to me."

"I love you, Harmony."

He easily picked her up as if she were still a little girl and carried her to bed.

"I believe what man whispers of you, my love," he whispered in her ear as he caressed her naked body.

"What is that?" she said, breathless.

"That you are a witch. You have bewitched me. *Me*, a god. I am yours. I, a god, loves you, Harmonia. I love you more than anything else in this forsaken world."

15

THE THRONE ROOM

HARMONIA DID NOT NEED TO FIGHT THE FINAL BATTLE TO TAKE the fortress. With the ice storm and her continued show of strength, the enemy surrendered. Yet, as she sat atop her gilded throne, she felt worn down after ten years of war. This war was supposed to have moved as quickly as the first battle. But just as time had made her a proper Azure queen, as days passed her Amazon army grew. With her own steed, she bred hundreds of monokera. And it was this force, her flying unicorn Imada surrounding the castle, that finally brought the dwarfs to their knees.

In servitude, the dwarfs built a masterful kingdom of glass. They coated their ancient fortress of ramparts and towers in crystal. This project took three years, but the result was a master work of beauty, some dared say greater than the beauty of Olympus in the clouds. Only the defensive wooden towers of the Mandrigel remained, as before, for defense. Her bedchamber, great dining hall, lookout upon her balcony stairway, and gilded gates left all visitors awestruck. Still, everything paled in comparison with the greatest structure of them all. The throne room.

Now the queen sat on her dais with three marble steps. She wore a delicate gold crown and Caravian kohl. Her hair was wrapped in a black cloth over a long, flowing blue peplos. There was a sapphire necklace around her neck, which seemed darker in contrast to her light azure skin, studded with diamonds and red rubies. And she had many rings of gold and diamonds upon her fingers. The Mandrigel had fashioned the thin crown of gold on her head and all the jewelry on her hands. Only her blue-green dress had been sewn by her own people.

Her eyes fell upon the only area unchanged since antiquity, through her crystal windows surrounding the hall: the blue-green gardens. The genius of these little men! They had constructed the grand throne room with huge floor-to-ceiling glass windows joined by black marble columns, giving her a glorious view of these gardens. Beside the columns, statues had been made, some by nymph artists, of man, nymph, and Mandrigel. But there was only one god represented. Hades.

The massive hall seemed to be outdoors. Dark-blue and cherry-red vines and branches surrounded the black columns, vases, and benches, blending the whole room with the blue natural environment surrounding them. The green sun had set, no longer visible above through the glass dome. It was getting dark enough to see the stars through the crystal dome ceiling. And large torches flickered along the aisles to light the hall. The hall was large enough to seat three hundred of her people, and she used the room to address them nearly every fortnight.

Such was the brilliance of the dwarfs, rivaling any engineer of any age. And why wouldn't it? Legend claimed that they helped construct the lakes and plant the fields of Olympus.

She yawned. A royal delegation of Mandrigels had asked for a private audience with her this evening, on the third and last day of the Fall Harvest celebration.

Oh, sard it all! I'd rather sleep. You've had too much wine and cake, sweet Harmony. She laughed. *You've been a bad, bad girl. Now how will you properly entertain your guests? Well, I must honor them somehow. Hades was so right about them. They are such weak creatures.*

Her chief guard and general, Jaida, walked through two great doors, bowed with a smile, and then stood tall stomping her staff on the ground. Jaida wore polished armor: a scarlet helm, matching breastplate, elbow and knee pads, and pteruges. The armor had been built by the dwarfs—a few thousand panoplies for her army.

Jaida gestured with a broad sweep of her arm for the guests to walk through the two huge wooden doors. Three master builders and their king, the eldest and wisest of all the Mandrigel, walked down the central aisle. They were dressed in their finest gray and brown tunics and pants. As the little men trudged along the long passage, their shoes echoed upon the smooth, waxed marble floor. By now a full moon was shining down through the dome, and its light reflected from three of the men's bald heads.

"Queen Harmonia," King Pangrin said with a low bow.

"What can I do for you, old friend?"

"We've finished the palace as requested. This serves to complete all agreements for our treaty of peace. You told us many times how pleased you are."

"Oh, it is so lovely. So incredible. A wonder to behold. Your work is better than any other, and I am so pleased."

"Thank you, Your Majesty," said a younger dwarf with thin blond hair with another bow.

"Please join me in drink." She yawned again and pointed to four glasses already filled with red myrle berry wine on a table near a window. Then she picked up her own glass of pomegranate wine from a step below. It was her fourth. There was also a tray of pomegranate seeds, and as she took another sip, she took a handful of those too. "Let us drink to peace, friends," she said with another smile, raising her glass. "Come closer to your queen. Indeed, you have all made me so very happy."

She gestured to four small wooden chairs near the throne.

"We are pleased," sputtered the younger blond dwarf with a nod. "You are nice." "You are nice" was a term of affection from their people. This youngest dwarf was the only beardless one. He took a glass and sat down. Then Pangrin looked at him. Their king nodded.

"We met in our village, and the people are asking what shall be done now," said the young dwarf.

"I hope you are joining the festivities outside, friends," Harmonia answered with a nod. "Our people are performing the famed dance of the games in celebration of the palace's completion. It is the first time in so many years. It is wonderful."

She could hear the drums, laughter, and revelry outside, though faintly.

"Just say it, Antilees," snapped another dwarf. "Get to the point of our visit. The queen does not wish to be bothered."

"Hmm?" Harmonia smiled and leaned forward, amused. She leaned toward the dwarf as she sipped more wine.

"Our people speak of...payment, Your Majesty," continued Antilees hesitantly. "We've worked tirelessly to build your palace. We have lived and breathed its construction for three years now. And we've constructed your armor and weaponry. We even constructed your tower stables for the monokera. But you have offered us...little. No gold. Nothing. Why?"

"I have no gold," she said, laughing. Then she glanced at Pangrin. The king looked away. She showed them the rings on her hand. "Your people give *us* gold. We have none. This was all given to me for the queen's promise of peace. And peace is what she shall give you. The nymphs hold no treasures, but we shall die in your defense."

"You can get gold," said a dwarf with a long brown beard. "There is word that a treasure lies bountiful at the foot of the pyramid. Originally mined by our people centuries ago. Now it is guarded in Hermes' lair. And you are a friend of the God of the Underworld. You could arrange to speak with his guard at the gates."

She had some difficulty swallowing her wine. Then she felt dizzy.

Too much wine, Harmonia. Too much wine.

"What?" Harmonia said after some silence. "What are you saying? Oh, gold? I thought it was clear that your people would craft our armaments to prepare for war with man. Such a war will bring your people bounties soon enough. Perhaps, yes, gold, if that is what you wish, though I don't know what your people would do with it. I can bring gold to you. But the guard you speak of is the messenger god. Though I worship Hades, the Amazon queen does not hold any allegiance to Hermes."

There was silence. All of the dwarfs nodded, but Harmonia knew they were silent due to fear. She terrified them. She used that, just as she had learned from her champion god, to control weak people like these idiotic things.

Their small women and children disgusted her even more. These small females were actually subservient to these fools.

Harmonia heaved a long sigh.

"This palace ..." She stood up with her crystal glass of wine and walked carefully down the marble steps, gesturing at the hall with an outstretched arm. The dwarfs seemed to lurch back. "This is payment to your queen, Harmonia, the ruler who protects you. For when we travel over the strait, man will threaten us. And if they dare threaten your little villages, your small women and children, they threaten me. But Queen Harmonia promises her own blood for your defense. That should be enough payment. And, anyway—" She laughed. "I repeat, why would your people need gold? Gold will buy you nothing in Azurea." Then she wagged her finger at King Pangrin. "But friendship, ah, friendship with the Amazon shall buy you everything, old friend. For, as I have told you in the past..." She stood over them. "We shall one day rule the world. This magnificent crystal palace shall be the center of all of Gaia. Thanks to you."

She smiled brightly. Then she stood right over the young blond-haired dwarf, Antilees. She knew him. Antilees was a quiet man, always busying himself with supervising the workers in construction. She measured him up and down with her eyes. He was a leader, like Pangrin, but...less cautious. More mysterious. More...dangerous. The other dwarfs trembled before her, but Antilees did not.

"We don't come on our own accord, only upon your invitation," said the brown-bearded dwarf, "our people have asked that we seek audience. All our people are appreciative of your promise of peace, you are nice, but many feel slighted by your taking of the fortress and the surrounding Mandrigelian fields. They wish something else in return."

"I'm tired. Too much drink, I think," she said with a yawn. "Perhaps we can talk of gold later." She laughed. "Gold, yes, if gold be at the bottom of the pyramid, perhaps I can snatch it for you."

After keeping most of it for myself. Then she laughed again. She covered her mouth. She considered her thoughts might be too obvious.

"Perhaps, friends, I can discuss this with Lord Hades. Hermes is Hades' dog. But now, let us speak of pleasanter things. Perhaps a toast?" She lifted her crystal glass. "To celebrating the Fall Harvest with friends. It has been so long, and now this magnificent palace and fortress for the Amazon is complete. All because of you. To friends. This Crystal Palace's glowing light shall only spread peace to the entire island of Napea."

She raised her glass. They aped her, but many held their glasses with shaky hands.

Antilees was the only dwarf who didn't toast. He lowered his head. "Your palace was created because you decreed it. We never discussed payment. It does not mean payment has been rendered."

Perhaps I should kill you?

There was silence again.

Harmonia used the silence to let the mood fester. She slowly walked back up her steps and glared down at the young dwarf. "How dare you build something, something absolutely breathtaking and beautiful, indeed rivaling the home of the gods itself, and then turn around and tell me I owe you for it."

"He means no disrespect, my queen." King Pangrin raised a hand. "It is only—"

"The most the queen of Azurea gives is her deepest thanks," Harmonia said—but she said the last words grinding her teeth. "I give thanks for all of this wonder and I mean it. It is lovely. I have said this over and over to you and my people. I am so appreciative to the Mandrigel. I am very grateful. We all thank you. Now enough." She yawned loudly. "Is there anything else you wish to tell me?"

She forced more wine down. A couple of dwarfs shook their heads. King Pangrin looked ashamed.

"Of course," Harmonia added with a wicked smile at the young blond dwarf, "if you wish, Pangrin, I can *renegotiate* the treaty."

"No." Pangrin's eyes widened. "No. No." He raised his hand. "Your Majesty, no, that is not what we meant."

"Then why have you made a day of celebration bitter, old friend?"

"Hear Antilees, dear Queen Harmonia," Pangrin replied. "His objections do not come only from him, they come from our people. We are angry. You could see it yesterday during the celebration. You talk of payment and love for your brothers, but we see no gold. You speak of protection…" He gestured around the room. "Where's the need for protection? All we have is peace in the Azures. There's no invasion from east or south. There's no enemy. If you provoke them, they will come. You speak of armies from Minoa, Egypt and Canaan, Mitanni, or Assyria, but no one dares cross our shores. The gods protect us."

"No god protects you, Pangrin," Harmonia snapped. "At least…not anymore." She laughed, quickly covering her mouth.

"We've built this for you," said a long-bearded one, bowing. "We've built you swords and shields. We've provided spices and oils. Taught your people herding and tilling. Your stables are full, tower stables in this palace built by our own hands. Now you have the most beautiful lands in all of Gaia. Yes? And all the defenses we could desire. But you talk of the outside world. None of our families are interested in anything beyond the strait. Listen to Antilees. He speaks for our people. It is not only this delegation, but all our villages that object to your offer. Our wives and children, others of our villages unable to meet with you tonight, are petitioning for gold."

Harmonia opened her eyes wide. Then she gazed across the vast hall toward Jaida, but her guard had stepped out and closed the great double doors. She had every intention of ordering Jaida to throw them out. Or perhaps bring the young guard over to knock some sense into them.

"Are you stupid?" Harmonia said, standing again. "Don't you understand? The gods have abandoned you. Olympus doesn't protect you. I do. One day man will travel over the strait. It's been predicted by the grain goddess that Amazons shall wage war with man. And when that day comes, they will burn your little homes, all your little boys and little girls and little fat wives. That day is assured. Now that you have helped build my palace, we will fight for your protection. Queen Harmonia swears to it. But if you do not give me your solemn allegiance, your queen shall abandon you. And then, you will not ask for payment, you will kneel before me begging for your very lives."

I protect you under Hades, you rancid, curdling turds! What defense would this land have if I weren't here to rule? Hmm?

I'm…so tired. By the gods, I'm so tired… Too much drink? Or too many years of fighting for nothing. If I can only just…sleep. Hades suggested I kill them. Perhaps he was right.

"My protection," she said more quietly, falling back in her throne, "Your lord queen's protection, dwarfs, is more valuable than gold."

"*Protection from what!*" cried Antilees.

"Antilees, silence yourself!" said Pangrin.

"We've met man," the young dwarf raged on. "We know King Dracus. Karthra, Aram. They're no threat. No one talks of war except you!"

"*Get out of my chamber, you sarding shit!*" Harmonia cried. She nearly stumbled down the stairs in rage. "*Get out! How dare you speak to your queen in that tone of voice!*"

Pangrin shoved the young blond dwarf back into his chair. Then he put his hand up and bowed repeatedly before Harmonia. "Wait… Please…"

"Just go," Harmonia said with her head in her hand. She was getting a headache. "Get out, Pangrin. Leave me. All of you. I will forgive this outburst if you walk away now. This was supposed to be a celebration."

But no one left. That incensed her.

"*You will remove this worker from my Court, King Pangrin,*" Harmonia shouted, pointing at the young dwarf. The dwarf dared challenge her gaze. "*I will not speak another word until he has left the hall. Remove him this instant or I will cut out his tongue!*"

"I speak——"

"Shut up, fool!" snapped Pangrin.

Antilees stood up. With an exaggerated bow, he walked out.

"He's young, my queen," said Pangrin. And he bowed deeply before Harmonia. "I apologize profusely, Lord Harmonia. I don't know what's gotten into him lately. Please accept our greatest apology."

Antilees walked down the hall. The others still stood by Pangrin, glancing back at him.

"How do I threaten you?" asked Harmonia. "Hmm? What do you ask of me, Pangrin?"

"Gold," another dwarf repeated.

"Enough!" said Pangrin.

Apparently, it wasn't enough. The other went on, "We request gold from the gate of the Underworld as payment. That gold was once mined by our blood. You wish conquest of Gaia, we wish gold. Not for the four of us, Harmonia, but for our people. And if you are unwilling, allow us to mine for it like in the old days. Grant us our request with Lord Hermes. But allow us to keep our treasure."

"You won't stop," Harmonia said, shaking her head. She heaved a sigh. "Our treaty says that all items, including gold mined in Napea, are now subject to my possession. If you wish to renegotiate the treaty, I can bargain. But you stand on dangerous ground. One way, I suppose, to barter for possession of gold would be for you to enlist in our army in our upcoming fight in the South. If you wish to negotiate that, I might give you gold. Perhaps some of your ancient fighters can fight in the war. But if you claim that I owe you for a structure you built upon trust, I warn you, I take that as a grave insult to me, Imada, the elders of Napea, and all the nymphs of Azurea. And the war shall start again."

"*Then pay with your blood, witch!*" Antilees shouted from halfway down the hall. Then he pulled out a curved dagger. But he didn't rush her. Oddly, he turned his back on her.

Only then, as fear rushed from Harmonia's chest to her head, did she finally understand the treachery of their plan.

Two dwarfs rushed up to the throne with daggers. Pangrin was shouting for them to stop, but they ignored him.

Harmonia spun around behind the throne reaching for her sword, but it was too late. As quick as she was, she could not reach it in time. Harmonia had once faced four dwarfs with ease, but now she was unarmed and foggy from too much pomegranate wine. The two fiends stabbed her repeatedly with their curved daggers. They easily shredded the aqua-colored cloth of her formal dress and cut her. She fell face first to the bottom of the steps. Then, from the corner of her eye, she saw Pangrin, of all people, throwing them off her.

"Harmony, oh Harmony!" cried Jaida.

But Jaida sounded like she was outside. After another sharp stab in her back, she watched Jaida sprint down the main hall and impale Antilees with her staff. But the sharp stabbing to her back did not end. Jaida fought all of them, killing every one of the traitors. Then Harmonia heard more nymphs enter the hall.

Harmonia lay on the ground, blood dripping down her dress and the marble steps. She looked up at Jaida as her favorite soldier held her in her arms.

"Oh, Harmony. Harmony!"

"Our queen!" Milda screamed to her people. *"By Hades, our queen!"*

A torrent of nymphs had rushed into the chamber, filling the great hall. *"Our queen is dead!"* Milda's scream of madness echoed in the large hall. She ignored Jaida and fell to her knees beside the queen, bashing her breasts and wailing. And with her cries came the cries of a hundred others. Then Milda whirled around to Jaida. "Small dogs attacked our majesty? Small vermin? Mandrigels? Under your guard! How incompetent can you possibly be, sister! Or did you join in the attack?"

The only dwarf who was still alive was King Pangrin. He was screaming as he was pummeled by nymphs entering the palace. A nymph was about to run a sword through him, so Jaida unsheathed her own sword to stop her.

"Pangrin was trying to protect her!" cried Jaida.

"Oh, Harmonia," cried Milda over her limp body. "Harmonia!"

Milda turned to Pangrin, who was now held by three nymphs.

"Kill him!" Milda ordered. "Kill that dwarf now!" She pointed at Pangrin. "Kill him! How can you not kill their king for this outrage?"

"He was protecting her!" objected Jaida. "He deserves justice."

"This from Harmony's so-called guard!" cried Milda to the other nymphs. "*Kill their king!*"

Pangrin looked defeated. But Jaida blocked every assault with her body and sword, now perversely protecting one of Harmonia's attackers.

"Stop!" Jaida cried. "Back away from him!"

Although Milda was the queen's assistant, Jaida was still their head guard. The nymphs released the Mandrigelian king. And then, to add even more bizarreness, the king of the Mandrigels buried his head in his hands and started weeping.

Everything had happened so quickly. Jaida had been detained by a fight outside the hall. The three Mandrigels had obviously fought to distract her. And now, with many still drinking and reveling with the Fall Harvest festival outside the palace, Harmonia, her dearest Harmony, was mortally wounded. Under her watch.

More nymphs rushed into the palace. Jaida lifted Pangrin and pinned him against the wall, shielding him. Dozens of nymphs now surrounded them, wanting the king dead.

Milda released Harmonia and stood on a chair in the front row addressing everyone.

"Take torches. Tinder. Bring it to their little homes! Burn their little women. Their little children! Torch and burn everything to ash! Exterminate them! Our queen is dead!" And with that last proclamation came cries and screams. The nymphs' wails were so terrible that they shook the crystal dome above and the glass walls surrounding the Court. Milda lifted her fist. *"Go. Kill them! Just as they killed Harmonia Ambrosia! Burn every single one of the dwarfs until no one survives!"*

Nymphs stampeded out of the throne room, trampling over each other in the chaos.

JAIDA DISCOVERED LATER that they were running to the armory grabbing spears, swords, metallic scarlet armor, and shields crafted by the dwarfs themselves to fight man. Never would they have dreamed that the nymphs would use their own weapons to kill them. In one night, Jaida was given reports that thousands of dwarfs, women and children, had been slaughtered by the Amazons. In the madness, some were even attacked by elders and young nymphs on the isle who did not even have training in warfare.

Structures as intricate as the palace, dear to the dwarfs for centuries, were ransacked and burned. And the Napean nymphs did not fight in lines as they had been taught by their queen. They killed the dwarfs like animals, without order, thirsting for Mandrigel blood, torturing, mutilating, and burning them, just as Milda had ordered them to do.

Such was the darkest point in all Amazon history. Many nymphs were so horrified by their own actions that they blotted out the memory, denying to their daughters that it had ever happened. But Jaida never forgot. Nor did the Mandrigel dwarfs.

The few dwarfs that survived fled, ironically, toward the very river that once imprisoned the Napeans, the Stratos.

There King Pangrin regrouped all his people and fled into the base of the pyramid, where they descended underground. And there they saw the gold they had mined a thousand years before in Hermes' lair, only for the messenger god to hand them over to Lord Hades. Under the Dark Lord, their punishment would be to mine the caves and stoke the fires again, surviving only in servitude in the Underworld.

16

SPOILED ROTTEN

Harmonia awoke to the sound of a little girl's voice. Then a sharp nagging pain in her back so intense that it made her drift off to peace again. She felt sharp-nailed fingers run through her hair, over her forehead, and down her neck and back. Then she saw tranquil blue eyes gazing into hers. She closed her eyes tightly in unbearable pain.

"Ah, Harmony," Hades said quietly. "You were too trusting. Alas, your people had to finish what you started. Sometimes I wondered if you ever had the heart to seal their fate."

Harmonia stirred. She winced and forced one eye open. Hades was not alone. Her chamber was full of nymphs looking down at her. And, oddly, they all wore the scarlet armor of war.

"I need you to awaken from slumber now, my love," Hades said, patting her hand.

His voice seemed peaceful. But her bedchamber wasn't. Something was wrong. There was shouting. Then came the strange sound of a child's laughter mixed with breaking glass and vases, statues hitting the floor, and what sounded like her large crystal dressing mirror shattering. The nymphs were trying to catch some kind of animal. But it wasn't an animal.

Cracking an eye open again, she saw a little girl with long, unkempt golden hair rushing by wearing a short bright-red dress—nearly the same color as their armor. The young girl was rampaging in her royal bedroom.

"Unhand me!" cried the girl's voice. "You dare touch a goddess?"

"Come here," replied a nymph. "Stand still in the queen's chamber, child!"

"I am no child. I am your god!"

"Stop her, she's turning over the dresser!" shouted another nymph. "She'll break the thyine boards."

CRASH.

"Come here, Kore," said Hades. "Where are you?"

"I'm here, Uncle," she said, laughing. "I'm trying on Her Majesty's dresses."

Harmonia winced in pain. Another stab, this time from her stomach. She saw clothes being thrown across the room.

"*Come here!*"

Everyone finally fell back in response to Hades's thunder. The little girl slowly approached. She smiled and laughed. But then she lost her smile when Hades grabbed her by the arm hard. He pointed at Harmonia on the bed. The little girl squinted, her eyes changing to fiery red. And that's when Harmonia recognized her. This was Cora, the goddess Persephone, the demon child who had helped kill her family.

"Touch her again," Hades said, pointing. "She is the Amazon queen of Azure. She is a Napean Amazon. One day, she will invade Gaia and rule over all of man, as foretold by your own prophecy. Now, Kore, I need you to lay your hands on her one last time. I need you to stop her pain. She's not healed."

"*No!*" cried the girl. "*No, I won't! I won't do it!*"

Harmonia moaned. Hades grabbed the girl by the elbow again and practically threw her down on the bed.

"*Touch this nymph and heal her!*"

"No!" She shook her head. "Let me go! I won't do it!"

The child slipped out of his grasp and ran away from the bed. She might have left the room if it hadn't been for Hades grabbing her wrist and throwing her on the mattress. This sent a wave of shooting pain down Harmonia, making her groan.

"Whenever I heal them, it hurts me, Uncle!" cried Persephone. "It's like a sting. I don't want to feel it."

"You must, Kore. You didn't fully heal her!"

"Because this one's spoiled, Uncle."

"Try again."

One of the nymph soldiers drew her sword before the god. Hades looked at the soldier curiously. "She's just a child, Lord Hades," the nymph said. Her hand, holding an Amazon sword, shook before the god.

"Put that thing away," Hades said with a smirk. "I'm trying to help her. And that *child* is a goddess older than you." He turned back to Cora. "I swear, little wench, if you don't touch her, I'll hurt you! Are you worried about pain? Believe me, I will cause you far worse."

Cora started to cry, shaking her head violently.

"Just leave the girl alone," implored another nymph.

"Do it now!" shouted Hades. "Will you? We traveled far for this."

"It hurts," Cora said, shaking her head. "It hurts, Uncle! I don't want to. And I already touched her. Isn't that enough?"

"For a second. I need you to do it longer."

"There was no need. She only could endure a moment. She's poisoned I tell you!"

"Kore!"

"Who will help heal *my* pain?"

"Do it now." Hades' eyes turned red and the little girl trembled.

If Harmonia hadn't been in so much pain, perhaps all this would have been funny. This all-powerful god was begging a little girl to touch her. But Harmonia knew that this girl had not only the power of prophecy, but the magic of the healing arts. Legend said she had once healed Ares and her own mother, Demeter.

The girl kneeled and laid a palm on Harmonia. Energy grew inside Harmonia's chest. She felt the deep, festering pain in her back fade a little. Her vertebrae even moved and cracked. Then Cora wailed. Hades laid his hand on the girl's, locking it over Harmonia's chest. Harmonia began to breathe better. And some pain lifted. All the pain left her neck. Cora stopped groaning, but her tears didn't stop flowing. Finally, with her hand still locked on Harmonia's chest by Hades, she cocked her head back to her uncle and said, "There's nothing left, Uncle. This one's poisoned rotten, I tell you."

17

FROM BEFORE THE STARS

WHEN HARMONIA OPENED HER EYES, A BRIGHT GREEN LIGHT was shining through a crystal window. She looked around her bedchamber. Most of the furniture was gone now (perhaps destroyed by the grain witch). A step led down into another room. But surrounding her bed were large crystal windows. It was a clear, beautiful day in Azure Blue. She could see the purple fields. Beyond were large blue oaks. Further still was the distant strait. And on the other side, she saw the giant wall of gold, Ambitus Pyramid.

But she groaned from pain.

A tall man in a dark, hooded cloak sat in a wooden chair, leaning forward. Was he sleeping? She recognized the dark cloak. It was Hades. The God of the Underworld himself was holding vigil for her. And this time no one else was in the queen's chamber.

He looked up.

"Ah, Harmony," Hades said with a smile. "You awaken to a glorious day. Your beloved sisters have freed us. Maiden Milda led the charge. They raided the little ones' homes, their dwellings, their farmland, and the main square, and they searched every tree in the woods. Then they rounded up all the little rodents and exterminated them. All of them. It was glorious. The few that survived ran with their king into the depths of the pyramid. I told Hermes to not harm the fools. *Yet.* I shall allow them their exodus to provide false hope. Then in my kingdom I shall deal with them, and vengeance will be mine for what they did to you." He yawned. "I shall deal with the little shits. Some fools tried to fight us." He laughed. "But my Eruboi arrived from across the strait and helped Milda clear the rest of them. After what they did to you, the idea of more fighting was intolerable to me. The island this morning is, of course, now yours again, my darling."

"You had no right to bring your mercenaries."

Hades stared at her for a moment. Then he laughed heartily. He slapped his knees and got up. He walked to one of the floor-to-ceiling crystal windows and just gazed outside. "I see you're improving. Don't worry, my Eruboi guards left as soon as their job was complete."

"And Milda had no right to do this to Pangrin's people. I never asked for them to be exterminated."

"She had every right," Hades said, still with his back to her, staring out the window. Below the palace lay lovely blue-green and violet fields of grass. "They hurt you."

"And now you heal me?" But if Cora had healed her, why did it still hurt to move? Just moving felt as if a dagger were being thrust into her again. "Did you stay with me all night?"

"Aye," he said with a nod.

"That demon child healed me? Yes, I remember her screams. But I'm afraid, Hades, she didn't do a good job." She moaned some more. "I can barely move. I don't have any strength. You were with me here? The whole night?"

"Yes."

"Don't you have a kingdom to run?"

"We hold Azurea," he said, finally turning to her. "Now rest, my love. The dwarfs have been removed. All is well on your island. We finally have peace in Napea."

As HARMONIA OPENED her eyes again, the green sun was just rising through her window. Had she slept through the night? Or all day and all night? It must be morning? Again? Had she slept an entire day? She heard the nearby waterfalls in her garden. She'd had thin walls constructed near her bed so she could hear the nearby streams. It had probably been perfected by that fiend Antilees, the master builder. The dwarfs had built the palace overlooking a hillside with Azure's glowing blue water flowing in a waterfall, past blue-green foliage, into the valley below. And, amid the pain, she enjoyed the sound of the flowing water.

She turned and was surprised to see that the God of the Underworld had still not left. He sat in the chair staring out the large window.

"I blame myself," he said quietly. "I should have brought my men in long ago."

"You had no right to bring anyone onto my island."

"You're awake?" he said, whirling around. "Still upset about that? I brought Eruboi for order in Napea."

"This island is my responsibility. No men shall ever raise arms on it." She scooted up but then cried out in pain. She shut her eyes tight and fell back. "Never again, I tell you."

"Even when you were nearly dethroned? I disagree. The Amazon needed help this time. Without help, your people were well matched by the dwarfs. Many are trained soldiers. And a trained force fighting for their lives could have depleted a better trained Imada. I made your army for Gaia, not Napea. Anyway, I told you, I had all Eruboi leave the island after the fight was over. They're gone."

"Never send them again."

"As you wish," he said with a bow and a smirk.

Then she heard humming. This was so strange. She thought they were alone.

It was a child's voice. Perhaps Hades hadn't been talking to himself; perhaps he was talking to this child, his niece, the witch who healed her? She spotted the young brat sitting by another window, by a step, holding a black bird nearly her size and petting its feathers. The girl had the same long golden hair, but now it was combed straight. And she wore a white peplos in the fashion of the nymphs. Her eyes, gazing at Harmonia, were a bright azure blue. The little witch seemed tranquil now. And her brilliant blue eyes matched the eyes of this strange bird. Bright azure. The black bird also had a blue chest and multicolored wings.

"Thank you for healing me," Harmonia said to Cora.

"Humph." Cora squinted. Then she ran her fingers along her bird's feathers again. "You please Uncle. But you shall die soon. No one really cares about you."

"Shut up, Kore," said Hades.

"If I was granted power," Harmonia said to the girl, "I'd kill your family."

Cora opened her eyes wide. Then she grew a big smile, jumped up, and burst into laughter. "Funny! She's funny, Uncle. This one is very funny!"

"Yes," Hades said with a smile. "She is also the Azure queen. Now leave her chamber and go play with the nymphs. Leave us."

"Amazons fear me," Cora said with a shrug. "They're boring. And I have no one my age to play with." Cora jumped up and stood over Harmonia. "Boy, those dwarfs really hated you. Are you still in pain? Hmm? You hurt me. It hurt so much to touch you. They poisoned you, you stupid nymph. That is why my hands could not completely heal you. They hate you so much that they poisoned their blades. Now it's stuck in you and can't be removed."

"It can't?" Hades asked.

"*I told you it can't!*" cried Cora. "*I did everything in my power, Uncle, and I won't do any more! Stop doubting what I say!*"

"Or did you let go when you weren't done?"

"Don't speak to me like this! You can't!" Cora said, throwing her long blond hair back. Then she stood up straight and regal—strangely resplendent, for one who appeared so young. "Mother doesn't like you. And Father will punish you." Then she turned with a devilish grin to Harmonia. "You don't fear me, nymph? Hmm? Are you stupid? I could squeeze your chest and take your life in an instant. I did it to a dog once. I squeezed the deisa till it couldn't bark anymore. Its bark was annoying me. I don't care for dogs. I hate them. I can heal, but I can also kill. And killing doesn't hurt. Don't you fear me, Amazon?"

"I discipline what I can," Harmonia replied. "If there is something that I cannot put into order, I leave it be. Even my final breath. I fear nothing." Harmonia closed her eyes and sighed. "Get this spoiled child out of my chamber, Aidoneus."

"How dare you!" Cora whirled to face Hades. "How dare you...say that to me! I am a goddess. You will address me as Persephone, the goddess of grain, daughter—"

"Get out, Kore," Hades said, rolling his eyes. "Get out now."

"But didn't you hear her words?" Cora stomped her feet. "Didn't you hear what she said? My mother would never allow—"

"*Get out!*" cried Hades, his eyes blazing fiery red.

Cora trembled. Then she turned to Harmonia, stuck her tongue out at her, and stormed out of the room.

Hades held out an outstretched arm. The great bird flew to him. Then he walked to Harmonia's bedside and took her hand. He said quietly, "The poison needs to leave. It will take time. I didn't understand why you weren't completely healed by her hands. At first, I punished Cora thinking she did not finish the healing because of her anger with me. But then I realized I was being harsh. The brat heals, but she can't get rid of poison set in your bones."

"You heard what I told her. I don't fret. Even over my last breath." Harmonia closed her eyes tight and nodded. Then she squirmed, feeling another sharp cut in her side.

"My niece brought you a gift," Hades said. He let go of her hand and petted the bird. The bird cooed. "His name is Mainax. He is a phoenix. Some say he was born before we came from the stars. He is eternal. He will live forever, just as you will. Just as your name will. I have christened you and your daughter's royal family Ambrosia. Ambrosia is the food baked with the nectar of the gods. It is eternal, just like this gift. I wish to give you Mainax to help you in your recovery."

He used both hands to give her the great bird. But Harmonia didn't take it. She just stared at him. He held it, practically pushing it to her.

Every act from this brute had a purpose. What was this one? Love? Did the god truly love her? He stared into her eyes as if he did. And he kneeled beside her looking so tired. A god looked tired. For her. From the stress of her injury? Had he not slept because of her?

She finally accepted the bird and gently petted his multi-colored feathers. "Such a gift. Why do you try so hard to make me like you? Why so many gifts? I will die one day, Aidoneus. I am mortal. I will not live forever, like this bird. Like you. I've known this to be my fate since I tasted the myrle berry. Why don't you?"

Hades ran his fingers through her hair and rubbed and squeezed her hand. He just shook his head.

Harmonia laughed and went back to admiring the jewel of a bird gifted to her. Then she winced, for the laughter made her back burn.

"If only man knew the heart that lies in their god of death. I will die, my love. Perhaps not today, but tomorrow. You must accept it. But before I go to Charon, I shall give my favorite god a gift of my own." She gazed into his eyes. "All nymphs shall provide sacrifices to you and build you a great temple, only to you…*after* you bring my daughter to me. Bring Nephrea home now, Hades. No more delay. That was the deal. You say the dwarfs are defeated? The island is ours? Then bring Nephrea home to me. She is a far greater gift than this lovely bird. Send for my daughter now if you wish me to really be happy.

"As I sacrifice for my favorite god, your Ambrosia family will need an heir. I will teach Nephrea everything I know. I know the stakes as I push south, but somehow I think you don't. Give me an heir, Aidoneus. Bring her back to me now. And keep the gods from interfering as I take Atala under your very name. I am your champion…*only* if you give me back my daughter as promised."

"Even now you barter with a god."

She nodded.

"If that is your wish." He squeezed her hand tightly. "After you are strong."

"I am strong and I wish it now." Then she summoned all the energy she had to spare and glared at him. "And Hades… don't ever bring men onto my island again."

18

THE QUEST FOR KEMET

HADES SENT FOR THE CHIEF GENERAL OF THE AMAZON. HE SAT on a bench by a thicket of orange-leafed bushes under blue oak trees waiting for her in the palace garden. Jaida walked down the stone pathway in the scarlet iron armor and pteruges of the Amazon. Her long dark hair was tied in a ponytail. She approached him and took a knee, bowing deeply.

"My lord Hades, God of the Underworld. I am at your service."

"Rise. Let us walk and talk, General."

Jaida's eyes were sunken in, and she looked exhausted. Likely, like him, she hadn't slept. But not only that, this nymph had been fighting—not only killing dwarfs with his mercenaries but fighting with her own people in an effort to maintain order. Dry blood was still on her scabbard, matching the red color of her armor. The near death of Harmonia had nearly brought the kingdom into ruin. This Amazon nymph had helped it survive. Harmonia was right about her. Jaida was strong, possibly the strongest of all her race. Harmonia would need such strength to war in Atala.

She followed him along the garden walkway. They crossed

small bridges lined with torches—not yet lit, for the green sun still shone through a cloudless turquoise sky. They passed waterfalls and red and yellow flowers, and a lovely pine-like jasmine filled the air. Hades walked with his hands behind his back under his pitch-black cape. Some nymphs passed by. One carried an ampulla of water. An older woman brought oil to light the large lamps along the walkway. With the sight of them, the nymphs quickly rushed off.

"I love these gardens, Jaida. They were made lovelier upon the order of our queen. Did you know this?"

She nodded.

"First, know that I do not blame you for the attack on Harmonia. I have heard many nymphs accuse you of abandoning your post. I know better. The dwarfs are clever, as clever as some of the greatest elders in Gaia, and when they seek blood, their goal is fulfilled. You were just part of a trap."

"Thank you, Lord Hades."

"But you still feel guilty?"

"It was my job to guard her. Yes. It was my fault. But now I only worry over her health. I only care that she gets better."

Hades nodded.

They walked over an arched stone bridge, the largest, over a glowing blue stream. Then they were startled by giggling. By the great azure hedge maze, in the distance, they spotted a small red peplos rushing through openings in the thrush. Cora?

Hades stopped on the bridge and looked up. A wall made of glass stretched up six floors above him. The Crystal Palace shone blue and green, reflecting the land and sun, exactly as Harmonia had proposed it would. He shook his head in awe.

"She did it."

An older nymph in a simple white peplos, accompanying her daughter, about Jaida's age, walked along an intersecting walkway. But as they approached the bridge, they both fell to their knees. Jaida helped them up and, like the others, they quickly left them alone. The nymphs gave their chief general and god a wide berth.

"Azure Palace is a wonder to behold, Lord Hades," Jaida said as they left the bridge. "I'm so proud to serve under Harmony."

"No, General. Truly I tell you, this is the greatest wonder in all of Gaia. It is the most incredible sight, next to Olympus. I should know. I have been everywhere. You cannot fathom how many seas I've traveled. Every land beyond the farthest imagined boundaries. Lands you'll never see. Already, before you touch down on your enemy's soil, when delegates come to visit, they shall be in awe of this palace. The mere sight will raise the majesty of my beloved. I tell you, this is the greatest jewel in the world."

"What is it you wanted to ask of me, sir?" she asked.

"The land needs an heir."

"An heir?" Jaida said, shaking her head. "I don't understand. You just revived Harmonia. The queen lives."

"This assassination attempt tells us that we don't have harmony, we hold discord. And the queen will still take many moons to recover from the poison. Harmonia and I have spoken of this many times before, but it never seemed like the right time. But now, with fortune brought from my own suffering, I can work this in Harmonia's favor. I can finally safely bring back her daughter. Now is the time for you to go fetch the princess. Of all your people, Harmony trusts you. And she will trust you with her daughter. She has asked that Princess Nephratee come home now. I ask that you bring her home."

"Harmonia has a daughter?" Jaida said, shaking her head. "She has never told me about her. Why'd she never look for her before?"

"In Egypt, Nephrea will go by the name of Nefertiti. The young girl, now nearly a woman, lives in Aneb-Hetch in the town of Busiri. Ask for Nefertiti in Memphis. She resides in a village off the river within sight of Giza and the great

Southern Pyramids. Find Hustaph. There by the Nile, where no nymphs reside, simply ask for the "blue" girl, and you'll find Hustaph's house. Hustaph cares for her. There is only one blue girl, one nymph, that far south of Azure Blue." Then he reached into his long robe and pulled out a small piece of soft violet cloth, about the size of his palm. He handed it to her, and she touched its smoothness and gazed at it in wonder. "And show him this cloth. He will recognize that it comes from me, and then he will trust you. There is no such soft cloth in Egypt or Atala. The fabric is our signal that it is time for her to come home."

She nodded.

"Good. My will be done."

Jaida took a knee before him.

And with that, Hades walked off toward the garden maze. Then he grew angry and cried out Cora's name. He snatched the little girl's hand and walked with her out of the garden.

"Will the queen of Azurea live, Uncle?" Cora asked Hades, holding his hand.

"You tell me, Kore. What do you prophesy?"

Cora laughed and shrugged. "I don't really care for her. I think I prefer her daughter."

19

NEFERTITI

Nephrea ran with a goat by her side, along a dirt path, past mud stone houses. She wore a thin kalisiris made of black-lined linen. Her long hair was tied to the side. Her eyes were darkened with kohl, but her skin was its natural blue. She had spent her entire life along the Nile hiding her color. She quickly learned when she was young that being different was dangerous. When she entered the capital of Memphis, which she rarely did, she had to cover her face with a veil and her hands with gloves, but she learned in Busiri to hide some of her skin with flesh-colored makeup. But not today.

She smiled as she glanced at the great river she ran beside. It had been such a temperate day. It was always nice this time of year, with the sun reflecting upon the waves of the Nile, not hot like it had been only a few weeks ago. Summer was ending and soon it would be cold. She already could feel a light breeze.

She rushed the gray goat into a pen, then she came inside her cottage. She approached a wooden table by the stove and looked at a small wire cage. It was empty!

"Etkus… Etkus! Oh, Etkus, where are you?" She searched

under a table, then she looked under a drape, then under pots. "Oh, where did you go!"

"Nephree? Nephree?" hollered a male voice from outside.

"Stupid mouse," she said cocking her head toward the door. "Yes, Papa?"

Her father stepped in with a dead chicken flung over his right shoulder. His eyelids were painted dark, like Nephrea's, and he had curly brown hair and a thin beard. He was shirtless with a rounded belly. He threw the chicken down on a table. Then he looked about fitfully.

"Do your chores, Nephree?"

"Yes. I put them all in their pens. I even got the water."

"Good girl. Why are you out of breath?"

"Huh? Hey, Papa, have you seen Etkus?"

"Did you lose your mouse again?" he snapped. Then he turned and latched the wooden door behind him. He walked over to the curtain over a hole that was their main window and looked out cautiously. He checked the lock on the front door for a second time. Then he squinted at her. She was sure she looked guilty, so she nodded and giggled. The giggle brought a smile to his face.

"You know the last time you lost him, I almost broke my leg," he said.

"He's around here…" She put a finger on her chin. "Somewhere."

The man took out a knife and laid it down on the table beside the chicken. Then he ran his hand through his dark curls. He walked over to a stool and gestured for her to sit, but Nephrea had already forgotten about him, searching the house for her mouse again.

"Come here, Nefertiti. I need to speak with you."

She looked up. Then she ran a finger along her chin again. "You know, I bet I left her at Yuya's house. Yuya and I were playing with him. Stupid mouse."

"Why aren't you wearing your color? Did Yuya see you prancing about without your paint?"

"It's such a bother. Yuya knows I'm blue. So do half the people in the village. Why can't I just ignore it and be like everybody else?"

"Because you're blue. Now come here."

For the first time, she noticed he looked upset. She was about to wander outside again, but he looked so serious. Her father was usually a joyful man.

"What's wrong?" Nephrea asked.

He pointed to the ground. She grudgingly sat cross-legged beside him on a checkered rug on the dirt floor.

"What is it, Papa?"

"Trouble," he said very seriously, standing over her.

"Trouble? From what?"

"There was a fight in the marketplace. It happened yesterday."

"There's always a fight in the marketplace, Papa. You shouldn't worry so much. You're always worrying."

"Three soldiers were killed. There's rumor that the culprit was a nymph. There are never nymphs wandering in these parts. The criminal was said to have your blue skin."

"So? I've seen a few nymphs in Memphis before."

"You haven't," he said, shaking his head.

"I swear I have."

"No, they'd be smarter than you and cover themselves if you had. And this one committed murder. The pharaoh's soldiers will be looking for the culprit. And, Nephree, your skin is blue. Do you understand? They'll come here first. Do you understand what this means?"

Nephrea just lifted an eyebrow, and she and Hustaph were silent for a moment. She started giggling.

"I've got it!" She jumped up and ran to the door. "Etkus is with Kaya! I loaned her the mouse when we sailed last week. I hope she kept him in her cages like I told her to. Kaya is so careless. You might have almost fallen and hurt yourself, Papa, but her mother really did."

"Nephree, get back here!"

"No." She shook her head. "I've got to go tell Kaya. Don't worry, I'll be right back."

"Listen, young lady, it's nearly supper and I'm not done!" He pointed again to the floor. "Come here! We need to talk."

"It'll just be a moment. I'll be right back. Bye, bye Papa."

And then she ran out of the house laughing heartily.

"Nephree! Nephree!" he shouted at the doorway. She still heard him hollering from their house. "Oh, Nefertiti!"

NEFERTITI RETURNED BY NIGHTFALL, and her uncle had arrived. She quietly hid against the wall outside by some bushes and snooped, listening in on the two men.

"You should message Orcus, Hustaph. Tell him what's happened. She can't stay. It's too dangerous."

"I haven't spoken to Orcus in years. Anyway, you don't message a god, a god messages you."

"It's trouble, Hustaph."

"I don't want her to go. By the gods, she's all I have. She is everything to me. But I will do whatever I can to keep her safe. We must leave and we must leave now."

"I know of a ship. I thought you'd go tomorrow morning, but you're right, you should leave in the darkness of night—tonight."

"Yes. Yes. Where is she, anyway?"

"Here I am!" Nephrea said with a laugh. She jumped through the door.

"Nephree! Where've you been?" cried her papa.

Her uncle walked over and gave her a tight hug. Her uncle was much younger than Hustaph. He was bald with a hairless tanned face. Both men were shirtless, wearing only plain short skirts of Egypt, or shendyts, with sandals.

"It's good to see you, Uncle." Then she giggled again. "And you too, Papa."

"I swear, you run out again and I'll find Etkus and serve him for breakfast!"

"I love you too, Papa," she said with a laugh. Then she leaned over and kissed his cheek. She carefully placed the mouse in its cage. "Back home where you belong, you naughty, naughty little mouse."

"Where've you been?"

"I told you, Kaya's house to fetch Etkus."

"It's time," said her uncle to Hustaph, running a hand over his bald head. "There is a boat that can take you two across the Strait of Aethiopia into Atala tonight. In Jedithian, you can head north. Atala is surely large enough for anyone to hide. The pharaoh will not chase you across the strait into Caravia."

"What are you talking about?" asked Nephrea. "I'm not going anywhere."

"I told you," said Hustaph. "It's unsafe, Nephree. We have to leave Busiri."

"And then be killed by barbarians," Nephrea quipped with a nod. She yawned and lay down on her bed at the other side of the room. "You two really should think this out a little bit more. What I really would love to do is just rest here at home now."

"We're leaving. That's final, young lady. And don't be running off again."

"No. I'm not going anywhere." She rushed to open the door, but when she put her hand on the latch…

Knock. Knock.

A loud rapping shook the wooden door. And then another. Then a bang. Nephrea opened her eyes wide. Her uncle's eyes bulged too.

Hustaph ran and pushed Nephrea to his brother. Her uncle snatched her by the elbow and pushed her behind linen sheets near her father's bed. Then he sat in front of her. She watched from under the sheets as Hustaph opened the door.

Nephrea had expected the pharaoh's men. What she saw was far worse. There, standing at the threshold, was a lady in a dark violet cloak, over red leather clothes, wearing a hood. She had a sword by her side and a quiver of arrows on her back. She lowered her head but, in the moonlight, Nephrea had already seen blue-tinged skin along her neck. Now she had truly seen her first nymph. The sight of blue skin gave her mixed feelings. On one hand, seeing one of her kind made her curious and excited. On the other, she was scared because of the story her father had told her. It meant this nymph was a murderer.

The stranger said something foreign with her head still covered. It was a language Nephrea had heard from travelers on the docks of the great river. She thought it was from the continent of Atala.

No one answered.

The hooded figure walked in. Then she gazed about the room. She turned and removed her hood. Her blue-tinged face shone in the light of the candles and lanterns in the house. Hustaph's brother gasped, likely having never seen a nymph before.

"Where!" the nymph snapped in plain Egyptian. "Where?" Then she added the Egyptian word "blue."

Hustaph quickly muttered strange Atalan speech. And the nymph responded.

Then Hustaph said to his brother, "She speaks Atalan. She wishes me to translate." The nymph spoke more of her strange tongue. Hustaph interpreted, "She says her name is Jaida, general and chief guard to Queen Harmonia of Azure Blue of Napea. She's being pursued. Probably tonight, they'll find her. Then they will find us. She's spoken to many of our neighbors, some at the tip of her sword. All of it, after days of searching, points to this house. Now she is very weary. And she's asking for the girl. The blue nymph of Busiri."

Nephrea lifted the sheet higher and watched the stranger, with her back turned, open a saffron drape at the window. She peered out. It was getting dark outside. Had Hustaph or his brother been soldiers, this would have been a great time to ambush her from behind. But her father was a simple fisherman.

Hustaph spoke more Atalan.

The nymph shook her head with her back still turned. Then he shouted something foreign to her and grabbed her wrist from behind. It looked like he was just escorting her to the front door, but the minute he laid his hand on her wrist, the stranger threw her father over her shoulder. Then she unsheathed a sword and pointed it at her father's neck. That sent Nephrea out from under the sheets screaming.

"Leave him alone! Get out! Get out of here! Don't touch him!"

Jaida's eyes opened wide at the sight of her. She stared at her Egyptian kalisiris and face. And as the girl kept screaming in a language Jaida didn't seem to understand, Jaida sheathed her sword. Then she fell to the ground and bowed deeply before her.

Hustaph's brother ran to him and helped him up.

"Who are you?" Nephrea asked. But she spoke in Egyptian, and the stranger did not seem to understand. But all anger left the stranger's face.

"Who are you?" Hustaph translated the Atalan into Egyptian.

Jaida faced Nephrea and spoke that strange tongue again. Her father said, "She's a general in your mother's army, the Amazon army that serves Queen Harmonia Ambrosia. The queen, your mother."

Jaida turned and asked Hustaph something.

"She's asking me if I cared for her," Hustaph said. He

nodded. "She said, for that, the kingdom of Azure Blue owes me. She is eternally grateful. The queen says she will repay me. She wishes to pay me in gold. Please, get up," said Hustaph in Egyptian. Then he shook his head. "I don't want your money."

But Jaida ignored him. She remained bowing before Nephrea. Nephrea realized she was waiting for her to give the order to rise. Nephrea took Jaida's hand and helped the warrior up. She stared at Jaida's dark-blue hands. They were dirty and stained with dry blood but…blue.

Jaida spoke quickly to Hustaph again.

"What is she saying, Papa?" asked Nephrea.

"Nephrea, this is Jaida," Hustaph said. "She's introducing herself again. She was sent by your mother to take you home."

"Mother? Home? I am home. I have friends here." Nephrea shook her head. She looked at Jaida. "Kaya, Yuya. I… I live here."

"Nephratee," said Jaida, grabbing the girl's hand and grimacing. She spoke in her strange tongue again.

"She says she's going to take you to your mother," Hustaph said. "She's going to take you home to where you'll be safe. Where you will be her princess."

"But I don't want to, Papa." Nephrea said, snatching her hand back. Then she felt frantic. "What about my friends? What …" A tear ran down her cheek. "What about you? I can't leave here. Tell her to go. Tell her to go away. *Tell her to get out of here!*"

Hustaph kneeled before Nephrea just as Jaida had, but she knew he was doing it to calm her. And then Hustaph hugged her tightly. That made Nephrea weep in his arms. He ran his hand through her long black hair and kissed her forehead.

"Oh my Nephree," Hustaph said with tears of his own, "Nephree, I would do anything for you. But this soldier was sent by your mother, Queen Harmonia, to take you home.

You are a princess. Harmonia is your mother, the queen. Napea is your home, not Busiri. I told you all this before. I said one day you'd have to leave. The Isle of Napea is your home, princess, not Aneb-Hetch. Not Busiri."

"Aneb-Hetch is my home! And I am not a princess! Tell her about my friends. Tell her about Uncle! Tell her about our lands. About the river. I can't leave, Papa. No!"

"Nephree," Hustaph said, holding the girl's chin. "Don't you see it's unsafe now? Even if you don't go with her, we'd have to sail across the strait anyway. Even then you could not stay here."

"But I'd be with you!"

"Oh, Nephree, you have to go," Hustaph said, growing stern, shaking his head. "I knew this time would come. You have to go see your mother."

"No." She jumped from his grasp and ran to the door, shaking her head. "No! I don't want to go! Leave me alone!" And she ran out the door crying.

Hustaph didn't chase her. Jaida just stood by the door. Only her uncle pursued her. Hustaph turned to the general. Jaida still had a big smile on her face, seemingly not caring that the girl had run.

"How can I trust you?" he asked in Atalan. "Perhaps you've been banished for your crime, like Harmonia was long ago. For all I know, you're a simple nymph thief that doesn't even live with nymphs anymore."

"I come on behalf of the God of the Underworld," she said, walking back inside. She ran a finger along some pottery. She shook her long black hair out of the tie and straightened it. Then she looked at him from across his small cottage. "I am what I said I am. I'm the queen's most trusted guard. I'm also her friend. And I was sent here by Lord Hades."

She reached into a pocket and brought out the piece of purple silk given to her by her god. He gazed at it and ran the soft cloth through his fingers with the same wonder as she had.

"The bargain is rendered," he said, staring at the cloth. And now, like his daughter, a tear ran from his eye. "I feared this day, but, even knowing it was coming, I did not know how hard it would be. Tell me when I will see her again? When can I visit her?"

"She shall be ninety leagues north on the Isle of Napea. Men are not permitted, except during the Spring Festival, but the games have been suspended until we have peace."

"Certainly I can see her?"

"No." Jaida shook her head. "I'm sorry. The queen said you can't."

"Get out," Hustaph said, shaking his head and looking down at the ground in disgust. "Leave me. Such a bargain is evil. Now I see that. I will visit. Ninety or nine hundred leagues, one day I will see her again."

"Then you shall be struck down by an Amazon sword, sir. I tell you, no man is permitted on our isle. And with the coming tide of war, no man will dare sail across the Strait of Azure."

"You are a killer. Without my Nephree, I will die."

Jaida nodded and opened the door. She was about to run for the girl, but Hustaph grabbed her wrist again.

"Take care of my Nefertiti. You will find her to be a jewel more precious than the Nile itself. It is her heart, you see. Her love flows greater than any stream I have ever known in this world. It is her heart that makes her sweeter than anyone in Kemet."

Jaida examined him for a moment. "Now you make me wonder if this girl is the princess."

20

SWORDPLAY

T HEY FLEW TOGETHER OVER THE S TRAIT OF A ETHIOPIA, BACK over the lands of Caravia and across the marshes of Logencia. Nephrea did not speak to Jaida for the first two days. She grabbed the food her caretaker gave her as if it was a bother and stared into the fire, playing with sticks. She figured she didn't know how to speak Atalan anyway. It was on the third morning in the marsh fields when Nephrea awakened to the sound of Jaida cutting the air with her sword. They were in a clearing between bushes. Nephrea stood up, walked to Antilus, and petted her horn and mane, watching the warrior practice with her sword. The exercises with the blade looked like a dance and she marveled at it.

"Ah, Nephratee. Come. Come here." She dropped her sword and gestured for her. Nephrea walked over cautiously. "Come here, child. Take my sword."

Jaida handed the girl her sword. It was heavy and she nearly dropped it.

"Raise it up," Jaida said encouragingly. "Go ahead. Go on, girl. You'll probably be as good with it as your mother. Here, I'll show you."

"No," Nephrea said. "No" was the only word she had

learned. Then she dropped the sword and walked away. "No *sword*."

"Come on, princess. Try it."

Nephrea hesitated. She walked over slowly and picked up the heavy blade again. Then she waved it around a few times with both hands, just like Jaida did. She liked the feel of it and the whistling sound as it cut through the air. Jaida showed her how to stand with her legs further apart for better balance. Then Jaida grabbed a long branch and twirled it around, asking the girl to mimic her. It didn't take Nephrea long to ape her movements. Then Nephrea laughed for the first time. Jaida smiled back. And they practiced swordplay for a while.

That evening, Nephrea said something to her in Egyptian. She knew her caretaker wouldn't understand. She didn't bother to explain. Apparently, Jaida did recognize one of the words, "papa."

"Ah, your father seemed to be a good man," Jaida said in Atalan. "Hustaph… Good man." But the name "Hustaph" wiped the smile off the girl's face. Nephrea quickly turned her back on Jaida again.

The next morning Nephrea adorned her eyes in the dark kohl she had brought in her travel bag. She tied her hair to the side and did everything she could to look Egyptian. She even chose her favorite Egyptian kalisiris from her bag. Then she plotted how she'd run away.

"Come on, Nephratee," Jaida said with a smile, mounting her unicorn. "Come up on Antilus so we can go."

"No."

"Nefertiti, we have to keep going."

"No."

The girl promptly turned around and started walking back the way they had come. At first Jaida seemed to think it was a joke and laughed. The journey was many days by foot, and at her age walking back alone would be ridiculous. But it wasn't a joke. Nephrea stubbornly kept walking south, through the muddy marshes, in the direction of home. After about a quarter of a league, Nephrea actually believed she might have gotten rid of the Amazon, but her caretaker flew over her on Antilus and landed on a clearing right in front of her.

"Come on!" Jaida said angrily.

"No."

"Nephrea, I'm taking you home to see your mother."

Nephrea broke out in a torrent of Egyptian: "If you want to please me, take your princess home to the Nile. If I even am a princess. I don't care about your queen. Mother? Where's she been? My mother, I don't even know her. You come to my house and ask for me to embark on a journey, abandoning Papa and my friends? How dare you. If I'm the princess that you say I am, then obey me and send me home. Why, you're just an Amazon."

Jaida squinted at her, not understanding a word. Jaida just repeated, "I'm taking you home to see your mother."

"And Mother," continued Nephrea, "*Mother*? Why didn't she come and visit me personally? She sends you to collect me, like a dog? Like scraps? I already don't like her. Does she cover her eyes, or does she walk around like you, looking like a slave? Why should I go with you? Just because Papa allows it? I didn't want to leave with him either. Leave me alone. Just fly away. Go! I'll find my way back myself."

And she kept walking. She could feel Jaida's stare behind her.

"Stubborn girl!" shouted Jaida. "Do you plan on finding food and shelter for a week? Do you even know how? Do you even know the way?"

Nephrea kept walking.

"Come back here!"

"No."

Finally, Jaida lost all patience. She flew again over the girl and landed a couple of yards in front of her. Then she leaped from the horse and stood before her.

"Get up on the unicorn! Now!" Jaida yelled, pointing at her unicorn. "Get on her, now!"

"No," Nephrea said, folding her arms and shaking her head.

"Get up on Antilus!"

"No …" Then in her best mockery of Atalan: "No *get up on Antilus.*"

Jaida let out a big sigh. Then the girl almost cracked a smile. But she simply turned and walked on. Jaida followed. They walked for the longest time. All the while, the unicorn circled overhead.

Nephrea finally came upon a stream. She cupped her hand in the running water and drank from it. Then she gathered branches and leaves and constructed a shelter. Afterward, she sat there and just stared at the ugly fart-stinking marshes surrounding her. Was this her mother's land? The kingdom she ruled? Probably. It was the ugliest place she had ever seen. She sat for the longest time as her pursuer stood yards back, looking at her.

Evening came. And with darkness came hunger.

She watched Jaida run to some trees and sneak up on a deer, quickly slaying it with an arrow. Then the general roasted the beast by a fire. When it was very late, Jaida took some of the meat to the princess's makeshift shelter.

Nephrea still sat staring out at the stinking bogs. She took a pin from her hair and let it fall like her barbarian companion. Then she looked down at her muddied favorite dress.

Jaida dropped some freshly cooked meat before her. The princess scooped it up and ate the meat without looking at her. Then, after she was full, she looked away.

And then she cried.

Somehow, although Nephrea didn't see her approach, Jaida sat beside her. Nephrea cried for the longest time. At times, she'd look over and see the stranger just sitting beside her and staring up at the stars and the crescent moon. Jaida said nothing, but she didn't leave her side. She just sat with her legs folded, looking up and seemingly waiting for Nephrea to stop her weeping.

After a long while, when the tears stopped falling, Jaida said quietly in her best Egyptian: "Here stay, Pharaoh Nefertiti?"

Nephrea turned to her with tears in her eyes and nodded.

Jaida put an arm around her. Then Nephrea cried on the Amazon nymph's shoulder. She cried until she fell asleep.

And stay they did. Nephrea couldn't move on. She had to stop. She didn't know why, she just had to. Everything had happened too fast.

By day, Jaida taught the princess the bow and sword. By evening, they taught each other their languages. The marsh was ugly, but tranquil and quiet. Her nymph stranger did not seem much older than Nephrea. So it seemed that the two of them were becoming friends. As they learned each other's language, Nephrea learned of her home. When Jaida used the word for her skin color to describe the lands of Azurea, Nephrea, for the longest time, thought she meant something else. In time she realized that her mother's lands were so different that they were *literally* blue—like the sky. And as Jaida taught her of her mother and Napea, the idea of journeying to this wonderful world became more and more appealing, even to the Egyptian girl. One evening, Nephrea called their home in Atalan ugly. They laughed. Then they picked up their things and flew north toward the lands of Azure Blue.

2 1

THE LONG-AWAITED GUEST

QUEEN HARMONIA SAT ATOP HER THRONE WAITING FOR THE arrival of her special guest. She supposed she had been waiting a lifetime. She wore a long purple-blue gown with her hair wrapped in a black cloth upon which she had placed a thin gold crown. It was the first time she had sat in this room since the assassination attempt a year before, but it was perfect for her reunion with her daughter, Princess *Nefertiti* of Egypt.

Jaida walked through the great double doors wearing her Amazon scarlet armor. She was smiling. Her shoes echoed against the white marble floors. Then a guard by the door hammered the floor with a staff. And the girl walked in, in a tight dress and long leather boots—not shy, more curious. And for a moment, just a flash, Harmonia lost all her excitement. For the girl's wonderment and curiosity reminded her of a villainous general from Caravia, General Azerius. Nephrea's dress was a simple thin kalisiris from Egypt. And her long black hair was tied to the side in the fashion of an Egyptian. And, like the queen, but unlike the other nymphs, she wore thick black makeup over her eyes. But her face was familiar, as if Harmonia were looking in the mirror.

With a broad gesture of her arms, Jaida kneeled before

Harmonia midway across the throne room. Then, at the sight of her dearest friend, Harmonia broke all formalities, rushed down the steps of her dais, and embraced her.

"When I heard of your return," Harmonia said in Jaida's embrace, "I knew I had finally found happiness, dear Jaida. So many moons. Four moons! I feared something terrible had happened. But Imada scouts told me you were safe." Then she turned to Nephrea, who kneeled before her. "Then, when I heard that the quest to find the princess was a success…"

Harmonia chided herself for stupidly ruining her charade. She had planned to sit atop her throne in a queenly fashion. Surely that would impress the girl. Nephratee was supposed to be in awe by the foot of her throne. But Nephrea had taken a knee by the entrance in the throne room.

Harmonia helped her daughter up. Nephrea looked up and surprised her mother. She held a challenging gaze.

"Nephratee. Oh Nephrea." Harmonia hugged the girl. It felt uncomfortable. She probably made it worse by running a hand along the girl's long dark hair and face. "I'm so happy to see you, my darling."

"I was told you were sick," Nephrea said in Egyptian.

Harmonia was caught off guard by the foreign language. She had been across the Strait of Aethiopia for only a few moons in her many travels, but she knew enough Egyptian to converse crudely. She smiled and glanced over at Jaida. "Must have been quite a journey," she said to her friend in Atalan. Then she turned to Nephrea and said in Egyptian, "Yes. I was hurt. But I am better now. You'll learn so much, my daughter. So much." She ran her hand across Nephrea's face again. "So much, my princess. My daughter. In time. It's been too long. And General Jaida shall help teach you. She makes the best teacher."

"You understand Egyptian?"

"You have your room, Pharaoh Nefertiti." Harmonia nodded, continuing in the Egyptian tongue. "Indeed, it is a room fit for a pharaoh. You will learn. You must learn every-thing about us. I will teach you too. But most importantly, you must learn how to wield the sword. I need you, Nefertiti, my daughter, my pharaoh. I need you to rule. But more so, I need you to fight."

"Fight? Fight who?"

"Man."

Then Harmonia clapped hard. The suddenness of the gesture made her daughter jump. Milda bowed very low by the door. Jaida scowled at her assistant.

"Show the princess her quarters, Milda," Harmonia said in Atalan. "Give her treatment fit for a princess. Fit for my daughter. Today is a great day for the Amazon. I request a welcoming feast for my reunion. My daughter has finally come home."

"Your Majesty," said Milda bowing again. "A great day, indeed!"

The old hag and Jaida traded more nasty looks. That made Harmonia's lips curl in a smile. She enjoyed their hatred.

"Jaida," Harmonia continued, running a hand through Nephrea's hair again, "stay here after the princess leaves. I'd like a moment with you alone."

Jaida bowed.

Milda led the girl out of the throne room, but before she left, Nephrea turned.

"Goodbye, Mother."

And then the doors shut.

"*Goodbye, Mother,*" repeated Harmonia, shaking her head in amazement. It had been said in nearly perfect Atalan. Only her accent revealed her foreign origin. She turned to Jaida. "*Goodbye, Mother.* Did you teach her those words?"

"Yes."

"A remarkable girl. So lovely and strong. But I wonder, Jaida, is she the princess?"

Harmonia walked back to her throne. She grabbed a glass of myrle berry wine from the steps, and she felt the searing pain in her back again, a pain that she knew now would never leave her. Jaida took a chair in the front row.

"What do you mean, Harmony? She's your daughter."

"I know. But can she hold a sword? Better yet, can she lead?"

"She's your daughter, Your Majesty."

Harmonia shook her head and sighed. "No, Jaida. What is your impression?"

"She has your strength and your stubbornness. After we left Egypt, it took me three moons just to get her to leave the outlying bogs of Logencia. She's quick with the blade and quiver. She learns faster than anyone I've ever taught. Like you. She's also more stubborn than anyone I have ever met. Like you. Though she doesn't know how to fight, I'm quite sure that if I had insisted on taking her out of Logencia immediately, she would have battled me. And she would have been willing to die. She is intelligent. Fierce. Strong. She is an Amazon, Harmony. And she is an Ambrosia. Yes, Harmony, she is your daughter."

"Quite a glowing report." Harmonia winced again in pain and held her lower back. Jaida jumped up for a moment, but the queen waved her hand.

"Are you all right?"

"Ask the witch infant goddess. She could not get rid of the poison. The pain shall go on forever, I think. But judging from the look of that demon child, I wouldn't be surprised if it was planned."

"I'm sorry. But I'm so glad to see you again, Harmony."

"I was so worried about you. I considered messaging you and bringing her here, but I heard you were with her in Logenth. So I decided against it. I figured you could handle things. And, as usual, I was right."

Jaida nodded.

Harmonia nodded with a grin. But then it faded and she suddenly felt sad. She walked down her steps again and to one of the large crystal windows. Then she leaned her head on the glass. It was cold and dark outside now. She could barely see the beautiful bushes and trees in front of her. But, being this close to the glass, she could hear the trickling of the water in a small stream.

Jaida approached her.

After a long silence, Jaida said, "Harmony, what did you say to her? I didn't understand the foreign tongue."

"I told her that we had to be ready for our enemy. We shall invade. Now that this isle is ours, and my lord god has provided me an heir, I shall move forth onto their shores. That is my dream. First I will take the Hinterlands. Then Logencia. Then I shall take my vengeance on Azerius and Caravia. Just as he once wanted to burn me and that beautiful girl, I shall burn him. I swear it, Jaida. And then the Amazon will take all of the continent of Atala. And then, I shall take revenge on Demeter and Zeus by crossing the endless waters until I reach Zeus's precious Argos in Mycenae. One day, perhaps we will expand our reach to the surrounding empire, the lands my daughter is so very fond of. We will extend our reach until the Amazon rule over all men everywhere in Gaia. And you shall rule by my side."

Jaida nodded. Harmonia turned and touched Jaida's hair, just as she had with her daughter.

"And I told her the truth. I need her, Jaida. Just as I need you. She seems smart enough to understand. She may not get a mother's love, but she shall get my dynasty."

Jaida embraced Harmonia. "I love you, Harmony. I've missed you so."

"Next to me and the princess," she said quietly, kissing her forehead, "you are the greatest of all the queen's Amazons."

2 2

ESSER

IT WAS SPRING. THE FOURTH YEAR OF THE OLYMPIAD. HAD IT been a time of peace, Azure would have been full of celebration. By the law of the gods, no men were permitted to cross the strait except during the Olympian festival. Harmony detested the edict, as she detested all edicts, but she used this one to her advantage. Just as she planned to take advantage of a crisis that had befallen one of her Imada.

She had sent messengers to all the barbarians of the surrounding nations of Azure. All these missions had been uneventful, except one: Esser. Esser was a young soldier accosted in Logenth. In tears, lying prostrate on the ground before her throne this morning, poor Esser had related how she was ravished by three men, such was the disrespect her soldiers were given. Then, by the end of her tale, she forced herself to stand tall like an Amazon, awaiting her queen's orders. There were gasps in the hall. That was Jaida and Nephrea. And her idiot sycophantic assistant, Milda, was there too, sitting on a chair in one of the aisles reading and scribing on papyrus. Esser was dismissed.

Now Nephrea stared out—through a floor-to-ceiling window taller than herself—at the garden outside the throne room. It was dark, but Harmonia could see shadows from the distant forest and the reflection of her daughter in the glass. Nephrea wore a very long porcelain-white peplos draping down to her hands and trailing down her back, and she wore sandals. Her hair was tied in a band. And her eyes were darkened with kohl. She was dressed formally for the meeting with poor Esser, having just come from another meeting with the elders. Nephrea's face looked Egyptian, but her dress looked Atalan. She was royal. Elegant. Her daughter had learned the ways of the Amazons quickly. Already, within a year, she spoke fluent Atalan. And she had proven herself as a soldier. But she would never lose her Egyptian accent. And judging by the look of her profile, and her clenched fists under her white lace sleeves, she was now enraged.

"This is a slap in the face, Mother!" Nephrea snapped. "We must have King Karthra pay."

"Indeed," said Harmonia, sipping myrle berry wine. "Indeed. And we shall. Witness, my daughter, intolerable and disgusting man. What do you think your queen should decree?"

"I think," Nephrea said, shaking her head, "a petition should be sent immediately—"

"I told you stories of your father," Harmonia interrupted, raising a finger. Harmonia's voice echoed over the large vases, growing lovely blue and red vines along the rows of empty chairs. "The fate of a great man that I loved dearly. If General Azerius had not taken the life of your sweet papa, Ornaius in Caravia, you would never have been taken from me. You would have lived by my side even as a child. But, alas, that was never to be. And you know the reason for it, don't you? I've told you the price of my misery after the death of your father."

"Is it time, Mother?"

"We've trained since your return, haven't we? Imada has grown under the tutelage of Lord Hades. And so have you, my darling. You've grown and become a strong Amazon. We have multiplied the monokera to over four hundred steeds in the tower stables. We have perfected every bow, arrow, sword, and shield." She sipped more wine and nodded. "Our people have tirelessly trained every day for the defense of our isle. And now this. This disgusting act." Harmonia turned her gaze upon Jaida. Unlike Nephrea, Jaida wore the red scarlet armor of battle. Now, thoughtful as always, her general had her arms folded, standing beside a column staring at the ground. "What think you, Jaida?"

"Order a special convoy of Imada in secret, Harmony. Fly to Logencia with Esser. Have her point out the perpetrators. And then allow me to slice each and every man's throat."

"No, Jaida," Harmonia said with a laugh. "No." Then she raised a finger again. "But not bad. A bit too tactful. You're thinking too much like the princess."

Nephrea finally turned from the window.

"Allow me to offer a solution," Harmonia said, rising from her throne. She walked down the steps of the dais. "I shall invite all men of the North to the Crystal Palace. We shall discuss these events and find out who our enemies are and who our true friends are. It shall be done now at the time of the games, the suspended games, mind you, but the games. When the men cross the strait to partake in their perversions, I shall ask King Karthra publicly to surrender his perpetrators. If I am not provided a list, I shall declare war on Logenth. If instead he provides me the names of the perpetrators and sues for peace, I shall declare war on him anyway for the crime. But we still might need to fly in secret to find the villains. Either way, Esser's pain will be avenged by my very life. Be assured, as your queen lives and breathes, Esser will have the honor of penetrating every one of these monsters with her own blade."

Harmonia clapped her hands together loudly. Milda jumped up in her chair in a middle row.

"Write this decree, Mildew! The queen of Azure swears to take revenge on the perpetrators. Send it to comfort dear Esser. What an atrocity. Do not worry, sisters, when we take man's lands we will do the same to them."

"Your Majesty," Milda said, rising and bowing.

"Blood from men shall spill in return for this disgrace," Harmonia added, pacing. "Witness, Esser will become our champion. What say you to that?"

Nephrea and Jaida nodded.

Then stupid Milda nodded repeatedly like a fool, bowing again and again before Harmonia in the central aisle. "A great honor, Your Majesty. A great honor."

Harmonia squinted down at her assistant. Then she hurled her crystal wine glass at her. It hit Milda's back and shattered across the marble floor. Myrle berry wine splashed all over her white peplos.

"Write the edict, Mildew! Defy me again with your idiotic babble, you stupid shit, and I may lose all kindness. As well as patience!"

Milda ran back to her chair in a middle row, still infernally nodding over and over, her whole body trembling. Then she grabbed the papyrus from a nearby seat and scribed.

"But if we fail," Harmonia said quietly to Jaida and Nephrea, raising a finger. "We won't." She chuckled. "But if we do, I shall ask my god for vengeance. No, friends, I welcome this horrible news. Not for Esser but for Amazon. Esser sacrificed for all of us. Her face shall be engraved on every shield so that every Amazon may be reminded of the filth and debauchery of man. Make it so. I welcome this, just as tomorrow I shall welcome man into this hall with my special guest, King Karthra."

Everything is going according to your plan, Aidoneus. What irony that this tragedy falls upon Karthra's kingdom.

"Jaida." Harmonia heaved a sigh. "Oh Jaida, and my sweet Nephratee, you two think like man. Don't do that. We are Amazon." She walked to a small wooden table and poured herself another glass of pomegranate wine. "In this war, there are no petitions. No apologies. No discussions. No secrecy. The Amazons are the greatest race to ever step foot upon this world. Never forget that."

"I shall personally avenge Esser, Mother," Nephrea said with a nod and a scowl. "Just as I will take my vengeance on Azerius. I swear it."

"Indeed, Nephree," Harmonia said with a smile, sipping her red wine. "Indeed. I'm counting on it."

23

AS SHARP AS A DIAMOND AND CLEAR AS CRYSTAL

HARMONIA FOUND HERSELF ONCE MORE SITTING UPON HER throne. On her left shoulder perched Mainax, her phoenix. Jaida stood on her left, and Princess Nephratee stood to her right. Both wore red Amazon armor and held long spears. In fact, the entire hall was filled with her sisters, wearing the same polished scarlet armor. But only Harmonia and her daughter wore black makeup around their eyes. And only Harmonia wore the long blue and turquoise peplos of a queen, and more blue makeup on her face to show pride in being a nymph.

The three hundred Amazon guests stood at attention, waiting. After years of training, not one spoke a word or even moved. Hades had taught Harmonia that in the face of tens of thousands of soldiers in the South, only with precise, sharp, and deadly order, as sharp as a diamond, could she destroy her enemy. The room was also lined with red flags bearing the insignia of her phoenix—a dark bird with multicolored wings.

It was somber, so different from the Olympiad when Harmonia was a girl. Back then, there was a frenzy of excitement whenever men crossed the water. During the games everyone drank and was merry. And in the games, even before her Amazon were taught to use the sword, the nymphs displayed their athletic superiority. Not now. This morning was somber.

The green sun rose and soon filled the hall with a green haze as it shone through the crystal dome above.

Harmonia looked through the large crystal windows of her palace, tapping her fingers impatiently on her gilded arm rest. A lovely day. The red flowers abounded over her blue and green thrush, flowers so different from those in man's world. And, as she peered harder, she could see the purple grasslands in the distance. She thought of how the barbarians visiting would be in wonder over her azure world—the same wonder she had felt when she visited their brown and yellow lands. Her land would enchant them. So would the Crystal Palace. They didn't even have glass windows in the Hinterlands—or chairs for that matter.

The two large doors opened, and sandals echoed along the hall. Milda, also in scarlet armor, bowed deeply before Harmonia.

"The Hinterland lords of the North have arrived, Your Majesty," Milda announced.

The first warrior to enter slowed his step at the introduction. "*Hinterlands?*" This was a term used by Greeks referring to barbarians. But the man's awe of the throne room made him quickly forget the insult.

Many wore long fur coats and had long beards, with gold and silver jewelry shining from their ears and neck. And many wore leather pteruges. A few were in military armor, some silver, others bronze. They walked slowly down the central hall with mouths gaping, peering at everything. Not only the giant glass dome above, but the sheer size of the room was a design marvel.

She smiled wide, recognizing one particular warlord. The

most powerful warlord of Atala—that idiot pompous king, King Karthra. His sparse, disheveled hair was now white. He had chubby cheeks, long, dirty fingers gilded with golden rings, and silver bracelets and necklaces over a long violet robe. He walked with a limp, and his long beard was as white as his nearly bald head. And many of his accompanying officials wore purple clothes.

Soon a hundred guests filled the room, and Milda closed the large double doors. But none could sit. Though the nymphs stood at attention, they stood along all the rows of chairs in the hall. So the hundred guests had to stand or sit in the central aisle.

Queen Harmonia rose.

All the hundreds of nymphs stood straight at attention and smacked their shoes against the marble floor, the sound echoing over the hall.

A nervous young man in peasant clothes, a simple tunic and pants, pushed forward and bowed before the throne. Harmonia looked down upon him.

"Great Queen Harmonia, ruler of the Amazon and sovereign of the Nepean kingdom of Azure Blue. It is with great honor that I introduce to you, with love, brothers from across the strait, great rulers with their entourage. Lord Iselborn of Azerbanith, King Aram of Sutsik, King Dracus of Akti, King Karthra of Logencia, King—" He went on and on, listing all the kings of the South. She stopped listening. Not only did it all bore her, but her eyes had fallen on something far more interesting.

A man midway down the aisle gazed with wonder all over her great hall. It was his curiosity and his eyes that drew her. He was one of the only men wearing kohl. And he wore light-blue metal armor. He was tall with graying curly hair. He was beardless with broad shoulders and a hard expression, but he walked almost with a limp, like frail Karthra. It was her villain! General Azerius. He had come! Had he known she was queen? Would he have come if he had known? He seemed to barely notice her. With the immortality of the nymphs, she wouldn't look different from when she fled his villa two decades before. But he had aged badly. He seemed to wear his years heavily, with wrinkles about his brow and eyes.

Harmonia glanced at her daughter. Nephrea stared at all the men, probably passing right over her father. But then she noticed how her eyes roamed curiously about the hall, just like his, carefully scrutinizing everything. That disgusted her.

"And great brother King Ruvillus brings oils and a solid gold statue of the God of the Underworld, Hades, in your honor, Queen Harmonia, from the furthest reaches of Wilusa for—"

"Enjoy the ceremony," Harmonia interrupted the messenger, tiring of the announcements. Then she raised her hand. "Sit, sisters."

Nephrea and Jaida slammed their staffs on the marble ground. All her nymphs sat down in perfect unison. Then she gave all her guests a fake grin.

"The games have ended," Harmonia announced. "I am so sorry to bring this unfortunate news, friends. But events in the East have made it impossible to hold them for you this year. I have gathered all of you to discuss foreign threats. And so, today, I hereby announce once more the end to the Olympiad games." Jeers echoed in the hall. "I am most concerned with the eastern shore by Sutsik. The bay in the East is contested by Egyptians and I fear—"

"My lands are secure," said a short, broad man in bronze armor walking forward with a quick bow. This was King Aram of Sutsik. "It is an honor to stand before you, Queen Harmonia. The legend of your beauty is heard from Mycenae all the way to Babylonia. The whole world speaks of your beauty, and I see that there is no myth to those words. I heard of your fears of the East in your letters. But I come to tell you, to tell everyone, there is no concern. The Egyptians wish only peace. And so, I believe the games should be reopened today."

"Here! Here!" cried many foreigners. "Here! Here!"

"Open the games!" cried another.

"The games! We come for the Amazon games!"

"And their women!"

"All is secure and safe in the East, Amazon Queen," decreed King Aram, gesturing with his arms wide and bowing his head.

"But I disagree," Harmonia said.

Murmuring erupted.

"There shall be order in the queen's throne room!" Jaida cried.

Harmonia smiled slyly at King Aram. "It is well known that your city is in your hands, King Aram, but you do not control the lands along the hills or, most importantly, along your bay."

"You discuss this publicly, Queen Harmonia?" objected an elder beside Aram.

King Aram raised a hand and chuckled. "Queen Harmonia, I had looked so forward to the games and seeing your people dance and feast today. We understood withholding the games during your war on the isle with the Mandrigel. But why now? In all truth, most of us here have come believing that you jest over suspending them. Many here believe it is a ruse to welcome us for celebration." Many of the barbarians cried out again. "But now you speak of things that would be better spoken of in private."

"This hall is private, sir," Harmonia said. "The delegation here represents merely all the leaders of the continent and my private guard. You may speak freely. There are no commoners, or *habiru*, in my halls."

She glanced at King Karthra. He was oblivious to the reference to vagrants, habiru. He was too busy drinking from a golden goblet and casting a stray comment or two to his advisors to notice the term or even be listening to her.

"You show us an army!" cried a man hidden from the audience.

"Perhaps *you* are the threat?" heckled another.

"Who speaks?" asked Jaida, searching the crowd. But the heckler would not reveal himself.

"I, sir?" Harmonia laughed. "Me?" She searched the crowds, but no one dared come forward. "Sirs, I am only a woman."

And that made the hall burst into laughter. The whole room, including all the rows of stoic nymphs, laughed. It seemed to relax everyone.

Harmonia smiled and raised her hands once more. Jaida and Nephrea hammered their spears on the ground. Then Harmonia spotted Azerius again. Now he was finally staring at her. For a moment, it made her lose her false smile. Her greatest desire would be to arrest and kill him on the spot. Or perhaps rush down from her dais and stick a knife through his throat. Did he finally recognize her? Good. Unlike all the other people in the hall, he wasn't joining her mirth.

"This is a serious matter," Harmonia said with a chuckle. "I welcome you, guests, to our home. Perhaps there might be...*a little* dancing."

The hall erupted in cheers.

Harmonia clapped her hands. "You all have traveled so far. You honor us with your journey. Perhaps some food and drink before I continue?"

More people shouted in joy.

Nymphs dressed in the thin, translucent robes of the games entered the hall. Their presence brought the smiles Harmonia was waiting for. Many carried silver trays full of beef and cakes and fresh mutton. They traveled slowly, walking around the crowds, having to walk over some people.

"Ah, this is more like it!"

The servers went to everyone, offering food and drink. Harmonia reclined on her throne. But that movement made her wince in pain.

She glanced at Azerius again. Now the general did not shift his gaze from her.

After a while, the crowd settled down. King Aram bit into a thick leg of mutton, seeming to have forgotten politics. Soon the hall was more like a dining hall, with people eating, drinking, and conversing joyously together. Everyone but her nymphs. Her nymphs remained in line, sitting up straight, staring ahead in rows, awaiting orders. And Azerius began to stare not only at her, but at her army in rows in the throne room.

A nymph bowed before Harmonia offering her a plate of food. She shook her head.

Harmonia then said loudly, "King Aram, I am afraid we differ in opinion. Our lands are not secure." He seemed shocked that she had brought it up again. So did many in the crowd. "If there was an invasion in the East, all the villages you control around your capital would be overrun. But I don't doubt that you have the strength to fend them off from the city walls of Sutsik. Sutsik is well fortified. However, my interest is in Napea. Our island. If your bay is used by Egyptians, sir, it shall be a launching point for foreign invasion."

"This is not the place to discuss this, before your subjects," King Aram said.

"But these are not my subjects. Some of my ladies are serving you food, others are guarding us from watchtowers, others are readying weapons in our armory." Many stopped eating. "Here in this hall witness my elite force. My Imada. They have every right to be privy to the situation threatening our homeland."

A nymph in a long azure peplos walked up the three steps of Harmonia's dais and bowed before her. She handed

Harmonia a crystal glass of myrle berry wine. Harmonia grabbed the glass and sipped it.

"Now that you have what you have always asked for, food and lovely women to serve you, I ask again for your assistance in guarding our borders."

"A wonderful invitation, Queen," said someone in the crowd. He walked toward the dais, coughing and clearing his throat. It was the foul king Karthra. Harmonia's eyes narrowed and she tightened her grip on the armrest. With a stupid fake grin on his greasy, filthy mouth, he raised a cup. "I am in awe of your palace. But now we shouldn't speak of foreigners, my lady. Let us all choose to partake in Dionysus's blessings instead. The edict of Zeus." He turned to the crowd, and many shouted his name and cheered. "I propose we hold the Olympiad celebration on this isle every four years with your wonderous people, just as before. Starting today!"

"*Hear! Hear!*"

Fool, have you actually forgotten me?

"King Karthra, I presume," Harmonia said. She stood up and stepped down from the dais. Jaida and Nephrea came to their queen's side. "Such an honor that you yourself, King, step foot before me in my throne room."

"Aye," he said raising his hand, holding a large drumstick of meat. "Aye." He bit into it before her face. "Aye." Then with his stinky full mouth, he said, "I am...in awe of Azure Blue, Queen Harmonia Ambrosia. How could I miss the chance? But I think you should reconsider the games. We so enjoy watching your people dance. And we welcome any competition upon the fields."

"*Hear, hear!*"

"I am delighted that we meet you in person," Harmonia said. "Unlike yourself, I did not have the courage to travel south and invite you personally. I wish I had. As my people are aware, I would rather harm befall myself than any of my sisters."

King Karthra nodded slowly, furrowing his brow in confusion. Then he bit into his drumstick again. A few nymphs in the room broke their stoicism, jumping up and heckling the king. A few others started to cry.

King Karthra looked all around him. "I... I don't understand."

"This was the next issue I wished to bring forth before the delegation," Harmonia replied. "One of my sisters was mistreated in your nation, sir."

"My lady?" Karthra said, stepping back, looking shocked. "My lands are safe. Tell me the charge and I shall look into it immediately."

"The crimes took place in your Hinterland kingdom." Then Harmonia leaned forward, speaking more quietly though still loudly enough to be heard by everyone. "There has been a great deal of unpleasantness over it, I'm afraid. I heard that my messenger was ravished."

"Ravished?" Karthra laughed. "What do you mean?" That elicited a whole torrent of shouts from the Amazons in the rows. Jaida quieted them by pounding her staff on the marble floor. A soldier in silver armor rushed to King Karthra and whispered something in his ear. Karthra shook his head and pushed the man away. "All people are respected who come to my Court. What do you speak of?"

"Rape."

The whole crowded hall turned silent. Nephrea was glaring at Karthra.

Harmonia slowly made her way back up the steps to her throne, picking up her glass of wine in the eerie silence. The throne room was as quiet as when she sat and delegated in private with her daughter and Jaida. Everyone now stared, her nymphs awaiting her orders and her guests awaiting her next words. She sat back down and gazed down upon Karthra. Then she raised her glass, as if in a toast. *To you, you decrepit, feeble old man, in celebration of starting the war.*

"Is it not a crime in these lands to assault a messenger?" asked Harmonia. She now spoke very loudly. "Assault on a messenger is a violation of peace." Then she sipped more wine. No one else seemed to be drinking or eating a thing anymore. They all stared at her. "I am, of course, a new queen. But I believe any nation that sends messengers is protected by our code of justice."

Karthra ran a hand down his face. He seemed to be trying to regain his composure and seemed shocked at the accusation —not to mention that the stupid king was already inebriated.

"Aye, such is the code," Karthra said. "Aye." A man beside Karthra quickly leaned toward his ear again, but Karthra pushed him away.

"Esser, come forth," said Harmonia.

"*Step away from the dais!*" thundered Jaida at a crowd of men. "*Five paces back!*"

Many were crowding too close to the dais. Then Jaida cried out, slamming her staff on the ground again, "Presenting Lieutenant Commander Esser of Her Majesty's Imada."

All the men who had crowded the aisles made way for the short young hoplite in scarlet armor. She walked down the aisle, stepping around men sitting in her path, and stood before the dais. She took a knee before Harmonia.

"Esser, dear," said Harmonia, forcing a smile, "is it true that I sent you alone to deliver a message to King Karthra, the King of Logenth in Logencia?"

"Yes, Your Majesty," Esser said stoically.

It was so quiet in the hall. Too quiet. The only sound was Mainax flapping on Harmonia's shoulder.

"And what happened after you delivered the message?"

"Upon leaving the king's tent, I was captured. Three men threatened my life if I did not *dance* for them—they asked that I dance the dances of the games. I told them I had never been trained in such a dance. That I was trained only to fight in your Imada. They laughed, saying that I was lying. They said the only worth of a nymph was dancing. Then a man rushed me. I kicked him off. But…others grabbed me. There were too many of them and I was unarmed. I was roped from behind. They removed my armor and clothes. Then came—"

"Queen Harmonia," cried Karthra. "Such accusations! And publicly? This is disgraceful. You speak of justice, is it proper to make an accusation before a royal delegation? Here before the entire continent? My men would never—"

"Assault a messenger?" asked Harmonia. "And now interrupt the victim to keep her from speaking?"

"But she is just a woman—"

"Jaida," Harmonia said, raising her brow.

Jaida thundered her staff on the ground more loudly than ever. But her army was now inconsolable, shouting like crazy at the men in the central aisle. Some even threw things at the men.

"Sisters!" Harmonia cried, addressing the hall and raising a hand, "*Ektaxis.*"

Every nymph, some of whom had held meat or crystal glasses of wine, dropped everything and stood at attention. Once more, three hundred shoes hit the marble floor. All the men in the hall looked about, perplexed.

Harmonia glared down at Karthra. "What is the punishment in your lands for attacking a messenger?"

"You can't be serious," cried another man. He was one of King Dracus's guards.

"If a messenger was a man and was assaulted, what would be the punishment?" cried Harmonia, rising. "Is it not death? Is that not our code? For a man? Then what may it be for a woman? An Amazon? Even at war, isn't there justice on our continent?"

"My queen," said Karthra, raising a hand with a nervous chuckle. "Any offense will be investigated. I assure you. We will find justice. Even if this allegation is true, it was not sanctioned by my people. It would be a terrible mistake. If your lady—"

"*Soldier.*"

"If your *soldier* was wronged, she shall—"

"Esser, did three men attack you? Repeat it once more, for I believe the king is getting too old to hear."

"Three men attacked me after I spoke with him. I was raped."

The hall broke out in deafening objections from nearly every nymph. When it was quiet enough, Harmonia said to her army, "What think you of this, sisters?" And that sent another torrent of shouts echoing about the hall. All the nymphs who had been standing at attention now cried and gestured at the foreigners, looking ready to leap over the chairs and kill them.

"But this is preposterous!" cried one of Karthra's guards. "You can't accuse us—"

"*There will be silence in the halls of Queen Harmonia!*" cried Jaida.

Then Nephrea and Jaida pounded their staffs on the ground. But there couldn't be silence. It was as if this was the opportunity for all the nymphs' disgust and rage over the treatment of their sister to finally be heard. The Amazons shook the great crystal windows and dome above with their cries. Finally, Harmonia rose and raised her palm, gesturing for her nymphs to sit. Her army sat. They grew silent.

Karthra gazed at the aisles in bewilderment.

"I invited men to my hall in order to see who can help protect the Amazon nymphs in Azurea," said Harmonia, addressing the crowd. "As we are now a nation north of yours, I expect the same respectful treatment that you give yourselves. If this so-called king—" Harmonia gestured with a sweeping arm at Karthra. "Would like peace, he will forfeit all perpetrators of the act against my dear Lieutenant Esser. If he does not, henceforth, in accordance with the edict of the land of Atala, we declare war upon his lands of Logencia."

"My queen!" objected Karthra in astonishment. "All we want is peace."

"Then you shall forfeit the three men," Harmonia said with a shrug. "Or you fight once more with the queen of Argos. If you choose to fight, I warn you that you will not only fight with Queen Harmonia, but once more with Lord Hades, my god, the God of the Underworld."

King Karthra stammered. One of his guards, a man in bronze armor, stopped him from falling. The king's eyes opened wide.

Recognize me now?

"Queen of…Argos?" asked Karthra quietly in disbelief. "What…what…what is the meaning of this?"

"I'm simply requesting fairness in law."

"No. What did you just say, woman? I… I know you. You were…but you were just a common thief. A habiru. A lake witch."

"I think you are mistaken. I am Queen Harmonia Ambrosia, the Amazon Azure queen of the Isle of Napea, sir. The first of my reign." She jumped up and gestured with a sweeping arm to her daughter. "There by my right hand stands Princess Nephratee Ambrosia. And on my left is my chief general, Jaida. You, sir, stand before the ruling Ambrosia family of Azurea. And now you insult me and call me a common thief? A habiru? I say before my daughter and people that I was never a thief. As for a witch, if even you, King Karthra of Logenth, call me that again within this hall, I shall order my guards to run a sword through you."

And with that came an explosion of objections from more than just Karthra's guard. It seemed to be from every man for, truly, Karthra ruled all the warlords of Atala. The shouts were finally stifled by Jaida's hammer and Nephrea's staff.

"We take our leave, *Queen!*" chided Karthra. "I have no

interest in uttering another word with you regarding falsehoods. This accusation is ridiculous. At first, I was amused by your summons and display. I had hoped that the nymphs had resumed providing entertainment. Now I am aghast at your behavior."

"Look about you, Hinterland King. Look carefully at every soldier in this hall. Heed my warning. If you do not forfeit the three men who attacked my messenger, you will meet this army on the battlefield."

King Karthra ran his hand down his face and beard again. Then he gestured for his men to follow him down the central aisle. And another fifty, many from other nations, stormed out of the hall with him.

"Milda," Harmonia said. "Log down everyone who leaves my hall with that king. Catalog all his companions and the nations they come from."

She waited until the double doors were closed. Then she turned her gaze to the remaining foreigners. They seemed confused. Angry. Others looked fearful. Azerius, once the love of her life, continued to infernally scrutinize her. Surely he had heard the "queen of Argos" remark.

Harmonia leaned back in her throne, and all of the Amazons sat down with her. Then she glared at the Caravian general. Azerius had examined, observant as always, each and every man who had left with Karthra too. "Why is a delegate from Caravia here? Hmm? I remember specifically not inviting Caravians, Milda."

Milda quickly shook her head. "There were no such invitations."

"Hmm, how interesting. That man over there." She pointed right at Azerius. "Right there. The one who colors his eyes like me. Is he a spy? Perhaps Egyptian? Assyrian? But his armor is blue. Why is there a Caravian in my throne room?"

"Perhaps he is enjoying this spectacle as much as I am," quipped King Dracus with a sly smile. Many laughed. And

then her arch enemy, the beastly General Azerius, maneu-
vered around some of the other men to approach the dais.

"I come—"

"Please everyone, drink, eat," Harmonia said, losing her
smile. "I've addressed the unpleasant crimes that had to be
brought out into the open. No more unpleasantness. We will
not have the games, but we will enjoy supper with friends.
Brothers, I trust none of you remaining are involved. Join us.
We have myrle berry wine and azure mutton." Then she
looked right into the eyes of her greatest enemy, her former
lover. "Those of you still here must be, of course, Amazons'
true friends. These foods, I'm sure, you will find richer and
more flavorful than the foods you are accustomed to back
home."

"Wine," cried one of them with a laugh. "Humph, myrle
wine suits delicate nymph women!"

Men burst out in laughter.

"Indeed, sir," Harmonia said with a laugh. "Red is the
color of blood, isn't it?" And she raised her glass to him in a
toast.

Then Harmonia put the glass down under her chair and
raised both her hands, clapping loudly once more. A group of
nymphs entered the hall with more dishes. She clapped three
times in succession, and all her elite soldiers, except a handful
of guards, exited down the aisle and slowly left the throne
room.

"Sit and join me for supper and pleasure, friends,"
Harmonia said. "But, Jaida, please escort this Caravian spy
out of my sight."

"I only wish to have a word with the queen of *Argos*,"
Azerius insisted, now directly before the dais.

"Oh, there can be no words between us," Harmonia said,
opening her eyes wide. "There shall be no words between us
ever again. Jaida, let this spy catch up with King Karthra, his
true friend, across the strait. Get him out now."

Jaida took him by the arm. He snatched his arm back. "We Caravians only want peace—"

"Peace was dreamt of once by an ignorant woman before a Caravian general ravished her too!"

"Our daughter—"

"No more words are permitted by this Caravian spy!" Harmonia raged, jumping up. *"Get this man out of my hall before I run a sword through him! Send word, sir, to your King Tolen that if he wishes to delegate with the Amazon queen of Napea, have him come announced, not in secret in the fashion you Caravians prefer!"*

Azerius squinted at Harmonia for a moment. But then he was grabbed by two more guards and led down the hall. As everyone settled down into merriment again, Harmonia watched as Azerius took his leave. But before he left the room, she walked down the dais steps and grabbed her daughter by the arm.

"Do you remember who I said killed your father, King Ornaius?" Harmonia whispered into her ear.

Nephrea nodded.

"That's him." Harmonia pointed. "That's the man. That is General Azerius of Caravia. See, he fears my revenge for dear Esser. And such a revenge it shall be, child. Something no one has ever seen. I shall avenge Esser and your father in ways never before witnessed in Gaia."

Azerius stood by a nymph guard at the door. He turned for a moment. Did he hear the word *father*?

"Will you kill him tonight, Mother?" Nephrea asked, narrowing her eyes.

"No. Not yet. I wish him to return and tell King Tolen II of my power," Harmonia whispered in her daughter's ear. "Man's fear aids us in battle. So teaches the Dark Lord. That is why, Nephree, we do nothing in secret."

"I will kill him myself," Nephrea said with a nod, glaring at her father. Then she said in Egyptian, "By the blessing of Montu, I swear I will take his life."

"There is nothing in Gaia that could make me happier, my dearest Nefertiti." And Harmonia put an arm around Nephrea and kissed her on the cheek.

Only half the men that had arrived remained in the hall. And, in a great irony, many were secret delegates she had requested from Assyria and Mitanni from the East. She would meet with these foreigners in private later tonight to assure peace along the borders of the continent and protection from Egypt during the upcoming war.

2 4

THE SALPINX

As Harmonia flew on Antilus near her general, leading the cavalry in the sky, she strained her eyes downward, peering through thick fog, searching for the sea below. She knew that the water had changed color from violet to blue, but the mist was too thick to see beyond her blue legs and red painted leather sandals. Finally, there was a break in the gray and white mist and a rush of yellow sand below. No one would expect her attack. At her delegation, she had drafted treaties with King Dracus promising peace and alliances against their mutual enemies in the South. But without a navy, the only way to push forward was to invade the coast. She'd be forced to first take Dracus's barbaric kingdom, march through the thick Shadow Forest, cross her ancient, treasured Crystal Lake, pass the marshes of Logencia, and finally climb the cliffs to reach her goal. Through the mist over her shoulder, she caught her cavalry bobbing up and down behind her. They wore the shiny red armor of the Amazon too. She gazed up, squinting in the wind, and through another clearing she watched the familiar turquoise sky turn azure. And hints of rays of gold beyond the clouds revealed man's yellow sun.

More fog cleared and the sand under her feet quickly changed to a rush of trees. The trees in these parts were not blue like at home, but green. It was as if the world had turned upside down.

"Harmony! Harmony!" cried Jaida, excitedly pointing at stone towers in a clearing.

As she dipped through another cloud, a farmer with an ox-drawn cart was moving down a dirt trail by a stream. Two children wearing only pants ran, laughing, beside a long wooden fence. Another three humans walked along a dirt path past a thatched-roof cottage. The cottage was surrounded by thick green thrush; it had a white flower garden and stone steps. Her eyes burned from the lack of blue. And she felt the pressure of the air weigh her down in this foreign world. She had been away so long that she had become accustomed to the lighter air in Azure.

Two cottages were lit aflame by fiery torches dropped by her Imada—the first sign of battle. As mist mixed with smoke, there was no turning back.

Within moments, she was approaching the stone ramparts of Dracus's castle—close enough to see soldiers in silver pteruges and breastplates rushing for cover behind the ramparts.

"*Aieee!*" cried a hundred nymphs. "*Aieee!*"

"Blessed be Erebos, Jaida!" Harmonia shouted through the wind. "Our first victory!"

Jaida nodded.

"This day we shall remember! This day, Erebos shields us. For on this day Queen Harmonia returns to Atala! Watch men fall to their knees before your queen!"

"*Aieee! Aieee!*"

Then came the blowing of the salpinx. And more battle cries with the sounds of a hundred unicorns whinnying through the air. And then more fire beneath.

Antilus shifted and Harmonia was almost thrown. Had her unicorn not turned, an arrow whizzing by her helm might have slain her. But the arrows from below were paltry compared to the rain of arrows falling down from her cavalry. Turning, she saw a hundred unicorns following close behind, rushing through wisps of clouds and smoke. They all bobbed down, nearly touching the branches in the woods and soaring close to wild green grassy fields. They speared castle defenders with javelins or struck them with more arrows. Then they quickly rose into the dense clouds for safety, only to descend and strafe their enemies again.

But then Cassias was thrown from her unicorn. Cassias was a sharpshooter with the bow, better than almost any other nymph, trained as an Imada sniper. It's likely she had been killed before she fell, but the drop alone from this high was enough to slay her. Cassias was Harmonia's first fallen nymph in the war and, as such, Harmonia would see to it that her death would be remembered. Any death of a sister was terrible, made more abhorrent by the fact that her nymphs were destined to live eternally if unharmed by violence. And Cassias was a friend.

Harmonia aimed an arrow in the direction of her killers. She saw one arrow fly through a helm, but many more hit shields or the stone ramparts of the tower walls. Then Harmonia pulled Antilus's neck hard and rose nearly straight up. She caught three other nymphs trying to keep up with her to guard her from behind.

Antilus, take me higher. Higher! Over the tower. You can do it, girl.

Then she turned her unicorn's head downward and dove, dangerously close to the roof of the tower. The nymphs guarding her were forced to break off, not able to keep up with her prized unicorn.

As the tower came crashing before her and Antilus, she leveled out and, when steady enough, she jumped.

She landed hard on the gray stone floor. In a flash, someone cried out her name from above in a panic. Her guards were shouting in a frenzy for her to return to the air.

Two guards in silver armor rushed her with swords drawn over their heads. They were huge, broad men, twice her size. She pulled her Mandrigelian sword from her scabbard, parried, then thrust. She cut and parried in the way she had been trained for decades, gracefully, with the elegance of a dancer. Her arm was cut as she ran a sword through the soldier's silver armor. Her enchanted blade cut through his crude armor with ease. But she felt the sting as blood dripped down over her blue hand, matching the red color of her wrist guards.

"*Aieee! Aieee!*"

"A woman fights me?" cried a thick-bearded man with clenched teeth under his silver helm. "So be it. Then a woman shall die!"

But her guards landed beside her. They too drew their swords and entered the fray.

One of them struck a man in the back as he charged her. Then she saw three more enemy soldiers rush up the stairs through a stone passageway. Harmonia struck another thick-bearded man's sword and splintered it in two. Then she used her shield in her left hand to strike the man in the face. He fell to the ground. She plunged her sword through his breastplate, finishing him.

It rained more arrows from above. More of her Imada were providing support.

"We must get back in the air for safety, Your Majesty," cried a nymph beside her. "Why'd you land?"

"Cassias. Did you see what they did to her? They shot her, Arava. The archers needed to be stopped or they'd shoot more Imada."

"I beg you to reconsider, my queen," Arava said. "We

must go." And as Arava blocked another throw of an enemy's sword, she said, "This isn't the plan."

Harmonia thrust her sword through Arava's assailant's chest. Then she looked about the tower. All the barbarians lay dead—for now. But she heard more steps running up the tower. And then she saw the scarlet body of another one of her nymph sisters lying dead beside enemy bodies.

"Call your monokera!" Harmonia ordered. "Yes, we rise back to the clouds."

"Look, my queen!" cried another nymph beside her. "Look!"

She was pointing excitedly through an opening in the stone wall. Hundreds of soldiers in scarlet were marching, through a clearing in the fog, from the shore. The weather had worked in Harmonia's favor. Her plan was, so far, a great success. Her foot soldiers were already approaching undefended gates.

But down below, by the front of the castle, enemy horses were finally rushing out to greet her Amazon soldiers in the fields. Some wore silver armor, but far more wore thick animal fur and carried axes. A horseman held Dracus's red and white flag. Hundreds of men from behind the castle walls were rushing to defend the castle.

"The time has come to breach the walls!" Harmony said excitedly, placing a hand on a young guard's shoulder.

Harmonia whistled for Antilus. Then came the whistle of all her guards at the tower. When Antilus arrived, she leaped upon her.

"Take to the skies and defend our sisters below!" Harmonia cried. "We shall have King Dracus by sunset! Haw!"

Antilus whinnied as she leaped off the tower. Harmonia raised her fist and shouted "*aieee!*" as she strafed the enemy.

Harmonia had seen armies in Caravia and Egypt. She had observed her lover's soldiers standing in perfect rows, which she had admired and then emulated. Now her enemy below was trying to ape such order. It was laughable. The nymph elders had warned Harmonia that these Atalan men would be harder to defeat than the dwarfs. She knew now that this was not so. Watching them scramble, she began to wonder if King Pangrin and his white-armored army could have conquered them. And then she wondered how Dracus maintained any defense at all against armies like Azerius's Caravians.

She spotted what looked like a general—only because he kept shouting at his men, trying to keep them together as the arrows continued to fall.

"Aieee!" Harmonia lifted her fist and spat down at their leader as she flew within feet of him. Then she fired arrows down at them. More arrows whooshed by her ear, one an inch away from her helm, mixing with the sound of howling wind.

She turned Antilus away from the castle toward her front line. Then she landed on the grass before her army. The mist was fading. It had done its job. Indeed, Erubos had been with her this morning.

She raised her fist atop her unicorn. That made all the Amazon foot soldiers shout and cry out her name. Five hundred nymphs in scarlet stood in perfect rows at attention before her.

She raised her fist again.

"Amazons, think you were abandoned?" Harmonia shouted. "Stepped on by false gods? We march with pride this morning, for Queen Harmonia frees you! She frees all from subjugation. Upon the words of mighty Orcus, blessed Aidoneus, Gaia shall be ours. The whole world. All of it!

"Enter their homes, enter their fields, free their women. Raise the flag of our phoenix over the pyres of their homes. Do not forget the message they sent to us by our dearest Esser. No longer are you slaves for man's subjugation. I free you. Free as Amazons, nymphs of Argos. No longer do we answer to wretched Cronos. No longer under the dung of false gods Zeus and Demeter!"

Harmonia was thrown from her unicorn.

All turned dark for a moment. Something had thrown her off Antilus. Then came a flash that burned her eyes and the sound of lightning ringing in her ears. For a moment, all she heard was the ringing. Then, lying on the ground, she saw some of her soldiers breaking rank, rushing to her with concern. The lightning had been close enough to burn her face.

As the ringing faded, it was replaced by pain in her ears. She stood up. Then she had to quiet Antilus. Her unicorn rose on her hind legs, kicking up and down, terrified. Then came another burst of lightning. This one, mercifully, a bit further away.

All she heard was ringing in her ears. Many of her sisters who had broken rank stopped rushing forward as Harmonia stood up. Then she heard the triumphant shouts of men from behind. The gods had fired lightning bolts.

Harmonia kneeled near Antilus's head and ran her hand over her hide. She kissed her unicorn. "It's all right, girl. It's all right." But Antilus's whole body shook.

Harmonia bowed her head. Quietly, she said only to herself, "Aidoneus, my love, alas, I am alone. My very life lies in your hands."

Harmonia ran her fingers along Antilus's soft wing. Then she hit the unicorn's behind hard in a signal for her to fly off. For a moment, the unicorn disobeyed. Harmonia swiftly hit the unicorn again with her palm. Antilus took to the air.

Then Harmonia drew her bloody sword from her scabbard. It took all her might to stop a terrible tremor in her wrist as yet another bolt of lightning struck beside her.

Harmonia looked up at the dark clouds. Then back down at her army.

The fog had cleared on the fields, and she could now

clearly see rows upon rows of her sisters in position, in perfect harmony, waiting for her orders. She raised her bloody sword again and cried as loudly as she could.

"I fight you! By the power of Erobos, from my beloved Lord Hades, I fight you! Take my breath if you dare. Cowards! I swear that as long as I breathe, I shall take my vengeance on all of Olympus!" There was another crack of lightning. One bolt came close to her again, nearly throwing her. But she used all her will to remain standing. Then she pointed her sword to the castle. *"Amazons, fight! Sisters, fight! Fight for freedom from these so-called gods! Charge with your queen now!"*

The multitude cried out the words *"Harmonia! Harmonia!"* and the thunder and lightning was exchanged for the thunder of their feet as they began their march forward.

But then...

It was not the rush of the Amazons that began the battle. It was the rush of the enemy. Hundreds of men wielding axes and primitive curved blades, wearing thick animal hides, rushed haphazardly from the castle walls charging them. Many of the warriors of Dracus were giant men, nearly twice the size of the nymphs. Yet, like their queen, where the nymphs failed in sheer strength, her army exceled in dexterity. And the nymphs had prepared for this fight for two decades.

As the men charged and hurled women through the air, slicing through them with their axes, many more nymphs counterattacked, spinning around and striking their swords through their enemies' stomachs, chests, and necks. And not one Amazon broke their place in line, even if they were stabbed, shot by spears, or even maimed. Upon the order of their sovereign, only upon death would they leave their posts. Only with the fall of their bodies would the enemies stop their advance. With shields in front of, atop, and beside them, despite the chaotic force and bedlam, they marched with spears forward. And many spears pierced the enemy in the mad rush. With Harmonia in the front line, fighting with them, they advanced to the fortress gates. As Harmonia hacked, she watched so many of her sisters get struck down. With the clang of swords, it was just a quick strike or blow to the head that slayed a nymph or an enemy soldier. She even saw some of her Imada fall from their unicorns in the sky. Blood stained the green grass. And any trace of fog was replaced by smoke. Then came the smell of war: metal, sweat, and excrement. The stench of death.

When her forces were close enough to touch the wall, arrows rained from above. Then terrible fireballs of oil splashed down. Her Amazons raised their shields over their heads to try to avoid the flames, but the fiery oil struck and burned many of her nymphs alive. Even then, the nymphs did not halt their march.

Charging through the metal gates, they entered the city. Then they brought destruction of their own, throwing fire from above on tents and cottages and burning everything in their wake. Citizenry ran, but many were smoked out and cut down. Others were taken prisoner. As twilight came, the entire city was blanketed in thick black smoke.

Jaida swooped down and met Harmonia near the main square. She watched her Imada fight on the streets, sword to sword, back to back, while enemy snipers struck with arrows or javelins.

Harmonia and Jaida trotted together on a long dirt road to the main tent structure in the middle of the square: the Great Hall of Dracus. This was a huge tent over a stone foundation, similar to Karthra's hall, which served as the king's palace. Jaida's face was bloodied and she was covered with sweat. And every part of her body, especially her back, pained her terribly.

Harmonia dismounted close to the entrance. In the distance, Imada were sword fighting the last remnants of the guards.

Jaida shouted excitedly amid the cries of pain and clashes

of metal, "Remaining armies in the fields are rushing back here to defend, Harmonia! What's left of them. They've completely given up fighting and are rushing to defend their king! But we've cornered them."

"Welcome them!" Harmonia replied. "We shall form a noose around this hall. And I shall have Akti by nightfall."

"We already have it, my queen!" Jaida yelled with a broader smile. "Rose said many have fled the city. And there's even greater news. Imada has received a message that most of the villages in the Moon Desert, all the way to the border near Sutsik, have bowed to the Amazons! Word is King Aram has fled his Court! Many of our enemies in the South are surrendering too, and—"

Harmonia hugged Jaida in joy. Then she signaled to her cavalry above. She whistled for Antilus.

"Follow me, General! Let us enter the hall and end this together. Let it be you, the queen's favorite, who enters first! What an honor!"

Harmonia kicked the wooden door open. Inside was a great amphitheater, just like the one she had once seen as the "crystal witch" in Logenth. And similarly, toward the center was a great wooden stage. When she had first come to Logenth so many years ago, the amphitheater was filled with people drinking and dancing as if in jubilee. Not tonight. Tonight it was dark and full of shadows as all but a couple of torches had been snuffed out. But it was crowded. It was full of townspeople who had come to hide as a final refuge. And at the sight of the Amazon queen entering the tent, many stampeded to exits across the hall, women and children clutching each other and climbing over one another desperately trying to fit through the narrow passageways.

"*Take them!*" shouted Harmonia. "*Don't let any get away!*"

"The king has fled," Jaida cried. Then as Jaida turned and saw Harmonia's stern face, she nodded and ordered the other guards, "Gather them up! Don't let one escape."

Harmonia grabbed Jaida by the arm. "Go back out and find King Dracus! Don't let that bastard flee from my grasp. You hear me? I want him. Do you hear? I want his head. Or bring him and I shall run my sword through him. Only with blood can we end all resistance in the North."

SIMPLE FARMERS

HARMONIA KICKED IN THE FRONT DOOR OF A SMALL COTTAGE. The house was dimly lit by a candle on a single wooden table. At the other side of the small home was a hearth and three mats on the dirty floor. It smelled of cooked mutton and spices. Standing by the hearth was a woman in tattered clothing, clutching a shirtless little girl and boy. Three Imada guards wearing scarlet, bloody and filthy, followed closely behind Harmonia. A shadow crossed her path. Then a man lunged at her with a knife. She parried and threw him to the ground. Whoever this was, he did not know how to fight. With ease, she flicked his dagger from his wrist and pulled out her sword, aiming it at his throat.

"No!" cried the woman, accompanied by screams from the children. "Please! Don't kill him! Please!"

Harmonia's three guards quickly grabbed the man and threw him against the wall. The whole flimsy cottage shook from the impact.

"Where's your king?" Harmonia asked, turning to the woman. "Hmm? I've searched every home in the village but this one. I'm running out of time and patience. And I'm running out of hovels to search for the coward."

"King Dracus is no coward," said the man.

"Quiet, Peter!" cried the woman. "No! Don't say a word!"

Harmonia whirled around and glared at the man. He was a young farmer with a thin blond beard, shaggy hair, and a stained tunic. His children were probably seven or eight years old. He looked young too.

"Does your husband know the king?" asked Harmonia.

"I'm just a farmer—"

"*Silence, Queen Harmonia does not speak to men!*" cried a guard. And she struck the man hard in the face with her staff.

Harmonia walked over to the woman and her children. Then she slowly removed her gloves and said softly, "Tell me what you know. Then the queen of Azurea leaves." Then she wagged a finger. "But be careful. If I discover a falsehood, I will kill him."

"My husband and I are simple farmers, Your Majesty. That is all. I cook and care for the children. We have nothing. We have never been in the Court. You must believe me. We seek peace. Truly, we don't know where our king is."

"I seek peace too. The queen of Azurea dreams that one day this continent shall live in tranquil harmony. Now tell me your name?"

The little girl started wailing. Harmonia hissed at the little girl, only making her cries worse.

"*Shut her up!*" cried Harmonia, staring down at the little girl. "*Shut her mouth! Do you have no control of your children?*"

The little girl froze under her glare.

"What do you want from us?" said Peter warily. "We don't know where our king is. And she is only—"

"No, Peter!"

The guard struck him with her staff in the stomach and then again in the face. Then another guard cut his arm with a knife. He fell to the ground crying out in pain. The third guard lifted him and slammed him against the flimsy wall, shaking the house once more.

"This is my final warning," Harmonia said, raising a finger. "One more word from the male's mouth and my guards cut his throat. As Imada has said, the queen does not speak to men." She turned back to the woman. "Tell me your name?"

"Sophia."

"Tell me, Sophia, where would someone hide in these parts? If you do not know the king's whereabouts, perhaps you can tell me where you think he would run. Where do ruffians and criminals run in your lands?"

"Shadow Forest. If anyone wants to hide, Your Majesty, they'd go there. It is dangerous because of this. Full of ruffians and robbers. And it holds great magic. Many villains are hunted in the woods. Not only by people, but by the shadows themselves. The trees cover everything, but legend says the trees can swallow travelers. If our king is hiding, he'd be there, Your Majesty."

Swallow travelers? Such ridiculous superstition. She had heard so many false beliefs from these simple villagers. Harmonia had traveled throughout Shadow Forest many, many years ago. She got lost, but there was no magic trying to eat her. But, indeed, it "swallowed" people by shadowing them in darkness all year around and creating a difficult passage. If the king wanted to hide, indeed he'd be there.

Harmonia walked to the door. "Very well, madam. Imada, take Sophia's husband along with the boy to the prison tent—"

"But you said you'd leave my husband and son be," Sophia said.

"Who made such a promise? I never said that."

"The Amazon princess promised."

Harmonia spun around and turned to her guards. "Was the princess already here?"

"Yes, my lord. Princess Nephratee has also been searching the village looking for the king, upon your orders."

"And our princess offered to leave the males free?" Harmonia fought a smile forming on her face.

"She promised," Sophia insisted, nodding her head. "She said you would."

"But I am not the princess." Harmonia patted her gloves against her hand. Then she put them on, shook her head, and turned to her guards. "Take the man and boy. My edict is servitude or death for all men who align against Azurea. This is our known law. There are no exceptions, even in this worthless village."

"*Oh, please, Queen Harmonia!*" cried Sophia. "*Please! Let my husband and boy be. Please. I beg you!*"

"*Beg!*" Harmonia shouted. "*Beg! You beg? Never beg like a dog! Stand tall like an Amazon!* I give you mercy, woman. I didn't say they will be put to death. They shall be spared. But…if you prefer to act as a deisa, the Amazon queen can change her order for this cottage."

"No, please!" Sophia said with wild eyes, panting and nearly falling at her children's feet. "Forgive me."

Harmonia raised her hand, ready to strike her in the face for her show of weakness, but then a bolt of pain ran along her spine, stopping her. She straightened, closing her eyes, and took a deep breath. Two of the guards approached her, but she raised her hand.

"Stand tall," Harmonia said to Sophia. She lifted the lady's chin with a finger. "Calm yourself. You are the lady of this household. Stand with pride." Then she turned back to a guard, walking out the door. "Take the men to the prison tent, Rose. I tell you, my daughter's infernal kindness shall be the death of me."

2 6

ENTU HEERD NERRI LAWIT

"Why'd you wish to speak with me, daughter?"

Harmonia heard the clap of sandals behind her as Nephrea stepped over puddles and mud along the shore of Crystal Lake. They both wore their scarlet armor, but they had removed their helms allowing their matching black hair to flow over their shoulders.

It was a lovely day in the world of man. The sky was azure, very much like the woods and grasslands back home. And the sun shone a golden yellow, warming Harmonia's face and reflecting off the calm water. Birds chirped and squirrels scurried up trees. After being in man's kingdoms for many moons now, her step had become light and she was accustomed to the weight of air outside Azure Blue. It was tranquil here. Except, if she listened carefully enough, she could hear the clatter of her army outside the surrounding tents where her forces had laid camp. The fight for Crystal Lake had been an easy one. Nearly all of Karthra's soldiers had retreated south to bolster their forces, along the castle walls, in defense of Logenth. But the battle they faced now would be difficult.

Harmonia cocked her head back after her daughter did not respond. For a flash, Harmonia squeezed her fist.

Nephrea's features resembled her father's. And once that turd of a man had walked with her just like this around this very lake.

"Why won't you allow me to fight in the front, Mother?" Nephrea finally replied, speaking Atalan with a thick Egyptian accent.

Harmonia laughed. She shook her head. It was the last thing she had expected.

"Nephree, when I walked around this lake long, long ago, I walked alone. You know this. For, as you know, I had been exiled." She slowed her pace so that her daughter could come by her side. "And then, unlike now, I resented my station. You can't imagine my misery. I spent so long feeling sorry for what I had done by the Stratos. I was not a whole lot better than—" She pointed to a squirrel climbing a tree. "That creature. And every day, I missed our sisters so much that I lamented my past. Such was my sentence. For so many years, I grieved my banishment. I told you what the gods did to me after we fought the Mandrigel on that fateful day? Demeter's true sentence?"

"It's horrible."

"I was blindfolded and gagged, and they watched those that ran to me, those that greeted me, those who loved me, and then they slaughtered them all. Your family. Terrible? No. It is beyond words. I had to live with their cries for years, for not only did they exile me, the gods destroyed everyone I loved. I still hear their cries."

"I know, Mother."

"Do you?" Harmonia shook her head and turned. She ran a dark gloved hand along her daughter's hair. "If you knew, you wouldn't ask your question. I was left with nothing. Until I met your father. Then I was betrayed again." She faced the lake. Leaves of the tall trees let in rays of golden light splashing along the shore. This was her greatest treasure on the continent—next to her Nephratee. "I won't let that ever happen to you. I would rather be sent to the ferryman." She touched her daughter's scarlet-clad shoulder armor. "You are like those that have left me. No, greater. You are a greater jewel than this very lake." She gestured at the water. "You're my Nephratee. My beauty. My Nefer. I will never lose you. I would rather die. Do you understand?"

Nephrea quickly shook her head. "You trained me to fight. I watch my sisters, my friends, those *I love*, get cut down. And I can do nothing to help them. You know I'm skilled with the sword. But you order me to stay back with every advance."

"I've allowed you to hunt men. You helped find Dracus."

"That isn't enough. As we gather in Logencia, I'm guessing you'll want me to stay back again? If I'm so dear to you, why won't you allow me to join the front? How can you not allow me to avenge what Azerius did to my father?"

"I just told you why," Harmonia said sternly.

"Oh mother!" Nephrea cried, shaking her head and turning her back on her.

"You won't fight in the front," Harmonia said, raising a finger. "You shall protect my rear. As we get closer to Caravia, the war will get harder. I need your protection. In my back."

"You need me as a trophy—"

"*Do not disrespect me!*"

Nephrea stopped walking. She turned to the lake, folding her arms, seeming to do everything she could to not meet her mother's gaze.

"You wish to fight?" Harmonia asked. "Is that it? Is that why you summoned me? Very well. Let us discuss things as queen and princess. You shall lead our sisters in battle, whether it be by air or on the ground, in battle, *in the back*. And if you continue to complain, you might find yourself not joining the battle at all."

Nephrea shook her head.

"*In my back, I tell you!*"

And then, as if the god Algea heard her on Olympus, a

sting of pain shot along Harmonia's back. It was enough to stop her from a further tirade. Nephrea turned and looked at her. Harmonia used all her will to hide the sting. Nephrea scowled.

Fight me? Ah, alas, but I adore your obstinance.

"If it's fighting you wish, captain," Harmonia said more quietly, "tell me now why you countermanded the queen's orders to imprison and execute men after our offensive in Azerbanith? I learned that hundreds of men were freed as I moved on to battle along their shore. Why? Do we not fight man? Was it not a man that killed your father? You know my edict of war."

"Those men were fathers of children."

What?

Harmonia furrowed her brow, trying to comprehend those words. It seemed like such a strange thing to say. But this was a part of her daughter too. Harmonia adored and respected her, but there was such a strangeness to her. Nephrea remained resolute.

"Revoke my edict again and I shall punish you. Princess or not. Daughter or not. You've been countering my orders ever since we first landed on man's shores. It seems that in every campaign I hear of Nephratee's maddening kindness. These enemies, may I remind you, destroyed your childhood. Why did you do that in Azerbanith? What is today's excuse for your infernal mercy?"

Nephrea, in predictable fashion, met Harmonia's gaze rebelliously—the only nymph to ever dare do it. Then she squinted, shook her head violently, and snapped, "*Entu heerd nerri lawit.*" This meant in Egyptian, "No child should be without a father."

Harmonia raised a black gloved finger, ready to scold her again. But then…she closed her fist. Instead, she resumed walking along the shore. And once more, she heard the sound of Nephrea's shoes clopping behind her.

"Speak Egyptian to me, Egyptian? You're something else, Nefertiti. You care of fathers, huh? Need I remind you that your father—"

"No, you do not need to remind me of a thing, Mother!"

Harmonia heaved a heavy sigh. "Oh, stop. Stop. Please. Forget it. Must we fight?"

And they fell silent. Harmonia squinted out at the lake once more. It was so bright from the reflecting sun. A bird flew across it, skirting by the water close enough to cause ripples. The ripples distorted the shadows of the surrounding trees.

"But this hints at something I've been meaning to request from you," Harmonia said. "Speaking of fathers, I need you to go to Egypt. Busiri. Hustaph must be quite old now, but the sight of you, now grown, will enchant him. You will enchant all Egyptians, I suspect. And because of the love Jaida told me your father has for you, your visit will fill Hustaph with joy."

Indeed, the news brightened Nephrea's face.

"Return to Egypt with Imada. Ask for an audience, as the princess of Azure, with Pharaoh Amenhotep III. And then show them your..." She stopped and gazed at her daughter from head to toe. "*Nafret*. Beauty, from the most lovely young maiden their foreign eyes shall ever behold. Show their royal family you and your entourage and then, with tact and wisdom, discern their loyalty. Do this in your native tongue, just as you just did with me. We are in desperate need of defense, child. A fight with Caravia *and* Egypt could ruin us."

"But what about Canaan in the East, Mother? The elders believe Sutsik to be the weakest point, and we should plan for a defensive, or even an offensive, stance there. While Caravia is still strong, why not send me to their cities in Canaan instead of Waset?"

"The lands in the East are as disorderly as the Hinterlands bordering them. I've sent letters by envoy ever since our first meeting with the foreigners at the dawn of war. The

Canaanite rulers can be bribed. They are not led by the pharaoh, but they obey the pharaoh. If anything, Assyria and Babylon will one day need to be tamed. But for now, if we sue for peace with the pharaoh in Waset, Canaan will follow."

Nephrea nodded.

"But as usual, you are sharp. More cunning than any other Amazon."

"I wish you'd share your plans with me. That's the other thing I wish you'd do."

"When you are queen, you'll learn that no one should know what's on your mind. Not even Lord Aidoneus. Not even me."

"I will never be queen."

"Why is that?" Harmonia asked with a chuckle.

"Because you will never die. If…you allow me to protect you, fighting by your side."

"Oh, Nephrea," Harmonia said with a laugh. "Truly, I say of all Amazons, you're my greatest treasure. I am so proud of you. There is no greater warrior with no greater heart." Then she surprised Nephrea by scooping her in her arms and embracing her tightly. Nephrea stiffened in surprise but did not move away.

"If I agree to travel to Egypt," Nephrea said, gently backing away, "will you wait for my return before the next offensive?"

"Why wouldn't you agree to see Hustaph?" Harmonia asked with a laugh. "But if the princess of Azurea wishes her queen to wait, the queen shall wait for her return."

"I must fight by your side. You must promise me."

"I grant your request for an armistice," Harmonia said with a nod. "To prove it, take Antilus for the journey to Aneb-Hetch. I promise there'll be no fighting until your return."

Nephrea walked past her mother exchanging position in front. That disturbed Harmonia, for it reminded her of a young crystal witch who once did the same to a Caravian general.

"Are we at peace, daughter? Making you happy has always given me peace. It's my only wish."

"No. I still wish to lead the front." But Nephrea smiled. "But, yes, I'll go to Papa and garner support with the pharaoh. Tell me why you like this lake so much? Why did you choose to live here all those years, Mother?"

Harmonia gazed at the water again. It was like a giant mirror reflecting all the trees and stones bordering the shores. Rays of yellow light filtered through the green trees. Then a mild breeze touched her cheek.

Her eyes fell on her daughter. Nephrea was truly *nefer*, the most beautiful of all the nymphs, even prettier than her. Her features were less blue, more like a human's, but with penetrating eyes—cunning, intelligent, like her own. And yet, unlike herself, there was such an innocent kindness. She ran a hand through Nephree's hair and said, "The lake is peaceful."

REMPTJU NI KEMET

Nephrea had to stop herself from leaping from Antilus in midair over the Nile, but she tempered her excitement and descended cautiously. She had to be careful. No one had ever seen flying unicorns in Egypt. Not to mention she had left her guard to descend alone. Busiri was not far from the Egyptian pyramids—great structures she had once considered unmatched, until she saw Ambitus Pyramid in Azure. Her father lived in the outskirts of town, among scattered orchards and fields, close to the river Nile.

As she neared the ground close to her papa's cottage, she smelled something wonderful: baked bread. It would be baked the Egyptian way, unleavened with even pieces of stone. She longed for the taste of it, the sharp spices.

A young girl ran, in a plain close-fitting kalisiris, through fields of wheat. When the girl gazed up, she ran faster, darting in the opposite direction. Not only was Nephrea riding a flying horse, but she wore her red battle armor.

Nephrea landed. Antilus neighed, tossing her head. Nephrea dismounted and kissed the unicorn's head. "Rise up and wait for me in the clouds. Okay, girl? I won't be long."

Antilus shook her head.

"But you have to," Nephrea said with a laugh. "You can stand guard for your princess above. I must visit Papa alone."

Hesitantly, the unicorn trotted forward, nodded a few more times, and took off in a gallop, gliding into the air.

Nephrea walked down a dirt path until she found her simple one-room cottage beside a stream. If she followed the stream another quarter of a league, she'd be beside the great river Nile. But as she came closer to her house, she wondered if her papa would even be there. She heaved a sigh. But then her nose caught another whiff of that delicious freshly baked bread.

She rapped on the wooden door.

"Omari?" asked a voice inside. Nephrea's heart raced. It was her father! "Oh, why has it taken you so long? I told you, you need to be close by. The sun's setting."

The door opened. A man she nearly didn't recognize stood before her. His skin was darker and more wrinkled than she remembered. He stood leaning on a cane, squinting up at her through sunken eyes.

"Nefertiti?" he muttered quietly. "Nefer—"

She grabbed him in her arms. Then her tears fell. "Oh, Papa! I've missed you so much!"

"Oh, Nefer, my Nefer." He patted her back. "My Nephree has come back home to me."

"Yes, Papa," she said with a nod. "Yes, I'm home."

He took her hand and excitedly led her inside their cottage. She noticed he hobbled. In fact, her father was missing a leg, replaced by a wooden stump. The stump was probably of the same wood as his cane. If he'd had hair, judging from all those wrinkles, she was sure it would be white now. His eyebrows were white. Actually, there was a very thin layer of white fuzz on the back of his head.

It was dark inside. Only one hole in the front served as a window. It was shaded by yellow linen.

Her father moved to the hearth, quickly gesturing for her

to sit on a large brown fur rug beside him. There they sat beside each other, leaning on their sides by the fire. So many years had passed, but in the darkness of firelight, it seemed she might have never left. She had sat so often with him like this by the fire.

"You're grown tall and strong now, Nefer. More beautiful than ever. You've grown into a woman."

Nephrea nodded. But then she lost her smile. "What happened to your leg, Papa?"

"Oh, it's nothing. It became red and useless, lame in the fields. I have Omari and Meripatu to help. And your uncle comes on occasion."

"Uncle is well?"

"Yes. Yes. He's fine. He'll be so happy to see you again."

Nephrea looked down and shook her head. "Sorry, Papa, but I doubt there'll be time."

"Never mind, Nefertiti. Never mind. Tell me everything. Are you well? Are you treated well in Azurea? Of course you are, you are a princess. But I've heard tidings of war. Many men fear your mother even this far south. I've worried only about you." He smiled a toothless grin with a hint of pride. "Otherwise, I don't care much for politics, and I only hope that the war will be soon over. But the people speak of your lady soldiers. And flying horses. Many of my neighbors and friends fear the Amazon… And, I must say…" He flashed the jolly grin she so loved. "You look menacing, daughter." But his smile left him for a moment. "But the last time I saw that red armor was when you were taken from me."

"All Amazon nymphs are soldiers now."

"And you fight? You fight…" He squinted. "*Men?*"

"Yes. We fight all who threaten Azurea." Nephrea gazed at the hearth. The smell of baked bread and soup was overwhelming inside the house.

"Care for some?"

"Oh yes, Daddy, I would."

He laughed joyously. "A soldier, but still my daughter."

He walked over to a metal pot on the floor and tore off some bread for her. And he gave her a dip she had loved ever since she was a child. Then he handed her a cup of yellow fluid that smelled pungently sweet. Mead. But before she could chew on what she longed for, her father snatched her hand. "Blue. I so love your skin. I was given the gift of a blue baby. The same baby that now sits before me, grown. A beautiful woman. So beautiful and fitting for your name, Nefertiti. And not only a woman, a princess. My Nefer. Tell me why you've come to visit me?"

"We wish support from the pharaoh," Nephrea said with her mouth full of bread. It tasted so fresh and wonderful. "After here, I go to Waset to seek an audience with your king."

"When?"

"Tomorrow."

Her father looked down, forlorn. He nodded contemplatively. "So little time, indeed." But then he raised his head and forced a smile. "It is good that you go to the pharaoh. Amenhotep III is very wise. So is his son. I believe he'll help you. You are an Egyptian, Nephrea. You are of Iteru. Just as, I see, you still darken your eyes."

"Yes. Even Mother does. We are the only nymphs that wear color over our eyes."

He nodded and fell silent. Nephrea enjoyed the food and drink from her past. The fresh bread and sweet mead. And she simply loved his company.

"Your mother lived close to here for many years," he said, breaking the silence, with a nod. "I remember."

"In ceremony, she wears bluer paint," Nephrea said, shaking her head. "She teaches our people that we should be proud of our blue color."

"Humph," her father said. But he smiled. "And all those

years I tried to hide your skin, Nephree. Does she still dress in the Egyptian fashion?"

"Caravian," Nephrea said, shaking her head. "Just the eyes." Nephrea felt her eyes narrow. "But that is why we fight, Papa. Mother told me that a Caravian general killed my father when I was a little girl. She and I have sworn vengeance on General Azerius. Why did you never tell me about Azerius and my father?"

"I didn't know of him," he said, shaking his head. "I wasn't told what happened before you came to me. I only knew that your mother was the nymph queen. But I never met her. Lord Orcus came to me and gave you to me when you were a baby. Orcus, or Hades, the god of Duat.

"Your meeting with the pharaoh should go well. Don't worry. Tell the pharaoh you are remptju. Tell him you were raised by Hustaph of Busiri. I live a simple life, but I have a good reputation, even in Waset. If he believes that you are one with Iteru, remptju ni Kemet, then he will consider you *his* daughter. And our people can be your friends. Your enemy is Caravia. So it is with the pharaoh."

Nephrea nodded. "I hope you're right. All I desire is peace." And she tore more of the delicious bread with her teeth.

Hustaph laughed. "Always so serious. You can be so happy but turn so serious so fast, even when you were little. Because you are so smart. Tell me, is there a man for my Nefertiti? Or, even better, am I a grandfather now?"

"Papa!" Nephrea said with a laugh and brushed his arm. "No." And she drank the sweet mead from the cup.

"Your mother has canceled the games repeatedly. It's a shame. You Amazons have such strange ways of meeting men."

"To us, your arrangements with women are just as odd."

"Yes, but between battles, whatever way you wish to do it, you must find yourself a man eventually." He pointed a finger at her and winked. "So that old Hustaph may have a grandchild."

Nephrea laughed heartily and raised her cup in a toast to that.

"Papa, tell me," Nephrea said, sipping more mead, "why didn't you move? Mother gave you gold. I can provide you so much. Why aren't you living like a king? You could be rich in Waset for caring for me. You deserve it."

"I don't care for gold. I have everything, Nephree. The fields. The birds. The will of Shu. In the distance, I see our river. I enjoy walking, even alone, along the water. Even with…" He slapped his false leg and Nephrea laughed. "My cursed leg. I'm happy. I have no need for gold.

"You know, when Hades gifted me a baby girl, he told me your mother had chosen me. Not only because of me, but because of this land. At first, I must admit the promise of riches enticed me. But as you grew, I cared only for you. That's why it was so wrenching when you left." He closed his eyes and shook his head. Then he took both her hands. "But now, with you here with me this moment, I have everything I could ever desire. I have no interest in buying things in the marketplace or living on some hill with servants. I only use money for help to till my fields. I wish to breathe this valley every morning as Ra rises. Come outside," he said, rising, "if you wish. Why not walk together and watch Ra set outdoors by the river? It is cool enough. Then in darkness, we can talk more indoors."

"I'd like that a lot, Papa."

And she walked with him slowly outside their cottage. He had to lean on his cane as they walked. The river was close and soon she gazed upon the water in wonder, watching the golden rays of sunlight reflect off the ripples, just as she had at Crystal Lake.

"I think, Nephree…you know, I think your mother loved this place too," he said, gazing at the water with her. "It is beautiful. That is why she chose Egypt for you. It is peaceful."

"*You* are peaceful, Papa."

"Hmm…" He put an arm around her. "No, I see peace only in you, Nefertiti. The tranquility of our blessed river Iteru. I so hope this war ends soon so that you may discover the peace I see inside you."

2 8

THE TERRACE

From a lovely fourth-story garden terrace, Nefertiti leaned on a stone ledge and gazed down at the torchlit vista of downtown Waset. She was alone but she knew her best friend, Jaida, stood guard outside the door. Nephrea wore a draping violet evening dress as she prepared for bed. Her hair was curled in preparation for her meeting with the pharaoh tomorrow. She had traveled so many leagues from home, but never in her travels had she seen such splendor. It almost matched the Crystal Palace back home. And she suspected the Egyptians had given her this view just to witness it. Stone buildings lined the streets below, and large vases covered in draping vines shone under large torches. There were strange symbols on the walls: men with bird or lion heads and ladies in headdresses. And below, even late at night, crowds walked and shopped in merchants' tents along zig-zagging streets and alleyways. Others danced with tambourines, flutes, and drums in courtyards. The view eased her mind a little over the proceedings tomorrow.

She turned and gazed at her three-room guest chamber. It had no less splendor. Ornate stone columns in the hall were torchlit, with grass and vines extending indoors. Upon the flickering stone walls were painted figures, like the ones outside, of men with orbs on their heads and women standing in fields. There was a marble bath with a trickling shower. The water was warm and flowed around vines down into an indoor waterfall. There were no windows. But unlike in the barbarians' dark homes in the Hinterlands, it didn't seem to matter in this warm climate. Huge linen curtains shielded the balcony from storms. It seemed everything was designed to make you feel as if you were outdoors. Still, unlike home, there were plenty of insects. Too many flies. She had forgotten about them. And in summer it would be unpleasantly hot. She remembered the humidity and terrible heat.

She heard laughter below. It was faint but it was wonderful. It was the sound of children. Even this late, children were running around having fun. Children's laughter was another thing she missed. With the banning of the games came the banning of nymph children. Her mother had not allowed relations with men for the past decade.

There was a knock.

The door slowly opened and in walked Jaida wearing her familiar scarlet armor. Behind her came a group of four men in long, draping robes. The large man in the middle was shirtless, and the other two wore leopard skins draped over their shoulders. Nephrea inferred that the shirtless one was their leader. Gold necklaces adorned a rippling, muscular chest. He had kohl around his eyes. But there was something strange about his face. His head seemed narrower than normal, and his neck was long.

"Pharaoh Nefertiti," he said with a smile. "I welcome you to Waset."

An older man with very thin gray hair rushed from behind, coughed, and said, "Presenting his eminence, Pharaoh Amenhotep IV, grandson of the great Thutmose the Fourth, His Majesty Amenhotep IV, pharaoh of Egypt."

"Pharaoh of Egypt?" Nephrea smiled. "But you're the

prince. I was expecting to be greeted by Amenhotep the *Third.*"

"And I was expecting to be greeted by Queen Harmonia of Azure Blue," replied Amenhotep. But he raised a hand, fearing that he had offended her. His voice was calm, almost soothing. So was his smile. "But I am hardly disappointed." He kneeled before her.

"Your Majesty!" cried one of the elders.

"May I take the hand of the Amazon princess?" he asked, gazing up into her eyes. "I only require it for one moment."

Nephrea furrowed her brow. But she nodded and gave the man her hand. She thought he had asked for it to examine it, for nymphs' hands were the bluest of all their features. He didn't. Instead, he kissed the back of it gently.

Nephrea giggled. "Are you always so suave, Pharaoh Amenhotep IV?"

"Only before beauty, Nefer." Then he stood up tall and looked back at his men. "Leave us."

"Your Majesty, I protest," said the elder. "Princess Nefertiti is an Amazon. She is trained in battle. I believe our presence—"

"Am I not a soldier trained in battle, Akiofey?"

"Well, yes, sire, but…"

"Do you object to the words of your pharaoh?"

"My Lord!" The elder and the other two men fell to the ground in a show of respect. It reminded her of her mother's power.

"Leave us alone," Amenhotep repeated with a smile.

A lovely smile. And such intelligent probing eyes. But he has a long, almost misshapen, face and neck.

"Jaida, you may stand outside the door," Nephrea said.

"Yes, princess." But Jaida seemed unsure too.

They shut the door behind them. But then her guest completely ignored her. He walked over to the terrace, leaned on the stone ledge, and stared out over his city. Then he gazed up at the clear, starry night.

"Let us finish the unpleasantness first," Amenhotep said with a sigh, still with his back to her. "Tell me your mother, the Amazon queen's, message. Tell me here in private, where no ear can listen. I'd like you to tell me before our meeting tomorrow morning. The real meeting…" He cocked his head back. "Begins now."

"Why?"

"I might be able to grant you what you ask. It'd be better if I try to convince the priests of Waset, not you."

"So this is a business meeting?"

He flashed a sly grin. Then he gazed down at her bare feet and up her thin dress to her face. He turned back to the view and shook his head. "No. But you'll find this conversation more comfortable than tomorrow's meeting. I can discuss your wishes with my father. Why are the Amazons requesting an audience with the pharaoh?"

"We're seeking a treaty," she said, walking to the terrace. "We've no interest in crossing the Strait of Aethiopia. Nor the eastern shore. You know our people aren't even permitted to sail by Poseidon's edict."

"But you can cross by air."

"We're stretched thin. Our unicorns' home is the tower stables in Azure Palace. They tire quickly and head back after only a few days, unless battle is imminent. And your lands are even farther. We have no interest in fighting you. You're too far away."

"For now," he said, nodding contemplatively.

She stood by his side. And she caught a glimpse of another grin. She liked this prince. This man. There was something about him. She felt safe around him. And she felt like he was kind. Perhaps he could help her?

"You said you were surprised when my father didn't greet you," he said more quietly. "That is because your mother insulted him by not coming personally. In my father's eyes, such an offense deserved a slight in return. So I'm here in his stead." He turned and looked into her eyes, then quickly gazed back down at the roads below. "Our people fear you. Your mother has not only proven a worthy match for any army as a woman soldier, something we have never seen, she's proven herself through brilliant tactics worthy of any general in Egypt. That's frightening. And now she sends her daughter. Why? Because she knew her daughter would please me."

Nephrea backed up and laughed. "I look about the same age as Mother now," she said. "We don't age like humans. If she had come, you would find her beautiful too, Amenhotep."

He furrowed his brow. Then he laughed heartily. "I wasn't referring to your beauty, though your looks are unmatched. I'm referring to who you are."

Then Nephrea felt stupid. Heat burned in her cheeks. She had just insinuated that he was complimenting her beauty.

Wasn't he? Well, he seemed to keep staring at her.

"I thought...well..."

Get a hold of yourself, idiot!

But I haven't even been alone with a man before.

"*Remptju ni Kemet,*" he said. "I meant, you are one with Iteru. Your language is perfect. You color your eyes, and you wear your makeup like our women. But that is nothing compared to your mannerisms, which are the same as our ladies. You might call yourself an Amazon, but I call you an Egyptian of the Nile."

"I am an Amazon nymph, sir."

"You're far more," he breathed.

He stared again into her eyes, seemingly hypnotizing her. He raised a hand to touch her hair. She let him. He ran it along her long curls and then ran a finger across her cheek. "You are of the Nile. You are Egyptian. That is why your mother sent you."

Nefertiti backed up again and giggled. "I allowed your

uninvited audience, Pharaoh, because I was curious. But now…I must protest. I will speak politics tomorrow with your priests, and I will plead my case. Why…why discuss these things now, alone in my chamber? Do you have other intentions? Whether I am Egyptian or pleasant to your eyes has nothing to do with my people's dire need for your trust. We offer a treaty."

"Again," he interjected, raising a hand, "you think I am here for you. I am Pharaoh Amenhotep IV. I came here to speak with you in private for the sake of my people." But she didn't believe him. In fact, he seemed smug. "Queen Harmonia should have come herself. Sending you was tactical. And tactics is precisely what my father fears about your queen. She is sharp, sharp like a knife."

"The queen sent me because we need help. Yes, she knew I could speak with you in your tongue. Was it wrong to send me for that reason?"

He tore his eyes from her and slowly shook his head. "No."

"My mother has never kept her planned conquests a secret. But we have no interest in the Nile."

"You have no interest in the Nile?" He ran a sweeping arm over their view from the terrace. "You have no interest in this? This is your home, Nefertiti. It is said your mother has traveled here before. I bet she loves it as much as you do. Do you believe that in your mother's thirst for land and blood she will not one day seek Kemet?"

"I can swear on my life that I will not fight you. If you swear to not aid our enemies. That is why I am here. I can give you that oath if you promise us peace."

Amenhotep's penetrating eyes met hers. Then he shook his head. "Indeed, if you could offer sacrifice for your life, Amazon, you could return to your mother and tell her that the treaty is a success. We would honor it and not step foot on the continent of Atala. If you swore on your life, I'd even swear on mine. And we could be friends. If we could trust that your mother would agree. But she'd never."

"My words are my mother's."

"Are they? You speak of peace? Your mother has turned your people into a warring race."

"We defend our shores."

"I have only just met you," Amenhotep said, turning away. "I've learned that you are intelligent. Honorable. But judging from your mother's actions, promising not to move further south or east across the sea will be very difficult, perhaps not for you, but for her. I think it is impossible."

"I can swear it."

He looked amused. Then he nodded slowly. "Make this petition to the priests of Amun tomorrow. They will say this and that, question you, but whatever is said, if you make this secret pact with me tonight, I shall fight for your request with my father for our people. Like your mother in your country, my father rules these lands, no matter what the priests believe. The pharaoh's word says all."

"You trust me?"

He nodded.

Then he leaned down to kiss her lips. She lurched back in surprise. His hand came close to her cheek again, running his fingers along her skin. That sent tingles down her spine. She caught his hand and threw it back.

"This has nothing to do with love!"

"Who said anything about love?" Amenhotep said with a laugh. "We just met."

Nephrea looked down. Then she shook her head. "I… I… I am ignorant in the ways of man. And you…you cannot, should not, act so, sir. You know our people are not permitted to be with men until peace shall reign and—"

He pressed his lips hard against hers. And for some reason —she wasn't even sure why—she let him. She fell into his grasp. Her right hand was still ready to slap his face, but she closed it. Then she embraced him. He entered her mouth with his tongue, holding her tight. Although she was now over twenty years old, this was her first kiss. He pressed her so close, and she desired this so much. But then she muttered, "I…I am…not…permitted…" She backed up. "To be with men. Except in the games. And the games have been canceled by royal decree. You seem to be taking advantage of me. I was right when I guessed your intentions. You…don't understand. Outside the games, we are hopeless and don't know how to deal with our feelings toward men."

"Then the pharaoh apologizes," he whispered, shaking his head and letting her go. "I'm sorry. But you are the one who doesn't understand, Nefertiti. Before your beauty, I am the one who is powerless. Please forgive *me*, a man who has never been in the presence of someone as beautiful as you."

Nephrea laughed. Then she leaned on a column and folded her arms. "I suspect you have been with many women, Amenhotep."

"Never as beautiful as you, Nefer. Never."

"So your attraction to me leads to this treaty?"

Amenhotep laughed and shook his head. "I already told you. You're Egyptian. Likely you're the only nymph in Gaia who speaks the language of the Nile. Right?"

"Except my mother."

Strangely, he left her then. He walked back into her guest chamber. Then he sat down on a long leather chair, the size of a bed. She considered remaining on the terrace. And, for some time, she did just that, enjoying the view. But she liked the fact that his eyes did not move from her. He just leaned on his side and waited. She walked a few steps inside.

He pointed at her, shaking his head. "Ever since I was a child, I was trained to judge people. It is for safety. My brother was meant to be pharaoh. So I was spared much royal nonsense. But my life as a prince has always been in peril. Many have wanted to poison me. Kill me. Now I judge you, princess. It is not your speech, it is your manner, Nefer. I trust you."

She laughed and turned back to the view. "Your father sent you to see me? To talk politics and then woo me?"

"No."

She discovered him behind her again and was surprised as he gently put an arm around her. She leaned her head back and found his lips. This time, she kissed him. He exuded so much strength and confidence. This was a great man with lovely eyes, intelligent and caring. She liked him. She liked him a lot.

"I saw you enter Waset," he said quietly, almost in a whisper. "I came here to meet you. Like you, I have no interest in talking politics. I wish only for peace. But it seems the world has other plans."

"I swear on my life we shall not invade," she repeated between kisses. "My word shall be held if you accept it."

"I will defend your proposal, Nefertiti, tomorrow. I will do what I can in your defense."

He ran a hand down her back, along her butt, and then up to her shoulder. Then he unfastened the brooch holding her violet dress. The dress fell to the floor. She was naked underneath. He ran his hand along her breast, and his fingers explored her form. She untied his belt. Then she removed his pants.

They were naked on the terrace. It seemed so indecent. But it seemed to draw them even closer. Perhaps some of the citizenry might catch them. So? That was even more alluring. Anyway, if his people saw them, that would be better. She had succeeded in making the Egyptians her friends, just as her mother had hoped. But perhaps not in the manner her mother had wished...

What am I doing? I just met him.

"Have you tricked me, Adonis?" she muttered.

"Adonis? The handsomest man in your mythology?" He

shook his head between kisses. "Behold, the most beautiful woman in the world has called the ugliest man handsome."

"I like you, Amenhotep," Nephrea breathed. Somehow she found herself naked in bed with this man, entwined in his arms.

"One night with you, Nefertiti, is a gift worth all the dreams in my life. You offer your life for Kemet? I think I shall offer you my entire kingdom."

29

HEM-NETJER

THE STONE-WALLED MEETING ROOM WAS SMALL, SQUARE shaped, dark, and musty. This far down below, it smelled earthen. The Egyptians had failed to cover the smell by burning incense, and the burning spices merely caused a thin cloud of smoke to fill the chamber. All the men reclined on one large carpet in a circle, wearing robes. Two of the ten had hair on their heads, but it was only a thin white fuzz. They all wore dark makeup around their eyes like Nephrea. And they all wore leopard skin draped over their shoulders. In the center of the candlelit room a man sat on the only chair. It was small and simple, covered in an animal hide. He wore only linen shorts and a headdress and leaned on a cane. But seeing him, and all the other priests in their robes, made Nephrea feel silly wearing battle armor. Had she already misstepped before the meeting began? This was not only a meeting seeking an alliance. It was a proceeding designed to calm the foreigners' fear of her mother's encroaching invasion. Why had she chosen battle armor?

Nephrea reclined on the floor like the priests. Amenhotep IV, the prince, was beside her. After a moment of silence, with not one elder speaking, they all turned to the man in the chair.

The old man smiled.

"Witness the bravery of the Amazons," he said in Atalan, waving an arm in her direction. "And the trust of their great Amazon queen to send me her greatest treasure in all the world. The lovely Amazon princess, Pharaoh Nefertiti."

Nephrea nodded her head.

"I am Pharaoh Amenhotep III. I hear…" He gestured to the prince, sitting beside her. "You met my son last night?" Well, she had done more than *meet* him. She caught Amenhotep smirking.

"I wished to make our guest feel at home, Father," the prince said. "She has indeed, if you have heard of her upbringing, returned home to our sacred river. She is fluent in our language."

"I never asked you to arrange such a meeting."

He didn't?

But then the pharaoh smiled and spoke in his native tongue. "Indeed, I have heard of you, Nefertiti. A blue nymph born in the northern lands of Caravia. Brought here as a babe to be raised near Sakkara by the farmer Hustaph Istari. Then returned home and trained, as all you Amazon women are, in the arts of war. And so you wear armor before us."

She had definitely chosen the wrong clothes. And to confirm her thoughts, a few of the priests looked at her armor in disgust.

"Unlike my son, whose eyes are dreamy, I've had to be grounded in Kemet to guard my father's lineage and the traditions of my people," continued the Pharaoh. "These traditions have existed in this valley for thousands of years, long before your island nation ever existed. We are of a race that was ruled by gods, ruled by demigods, and then united by Narmer. I am aware of my friends, my false friends, and my enemies. I smell fear in neighbors and aggression in nations. Before you address the blessed priesthood of Amun, I shall be as upfront with you as you are with the clothes you wear, in exchange for the trust and truth your queen provides me."

She opened her mouth, but he raised a finger.

"First, honor. The world moves through action. Though young, you've lived long enough to know this. I say again, I am honored and deeply touched that your mother sent you. We have watched the actions of your people, and it is said that you are the most valuable jewel in Queen Harmonia's possession. The fact that she offers you to me is a great honor."

Nephrea nodded. But she didn't say a word. She realized she hadn't said a word since entering the hall.

"Next, truth. Your clothes. Truly, the forwardness of Amazons impresses me. It is well known that your nation is a warrior nation, and I expect nothing less. It is also known that our two nations are at war—" He raised a hand to stop her as she almost jumped up in protest. "The war your mother has declared is not with Caravia. It is not with Kings Karthra and Tolen. It is with me. And my son." He gestured to the hall. "And with every man in this room. Because your people do not fight the continent of Atala, they war with man. That is truth."

Nephrea started to rise, but the prince gently touched her shoulder and quickly shook his head.

"That is truth, Nefertiti," the pharaoh said, shaking his head. "Bear witness to your clothes. I wish not to discuss *that* matter any further."

He coughed. It was almost violent and a man rose to aid him, but he quickly waved him away.

"Finally, Nefertiti Ambrosia, finally, let me speak of the woman before me. The one my son already favors." The old man smiled gently. "You are of Kemet. Although you are Amazon, Iteru flows in you just as it flows in every man in this chamber. Your mother knew this. That is why she dared send you to Waset. I swear to you now, if the Amazon queen had stepped foot on my shore herself, I would have met with her in the same dress in which you now greet me. She knew this. But although our people are at war, I do not war with Nefertiti. You will notice the hall we speak in now is not ornate, or even pleasant. This is a secret room that has been used only for private business for longer than anyone in our black sands region can remember. It has been here probably since before the white soil turned black. Any pact we make here, any struggle for peace, is in secret.

"My beauty, my Nefer. As you sit with us, I am studying you." He smiled again. "And I see a young woman, one with courage, strength, and hope. And even care in her eyes. One whose beauty entices all of us. One who has already beguiled my son. For you, Nefer, and only you, I shall allow you to speak in my temple walls. This is my payment for what your mother has done for me. For you must know that no other woman has ever been permitted to speak a word here. Remember this as you now use your tongue. And please honor us with your first words in our language. So that we may honor your past." He coughed again. Then he said, gazing intensely at her, "What message do your people send to the pharaoh of Egypt?"

This was it. This was what she had been waiting for since she left Crystal Lake. For a moment, Nephrea wondered if his son, the prince, would speak for her. She had already given him a personal vow. She had been led to believe that her case would be shared with the pharaoh even before the meeting began. Apparently not. He waited for her to speak.

"All that my people ask for," Nephrea said, "great pharaoh, is peace between our two nations. You mentioned my dress. Yes, I wear armor. Everyone in this room knows that my people are at war. But I don't agree that we are at war with you. Even if you believe that you are fighting us, it's my belief, and my mother's belief, that an agreement between us will benefit our people. Allow us to not fight one another. Allow us to find the water that sprouts forth and reaps our harvest."

The Egyptian expression of good faith. It was accepted by the pharaoh with a smile. But…not a genuine smile, a fake one. Her mother had sent that last sentence. It seemed to have been received as a slap.

Oh mother, you didn't tell me this would be so hard! You acted, as always, as if all our dangers are nothing. As if I were simply traveling to see my father.

Nephrea took a deep breath. From the corner of her eye, she saw the prince seemingly trying to reassure her.

"It is well known that my mother has her eyes set on Caravia," she continued. "There is more truth, great pharaoh. But the Caravians are not friends of yours. Queen Harmonia has sent me to see whose side you're on as we move further south. If she sees no sign of support, no soldiers or armament, she will stop our forces at Jedithian. You have her word. We shall end the war at the southern tip of the continent."

Another smile, this time from all the members of the hall.

"But if Egypt befriends the Caravians—"

"Our people will never side with—"

"Great pharaoh, you presumed I wouldn't interrupt you, but now you interrupt me?"

The pharaoh squinted his eyes in amazement. By her side, the prince stirred too. She had to remember that no woman had ever been permitted to speak before their king. There was silence and many priests seemed open eyed and wide mouthed. The pharaoh nodded.

"If Egypt sends men, or even supplies, in support of our enemies," Nephrea said, "you will, indeed, find that your people are at war with us. I have no power to sway my mother's hand over this. Be aware that the consequence of any such offensive is not a mere suggestion, but fact. We will fight you if you aid our enemies. The moment we see even a single spear, my mother will invade the Nile. These words I deliver directly from my queen."

Many of the priests scoffed. Some spoke quietly to one

another. But all grew quiet as the pharaoh raised his hand once more for Nephrea to continue.

"Now I shall tell you," Nephrea said, addressing the priests, "my other message from her. We are poised to strike at the city of Logenth. Amazons have taken Shadow Forest, laid flags upon our great desert, taken the coastal towns along Azerbanith, and captured villages over the fields surrounding our legendary Crystal Lake. All these lands, except Sutsik in the Northeast, have fallen. That is the state of affairs in the North. You all undoubtedly know this, but it is the timing that is important. Because after Logencia is taken, we will move on to your closest neighbor. Because once King Karthra is defeated, all the mid-nations will fall. That leaves the South and the kingdom of Caravia." She paused for a moment. Then she felt nervous again. She had not only the pharaoh's attention now. Everyone in the room was listening. "We have not struck Caravia, and we have not directly struck Sutsik because of the foreign presence within those lands. Although it is being done in secret, it is well known that Assyrians and Mitannites are ruling the regions in the Northeast. They came there shortly after Harmonia took power, presumably as a buffer from the Asian continent. But their secrecy ended a few moons ago when my sisters watched, with bitter hatred, their flags hoisted upon fortresses on the eastern shore. I've lost many women cut down by their swords, spears, and arrows. This foreign presence is intolerable. So as you consider us at war with you, we consider ourselves at war with the East. My mother will fight them. But we have not seen your flags, and we mustn't ever. And so…" She looked down and took a deep breath. "Queen Harmonia does not want war with Egypt." Nephrea rose and kneeled before him. "Lord Pharaoh…" She looked into his eyes. "This is truth from me, an Egyptian. Queen Harmonia asks that you simply swear no interference with us. If we fight all the way to Jedithian and do not see any trace of Egyptian forces, we will not move on into the sacred river."

"For how long?" snapped one of the priests. Nephrea slowly rose. The prince gestured for her to sit back down near him. He slowly nodded to Nephrea.

"I don't believe her," another elder said. "Or, rather, great Pharaoh, I don't believe her mother. As you said, their war is with man. It doesn't matter whether we live across the sea. The queen desires world conquest. She flew over her strait, and she shall fly over ours. She will attack."

Many nodded.

"She comes wearing armor!" thundered another, slapping his leg.

Prince Amenhotep rose. Everyone quieted. Then the prince bowed before his father. "I ask to speak."

His father nodded.

"I met the princess last night," he said with a smile.

"Yes, son, why'd you do that?" he asked, squinting his eyes. A few priests laughed. That finally seemed to lighten the mood.

"It's as you said, Father. I was bewitched by her beauty. But when she came to me, we spoke of politics. And she offered an exchange. If she'd permit me—" Nephrea nodded. "I will share it with you and the elders. I think it proves her word."

The pharaoh nodded.

"If her army steps foot in our lands, she forfeits her life," Prince Amenhotep said. "She swears by it. No matter what her mother does. She has promised to give herself up. And you yourself, Father, said Nephrea is Queen Harmonia's most sacred jewel. This is a great offering, Pharaoh."

Many scoffed.

"Such an assurance is not enough to defend the people," said another priest.

"But such bravery and sacrifice are what bring peace," objected the prince.

"Sit," the pharaoh said. "I ask for silence in the chamber." Then he turned to Nephrea and chuckled. "You and she are young." Then he raised his hand and peered right into Nephrea's eyes. "I love my son as much as your mother loves you. And I suspect I respect my son as much as your mother respects you. But you are young. Don't take that as an insult, it is a gift." In fact, he shifted in his seat after those words, appearing to be in pain, and coughed. "I judge you, Nefertiti. I told you that my position forces me to judge all. And I... believe you. I believe you, Princess. I truly believe you would courageously sacrifice yourself in the name of peace. Just as my son would. Yes, I believe you two would. But—" He looked down, forlorn. "I'm afraid, dearest Nefertiti, I don't believe your mother. Everyone in this hall has heard of the atrocities she brings forth in the wake of her conquests. All the men who have been killed *after* battle. Imprisoned. Many tortured. Far more executed. Many simple farmers, like your dear father in Busiri, captured and taken away from their daughters and wives and killed, as if for sport. Even the little boys have been captured and enslaved. No. No, I'm sorry, Nefertiti. I judge you and I trust you. If you ruled your kingdom, I could change my mind and we could have peace. But I cannot swear a pact with a leader who aligns with Seth. By Harmonia's own words, she wages war against man and seeks destruction of all men. As Iatep claimed, any treaty with her will only be temporary, broken later when she's able to gather more forces and move further east or south."

"Yes," said another priest. "Yes!" stormed a few others.

"Her word is sincere, Father," objected Prince Amenhotep.

"I don't doubt her words, son. But I cannot give this agreement to you or her. This is too dangerous to our people."

Nephrea stood up. Apparently, this was another great

offense, and she heard one of the priests gasp. "You must reconsider. I tell you, as strong as my word is, my mother's will is stronger. She will fight. All we are asking is that you stay out of it. I tell you, she will——"

"The fight, Princess," the pharaoh said, "is impossible to avoid. And this is where your mother will fail. Your Amazons are a mighty, terrible force, as good as any army ever run by men, but only a couple of thousand highly trained fighters cannot fight the entire world. She fights everything, so she will surely lose."

And then… silence.

Now the smell of smoke and incense seemed to grate on Nephrea's nose. She looked down at Amenhotep and furrowed her brow. She felt betrayed. Why'd she trust him?

"I came here to plead my case," Nephrea said to all the priests with a nod. "If I return home without peace, there will only be more bloodshed. Many of the things you speak of that we have done after battle are rumors and falsehoods. Our nymph sisters are a good race. Give me something, anything, I can bring back to her. Something I can tell my mother in the interest of peace to——"

"I have been kind to you," said the pharaoh. But now he sounded angry. "I see you, Nefertiti, as a good person. I have been kind only to *you*. You are the only woman I know of who has spoken in this chamber. Thus I honor you. But you, Princess, are the opposite of your mother. And I share with you one more truth. I believe you err. You are not seeing things clearly. You came here in secret as our enemy, not as our friend. That is why I granted you passage into Waset only under the cover of night. You asked for friendship, but your mother asked under the threat of the sword. Your loyalty aligns with a witch, a cruel, horrible woman with a poisoned heart. No doubt, I understand family and how foolish love can be. I understand and value love for your family. But now you come and *warn me*?"

"Silence her!" cried a priest. "This is enough!"

The prince looked down and said nothing. And Nephrea suddenly felt angry with him.

"If you feel you are returning from your trip empty handed," said the pharaoh slowly, "offer your mother this: if she stops advancing, we shall discuss peace with our sisters. But if her madness does not end, tell her that we have lived here for thousands of years, and we shall be here thousands more. Tell her that the day will come when her crimes will be paid for. And warn her, as she warned me, that if she does not halt her advance in Caravia, the moment she steps foot on Caravian soil, she will be advancing on the Nile."

That was enough. Nephrea turned her back on the pharaoh. Then, with no further words, she walked out of the room. This was probably another break from their stupid tradition. And, in fact, with her exit a torrent of shouts echoed from the meeting room.

She found her way back into the great hall, where her guards had been waiting for her. It was a huge stone hall with vases the size of people lighting up the columned hall with fire.

Jaida quickly approached, excited for news.

"We leave now," Nephrea said.

"You did what you can," Jaida said with a slow nod.

"These people, Jaida," she said, and many of the Egyptian soldiers turned, "they are old and stupid. There is no reasoning with them."

"They are men, Nephree."

30

WEDJA IB-EK IY

Nephrea stood on her garden terrace one last time, looking over the lovely city below before gathering up her things and leaving. She felt confused. She adored the view, the bustling streets, the ancient columned structures—some with strange paintings of bird and lion people, like those in the temple. People rode carriages on dirt roads, as they did behind her palace walls, traveling here and there to merchants. Others sold meat or clothing under linen tents. And half of her, the most daring part, even considered grabbing a hooded cloak and walking alone in the streets. The prince was right. She loved this city. But there wasn't any time. She had rushed her nymphs away from the palace to prepare for their return to Azure. And now that she knew the pharaoh saw her as the enemy, she didn't feel safe. But this was her home. And she was leaving after only a handful of days.

She heaved a long sigh. She had failed.

Someone rapped on the door. Jaida shouted something in the midst of some sort of skirmish, but it was too muffled to hear. Her door swung open and Jaida barged in. "Prince Pharaoh Amenhotep IV requests your company, Princess,"

Jaida announced haughtily. "Shall I run a sword through him?"

Nephrea looked down. She hadn't even changed out of her armor. Far worse, the makeup on her face was running. It was shameful, and now, she wouldn't have time to reapply the kohl or take it off.

Amenhotep walked in wearing the same pants and headdress as he had worn in the meeting. But not with his usual smile. He seemed as sad as she felt.

"Leave us," Nephrea said to Jaida. Then she turned her back on him, leaning on a column. She heard the door close and footsteps slowly approach.

"I'm sorry, Nefertiti."

"My name is Nephrea."

"You're leaving?"

She spun around over the idiotic question. Then she gazed curiously at his ugly, narrow face. This was the first man she had fallen in love with. Why? She asked herself why she would love a man with such a face. He forced a grin. Then he stared at her face too. And he looked sadder than ever.

"Perhaps… a delay," he said, stiffening. "Maybe a delay in a peace treaty between us…but peace can still be made? Unfortunately, my father and your mother seem to have plans of their own."

"You lied to me," Nephrea said, turning back to the view. "You said your word is the pharaoh's word. I would have kept my end of the bargain. And then I came to that meeting expecting to speak with the priests as only a formality. I never could have dreamed that I'd have to plead my case even harder. And worse, all of them, including your father, had already made up their minds."

"Nephrea," he said, shaking his head, "there are many things my father does that I don't agree with. One is his insistence on speaking with those old crone priests. The Nile is mine, not theirs. Meeting in the temple *was* a formality. And I hate it. But my father, though I love him, is short-sighted. He doesn't believe in changing the world. Truly, I swear to you that if I ruled these lands, your agreement would have been honored. We would live in a world of peace."

But it didn't matter. It didn't make her feel any better.

"Now we are enemies, Amenhotep. My mother must declare war on my homeland. She sent me here to teach me that, and that was cruel. But your father is right about her. She is cruel. I had come with every wish to keep that cruelty from my people."

He snatched her elbow and turned her toward him. The suddenness surprised her.

"Then why, Nefer, can't you speak with her and tell her to stop this? If she loves you so much, why can't you stop her? You know the terrible things she's done. I've heard stories that you are the opposite. You're known for mercy. It is said people petition your name whenever they're captured. You might be the only one who can change her mind. You must try. It's madness and a waste of lives. Can't you convince her to not push forward into Caravia? That's all you need to do."

"*My father was killed in Caravia!*" she shouted, yanking back her arm. The front door opened, only a sliver, then slowly closed. And for a moment, in fury, she thought of slapping him. "That is why I was raised here. Mother had no home after the death of my father. No, this advance is not only my mother's wish—it's mine. The Caravians are my sworn enemies. We shall never have peace with them. That's why I gave up speaking with your father. His request is absolutely impossible. The entire war is based on our fight with Caravia. We will move on until we ride over the Cliffs of Zonoch and take the city. If your father believes that is a fight against Kemet, everything is lost, I tell you, for you, my people. Everything!"

"I'm sorry," he said, looking down. "I didn't know about

your father." Then he sighed and nodded slowly. "I didn't know. It seems…there is no way then."

"It's not your fault." And she touched his arm. He looked down at her hand and smiled. "I don't blame you, Amenhotep. I… I believe you. I'm just so frustrated. There's no way to fix this. This world is ruled by fools."

"Yes. But last night, the agreement between you and me was special. Forget your mother and my father. What of you and me?"

"Perhaps when fools don't rule the world."

He ran a finger along her cheek. He traced her skin near her eyes with his finger.

"You cry for us. For all of us. You cry for Kemet. I believe you cry for Amazons *and* Egyptians. So I believe our words last night will happen. It wasn't all a loss, Nefer. There is you and me. One day, you and I will bring peace. I'm sure of it. One day."

"But I'm afraid today we meet on the battlefield."

"Then I'll drop my sword and give you my regards," he said with a chuckle. "I will shout *iy, wedja ib-ek.*" She laughed. "Believe me: when I swore last night, I believed my father would honor my word. He always has before. The trouble is, he can't over this. Even if he could, the priests would not accept it. My people love you, Nefertiti. Believe me. Even the priests were impressed with you. They spoke afterward about your intelligence, wisdom, and beauty. But they loathe your mother."

They held hands in silence for a while, enjoying the view of the city under them. It was a strange mix of pleasure and pain, the pleasure made bitter by the knowledge that she was leaving. Down below, people were baking bread and meat, and she smelled the familiar garlic, pepper, and cinnamon spices of her childhood. In the furthest distances, beyond the columned stone buildings and linen tents, lay the horizon, the Nile and, beyond that, the white sands of the desert. All of it shone under a brilliant golden sun in a cloudless azure sky. And although last night had been one of the happiest days of her life, today was sour.

"I love these lands," she said, playing with his fingers. "I'm sad to leave it. To...leave you."

"Our land, Nefertiti. Our land. One day you and I shall live in peace away from these fools."

31

BACK HOME

"So, Nephrea? Tell me." Harmonia smiled down at her. "How was the trip? Anything of interest happen while you were away?" Harmonia straightened the wrinkles along her long, flowing blue dress as she shifted her weight upon her dais. Then she fought to hide the sharp pain searing from her back.

Nephrea and Jaida stood at attention before the dais wearing their scarlet armor.

But her daughter said nothing. So Harmonia straightened the thin golden crown over the black cloth wrapped around her head. Then she sipped some myrle wine from a crystal glass.

It was raining. The water dripped along the glass dome above and down the large windows of the throne room. The room was lit by torches along the rows of chairs. And no stars shone through the dark clouds above.

"Hmm?" asked Harmonia. "Why so quiet? I thought you'd be happy seeing Hustaph in Busiri. It seems you're more depressed than ever. General, perhaps you wish to tell me—"

"I failed, Mother."

Harmonia squinted down at her daughter. Then she

wagged a black gloved finger at her. "No. An Ambrosia never fails. When is the last time your mother said she failed at anything?"

"They won't make peace with us," Nephrea said. "In fact, the pharaoh sent me back with a message. He said that they've lived over a thousand years by the Nile and intend to live a thousand more. He said that the moment we move into Caravia, they will declare war and consider that we have attacked them."

Harmonia burst into laughter. Nephrea looked completely befuddled. Jaida smirked.

"He also said," Nephrea continued, "that we're fools to think that Gaia can be taken by a military force of only a few thousand Amazons."

"*A few thousand of the greatest soldiers in the world!*" thundered Harmonia. Her eyes widened, and she leaped up from her throne. But then she touched her back again. The sharp pain quieted her. "The greatest soldiers, who shall ride steeds down from the clouds and rain arrows upon man, my darling. And their blood will flow in streams and rivers. Yes, a great river of blood. For, I swear to you, man shall be punished unless he kneels before me."

She jumped down her steps, in pain or not, and rushed to the window. Then she wrapped her arms around herself tightly, staring out at the darkness. It was so dark that she saw her own reflection, her dark head wrap, the long, flowing blue peplos, and the black makeup around her eyes.

"Rain. It will rain, daughter. Yes? Rain. Our arrows shall rain, just as water pours outside." She cocked her head and smiled. "You look glorious in scarlet, did I ever tell you that, dear? You both do. You didn't fail. You made it clear who our friends are. I sent my lovely flower, *you*, and they threw her back to me, defiled. Made her think she was weak, just like all the wives of sarding men feel as they're led on leashes in their sprawling empire of feces and dung. Failed?" Harmonia laughed again. "Huh. There is no failure with an Ambrosia Amazon. Never. We never fail, Nephrea." And Harmonia turned her back to the window. "Never." Then Harmonia said with a sigh, "I tire of all this, Jaida. Lovely as the palace is, I'm not made to sit on a throne in a crystal tower, eat, drink, and fart like an Egyptian dog. I miss the battlefield. But I've waited, as I promised, my princess. Impatiently. You asked and I obeyed you. But now that you're back, we have a glorious fight ahead of us with these ancient turds. The battlefield is an Amazon's home. And—" She turned to them, with her arms still folded around herself. "Why, look at you. I believe you both miss war as much as I do."

"I wasn't just a pretty flower, Mother," Nephrea said.

Harmonia smiled wickedly. But then she turned back to the window. Harmonia nodded to herself and said, barely audibly, "*defiled.*"

"*Mildew!*" Harmonia shouted, her voice echoing in the hall. It was so loud that it made Nephrea and Jaida jump. "*Mildew!*"

Milda came running in wearing a similar long, flowing azure robe. Then she fell to the ground, bowing before the queen.

"Scribe a message in Akkadian to Pharaoh Amenhotep III. Hurry up about it. Address him as *Great Pharaoh*. Tell him…of our deep appreciation for their treatment of the princess. It is my hope that one day he and our other brothers, particularly his son, can be received in the lands of Azure. Tell him that my daughter has relayed his warning. I have spoken with her, and we have decided that, in the name of peace, the Amazon people shall do, of course, everything we can do to avoid conflict in Caravia. After all, it is my wish, always has been, for the defense and peace of the continent of Atala. However, if it's deemed that the Caravian dogs have decided to side with King Karthra, both of our nations will be placed in a bind. For just as any attack on Caravia will be considered an attack on Egypt, any support of a force fighting my army in Logencia will be deemed a personal attack on me. War will be declared. So if the pharaoh wishes peace with his sisters as much as I do, he may want to warn his neighbors in the north not to interfere in Logenth. And then sign it, *with the hope of future peace, the great Amazon nymph queen, Harmonia Ambrosia, emperor of Atala.* Send the letter by Imada and bring with it, in the interest of peace, a gift: two ampullas, the height of a woman's head. Fill one with scented oils found only in Napea. Fill the other with gold bullion. Ensure that each bullion is fashioned into one of our new coins with the likeness of your queen, Queen Harmonia Ambrosia, but…add the word *emperor* under my likeness on each and every coin. Did you get all that, Milda?" Harmonia asked with a chuckle. "Particularly my new title?"

"Yes, my queen," Milda said bowing again. "*Emperor.*"

"Indeed. Emperor." Then Harmonia burst into laughter. "Good. I like that. That's very good. Now send the letter and get your filthy sarding ass out of my throne room."

Milda bowed a few more times.

But then she stood slowly reviewing the papyrus she had scribbled on.

"*Get out!*" Harmonia hurled her glass of wine at her. Slowly, as Milda ran down the aisle, Harmonia reached down for a second full glass of wine at the bottom of the steps. Then she returned to her throne. She sat and stared at her daughter and general.

"The pharaoh was right about you," Nephrea said. "That is a message of war."

"Of course it is." Harmonia raised her crystal glass. It was too full and some of it spilled on her blue-green peplos as she nodded. "Just as your quest was, my dear." Then Harmonia glared at her. "Is there something else you wanted to talk to me about? Anything else interesting that might have happened there? I am so happy you've returned. I wish to hear everything about your journey. Any other event that Mother should know? How were your relations with the Egyptian royal family?"

"I don't wish to fight, Mother."

"Ah," Harmonia said, grinning and wagging a finger, "this is something I hoped my general would have taught you by now. As we live and breathe, we fight to stay alive, Nephree. Right now we're competing for the very air we breathe within this very hall. But anyway, my beloved, you and I don't fight. I love you. And I am overjoyed that you have returned safely." She turned her gaze to Jaida. Then, after she drank most of her wine. "How about you, my dearest friend? Is there something else that you can report about while you were away in Egypt regarding royal relations with the Egyptians?"

Jaida quickly shook her head.

"That's not what I heard," said Harmonia, raising a black gloved finger. "I heard that the Amazon princess met privately with the Egyptian pharaoh Prince Amenhotep IV. And according to gossip in our Court, the two of you didn't only speak of politics. Indeed, from what I heard, you were his flower. His *defiled* flower."

"Mother, that's not your business!"

"Everything is my business, my dear. In fact, not only is it my business, it *is* business. I heard you sarded the brute. And from what I hear, he's deformed and ugly."

Nephrea spun around and rushed down the aisle, bent on leaving the throne room.

"Get back here, Nephratee! Mother hasn't dismissed you yet."

"No, I won't speak about my private life!"

But she was stopped by two guards in scarlet armor at the door. That shocked Nephrea.

"Come back," Harmonia said more quietly. "Our lovely reunion isn't over."

"You've drunk too much wine. Do you hold me prisoner? You wish me to fight the guards to be set free!"

"Oh, Jaida, Nephree would do it, wouldn't she?" Harmonia muttered with a chuckle. "So pig-headed. Why my daughter, the most beautiful girl in the world, chose to sleep with that disgusting man is beyond me. When I heard the news, I lost my appetite. I grew sick for days. It is so beneath you, child."

"He's the pharaoh of Egypt, Harmony," objected Jaida. "Amenhotep IV is a prince. And I found him to be a very honorable and strong man."

"Hmm." Harmonia slowly nodded, sipping the last drops from her glass. "But an ugly one. No, Jaida, my daughter sleeps with the enemy. An ugly brute. There are things in your head, Nephratee, that I shall never fathom."

"I don't care. Am I excused?" Nephrea asked, staring at the guards.

"I hope you don't meet the prince of Egypt in Trialga." Harmonia squinted at her. "Whatever sick tendencies you feel for the mutant, I expect you to drive a sword through him."

Nephrea didn't respond. She turned her back on her mother and faced the guards.

"I'll meet with you, dearest, before Logenth in three days. Gather the army. I am elevating your rank to general. You shall lead a force of five hundred of our foot soldiers into battle. I need your bravery and fool-hearted tenacity to drive phalanxes of Amazon foot soldiers across the river, whether I advance or die. If I die, I expect you to take the city in my stead. Burn it upon my death and then lay camp south of their gates for the next attack. Then complete our offensive and avenge the death of your father by invading Caravia."

"Yes, my queen."

"*Don't say 'queen' to me!*" Harmonia shouted. Then she fell back in her throne, feeling a severe jolt of pain along her neck and back. Her daughter stubbornly remained by the double doors with her back turned. "Don't say that. Let us…let us not end like this, Daughter. I'd like it if you joined me for breakfast tomorrow in the dining hall. Can we do that, Nephratee?"

"Very well, my queen. Am I excused?"

Harmonia laughed. "You are excused from my presence, Princess, but not for your antics in the Court in Waset. I found it disgraceful, and I am doing all I can to quiet our people and —for the sake of our love—my tongue."

"Hustaph is well," Nephrea muttered.

Nephrea looked down the large hall. Harmonia reclined in her throne and nodded slowly. "Hustaph was a kind man. He holds the same flaw as you."

"Why send me there if you knew they wouldn't ally with us?"

"I never sent you as a diplomat, I sent you as a threat. Truly, I thought they'd lie to you and sign a false treaty. But not only that, I sent you to return to your homeland, where you were raised. For you, so that you may see Hustaph again and be happy. I like it when my daughter is happy. Is that so wrong? I thought that would mend some of our differences. But then you did the most foolish thing you possibly could do. The minute you saw a man—" Nephrea was about to shout, but Harmonia raised a finger. "Finally, I sent you there, Daughter, because you are my shining jewel above all else. As clouded as you are in selflessness, I'm guessing your strength shone forth in Kemet. Of all the nymphs who could represent my people, I wanted it to be you."

"All the Egyptians showed great respect to your daughter, Harmony," Jaida said. Jaida had taken a chair in one of the front rows.

"Of course they did, Jaida," Harmonia responded. "They were in the presence of an Ambrosia." Harmonia heaved a deep sigh. Then she chuckled. "Oh, Nephree, don't be sore with me. Perhaps you're right. Maybe I've drunk too much pomegranate wine."

"You have."

"But I won't pretend that I wasn't furious when reports came by Imada. When I heard what you did."

"I don't care. Am I excused?"

"Till the morrow, dear. In the morrow, we shall have breakfast before you leave for your campaign in Logencia. Welcome home, Nephree. Your only failure was with the prince. Even that I shall forgive, for you are an Ambrosia. And I love you. Tomorrow Ambrosias shall meet Egyptians on the battlefield."

LOGENTH

NEPHREA SAT ON HER WHITE WINGED UNICORN, INGHORN, before rows of soldiers. For the longest time, she watched as her mother and their Imada fired arrows from the sky—indeed, they rained down, as her mother had said—across the river at her enemy. Some of the arrows were flaming, causing smoke and fire inside the city. But unlike the North, where the grasslands burned, most of the fire washed out the minute it hit the wet mud. This area was a part of the marshlands, the first lands she had become acquainted with in Atala.

After crossing the river before the great city, many soldiers were forced to swim. Others hitched rides on her elite guards' flying unicorns. Nephrea gathered them back in line. She was met with little resistance by the enemy. But torrential rain began to blur visibility. Then came their phalanx. Those in the first row brandished spears. Legend said that her mother, or her champion god, had invented this military formation. Others said it was invented in ancient times in the land of Sumer. Whatever the case, none of the Hinterland barbarians knew how to break it. Unlike her enemy, whose army spread out haphazardly—some in metal armor, some not—her Amazon marched forward in their scarlet armor in perfect harmony. To the beat of the drum, Amazons walked in perfect step, like some perverse dance, and would not halt come arrow, sword, or mutilation. Only their dead bodies would stop their advance.

Nephrea signaled for the salpinx to be blown. Then her unicorn, Inghorn, flapped her mighty wings and she rose above her army.

Her mother, who had been advancing since morning, had now given Amazon forces free passage to the city gates.

Like the kingdom of Dracus, Logenth was not a fortress like Azure. One high stone wall with tower ramparts stood at the front. Beyond the walls, a few cottages and tents dotted the fields. It seemed the only function of the wall was to shield sparse crops and grass, for herds of sheep and cattle, from the wet bogs. Nephrea did not spot any grand roads or buildings. A large central tent, like Dracus's, served as a throne room.

The enemy attacked. Many men stupidly hurled their bodies at her front line and were speared and then carried with the steady wave of scarlet. Some hurled arrows. Others in silver armor, likely their best soldiers, brazenly broke through some of the shields and fought hand to hand. But they were cut down.

Not all nymphs were brave. In every fight, Nephrea saw some nymphs run from battle. The deserters were never seen again. Far worse, her mother ordered that they would be refused all rights of burial—a major slight, for all nymphs believed that a wondrous afterlife was promised in the Underworld by their champion god, Hades.

Nephrea spotted a nymph on a black unicorn approaching her in the air. It was Jaida. The smoke glowed behind her, brightened by more flames from the violence below as the first foot soldiers advanced. Unlike Nephrea's shining red armor, Jaida's armor was muddied.

"Your mother messages you, Princess," Jaida shouted, hovering near her in the wind and rain. "She welcomes your advance and applauds your courage. Imada flies over the gates now, invading the city, awaiting your arrival!"

"I take it she wishes me to stay back?"

"Behind, Princess," Jaida said with a nod. "Behind. But she plans to give you great honor! After a passage is cleared, she wants you to trot with Inghorn through the gates like man! She wants you to enter first! She has sent word that you, her daughter, the princess of Azurea, shall be the first nymph to walk through the gates. What a great honor, Nephrea!"

More like a stupid formality.

A javelin whooshed by her helm only a few yards away. Jaida pulled the neck of her unicorn and retreated. Then she grabbed a quiver and threw an arrow. But there was no need to fire. Whoever threw the spear was likely stampeded by the continued march of her regiment.

"We think the town will be taken by nightfall, Princess!" Jaida cried, heading toward the city. "Blessed be Erebos!"

The rain poured so hard that Jaida seemed to fly into a cloud and disappear.

Nephrea squinted down at her army. Past the beat of Inghorn's wings, fire was finally raging in the wet mud. And the enemy halted their futile advance on her phalanx. The enemy's bodies covered the ground as her army moved forward. For a moment, in disgust, she wondered if their bodies were serving as kindling to finally stoke the flames.

So her mother had planned a ceremony with her stepping through the gates first? So? Did she think this is what she meant by fighting in the front? It was the same as the pretense of leading an army *after* Imada had already cleared the way. Even her leadership in the clouds, upon order by the queen, was a way for her to avoid the fight. But then, as if in answer to her false sense of security, an arrow came whizzing by her helmet nearly striking her. If she had been only a foot to the right, the arrow could have been fatal. That was enough to make her descend.

She galloped beside her troop formation. They cried out "Nephratee! Nephratee!" as her unicorn splashed over water and mud.

Then came another offensive charge. This wave was far worse than the first when, seemingly, the entire army rushed from the gates. They planned to overrun them, not a bad strategy, for the nymphs were outnumbered five-fold.

Nephrea drew her sword atop Inghorn and galloped before her front line. Although she no doubt looked brave, her knees trembled. Then, before she could stand her ground before the onslaught, she heard Jaida's voice again. The general was shouting an order over her.

For the first time, the front line formation dropped their shields and spears. Nephrea was grabbed. Her soldiers swallowed her into their formation before she could countermand the order. Two nymphs yanked her off her unicorn. Now she could see nothing beyond red-metal bodies. Only the drums and the shouts of nymph commanders ordering the army to stay in line.

She was forced to walk forward with the foot soldiers.

"Nephratee!" they still cried in celebration. "Nephratee!"

But stuck within her formation, she could only hear the incoming assault.

The incoming clash finally came. It was an explosion with such violence that it forced her to move in varying directions without any control. She saw one nymph a couple of rows down fall and shout in a panic. Then the poor nymph's eyes closed, and she fell over, trampled to death under the feet of her own army. The formation slammed Nephrea away from the violence in the front, nearly tripping her. Backward, and side to side, she kept being thrown by the shock waves of the advance. Was this war? She couldn't even fight. Then, even stranger, among all the chaos, she heard the sound of her army blowing the salpinx again.

Then came the screams of men. Nephrea couldn't see, but

she imagined so many of their men running headlong into the formation and impaling themselves on the spears. She had seen it before. Their defense was tough. The shock waves kept repeating and moving her, over and over, but no one broke rank.

Inghorn fell on a few nymphs beside her. Struggling to get her up and avoid burying her sisters, Nephrea tried with many other Amazons to lift her up. Then she heard a poor girl's screams under her unicorn. Within moments, somehow, the nymphs heaved Inghorn back on her hoofs.

There was the clash of swords and, for a moment, Nephrea saw a gap in the bodies. There were so many enemy soldiers now hacking against Amazon shields. But despite the cracks and openings, the phalanx moved forward. Their war machine was not stopping.

After what seemed like an eternity, the violence broke, and Nephrea and Inghorn were able to push their way out of her formation. The rain and wind had died down, but the sun had fallen. It was turning dark, but it was too misty or smoky to see the stars. Looking up, she saw the great gray stone wall now towering over her. Logenth's army had run behind their gates. The wall of the city now stood before her.

She mounted Inghorn, raised her fist, and signaled for the phalanx to move through the metal gates. Her army shouted out her name once more.

It was then that she was surprised by her mother, who landed beside her. She quickly embraced her. Harmonia was wounded. Her left arm was dripping blood down to her hand. She didn't seem to notice or care. She was smiling under the pouring rain.

"So close, daughter," she said in her arms with a big grin. "We are so close to victory!" Then she pulled back. "Are you all right? Are you hurt? I was so worried! I saw you nearly trampled in the advance."

In the background, the screams of her sisters and of men

could be heard among the crash and clang of metal. And the fires started by both armies now warmed her face, and the smoke made her cough.

"I'm fine, Mother."

"Are you ready? When Imada clears the way, they shall behold the Amazon princess of Azurea, Nephratee Ambrosia, trotting through the gate. Here in the center of the continent, so many sarding men shall bear witness as Ambrosia takes their precious city of Logenth. Then, by your order, Nephree, our Amazon shall breach the walls and storm the city. By *your order*, just as I saw you bravely order my advance. It will all be your honor, my love. I gift this to you tonight, dear Nephratee." And she hugged her excitedly again. "My sweet child."

"Yes, Mother."

"Behind the city walls, I shall regroup," Harmonia continued with a nod. "The fighting will be hard within. No longer will we have the phalanx. We will have to fight as men fight. But we shall kill as they kill. We shall slay all the men within the walls."

Nephrea nodded.

"The queen!" a nymph shouted, pointing at Nephrea and Harmonia. "The queen fights by our side! The queen!"

It was right then that a large man in brown leather armor and pteruges rushed Harmonia on horseback. As if batting off a fly, her mother unsheathed her sword. Then as the ape raised his sword over her, she struck him right in the gullet. Another three approached, but they were cut down by arrows from the sky.

"I must go," Harmonia said, returning to Nephrea. Her grimace revealed no loss of her excitement. "After you pass through the gates, darling, I ask that you step back and allow the army to advance through the streets. Guerrilla warfare will be hard, and I want you to stay back. Allow Imada to do most of the street fighting. Even I shall wait by the grand hall. Then we shall advance together! I witnessed your courage, my child.

Thank Lord Hades that Jaida was with you to protect you. It was glorious. Now you shall show that same courage before the entire world, to all our people, to every Amazon who fights to the death for you and me tonight. And it will be my pleasure, my dream, for you to walk into King Karthra's Court with me once more. I am so proud of you."

"You did it, Mother," Nephrea said, embracing her again. "You took Logenth."

"No, my dear," Harmonia said, kissing her cheek. "The people shall bear witness to the victory under my Nephree. Their princess. My Nephratee Ambrosia."

3 3

THE CRYSTAL WITCH

THREE AMAZONS IN SCARLET METAL AND LEATHER ARMOR brought the old king, King Karthra, with hands shackled behind him in chains, to his knees. Karthra wore only a shirt and pants, like a peasant, and his flabby stomach hung over the waistband. And even now, after a life of deceit, he did not carry himself with the sorrow he no doubt felt. Instead, he looked up with false pride.

Harmonia greeted him sitting atop his stage on his animal hide chair. She had changed into a beautiful long azure peplos flowing down to her ankles, and her small golden crown lay over her black cloth head wrap. She had applied extra blue makeup on her face. And she mused that now their fortunes had reversed in a picture not too different from when he had sentenced her to death so many decades ago. To her right and left on the stage stood Nephrea and Jaida, proud in their battle armor.

It was dark, for it was now late evening, and only a handful of the usual torches lit the empty chairs and benches of the huge tent. Harmonia gazed upon her audience. A large party of over fifty Amazon Imada, all in scarlet armor, the best trained in her army, stood around the abandoned throne.

The dim light fit the mood for, as proud as the nymphs were of victory, many were somber over the sentencing of the king.

"You stand trial," Harmonia said, waving her fingers listlessly in the air. Then she straightened her gold coronet atop her head and smoothed her long dress.

"Is that why you brought me here?" he asked with a smug smile. "A mock trial before a lake witch? Back when you invited me to your palace, you never gave me a chance to tell your people who and what you were. You were a monster who took men to bed with you and then stabbed them in the back. You were nothing, a habiru, no different from now. But I see that the Crystal Lake witch adorns herself in my gold and jewelry, no doubt stolen from the men you slaughtered. You are no queen." He spat at her. "And your army, they are mere puppets for the snake who rules in his den beneath us, bent on the destruction of the world. He rules over you and uses you as his puppet. All to destroy Gaia."

He spat at her again. He was many feet away, but it was intolerable in the eyes of her Imada. One of the nymphs took the dull end of her spear and struck him hard in the back, making him fall to the ground.

"King Karthra. I—"

"You are nothing but a crystal witch whore!"

The nymph guard was going to strike him again, but she raised her hand. Then the defeated king laughed.

"Do you think you can take my city and fare long? Aye, you might want to give bountiful libations to your champion god, for I may not be a soothsayer, but only an idiot cannot predict your downfall."

"Where are the Caravians who were supposed to protect you?" Harmonia asked. "Where is Tolen's chief general, Azerius?" Harmonia was amused by the rage in Nephrea's eyes.

"Why, he's gone to fetch help, nymph witch," Karthra said

with a grin. "He will ask his brothers across the sea to burn you."

She walked down the two steps from the grand wooden stage and stood over him. She said quietly, "*Where is he?*"

"He seeks help from foreigners."

"Where?" Then Harmonia turned and looked behind her. Nephrea and Jaida still stood on the stage watching. "General, Princess, leave us. Go tend the wounded and the dead. I will join you two shortly."

Both at first looked at her strangely but then obeyed, bowing before her. When the two had left the giant hall, Harmonia turned to Milda.

"You have his wives?"

"All twelve of them, my queen."

"And his children?"

"Yes."

"A whole litter, I suspect." Harmonia turned back to him. "Where is General Azerius? I received word that he is with his unit standing guard at the southern border in the Shryer Valley of Trialga. That could be false intelligence. We aren't sure. It's very possible he still hides here in your kingdom."

"Are you threatening my family?"

"I can protect your women. If you answer me."

"Azerius is likely far beyond Shryer. He was dismissed by me. I sent him home to tell of your massacre. By now, he is probably heading to Aethiopia or Canaan. He will ask for support, and at the threat of losing Atala to a witch, he'll get it. Then he'll return to Caravia to organize his army in defense. You won't get further than this hall."

"We shall see," Harmonia said, walking back to the stage.

But news of Azerius's absence brought her spirits down. She had so hoped she could apprehend and kill him tonight.

Memories flooded her head. It made her clench her jaw and tighten her fists. She remembered lying in the man's arms on a grassy field beyond these dark and dank marsh fields, in the valley in Shryer. Azerius taught her that morning that the Caravians and Egyptians hated each other. That they had warred for centuries. And Assyrians, Mittanites, and even the Hittites still waged war with Caravia. In fact, this had been Azerius's excuse for leaving her repeatedly at his villa—to prepare for defense from those foreign neighbors. The memory was unpleasant, but the meaning was clear. She doubted this king's confidence in garnering support beyond the sea.

Then she thought of Esser.

"How many wives do you have?" she asked.

"I have over twenty wives," he said proudly.

"I thought as much," she said with a laugh. "And how many children?"

He gave a large grin showing his mottled teeth, further disgusting her. Then she caught wind of his rancid breath. "What's the difference? Over a hundred, I think."

"That should be enough, don't you think?"

He said nothing but furrowed his brow. Harmonia turned to Milda. "My will be done."

"My queen?"

"Do it now. His sentence in Logencia shall be carried out here. Make the former king of Logenth pay before Imada."

"My lord?" Milda asked. "Here?"

"Yes. Do it now so that I may hear his objections. But be careful, Mildew. Make sure that the king still lives."

The Imada, the bravest nymphs, seasoned in war, having seen the most terrible violence and bloodshed, gasped.

"What do you intend to do to me!" cried Karthra. "You've already planned to kill me by sunrise!"

"Why, no," she said with a sudden nasty smile. "I've decided to show mercy, man. For a handful of days. Much longer than you ever planned for me. I will spare you after this act...if you live. I want to see if you'll live even an hour without your vigor. We shall make certain that no other woman is defiled by you. I wager you won't make it to your drowning in the sea anyway. You'll likely die from the act, and I'll be floating a dead body over the waves."

Then she burst out laughing. But no one accompanied her mirth. Then the queen turned very seriously to Milda.

"Obey my order and do it here in his hall right now, on his very throne, this very moment! Imada, unsheathe your knives! Let me enjoy the sound of his objections. This beast shall sire children no more!"

"Yes… my queen," she said, unsure. "If that is your order."

"My will be done. As for his living ones, kill every boy tonight."

Harmonia gracefully stepped down the steps of the hall and slowly walked out of the large auditorium. As she walked to the door of the tent, she heard Karthra screaming behind her as her guard grabbed him, threw him on the wooden stage, unsheathed their knives, and obeyed her order.

34

HAPPY BIRTHDAY

Harmonia climbed one side of a dual spiral marble staircase in the palace. This was her favorite, and the most majestic, room in the castle, an architectural masterpiece designed by the dwarfs. Azure guards stood on either side of the base of the double stairwell. There at the top was a lookout. One could stand and lean against the rail peering over the blue-green fields of Azure. The glass stretched from floor to ceiling, over three stories high.

It was near the top that Harmonia finally came across her daughter. She had been searching all over the palace. Beside Nephrea was a short red-haired girl giggling with another in short black curls. It was Nephrea's friends Ilia and Vainya. The two friends dressed simply in brown tunics and pants, which contrasted sharply with the princess's long, ornate blue robe. Nephrea's hair was tied back in a ponytail. Her blue dress came up into two large glistening green collars.

Harmonia stared for a moment, a few steps down, in wonder. Her daughter looked older, now a woman.

"Happy birthday, Nephrea," Harmonia said, approaching quietly. She reached out and presented her a golden bracelet in her blue hand. Her friends quickly bowed.

Her daughter seemed to wince in her presence. It had been this way for the past few weeks, since her campaign in Logenth. She had fought with her in the past, but now it seemed that being anywhere near her disgusted her daughter.

"My birthday was a few days ago, Mother," Nephrea replied. But she put the band on her wrist and looked at it. It had multicolored gems and shone bright gold. "It's very beautiful. Thank you."

"It is Mandrigelian, my dear. It's said that it had been meant for Aphrodite. It is one of my greatest treasures in our treasure chest, but it fills me with joy to know that it shall be worn by you."

"We should go," said Vainya, with a deep bow to the queen and the princess. Harmonia simply nodded.

Then Harmonia turned and leaned on the gilded rail, peering out at the view. Harmonia had on a long, flowing dress as well, but hers was saffron.

"Thank you," Nephrea said after a long silence.

"You're welcome. Funny, I thought the day was today. You're twenty-two now, I think? I can't believe it."

"Yes."

Harmonia looked out the window.

"You did magnificently on the battlefield," Harmonia added after some silence. "Your entrance in Logenth will be sung for an eternity. Logenth was our first true challenge, and you fought honorably and with immense courage."

"Yes, my queen."

That stung.

"There it is again," said Harmonia quietly. "There you go calling me by my title, instead of your mother."

"What do you want?" Nephrea asked, heaving a sigh. She leaned on the rail and gazed out at Azure with her. "I don't agree with so many things you do. Having me ride into Logenth is not what I meant by fighting in the front. I was whisked inside for protection from my unit the moment I faced the enemy. If I am to avenge my father, I expect to do what I was trained to do. Fight. That wasn't fighting." Then her daughter squinted at her. "Then I heard about your treatment of the prisoners. And then I heard what was done to the king. I hope what is said—"

Harmonia raised her palm. "I let you ride before our people. I gave you glory. Don't spoil it by speaking of rumors or lies spread around the Court. Take care what buzzes in your head, Nephrea. Your enemies would drag you to a tree and burn you, if they had the opportunity. I regret nothing I've done. I care only for you, my dearest daughter."

"Tell me the truth then," she said, staring into her mother's eyes. "No more lies."

Harmonia grew a smile and nodded. "Only my daughter dares gaze at me so." Then she ran her hand along Nephrea's arm. "What is it?... I think we should celebrate like last year? What do you say? I've arranged dancing and drink in the fields, the dance of the games. We will celebrate the birth of my princess. Can't we enjoy this for you, my love? It would make you and me happy."

Nephrea turned from her mother and faced the rail again.

"I hear rumors of what you did to King Karthra. If they're true, it's terrible. All prisoners that were under my responsibility were treated fairly. But gossip tells quite a different story about your actions, Mother. Many, it is said, were put through great pain for no reason before their execution. Particularly the king."

"Let's not speak of it now. Let us speak of your birthday."

The green sun was falling. Harmonia gazed out over the sea to the horizon with her daughter. Then she gently ran her fingers through Nephrea's black hair, but the princess did not look back.

"You fought bravely," Harmonia repeated. "I am so proud of you."

Nephrea smiled, seemingly in spite of herself. Harmonia took a deep breath.

"Jaida protected you on the battlefield," Harmonia continued, "because you would have faced death if you weren't corralled into our phalanx. That was brave, but an act of suicide. But I rewarded you for your courage. Now we will have a grand celebration for you. What do you think of that? We can celebrate in the violet fields. We can dance. You can bring your lyre. I can bring Neala. I think she's mastered the ancient songs of the dwarfs. And your friend Vainya, she is very good with the drums. How does that sound, Nephree? And drinking with Ilia?"

"I would rather not celebrate while we fight." She turned and leaned on the rail, running her fingers through her hair. "Not now. We aren't ready. Our people still mourn their dead. We are at war, Mother."

Harmonia turned away and clenched the rail tightly, seemingly trying to hold back her infamous rage. "Stop it." Then she closed her eyes tightly and shook her head. "Stop it. Stop it, by Hades, stop this, Nephrea."

Nephrea surprised her by nodding her head slowly.

"I already told you," Harmonia said, "our people spread rumors."

Then Nephrea made Harmonia almost jump as she gently leaned on her mother's shoulder in a partial embrace. "Forgive my disrespect. I love you, Mother. It's just, so many of our sisters have died."

"Well, we fight. But I love you, child. And I'd like to celebrate your birthday," Harmonia said as she caressed her daughter's head.

It was then that the guards far below her staircase began to stir. Both Harmonia and Nephrea quickly glanced downstairs. A man wearing a long black cape with his face covered by a hood briskly strode into the hall with three huge black-armored guards. The nymph guards quickly looked up for orders from their queen, but they were too late. He came in with such bounding energy that he was already ascending the stairs, a couple at a time. Harmonia walked to the top of the stairs and nodded. Nephrea fell on a knee and bowed.

"Hades," Harmonia said.

"Dear Harmony," he said, stopping a step from the top. Then he ran his hand along her hair, as Harmonia had just done to her daughter. Hades turned to Nephrea. "And you, child. Look how you've grown on your birthday. But I see you no longer cover your eyes in Court, pretty girl." Then his hands wandered along her face as well. "So beautiful."

"Leave us, Nephree," Harmonia said.

"Good day, Mother," Nephrea said hesitantly with a nod.

"We will have your party, my dear," Harmonia said. "We will celebrate. I promise."

Nephrea nodded again and quickly descended the steps.

When the coast was clear, Hades came up the last step, took her hand, and embraced Harmonia tightly. Then he lifted his hood and kissed her hard on the lips. If he had been any other man, she'd have slapped him across the face. But she yearned for him. He squeezed her hard, and she fell under his spell. Then he gently released her.

He leaned on the rail and looked down.

"She is watching us," Hades said quietly in amusement. Harmonia looked down and saw her daughter still in the Hall on the bottom floor. Indeed, she was looking up at them. "I don't care for her. I worry, in time, her allegiance shall be with her father, not her mother."

"She will never side with that shit," Harmonia spat. "Anyway, she is *our* daughter, Aidoneus."

"*Our* daughter," he said, turning to her with a laugh. "I see. Well, I must say, I do like that. Perhaps I shall change my view of her then."

"Why has it taken you so long to visit? We give libations.

My people pray to you at your temple. I need you now more than ever. Why now?"

"Yes, well," he said, turning back to the view. "You are the sharpest blade. But I no longer walk above Gaia. It is with great difficulty that I visit you at all. But, anyway, today is an exception. Today is *our* daughter's birthday."

"I was wrong. It was a few days ago."

"I see."

She looked up at his face. The beard was the same, but his forehead and temples were more wrinkled than she remembered. He had aged terribly in only a few moons. That was so strange for a god. His cloak was wrinkled and dirty, and there was a sadness in his gaze. And he seemed weaker. Whatever was happening, he was suffering terribly. He looked like a shell of the man he once was. But he was still a handsome brute.

"It is pleasant to have quiet before the storm," Hades said.

"The Caravians are preparing?"

"Aye."

"And foreigners? The strait?"

Hades turned and faced her. "No." He quickly shook his head. "Not yet, Harmony. We may celebrate *our* daughter's birthday."

She nodded and squeezed his hand. Then they fell into uncomfortable silence staring back at the view. Her god held her hand and stared out with her as the last bit of green light fell off the horizon.

"There will be some time until the girls light the torches along the fields for our late celebration," Harmonia said quietly by his ear. "We have time. Alone. I wonder what we can do alone together?"

He turned to her and smiled. "Is Harmonia, the Azure Amazon queen of the nymphs, asking *me*, a man, what to do with her time? That's not like you at all. Well, how is this: I intend to take you to bed and ravish you, as is a god's right. If the Amazon queen of Azure Blue will permit it."

"Yes. I will. I've missed you so much, Aidoneus."
"Aye. A god loves you, Harmony Ambrosia."

35

THE FALCON'S BEACHED

NEPHREA WAS RUMMAGING THROUGH MAPS BY CANDLELIGHT IN her tent when she was startled by shouting outside. There was a crash. And a scream. She dragged herself up from her wooden chair. She had on her heavy scarlet armor. In fact, over many moons now, she couldn't remember a time when she hadn't worn it. She couldn't remember a time when she had gotten much sleep either.

Right outside her door she saw an explosion of fire and smoke from across the camp. Amazons were running by her tent in a panic. It hadn't been the first sneak attack. Half the camp was set on fire a fortnight ago. As the camp was on the southern border of Logencia, her nymphs were under constant invasion. Shadows above rushed over her in the moonlit sky. These weren't birds; they were the monokera of the Imada striking enemy forces.

"Are you all right, Princess?" cried her guard, Rose, rushing to her.

"Another attack?"

"We think so," Rose said. "Stay put in your tent, Your Majesty."

"I'm the commander of this regiment."

"The queen's orders are for you to stay indoors."

Of course.

But Nephrea had no intention of following her mother's orders. She was about to run over, but then an older gray-haired nymph named Gashina, a dispatch rider from her mother's Imada, arrived down a dirt path in the opposite direction of the fire. Gashina was a soldier in the Imada and had likely come from the front lines. Where those lines were, her mother never told her, but rumors said Harmonia was already striking the town of Jedithian and the sea with her elite force.

Gashina's dark hair was disheveled, and her red armor was dirty and brown. She had white bandages over her left shoulder and scratch marks and dry blood on her forehead. Now she was panting.

"Your Majesty," Gashina said, gasping for air. She was about to kneel but Nephrea held her up. In the distance, there was the sound of the salpinx. In battle, it would be used mainly for intimidation. At their camp, it was to corral troops in defense. "My princess, I have an important message."

"More important than this?" Nephrea asked, pointing to the flames.

"Yes, Princess. Even more important than this."

"No formalities, Gashina. Just tell me quickly."

Nephrea gently took her inside her general's tent. Then she threw some rolled papyrus on the ground and helped Gashina sit by a wooden table.

Nephrea went over to a fire with low flames and picked up a bowl. She grabbed a porcelain cup and poured warmed red wine in it. She handed it to the soldier. Gashina's hands shook. Nephrea doubted it was fear. She believed the poor soldier was just exhausted.

"You are so kind, Princess. All the rumors about you are true."

"What is it? How is the front?"

"Your mother can barely keep this up. There are rumors that King Eriba and Amenhotep have sent men onto the continent. Well, not really rumors anymore I suppose. You saw some soldiers fighting in Logenth. But these are entire regiments. And they are only growing. The queen believes we need you to gather your soldiers and strike near the Shryer valley to stave off the Egyptians. She thinks it's time to move forward to Caravia."

"Shryer is secure. Why strike? We should be retreating."

Gashina shook her head.

"Shryer is not secure." She put down her cup, which shook in her hand. "Not anymore. The outsiders have taken most of the valley back. The Egyptians. Jaida even suspects mischief from Phoenicians and Myceneans. There are just too many foreigners entering the continent. They don't wait for your mother to advance, they keep snipers in wait everywhere to attack our camps. Just as they are doing now to the largest one. Yours. They are infiltrating all our outposts. Even in the very north near the Azure Strait. It's a wonder they haven't hit Napea yet. Only a fragile treaty is keeping them at bay at Sutsik. But for how long? If we lose more ground in the South, they could invade Napea. That is why your mother wants you to meet with her for one last great offensive. It would be unexpected. If we can take Caravia, it could weaken resolve—"

"And we can take the continent."

"Umm-hmm," Gashina said with a nod, sipping more wine. "Yes. And then we can stave off the foreigners' further advances. They might run."

"But there's no way such an offensive can succeed. Not if there are so many forces."

Gashina didn't answer. She just drank more wine. Then, with her tremulous hands, she put the cup down and lifted a finger. She dug into a satchel she had been carrying and took out a papyrus scroll.

"I'm not sure what this is, but it was given to us by the enemy. It was delivered in secret to Imada, during a truce, near the Strait of Aethiopia. There, Nephrea, I saw Egyptian mercenaries killing our sisters. This letter is written in Akkadian. Of course, none of us knows what it says except your mother and her scribe. The queen glanced at it. After breaking the seal, with a look of disgust, the queen pushed it into my chest and ordered that I deliver it to you. She said derisively that it's addressed to Pharaoh Nefertiti Ambrosia."

"Thank you, Gashina."

"Why is an enemy prince messaging you personally, Nephratee?"

"The Egyptian prince and I have been sending letters to each other for nearly a year now...but many were when we were at peace, not at war. I met him when Mother was trying to drum up support among the Egyptians. She thought, because I was raised there, I could convince them to take our side—or at least not interfere. I failed."

"No, princess," Gashina said with a smile. "They know your mother's plans, that's all. You didn't fail."

Nephrea smiled at Gashina. Then she unrolled the papyrus.

My dearest Nefertiti,

I beseech you. You spoke by the river of the coming wave of war. Surely you have heard that the falcon has beached. Our armies are marching on your shore. Of all Amazon in Atala, you are closest to your mother. Tell the queen to turn her army away now and retreat. Implore her. With my knowledge of the incoming force in the East and South, there is only defeat in store for your people. She cannot win.

But if she cannot be persuaded, come to me. Remptju ni Kemet. You are not of Atala, you are of Iteru. You are of the Nile. Come to me, my Nefer. Return to me. Leave your mother and come home.

Alas, I already know your mother's decision. And so I have included instructions detailing the way in which you can evade the border and cross the Strait of Aethiopia. Merely present your seal.

Do not think that your escape is cowardly. Or that this be some sort of trap. Truly, I tell you, I ask only for you. There will be no more negotiations with your mother. The war is over. Return home to me, dearest Nefer.

Oh, Nefertiti, do not believe that this world controls us. Let us make the world how we dream it. With you, my love, I know I would have everything. If our parents wish to kill each other, this is not our fight. You and I can live in peace. We can make our world our way.

Oh, how I wish we could be as before, close as before. I yearn so much for your touch again, Nefertiti, the feeling of your embrace, your very breath. I yearn for every part of you, the blue of your cheeks, or just the sound of your voice. I miss everything about you. Everything, Pharaoh Nefertiti. Through war or peace, you have my heart.

With love,

Pharaoh Amenhotep IV

Son of Pharaoh Amenhotep III, grandson of Thutmose IV

"WHAT DOES IT SAY?" asked Ganisha.

But Nephrea couldn't answer in time. There was a terrible scream right outside her wooden door. They leaped up and opened the door. Rose was dueling with two shirtless men in shendyts and headdresses attempting to enter her chamber. Another nymph lay dead at their feet. Nephrea grabbed her sword, hanging from the wall, and attacked the tallest man. As she thrust and parried at the Egyptian fighters, she was shocked to see how many men in blue armor were running at her with raised swords. With her sword, Ganisha struck the man Nephrea was fighting. But it seemed a mob was rushing down the dirt path at her.

"Get back in the tent, Your Majesty!" cried Rose. Rose was now dueling with a large, blue-armored man.

"She's here!" cried a man rushing their way. "The princess is—"

"*Aieee! Aieee!*"

The cry came from above. The moonlight was shrouded by what Nephrea thought at first was a cloud, but there came a shower of blades. A hundred arrows showered over her camp. It was Imada strafing overhead. Rose lifted her sword for another strike, but her foe now lay dead, pinned on the ground by a dozen arrows.

"Stay in your camp, I tell you," Rose insisted, touching Nephrea's shoulder. Nephrea shrugged her hand off.

"Where is the largest breach?" Nephrea asked Rose.

"From the east end, Your Majesty," said Gashina.

"Gather my army. We shall march east and take back that side of the camp."

"I think you should retreat and abandon the camp, sire," Gashina said.

"I can't. They'll pick us off if we run."

3 6

THE QUEEN OF ARGOS

HARMONIA SAT ATOP ANTILUS ALONE OVER A HILLSIDE, FAR from her army, looking out toward the horizon. This was far enough south to be away from the ugly bogs in Logencia, among vast green grasslands. But this far south, and alone, she was on dangerous enemy grounds. She was close enough to Caravia to see the tall Cliffs of Zonoch. Up there resided the fortress of her greatest foe.

The sun was setting, and the land was darkening along the trees and thrush. She stared at the falling sun, trying to keep her mind off all else.

She was alone. She had been abandoned by everyone. No, she had always been alone.

But...no, she was not alone this evening. From the corner of her eye, she saw a nymph in the same scarlet armor, her white unicorn trotting along the grass with its wings folded. Few nymphs ever rode in the country like this. Only her stubborn Egyptian princess.

Antilus neighed and shook under Harmonia, likely spotting the princess and Inghorn too. Harmonia ran her hand along Antilus's feathery side.

"Happy to see her? Eh?" Harmonia asked with a chuckle. Antilus nodded and neighed again. "Me too."

But she turned back to the sunset, cocking her head as the princess approached. "My dear Nephree," Harmonia said when her daughter was close enough. She took a deep breath and closed her eyes but smiled. "However did you find me?"

"I've been looking all over the continent, Mother," Nephrea snapped. "I couldn't believe it when I had to fly this far south, over the Black River, into enemy territory—land the enemy has taken back."

Harmonia opened her eyes and gazed back at her beautiful daughter. They were almost twins now because, as a nymph, she aged so slowly. She often felt like she was gazing in a mirror.

"Do you know why I love the sun?" Harmonia asked.

"No, Mother," Nephrea said, heaving a long sigh. "And I don't care. Why are you here? There were raids all morning. I nearly lost my base."

"But you didn't, did you? Because you are my Nephratee Ambrosia. The most beautiful, brave general and princess in all of Atala. Do you know, my beloved, why I love the sun?"

Nephrea said nothing.

"I love the sun because it is yellow. Here, it is yellow. The sun in these lands is not tainted by the gods. Not like our home in Azure. Our sun shines green. That is because our sun was manufactured by the gods, this sun was not. This is the sun of Sumer, of Ur, of Argos and even, it is said, of Olympus. It is golden. You see, the beautiful blue lands of Azure Blue are blue—"

Nephrea trotted her unicorn right in front of Harmonia, blocking her view of the sunset.

"Why aren't you at camp, Mother? Answer me? I couldn't believe it when Imada told me they didn't know where you were."

Harmonia gave her a stern look. "Because I'm taking time

to watch the sunset. We all should stop what we're doing on occasion and find the time to do that."

"Sure, Mother."

Nephrea cocked her head back at the sunset.

Everything felt somber. Terribly morose. It was as if they were in mourning. She wondered if her daughter understood why.

"You have come to bring me news of Egypt, Egyptian?" asked Harmonia, straightening. Her back burned. She did her best to sit tall and disguise it from her daughter. "Remptju ni Kemet? I read the letter."

"I know you saw the letter. You broke the seal. But I bring news from Jaida and Imada. Jaida said the Imada spotted—"

"I know everything Imada sees. I *am* Imada. I'm afraid, my beloved, we've been betrayed. And now you come to bring me news? There is nothing you can tell me that I don't already know. It was clear the moment the Egyptians splashed down. They used Phoenician ships, you see. So bent on our destruction that they traveled with the help of foreigners. Even the Myceneans greet me. The entire world, my daughter, is against me. As it always has been."

"We don't know for sure," Nephrea said, shaking her head. "I'm not so sure the Egyptians will stand with the Caravians when it comes time to fight. They are sworn enemies."

"You read the letter. The falcon's beached."

"But I don't trust him."

Harmonia laughed. "Don't palter with a fox."

"I'm not here about the letter. I could run. If you're enough of a fool to bring more death to our army, I think I should. I came to convince you to retreat. I've secured my camp, but not for long. I didn't retreat during the attack, as I believed it would lead to more deaths. But now, we can—"

"Watch the sunset before it leaves me, daughter." Harmonia attempted to look over Nephrea's shoulder. "It is nigh. Just as our time is nigh. But we can see this glorious gold not manufactured by any so-called god. You and I together. And that is glorious, my child."

Nephrea sighed and her unicorn, Inghorn, stirred and trotted to the side a little.

"I have learned," Harmonia said with a nod, gazing back at the breathtaking vista, "a secret that your queen shall now impart only to you. For only you deserve such gnosis. Not because you are the queen's daughter, but because you are my Nephratee." But she paused and shuddered. She felt the sting in her back again. And then she felt the memory of the screams of Nephrea's ancestors by the Stratos. "Man does not seek freedom. That is why, unlike the Amazons, Nephrea, the gods remain in their favor. Myceneans of Hellena break bread with the gods. They build great temples in the gods' honor, serving libations and kneeling before them. They pander to them, so Zeus bestows honor. The Egyptians do the same, just under different names. The men who now face us in the Hinterlands—" She straightened and winced again from a sharp pain in her back. "Do the same. I have willed that my children never worship any god. Except my beloved. But now, after his final betrayal, I shall order them to stop our libations to Hades too.

"There is word from Imada that a great army is marching north from Jedithian after landing by the Strait of Aethiopia, Mother," Nephrea said with a sigh. "This army will be ready to advance on us within two days and stop us from entering Caravia. They are far more numerous than the attackers who have been assaulting my camp. Probably, the force will be three to four times greater than the army we faced in Logenth."

"I am well aware of this, Princess."

"And so," Nephrea said, turning her horse and moving in front of her queen and Antilus again, "I've been asked by leaders and elders to talk to you. Not only the pharaoh prince, but our elders seem to think I'm the only one you'll listen to."

"You can always talk to me," she said with an amused smile. "But not if you block my view of the sun."

But Nephrea didn't move. "Thousands will organize by daybreak."

"What fortune, by the grace of the gods, that the two of us can watch this, mother and daughter," Harmonia said, guiding Antilus to the side to gaze at the valley and the sunset, "in twilight before—"

"*Why do you care about the sun!*" Nephrea snapped in fury. "*We must turn back, Mother!* For the sake of our sisters. We should return them to Logenth, gather all our forces, and fly home. Those not able to flee can take shelter in Shadow Forest. I can take one of my units and lie in wait in the forests and defend our position. Our smaller numbers won't be spotted beneath trees and bushes. I've already come up with the plan with Jaida."

Harmonia smiled again with a nod and turned back toward the horizon.

"*By the gods, look at me!*" cried Nephrea. "*Are you even listening? It's over!*"

"Calm yourself," Harmonia said, raising a finger.

"Why do you care about a sarding sunset?"

"Because it's yellow."

Then she gazed at her daughter. Nephrea's nares flared, and she seemed ready to strike her. She looked intimidating in her armor. That amused Harmonia. She smiled.

Oh, how you've grown. In your armor, you are a great Amazon, maybe the greatest there ever was. I am so proud of you… But your heart is soft. Too soft, like Jaida's. If my mother acted in such a way, I'd ride off and be done with this. But not you. Not my beloved and most loyal daughter. My Nephree.

"Will you have me miss the sunset, my dear?"

Nephrea just glared at her.

"I brought our people here," Harmonia said. "Your queen. Gaze at the gilded treasure I've gifted you. I gift you this view. Let us enjoy it together. This view is for no one else. Not even for the god Hades, for though I love Aidoneus dearly, he is still a god. Now watch as the yellow sun falls beneath the horizon and—"

"*Oh, Mother!*" said Nephrea, "*no one will cross you, but someone must—*"

"*Are you so presumptuous as to think you can?*" Harmonia cried. Then she closed her eyes and shook her head. "Oh, Nephree—"

But her daughter turned her back to her. And for a moment, Harmonia thought she would just ride off.

"Nephree," Harmonia repeated quietly, trotting close enough to touch her daughter's shoulder. "Nephree. Out there if we leaped into the sky with Antilus and followed the sun, like the great Phaethon, what do you think we'd see?"

"Who cares?"

"What would you see? Tell me. It answers your question."

"Is this another lesson?"

"Answer me."

"Phaethon took Helios's chariot and lost control, so goes the myth," she responded with a sigh. "He was blinded and burned by the sun. He saw nothing."

"But that is myth. That is what you were taught. However, I once made the journey. Atop Antilus, I followed the yellow rays of the sun as it set. I traveled further than any of our sisters. I was in anguish after what had become of you and your father. I was so distraught that I was willing to fly Antilus to her death and be blinded and burned. I pushed Antilus so hard as we flew west. But I was not thrown, burned, or blinded atop Antilus. Do you know what I saw?"

Nephrea shook her head.

"Argos." She raised her fist as Hades had done many times. "If I could take Argos and Hellena, I would humiliate Demeter and all of her gods. That would complete my revenge. Then my conquest would be over, and I could die a happy Amazon. But alas, you and I have been betrayed. And with the greatest irony of all, we were betrayed by your people. I think if I had to battle a handful of Mycenean Greeks, we could prevail. Alas, Hellena is too far away. But your people, who live only a short distance across the Strait of Aethiopia and across the eastern sea, surround us. They will ruin us. Just as your lover said. Perhaps the conquest of Argos will fall one day to you when you are queen. Or perhaps your granddaughter. But Argos is all I've ever wanted. Now it is slipping from my fingers. But if I could take Argos, I would retreat with the army, as you implore me to do, and return to our palace in peace."

"Then perhaps we should retreat, Mother," Nephrea said sarcastically, "regather the army and fight Argos instead."

"Ah," she said, raising a finger and laughing, "but then, my dear, we would not be able to kill Azerius."

Harmonia looked toward the rays of the sun, which had almost vanished from the sky. The yellow now mixed with red, like the color of blood, darkening the lands.

"Know, Nephrea, that the gods in the clouds move us like puppets. Know this when we meet the enemy before Zonoch. It was the gods that led us to this moment. Open your eyes and do not be blinded like Phaethon. I think even my blessed lover does not yet see this—or admit to it. For I don't believe he led us to ruin. He gifted us so many weapons. Yet it was a lie when I told Amazons that man was our enemy. Ever since the day I was exiled, I have known it is not man. It never was. It is the gods. This secret I give only to you now, for you are dearer to me than anything else in this world." Harmonia paused, because of the poison that had never been removed by the demon child. "Azerius killed your father, but Sara murdered mine. It may seem that our only enemy is man but, in truth, it is the gods. It always has been."

"I don't care, Mother. I need to know what to tell the

elders back home. My regiment. If we do not retreat, we will lose everything."

Harmonia leaned close to her, over Antilus, and said almost in a whisper, "It doesn't matter if we lose." Then Harmonia sat up straight, ignoring more pain running along her back, and nodded. "It doesn't matter. It only matters that we fight. This fight shall be glorious and remembered for all time. I shall kill Azerius. His end is the only reason I lead our army to my last breath. If I slay him, I will withdraw the army and do exactly as you suggest—for now. Then perhaps we can hide like the apes we once were in trees in the Shadow Forest. Regroup and go west to Argos. But for now, whatever forces that turd Zeus sends my way, I shall fight them to the death. And I shall not stop fighting until I dig my sword into Azerius's chest."

There was silence, and Nephrea seemed to ponder her mother's words.

They both turned and looked toward the sun. Now there was only a sliver of orange red.

"Now look, look what you've done, Nephrea. You made me miss the sunset! That was very cruel, daughter, when it might have been my last."

"I don't agree," Nephrea finally said. "Man is coming from Caravia and beyond the continent to fight us. The Imada have seen naval forces coming by Canaan across the sea in the East. Mitannites, Hittites, and Assyrians fight us in the North. They shall come down from Sutsik. Egyptian forces number in the thousands. We can't win this. There are too many of them. And this time, your stubborn commitment to revenge not only risks yourself, you are sentencing your people to death. Not even you have that right, Queen."

Harmonia raised a shaking hand in sudden rage. But her daughter seemed desperate.

Nephrea shook her head violently. "This is wrong, Mother.

If it's all for vengeance, I don't agree. You have no right to sacrifice our people for your revenge."

"I have every right! I made them who they are!" *Shall I tell you the truth? Your own father wanted to burn you alive under a tree as a babe!*

"I brought my nymphs everything with my own hands! My people! They are as much a part of me as my own fingers. If I ask them to walk into a burning pyre, submerge themselves in a boiling pot of oil, or run a sword through their gullet, they do it. I made them who they are! Our people are mine! And I have every right…"

"*Oh, Mother, this is wrong!*" Nephrea cried, shaking her head. "We won't survive! There is only one logical choice, and that's to retreat. We can fight another day."

"What of Azerius? I saw the way you looked at him in the Court. The way you fought with our sisters for his blood. Have you forgotten your father?"

"What of my unit? What of my line? What of my sisters who have sacrificed in battle for years? No, this is wrong! Are they any less important, Amazon Queen?"

"*Amazon Queen!* How dare you wave my own title around again!" Harmonia turned her back on her daughter and gazed back at the sun. Then she lurched back, feeling another sharp cut from her spine.

The last rays of the sun had already descended below the horizon.

"Wonderful! Now look what you did! You made me miss the sunset!" Harmonia said, slapping her leg. "That could have been my last! I think you know that if any other nymph spoke to me as you just did, I would cut out their tongue. But alas…you…you are no ordinary nymph. You are my Nephratee… Know that…I love you … You have become a true warrior and—"

"Oh please, Mother! *Your Nephratee*, I don't care! This isn't about me, selfish woman. It's about your people. You have no right to take—"

"Very well, scrupulous shit! Return and tell our sisters that anyone who wishes to not fight can go. Tell them I've made a special edict tonight with the venerable Princess Nephratee to not punish them for deserting. Apparently, the princess doesn't care enough about her father's killer. And they can mourn the death of their queen back home in Azure after I die. For everything I have given *my people!* For my—" She straightened her aching back again, closing her eyes hard. "*My broken back! My weary bones.* For all sacrifices given to them by me in the name of a better life. Let them run! And then perhaps, Nephrea, as you cower with them back home, under the chairs in our throne room, you will await man's invasion. Because after you and Jaida take my army to hide in the trees, man will cross the Strait of Azure. Oh, believe me, they will. And they will take the palace. But don't you and the people dare cry for Harmony when I'm gone. As my dead body rots at the foot of the cliffs of your childhood home, I'd better not hear people cry out my name! My spirit shall rise from Hades, tear the hair from my roots, and bash my chest if I hear any such dishonor from my beloved dust. I ride the cliffs up to Caravia now! If I must, I will battle the entire enemy force myself!"

"*Oh Mother, no one will abandon you! But you lead us to ruin!*"

Nephrea pulled the neck of her horse, finally ready to ride away.

"*Never leave without being excused by your Queen!*"

Nephrea held her unicorn back. "*May I be excused?*"

Harmonia cracked a smile. But her body still shook with rage. Harmonia reached over to touch her daughter's shoulder gently, but Nephrea yanked away.

"Daughter," she said quietly, "my…dear…daughter. Join me. To avenge your father. We finally fight the Caravians tomorrow, Nephree. You've dreamed of it for so many years.

You've asked so bravely to fight in the front. Whatever danger I've forced upon you, you must be happy about that?"

"I will follow you. You know that. I'll do whatever you ask. But I don't agree with this. Please, Mother, let's regroup and fight another day."

"There is no other day."

Nephrea nodded. Then she turned her back on Harmonia and rode off. She rode away on the ground with her unicorn's wings folded.

Harmonia looked back at the horizon. She pressed her aching back. Then she petted Antilus's head. The horse neighed. The sun's rays had passed, and it was getting dark. And cold.

"Oh, Antilus, I suppose she's right. But it was so cruel for her to not allow an old woman to see the yellow sun fall one last time."

The horse nodded her head as if understanding. Then the smile left Harmonia's face.

"Aidoneus," she said, looking up at the night sky. The stars were faint. Her hands trembled as she clasped them together. "Give me the strength in darkness. Watch with pride as your creation fights with honor and courage tomorrow. I shall gladly sacrifice my life. But you know the will of the gods is to destroy us all, my love. Whatever may come of it, protect the princess. Please, protect my sweet Nephrea." Then she looked south toward the Cliffs of Zonoch. Under the night sky, they seemed as remote and unpassable as the Napean Pyramid itself. "And grant me a steady hand so that I may kill her father."

TRIALGA

Nephrea watched as her regiment stood at attention in rows on the grassy field, holding their phoenix flags, their swords and shields in hand, and their bows and quivers carried on their backs. Two thousand Amazon nymphs standing at attention under her command. Her feared army would stand their ground before the Black River in the north. The river was called "black" because it was, indeed, shadowed by trees and shrubs and the water was dirty and opaque. The woods made it dark because it was narrow. And because it was narrow, it was crossable in many areas. This area, where her soldiers would march across, was shallow enough.

But her force made up only the first half of the field. The second half was led by her mother. In the far distance, she could see her queen atop Antilus inspecting the front line. The entire Amazon army stood at attention there too, so vast a force that she had to use a special Mandrigelian crystal lens to see in the distance.

Harmonia raised her fist and spoke, but she could not hear her. Instead her people echoed her word, "Esser," and then banged their shields and shouted. Others cried "Harmonia." Still others shouted "Nephratee."

At the base of the cliffs stood the enemy. Though not as disciplined, these soldiers were more menacing than those in the North, all wearing blue metallic armor. And their numbers seemed to cover the entire valley under the cliffs. And they held light-blue flags. And further west at the farthest field, she saw chariots and silver armor with foreign flags. And even beyond that, she saw soldiers wearing shendyts with orange Egyptian flags. Like the Amazon, the Egyptians had a bird on their standard.

Above all this stood the menacing, tall cliffs. And up there high in the mountains was a blue shimmer: Caravia, she had been told. The kingdom and home of the general who had killed her father.

Drums hammered and the salpinx blew. But then the tradition of war changed. Queen Harmonia, and another hundred riders, took off into the sky. Then Jaida ordered the foot soldiers, in a phalanx at the front, to march forward. In the clear blue sky, her mother formed lines even up in the clouds. And as her arrows fell, the terrible battle began. Arrows cut down countless soldiers in silver and blue. But then a far larger wave of arrows, more than Nephrea had ever seen, flew right back at them. Many nymphs beside her gasped as the sky rained arrows. And then many more cried out as Amazons and monokera fell like stones to their deaths.

Nephrea raised her hand and ordered her soldiers to start their march across the water. Her mother, as before, had already cleared the enemy from the other side of the river. Spears pointed in front, their shields above and to the sides, they marched slowly forward, first knee deep in water and then on dry land.

The enemy charge came, but it was more heard than seen or felt. It was so far in the front that it did not affect Nephrea's march. But she heard the whinnying of horses, a terrible clash of metal, and the screams of soldiers pierced by the long staffs of the phalanx. Then, as planned, she took off to lead her own small cavalry guard from above.

Up in the air Nephrea used her scope again to gaze at the battle at the base of the cliffs. Despite the slew of arrows, her mother kept strafing the valley. A spear entered the side of one of the queen's guards: Rose. Fortunately, they were close to the ground, and Rose's fall might not have been fatal.

Jaida rushed beyond the protection of the front line of her phalanx to help Rose. Then a huge burly man charged Jaida with two double-headed axes. Nephrea watched helplessly as Jaida turned her sword on the giant. Then two other blue-armored soldiers rushed Jaida with swords drawn. Other Imada soldiers left Harmonia to protect their chief general.

None of this was planned. But nothing in the first strike was going right anyway. For the first time, there were breaks in the Amazon war machine. Many of the enemy broke through their spears and shields and were fighting them hand to hand. Soon, as Jaida was still fighting a desperate battle with little support, the queen herself descended to help her. Ilia, her friend and expert at the bow who had the honor of fighting with her mother, was struck in the arm by an arrow. Fortunately, the arrow was deflected by the Mandrigel armor. But then a sword slid across Jaida's back. Finally, Ilia managed to carry Rose atop her unicorn and fly back to Nephrea's forces.

"The front needs our aid, Princess," cried young Dendera, flying beside Nephrea. "The phalanx is falling apart. We must rush forward to aid them. Why wait? She needs every one of us!"

"It is upon orders of the queen!" cried another guard. "We are ordered to stay back."

"But why? The line is broken!"

"We have to be able to retreat!" cried another.

Nephrea readjusted her helm, feeling stifled. She was sweating inside the helm, and sounds echoed from it. She hated it. Then she grabbed her eyepiece.

The battle on the ground was only getting worse. For the first time, there was a break in their military formation, and many soldiers were charging the queen and her guards. Her fierce Imada guard, being outnumbered, amazingly fought many more soldiers, but the force was nearly four times greater than hers. Harmonia continued to stubbornly hack at the resistance.

"Nephratee," cried Dendera again. "The front needs your support. You should order the unit—"

"It's not allowed!" said another guard. "Shut your mouth or you risk insubordination if you—"

"I am also Nephree's friend!" cried Dendera. Then Dendera flew to Nephrea and gazed into her eyes. "Your mother, Nephrea! Jaida! All the Imada. We have to provide support, Princess! We can't wait for their order. They need us now!"

Nephrea hit her leg hard. She did not disagree with Dendera. But a few other guards close by looked ready to shoot down Dendera for her disobedience.

Just when it looked like Harmonia would be either captured or killed, she climbed into the air again on Antilus. And then she did something very odd. She flew her Imada over the enemy and *away* from her army. She traveled past Jaida and her desperate front line, appearing to desert them.

Where are you going now, Mother?

Nephrea shook. Then her blue fingers lost their grip on her small eyepiece. She tried to grab it, but it fell from her grasp. Now she squinted as hard as she could, like Dendera.

"What are you doing, Mother!" Nephrea cried.

"What is it, Princess?" asked another nymph, hovering beside her. She hadn't even realized she was speaking out loud. "Is everything all right with the queen?"

Without an eyepiece, her guard probably could not make out what she had just seen. From here, her mother and her guard looked like insects flying off in the distance. But the destruction of half her red-armored front was visible enough.

"What is it, Princess?" asked Dendera.

Nephrea looked again and shook her head.

But then the strangest thing happened. A wave nearly as high as her unicorn came rushing down the Black River. The water was drowning all the soldiers in its wake who had been standing at attention along the shore. Such a wave forming from nowhere had to be the meddling of the infernal gods.

"Save all you can, Dendera!" cried Nephrea. "The gods are trying to force our advance to the enemy so that they can spear or drown us!"

HARMONIA FELT DESPERATE. Looking back at her army below, she saw that her war machine was finally stalled. This was the first battle where her sisters could not push forward. Her force was four thousand. Her enemy was likely twenty to thirty thousand. Indeed, the battle was hopeless. She knew, just as her daughter had told her, that the only answer now was surrender. But…what of Azerius?

As she held the neck of her unicorn, touching her feathery soft wings, she felt Antilus laboring in the air. Then she thought of her guard. The Imada soldiers accompanying her still numbered two hundred. From here, and with dwindled defenses, she might strike the city? Even if it meant certain death, couldn't she move up the cliffs for a final strike against Caravia from above!

She had never seen Caravia. For so many years, that bastard Azerius had promised that he would take her there. He never did. Today she could see it. Her army might be forced to retreat, but her guard could advance.

An arrow hit her lower right leg. Then another hit her unicorn, making Antilus quake and nearly fall. She strafed over the last lines of the enemy. Two more arrows struck Antilus. Crimson now flowed down her beloved unicorn's white hide. But soon, they flew too far to be reached.

"Where are we going, Your Majesty?" shouted Tyra, a prized sharpshooter.

"To the heart of the enemy, sister!"

Tyra's eyes opened wide and Harmonia caught a grin. Yes, even her guard wanted to finally bring the battle to their homes.

Her guards swarmed around her in the clouds. Antilus swooped up the steep cliff walls, and they followed a trail. Harmonia remembered it well, for on this wide dirt trail, a cavalry had once descended the cliffs with torches, bent on burning the "witch."

"We fight Caravia!" cried Harmonia, lifting her fist. And her guard cheered.

Harmonia glanced back at the valley below. She had to peer through smoke from the fire and ash. Through openings in the dark clouds, she saw all the fields now covered by fallen soldiers. Her phalanx was in shambles. No longer did her Amazon fight in order; they fought hand to hand. And she smelled the putrid iron and smoke, mixed with vomitus and excrement. The smell of war. And the water in the river and surrounding fields was soaked red. No…worse, the river was rising and as if the chaos of battle was not enough, a huge wave was forming, crashing over her foot soldiers in the rear. The gods were interfering again.

Tyra rushed beside her once more. For the first time, the young nymph looked afraid as she watched the flood below.

"Should we turn back?" cried Tyra. "Poseidon is flooding the rest of the army!"

Harmonia looked up and, at the cliff's summit, dirt roads converged on the main gates. She had never been this close.

Harmonia shook her head. Tyra bowed and signaled for the Imada to fly on.

Harmonia looked back. Four unicorns with the army's markings passed through the smoke. Runners. These were messengers, and they were flying fast, desperately trying to catch up to her Imada.

"Queen Harmonia! Queen Harmonia!"

They were frantic. But Harmonia and her Imada were near the summit, approaching the city gates. And as they came by air, this far into enemy territory, they met no resistance. She could easily pass through the gate in just another moment and invade Caravia.

"Queen Harmonia! The princess. Princess Nephratee. She's fallen."

LOGENTH AGAIN

UNDER THE FLICKERING TORCHLIGHT OF A LARGE HALL, QUEEN Harmonia stood vigil over her daughter. Nephrea's eyes were closed and she appeared tranquil. But every time she awoke, she winced and squirmed, closing her eyes tight. She seemed happier lifeless. Those who had seen her fall said she fell from a height that instantly killed all Amazons, from about the height of a five-story building. Yet, in a great irony, Poseidon had spared her life. Flooding water had cushioned her body. When the Amazon soldiers had recovered her, after a fall from that height, they were astonished she still breathed.

They had brought her to the main hall of Logenth—the former hall where the "lake witch" had once stood. Her entire army had retreated.

Now Nephrea lay on the wooden stage. Unlike in Karthra's time, only a handful of torches were lit. It was dark. Quiet. And Nephrea's eyes were closed.

"This is why I never let you lead the front," Harmonia said, her words barely audible but still reverberating. She touched her cold hand. "My love. My dearest treasure."

It was quiet, but Hades had entered the hall a while ago.

He was pacing by the door. And a hundred more nymphs were outside.

"I don't understand it," Hades said quietly, almost murmuring to himself. "Why would so many come to the aid of Caravians? Who cares for them? No one. But there are a lot of people who don't like you, I suppose. Not only on Olympus."

"The Caravians had help from your family," Harmonia said. It seemed to take all her energy to turn from her daughter. "Your brother drowned her."

"When is the last time your people gave libations to Lord Zeus, Queen Harmonia?"

"It was always only you."

"Just as Zeus betrayed me and sent me to the depths, he and my cursed family fights you," Hades said, approaching her. "But your army performed honorably. Why else has the enemy not pursued you? You retreated, but they haven't given chase... yet. Man fears you, Harmonia. For that, you've become my sharpest weapon. As I now live an eternity under the cold, dark earth, Zeus busies himself in the lives of men." He stood by her side and gazed down at Nephrea. "The future is Mycenea. Hellena. Not Atala. This future is for Greeks. Unfair? Of course it is." He turned her face toward him and ran his hand along her blue cheek. "Ah, poor Harmony, I shall make this up to you, my love."

"How?" she snapped. "You promised me Azerius's death. Now look what's been done."

"Who's to say you can't still have him?"

She furrowed her brow then turned back to her daughter.

"Bring the child goddess here," Harmonia said, touching her daughter's cold hand again. "Bring Kore. Nephree still lives. Heal my child before it's too late."

"From death?" Hades asked, shaking his head. "She is mortally wounded."

She gazed deep into his eyes and nodded. He squinted and raised a finger.

"A heavy price you'd pay for it. You'd never accept my sister's trade. She will destroy you."

"I will give anything for my Nephree to live."

"You won't." He shook his head and reached for her hand, but Harmonia snatched it away and turned from him. For the first time, she shed tears.

"No," she said, shaking her head. "You will do this for me. You will heal my Nephree out of your love for me."

"It's not in my power."

"*What is in your power?*" Harmonia spat. "Go away then! Come to gloat? Come when everything is lost! Where have you been? Did you wait for me to be defeated to finally see your *flower*? If you can't revive her, the only thing I have left, then you are useless! Go bury yourself back in dirt! How dare you come and offer me no solution, no reparation for this. If anyone deserved to live, it's my Nephratee. Not me. Certainly not you! Go! Get out of here." Harmonia stopped talking and pushed him. "*Get out!*"

But then she landed in his arms and wept. "Go." And the sound of her own crying echoing in the darkness only made her cry more.

"I can't," he said quietly in her ear, almost in a whisper. "Because I don't hold the power to revive her. Kore is Sara's daughter, the goddess you have forsaken. Your greatest enemy. I'd help if I could, but Sara will never help you."

She pushed him away gently. Then she stared down at her daughter.

"Then everything was for nothing."

"No," Hades said. "I cannot revive your daughter. But I can help you complete your quest. I can help you get your revenge."

She was surprised when he smiled. He took a deep breath and reached into his long black coat. He took out a small golden rod and laid it on her blue palm. She gazed with disgust at his hands in the flickering firelight. His fingernails were long and his hands worn and dirty, as if he had clawed out of the ground in order to see her. Just as his face had flecks of dirt. Indeed, he was a god of the depths now.

"Do you recognize this?" he asked quietly. "Do you remember when I last let you touch it?"

"Azerius's garden. To revive the flower."

Hades nodded. "It was a very long time ago, wasn't it? Once again, I need you to revive a flower. This time, *your* flower. I need you to revive your people." He closed her hand around the staff. "Here. This time not to touch, but to have. A present. One that comes well deserved for this most terrible fall. First your life, now your daughter's? For all this pain, I bequeath this to you."

"You're gifting your staff to me?"

"Take it."

She ran her blue fingers over the golden wand. She had forgotten how light it felt. It was made of solid gold with embedded diamonds and rubies. It was short, not much longer than her forearm. And it felt as light as a feather.

"My scepter," he said as she stared, "is now *your* scepter. Made for me by the hands of Hephaestus. Zeus has the golden thunderbolt, Poseidon the trident, and now you hold my staff."

"You're giving this to me?" she asked in amazement. "Are you serious? Why?"

She approached a torch and looked at it in the firelight. It seemed to glisten and become multicolored in the flickering light, not unlike a unicorn's horn.

"Every god holds something of our ancient power from the stars. Cronos once held the thunderbolt, before it was taken by Zeus. Poseidon controls the sea. Sara, with her witchy hands, the clouds and snow and the fate of the harvest. Her daughter, Persephone, the power of health and foreknowledge. This staff is my power. Its power is cold, Harmony. As it grows, utter the ancient words of the stars, *Eneich Aneu Loriaan.* It will give you the power of the most frigid snow. In my love, just as you say, I give you my gift to destroy. For only by fire and cold can life be born anew. It can freeze a pebble. A mountain. Or…my dear Amazon, it can ice an entire *army.*"

And as he said the last words, the staff elongated in Harmonia's hand. She dropped it in surprise, and it echoed as it fell on the ground. Then she snatched it up again. It was now a staff nearly the size of her body, but still as light as it had been before.

"Careful," he said with a smile. She waved it around in wonder in the air. "You are now the only mortal who wields the weapon of a god."

He walked over to her and embraced her, touching her cheek again. She let him this time. She didn't shed any more tears, she just let him hold her.

"You're right," he said softly. "You've been treated unfairly. For this, I gift you my greatest possession. You are my flower. You, not the staff, is what I choose to wield on Olympus."

But then she turned again to the stage where her daughter lay.

"Now that you have my staff, what will you do with it?" asked Hades.

"Eneich Aneu Loriaan," she said quietly. A cloud of white shot from the staff, and ice froze air before her. Then she turned and looked at him with suspicion. "Mine?"

"Amazon Queen, what you think of as a defeat is actually a great victory. You have singlehandedly brought your species out of the trees. Now you defeat all man. Your presence and your conquest shames and humiliates Theoi. You are my weapon. And you are my flower. Take this scepter and revive the Amazons. Freeze and burn man. Then plant their cities anew. After you take your vengeance, not only on

Azerius now, but for your daughter, rule our world with me."

He kneeled and gently kissed her lips. But behind him, she was still looking at her daughter.

"I shall take vengeance under your name," she said quietly. "But when I return, I ask that you bring me the child grain goddess. Bring me Kore so that she may revive *my flower*. Bring her so that my daughter may rule as princess again. She could still live."

Hades turned and gazed at Nephrea. He quickly nodded.

HER FLOWER GARDEN

SHE LEFT HER VIGIL. SHE COULD NO LONGER STAND IT. BUT she still saw Nephrea suffering in her mind. Even as she flew twenty leagues with her elite force of Imada back to the cliffs, slowly and stealthily scaling the walls of rock, she could still see her daughter squirm. Guards stood in blue by the wall, but they were none the wiser at her approach. Her elite force were the best warriors in Atala, and only the steady flap of wings would be noticed. Even their wings flew over unheard, easily passing the wall's defenses.

It was dawn. Merchants and peasants walked animals and carts beside thatched-roof houses and along flowing streams. Harmonia had not seen a city with so much order since the Fortress of the Mandrigels so many years back. She turned and gazed back at her cavalry. They stared down at poles lit with flames to light roads and cottages. Merchants were already readying their tents along the side streets, but it was dark enough this early in the morning to still need fire to fully light the broad streets.

She was spotted. Not by soldiers but by the townspeople, who lifted their hands and pointed. It was too late.

In the center of this city stood a large busy stone court-yard. The stone paths were arranged like spokes of a wheel, surrounded by green grass. And among the grass were large vases with flames. There were lovely red roses, lilies, and blue tulips planted around bushes in the grass. And noblewomen in long, elaborate peplos walked the stone roads from intersecting passageways and alleys leading from surrounding stone buildings. Others rode by carriage to this town center.

In the very center of this convergence was a large grass field. This was dead center in the entire kingdom, and a perfect place for Antilus to land. Before this stood a large stepped structure made of limestone and painted alabaster. In the afternoon sunlight, Harmonia imagined the building glowed. It was a ziggurat that Azerius had once explained was their temple to their gods. Somewhere by the temple still slept the royal family and, perhaps, King Tolen's brother Azerius.

Despite being early morning with the yellow sun still rising, the plaza was already crowded. And now with news of their approach, more townspeople were rushing over in curiosity—so peculiar and misunderstood was her method of invasion.

She heard gasps as she landed. Then she leaped to the very center of the green field, crouching down in an Amazon fighting stance. Alone, she brandished her enchanted gilded staff. It lengthened. That sent people running.

"Aieee!" she cried. "Aieee!"

Ten unicorns flapping their wings slowly descended beside her in the town center.

"Stay behind!" Harmonia said, cocking her head back. "Make a clearing so that I'm free to fire."

They obeyed and formed a tight circle, back to back, ordering the citizenry from the plaza to stay back, though many people surrounded them, watching in curiosity. In fact, their numbers grew, seemingly emboldening them to shout and throw stones at them. Some of her own soldiers in their polished scarlet moved back from the mob. Did her army believe they were trapped?

ALL GREW DARK. Harmonia found herself transported back to that dimly torchlit room. Now a tomb. Below her lay her daughter's body, writhing in pain.

"*AIEEE!*" cried Harmonia, shaking her head and opening her eyes wide. She waved the staff, and some of the citizens screamed in fright. "*Bitree! Bitree!*"

A soldier in blue armor rushed Harmonia with a sword. She twirled the scepter in her hand, and the enchanted sharp gold edge sliced his breastplate in two. Harmonia was surprised at how easily the tip cut through his armor. Then she plunged the staff deep into his chest. There were cries of shock, not only from the citizenry but from her guard.

"Stay back!" she warned her guards again. "Stay behind me, I tell you."

It was then that the salpinx blew. What great irony. The Caravians were gathering forces to march toward the center of the city, *away* from their city walls—something they assuredly had never planned for.

Harmonia turned to the cries of children screaming only a few yards off. A group of women clutched their children tightly, seeming to be in too much shock to run. Another group of men close by, in the finest purple robes with diamonds and rubies around their necks and shimmering golden bracelets, shouted at her. The faces of these nobles were adorned in lovely makeup. They were no doubt scented with the finest perfumes. This royal attire rightfully belonged to her. This was the affluence she had once been promised by her lover in the Shryer Valley of Trialga.

"Stand behind me!" Harmonia warned her guard, Arava, who was right beside her atop her unicorn.

Soldiers in blue armor started moving people back behind her flank. And in the distance, between buildings, an army of over a hundred were marching into the town center.

When the marchers came too close, she pointed her scepter in their direction:

"*Eneich Aneu Loriaan! Eneich Aneu Loriaan! Eneich Aneu Loriaan!*"

She froze all the soldiers in the front row. She heard the cries of women and children. Then she iced them too. A hundred people surrounding the Amazons instantly froze, becoming icy statues.

She heard gasps close by. They were not Caravians. All the men and women near her were dead. It came from behind her. Her Imada guard. And then…

The courtyard became very still. She looked at her Amazons, and they stared back. And then …

She laughed. It was the happy laugh of all nymphs. It was said that a nymph's laugh was endearing to man's ears in the games. It was said to be an utterance of pure joy. Today the sound of joy, before a hundred frozen leather-faced statues, was twisted, wicked, and cruel. Its pleasantness mocked joy. And what started as laughter became a great guffaw.

The queen walked to the closest woman. The iced woman wore an elegant peplos in dark purple, the most expensive dye in Atala. She wore long gold earrings and a lovely, ornate necklace, now icy blue. Icicles ran from her wide eyes and down her chin. Tiny icicles dangled from her ruby bracelets. And there was frost on her skin. She had crouched helplessly, trying to shield her daughter. Her daughter was frozen too.

Their eyes were disturbing. So afraid. With swift blows of her staff, their bodies shattered into pieces.

And she laughed some more.

Screams broke the silence. Many noblemen and women had witnessed the act and were now crying out in terror. But as Harmonia gazed around her, all she saw was motionless statues. It was as if these statues were emitting the cries, and it was unsettling.

The people left in the plaza, including the soldiers, now stampeded over each other, running from her, clawing, pushing, and shoving to escape.

Harmonia turned and saw Arava staring.

It was the sound of the Salpinx that made her finally lose her mirth. Then came the sound of their steps. Marching. The Caravian army had come, but the commanders remained by the outskirts of the great square.

Harmonia walked past the statues. She lurched back, startled, as a woman fell beside her and shattered to pieces on the ground. She walked east, where the sun had risen, passing frozen bodies, to another field, surrounded by columned stone buildings. A couple of hundred blue-armored soldiers entered the plaza.

"Rise in the air, Imada," Harmonia ordered. She whistled and mounted Antilus. "Leave your queen for the clouds."

"Your highness," objected a guard. "But you need our protection."

"Their army is marching, my queen," said Arava. She bowed deeply over her unicorn. "I think we should abandon the city for safety."

"I will remain, Arava, until I find their general," Harmonia replied.

"Their general?"

Harmonia turned. Arava spontaneously reeled back from her expression.

"Rise into the air and protect your queen in the clouds! Obey me now!"

Harmonia trotted by more frozen bodies until she sat atop Antilus before their army.

"I ask for King Tolen," Harmonia shouted. "Bring your king and his brother to me. Bring them to me and my destruction will end!"

"You're outnumbered! We demand your surrender, witch!"

"I claim this land," Harmonia shouted back. "All that surrender, I spare. Those that stand against me will forever chill. Like your false god, Thesmophoros, witness cold death if you defy Queen Harmonia Ambrosia."

The salpinx blew again in response. And the front line of soldiers crouched down, readying their bows.

"I have a hundred archers pointing arrows at you, ice witch! Surrender now or you will die."

Harmonia dismounted Antilus. Antilus neighed and jerked, shaking her head as if objecting like her guards, but Harmonia hit her unicorn's butt with her palm, gesturing for the unicorn to fly off.

"Bring me King Tolen!" cried Harmonia, walking briskly to the front line. "General Azerius and his brother! Bring them to me now or I shall kill everyone in the city!"

When it was clear they wouldn't obey, she did not speak the incantation—she thought it. That was enough. Just as before, perhaps with even greater fury, her staff blew out a gale of ice toward the rows of soldiers. But she found she could control the flurries. She willed the ice to hit whatever archer she chose. In seconds the entire front line was frozen solid about a hundred yards before her.

The army lost all reason. Hundreds rushed to the front to help their companions. Then, as before, the army's wails could be heard as they tended their fallen.

"Bring me your king or I will take every other soldier in the city!"

A hundred arrows were launched into the air. These were

not from the front; they were from behind. All these arrows were aimed solely at her. She waved her staff before her, freezing the blades midair. Every blade fell in front of her like hail.

The army charged. Thousands of foot soldiers raised swords and shields and rushed her. At this point, it was possible they had never been given the order to charge. Indeed, behind all the shouting, she saw men who looked like commanders trying to corral some of them back. With a wave of her staff, she froze them too. Hundreds of soldiers froze in running position, adding more specimens to her grotesque sculpture garden. The ice spread unevenly. Some did not die. Some were mutilated, losing frozen limbs.

She did not stop and would have smitten every single one of them if it had not been for a rider in a black linen robe, who wore a black cloth wrap and a gilded crown upon his head and gold chains about his neck. A blue Caravian flag was draped over his saddle. The man had a thick gray beard and short curly brown hair. His penetrating eyes looked about him with wisdom and curiosity, like her daughter—or worse, like her former lover. Beside this rider were five others on equally ornate steeds.

The soldiers dispersed to make way.

Harmonia whistled and signaled to Imada to come down.

General Azerius was with the king. Now old and weathered, her archenemy sat on horseback beside his brother. He had a gray beard too, but with the same cold, emotionless expression as on that fateful day when he came to kill her and her daughter.

"That's far enough," said Harmonia. She nodded to her Imada. The Amazons dismounted and led the men off their horses. They tied their hands behind their backs with rope. Then the men were forced to kneel before the Azure queen. But Azerius looked up, challenging her gaze.

"You are the Azure queen?" King Tolen asked.

"She is," Azerius said, beside him, on his knees. "This is the *witch* of Crystal Lake."

"I am Queen Harmonia Ambrosia, the Azure queen, King Tolen." She smiled down at Azerius and he squirmed. "I've become acquainted with your spies over the years. Never with the courage to reveal themselves. Of course, some of your people know me. Your brother in particular."

"Witch!" Azerius cried, spitting at her. "You murder an entire race and now freeze a city!"

She had never seen him so angry. She loved it. It made her smile more.

She hopped off her unicorn and held her scepter before his eyes. Those curious eyes. She could cut them out. Slowly, one at a time.

"Come here, my love, so that we may embrace."

She ran the scepter along his cheek. Azerius did not freeze, but his skin paled and shone with a tint of blue. Then one eye watered terribly and he could not close it. His whole body began to shake.

"Arrogant man," she said, as whirled puffs of freezing white air surrounded his head. "Was I an embarrassment to you? Your nymph lover? A disgrace to your Court?"

"Leave the king," Azerius said, shuddering. "That is all I ask." He squinted his eyes hard, finally managing to close them, but tears continued to flow. He couldn't brush them away, for his hands were tied behind his back. "This is between you and me. It doesn't concern my brother."

"But it was his order to kill our daughter, wasn't it?" Harmonia asked, gesturing to the king. "I believe he's more guilty than you."

"Don't kill any more people over a squabble between me and you, Harmony."

"A squabble? A squabble? Is this—" She gestured to the courtyard. "A small family dispute, little man? Aren't you aware that you're at war with my Amazons? Do you not know that Caravia is Azurea's greatest enemy? You attempted to kill my daughter in Trialga. Wasn't it enough to try to burn her and me by your tree?"

"I searched for her, Harmony," he said. He was still squinting and shook from cold. "I looked all over Egypt. I wanted her back. Why would I hunt Nephrea? I wanted my daughter to return to me."

"To burn?"

"To raise as royalty," Azerius said, shaking his head. "I had done you wrong. I thought I could mend the past with her."

"What's all this about?" asked the king.

"As if you didn't know," she replied. "Your puppy protects you. He knows his only defense is your order. Are you not the one who ordered his army to burn the witch and her daughter to protect your family from disgrace? Do you deny this? Azerius's illegitimate daughter? My Nephrea?"

"I don't know what you're talking about."

"The affair," Azerius blurted.

"This is the nymph?" Tolen asked in shock. "The nymph at your villa?"

"Do you deny your order, King?" repeated Harmonia. "Do you deny that you sentenced his lover and her daughter to death? Because we were Amazon nymphs?"

The king grew an arrogant smile and said, "Madam, I don't speak of my orders to women."

Harmonia's eyes widened. Her whole body shook in rage. She raised her scepter and swung it at his face. The cold metal shattered his flesh, and shards of the king's skin fell onto the ground. He screamed in pain.

"Leave him alone, Harmonia!" shouted Azerius. "Please! The king is innocent!"

"No," Harmonia said, turning to Azerius. "He killed thousands of my sisters. He's not innocent, my love."

"If you came to kill me, then do it! But leave my brother. Please, leave him and my people out of this!"

"Such loyalty, my love," she said with a smile. "I respect that." And she meant it. She always respectably loathed him.

"Don't say *love*. There's no love between you and—"

"Immaterial. You two are now prisoners," she said, turning from him. She began pacing. "I'll decide what form of justice befalls you. I believe—"

She was interrupted by the sound of an arrow rushing through the air, fired by one of her guards. It contacted a soldier a hundred yards away, on the third floor of one of the stone buildings—likely a Caravian sniper trying to kill her.

"We have seen your 'justice,'" remarked the king, panting. "We have heard of your treatment of King Karthra."

"He's better now, isn't he?" she asked with a chuckle.

"You are a witch," the king said.

"I am emperor of Atala," Harmonia said. "Zeus holds Argos in Mycenae, I now hold all of this continent. You two do not need to kneel before me in order to accept defeat. Your defeat is incontrovertible. You two bow before me so that I may pass judgment on you. And it is not a question of death, but how the deed shall be done."

"Just leave the king, Harmony," Azerius said. "Please. If you must know, I arranged everything that night. He had nothing to do with your execution. I planned the whole thing."

"Liar. How am I to believe that? I suspect you're simply doing your job, Azerius. Protecting your king to your last breath… What say you, King?"

King Tolen II looked up. He gnashed his teeth again. "You are correct. I ordered the execution of you and your blue abomination. Azerius had little to do with it. He was a fool falling in love with you. You've destroyed him, his reputation, just as you have now come to destroy me."

She swung the scepter again. Bits of frozen muscle from

the king's cheek fell to the ground. Even her Imada guard gasped at the act. There were shouts from the Caravian army across the field, now standing at attention in the distance.

"*Leave him alone!*" shouted Azerius. "*By the gods, I beg you!*"

"*There are no gods, Egyptian aper! Only two sovereigns: Lord Aidoneus, and his lover, Harmonia Ambrosia, emperor of Atala, Amazon queen, and ruler of Caravia!*"

The king squirmed on the ground, unable to clutch his face, which now bled profusely. Azerius tried desperately to aid him, but one of the nymphs stopped him at the point of a spear.

"Is something wrong with your king?" Harmonia asked Azerius, chuckling. "He seems to be in distress. Perhaps I can help him?"

"Please, Harmony. No. I beg you!"

She removed her sword from its sheath, kicked Azerius to the ground, and put the blade right beside his face.

"Do you know what this is?" It was his sword, taken by her on that fateful day when she fled from his villa. "I brought it for this very occasion, my love. To kill your brother."

She plunged the blade deep into the king's chest. His guards, though tied, moved to help him but were quickly corralled back by the Imada. The king toppled over onto the ground, and a hundred cries were heard from soldiers and bystanders outside the stone buildings and in the distance.

Azerius fell upon his dead king, his brother, weeping.

The army could not be held back from their commanders. They charged on horseback or even on foot.

Harmonia leaped on Antilus and began to rise in the air. Then she turned to the approaching soldiers, holding her scepter aloft. It lengthened before the enemy once more. Azerius, even as he wept over the death of his brother, shouted for his army to stand back. It was too late. Once more, Harmonia froze every offender. When it was done and the general's yard was covered in more frozen bodies,

Harmonia trotted over to Azerius, who now held the slain king.

"Take this man," Harmonia shouted to Arava. *"Tie him to a tree! Then burn him before our lovely new flower garden."*

"Burn him?" asked Arava. "Burn him, Your Majesty?"

Azerius wasn't listening. He continued to clutch his brother, weeping.

"Take sticks and leaves," Harmonia said contemptuously, as if she had to provide instructions, "and build a pyre. Then rope his body to a pole over logs in the town center. Let the kindling mix with the body of his brother, the king, until it is all engulfed in flames under their unholy temple. When he is ash, scatter his remnants to the wind. We have to sacrifice the witch. Do we not?"

"No, my queen," sputtered Arava bowing before her. "I mean …yes…yes, my queen."

"But before you do," Harmonia said, putting a finger to her chin. "Find Lady Ila, the villain's wife. Find his children." Azerius finally raised his head. His eyes were bloodshot with tears. He seemed perplexed, as if confused by her words. "Make certain that you burn his family too. Let the general experience what it feels like to lose everything he holds dear. All the love, let it scatter to the wind, in the same fashion he arranged for our beloved daughter."

"Don't do this," Azerius pleaded. "Please, Harmony."

"Now don't be weak," said Harmonia, wagging a finger at him. "I was never weak. Once I walked with my love, the great General Azerius, and I waited for him to burn me by the oak tree. I will be just as merciful and quick as you offered to be that night. He offered me the gift of a swift execution, Arava. I, too, am merciful. You'll be torched quickly. I promise."

"I beg you. Do not touch Lady Ila and the children. Don't."

She dismounted from Antilus and gazed into his eyes. "Why?"

"They're guiltless. Do what you wish to me but leave them."

"The woman, Ila, I doubt she is guiltless."

"Don't do this. You will suffer for it, Harmony."

Even now, despite having killed thousands of his men, tortured him, and slain his king, she felt as if he was not just threatening her, but genuinely warning her. For a flash, she felt that old attraction for him. His tears were not shed out of fear —no, not from this brave man, the bravest she had ever known—but out of remorse for his people and his king. But this realization burning inside her stoked her fire with even more fury.

"*Who would dare punish a god?*" she cried, turning her back on him and gazing at her guard. "Any nymph who lacks the stomach to carry out my decree, Arava, kill her! We are Imada. And I remind you that, upon Imada's sworn duty, though our sisters may hear of my glory, not one of you shall speak of anything you witnessed on the plaza this morning, punishable by death. No one will say a word. Especially to my daughter. Do you understand?"

"Yes, my lord."

"Yes," said another.

"But...Harmony," said Arava, "the princess has surely passed."

"*What!?*"

"She...the princess is, Nephrea, is... I mean, yes, by your order."

"Get the pyre and do it quickly, but be merciful. Run a sword through Azerius before he burns. He once promised his lover the same mercy."

"Harmonia!" said Azerius. "Please, I don't care about me, but spare my family!"

"Are you begging?"

"By the gods, yes, I beg for my wife and children! Yes. I beg you. My wife and children! Please spare them!"

She stood over him and examined him with her eyes.

"Very well. In memory of our love, you shall find that the Amazon queen is merciful. She was given the blessing of a child herself, and I understand your love for them." She turned to Arava again. "Execute the Lady Ila but Nephrea's sisters may be spared."

"What of his sons?"

"That is all." Then she looked down for the last time at her former lover and said, "My will be done."

4 0

MOURNING

Harmonia sat atop her throne with her chin on her fist, staring out at the empty throne room in the Crystal Palace. Not one subject, no one, was in the hall. No one dared. She stared forward into empty space. Even the torches had not been tended, and it was darker than ever as night fell. It was, fittingly, raining and the water dripped along the crystal dome above. It was quiet. Except that far from the throne room, echoed by the empty walls of her hall, she heard crying. Now her people cried not only over the thousands of nymphs who had died in the battle for Trialga; now they cried over the death of the princess. Her daughter. The princess, who was loved by her people far more than she had ever been.

She didn't dare look to her left. In her periphery, she could see the outline of a body. Lying upon a simple wooden board was the body of her daughter. She had been told the body had turned lifeless in Shadow Forest during transport from Logenth. But there had not yet been a funeral, for Harmonia still had hope that the young grain goddess could revive her. But how? She had committed the greatest hubris of all time.

The double doors opened. Jaida bowed hesitantly and let in a giant of a man in a black cloak. His steps echoed as he walked down the central aisle of the hall. Then Hades bowed before her.

"It is good to see you," Hades said. His voice echoed.

"Get out."

Hades walked over to the body, removed his gloves, and dared to do what she couldn't do again. He looked down upon her daughter.

"Unfortunate," he said. "She was a mighty soldier. Much like yourself. A very brave woman."

"Have you come to revive her? Did you bring Kore?"

"You know I can't do that."

"Then get out." But she repeated the words weakly, as if she lacked the strength.

Her Amazon Court smelled of fresh flowers and jasmine. She hated that. Those were funerary scents. And Nephrea's body was ornamented in gold necklaces and braids and dressed in a long formal azure dress. Her black hair, always slightly wavy, was tied back. Upon her chest lay her Mandrigelian iron sword and shield. She looked neat and proper, like a knight sleeping. There was no sign of her broken spine from the fall. Her shattered skull and legs. Or her lungs, no doubt scarred by her efforts to breathe in the flooding waters of the Black River. Her eyes were closed. She appeared tranquil. This was how she had appeared, anyway, when Harmonia had first entered the room. She hadn't looked since.

"It's your fault," Harmonia muttered.

Hades looked surprised. "What?"

"This is what your weapon, your flower, has accomplished. I conquered Atala, not with my bare hands as men have whispered, but with your staff. I've destroyed my people with my hubris. And now my hubris has killed my daughter. My daughter lies dead as a symbol of your failure. How dare I challenge your family? The gods have taken their revenge. Lord Zeus knew exactly how to hurt me."

"The Crystal Palace is unharmed," Hades said, shaking his head. "There are still a great many of your warriors who can fight. Your Amazon army is strong. And now every single man in Gaia is terrified of you. No, you've completed your quest. You are greater now than you have ever been."

She finally looked at him. Then she said in a broken voice, "Stay away from me."

"Now don't be weak," he said, raising a finger. His hand closed in a fist. "I gave you an instrument to take all of Gaia. You still have everything you've ever wanted. Ever since you ran in the forests, all you've ever wanted was to rule the world. Now you do. You rule a great kingdom and are emperor of Atala. What did you expect? Indeed, you took my staff and terrorized Caravia, crushing an entire empire singlehandedly. Do you not think my brother takes offense? Do you have any idea what I had to do to prevent my brother from striking you down with a bolt of lightning?"

"Striking me down would have been merciful."

Hades laughed. "Ah, Harmony, you have to brush this off. Have a respectable funeral for your beloved warrior daughter then move on. Honor her with a great marble statue. Perhaps plan a yearly festival. In a century, perhaps—"

"I will say this once," the queen said, finally meeting his gaze. "If you do not leave my Court, Hades, I shall fight you myself. Get out of my throne room. I don't love you. And I am no longer your friend. First you murdered my family, then you used me as a weapon for your own gain, for *your* Imada. Nothing you ever gave me was for anyone but yourself. I hate you. But I love my Nephrea. She meant everything to me. She's the only thing I ever cared about. And now she is…"

"That's not what I remember. Perhaps I err, but didn't you abandon Nefertiti in Egypt as a child?"

"By your order."

"And then you asked on your death bed for her to return simply so that you could have an heir. You didn't know her.

You don't love her. You love the idea of her. Your heart can't love anything. You are queen and absolute ruler of Gaia. Witness what you did in Caravia! You're ruthless. My dear child, *you are Imada.* You're now known by man, everywhere in the entire world, as the Ice Queen. Your reputation spans Mycenae and beyond, even beyond territories you cannot fathom. You are a terror that was born to inflict pain on man. My champion. This is what you are, and this is what you've always been. You're my answer to Zeus's arrogance. To Cronos. To my family. You mock the crumbling, incessant, violent, unjust, falling mockery of order that man calls society. Even as my family oppressed yours, you stood naked before the gods and met my sister's gaze. I knew then that there was no one with more courage than you. Ah, Harmonia, you're my favorite of all mortals. You've been slapped for your omnipotence, sure—but how is this any different from before? The thing of it is, you always rise to fight again. Like your phoenix. You are an eternal Ambrosia. And now you hold my staff."

"*Take it back! Your bird, your scepter, your kingdom! Take it all back!*" She jumped up and walked behind her throne. She brought out the scepter and pushed it into his chest. "This is evil. At first, it gave me power. I felt as a god. Now I blame it for everything. Take it and get out of my sight! The horror it brought me disgusts me!"

"It's too late, my love," he said, shaking his head.

She shoved it against his chest again. For the first time, Hades' eyes flickered red.

"Careful. You are not the only one who's suffered. I gave up my station beside my brother at the very top of Olympus for you. I was banished into the depths, Harmony, for you. I've suffered. For you. Do not stand here and act as if you have a choice in allegiance. We're bound together. Your arms have always been open to every gift I've given you. Antilus, your army, your monokera, your Crystal Palace, and every other gift I gave you offered an affront to the king of gods himself, Zeus. There has never been deception by me. It was never something you didn't yourself desire."

"But I never asked for any of these things! You gave them to me in order to use me. All to make me your weapon. But I see now that you're just a man. Like Azerius. And I've been your slave."

"*My slave!*" he shouted. He turned his back on her and walked down the aisle, gesturing at the great hall with open arms. "*My slave?* Look around you, *slave!* Perhaps *I'm your slave?* Look at what a god's gifted you. There is not a mortal in this world that has been given more. If you want to see a slave, I can take you to my home that lies now under the dirt. That's my lot. That's my sacrifice. For you! There you'll find true slaves. Dwarfs. They are slaves. From our conquest.

"No, Harmony, you're free, freer than any soul I know. And all your enemies shake before you now. Even me, a god, shakes before you. Even my family. Even my brother. My sister. Your actions in Caravia have made you the most powerful force in this world. And now you have your dream. Take Argos. Take Hellena. Be the emperor of the entire world. And with all the justice that my brother lies about, there will be nothing his justice can do to stop you!"

The red in his eyes faded. He walked to a black column by a window. Beside it was a statue. He touched the porcelain as if admiring the work. It was a life-size statue of a man crafted by a nymph's hand. The statue was naked, carrying a sword and shield—more like dropping the sword.

"Such artistry," Hades said with a laugh. "This is how your people envision man? I see…" he put a hand on his chin in thought. "You mock man's strength. And I see now that you see *me* like this. For I am a man. Yes? And yet you hate men? Well, who or what do you not hate, Azure Queen?"

"Nephrea," she breathed.

She approached the body of her daughter for the first

time. "It's over, Aidoneus. I'm finished. Everything was for her. It's all over."

"I gave you everything because I love you," he breathed beside her.

"Leave me. Go away and leave me alone with my dead daughter."

"I can tonight," he said gently, almost carefully, touching her shoulder. "But I shall return when your mourning is over. Then we can discuss the next advance in the West."

41

AMBROSIA

HARMONIA DID NOT TELL HER PEOPLE OF HER DEPARTURE. NOT even her best friend, Jaida. She took the body of her daughter upon Antilus alone and flew to faraway lands never seen before by any nymph from Azure Blue. She made a long and arduous flight to the west that lasted an entire day. She reached a group of islands she had once visited for a short while when, like now, she felt as if her entire world had ended. The journey was very hard on Antilus. They stopped on the great island of Minoa for a short while, but then they were off again.

She had learned that Demeter lived in Mycenae in the land of Argos. So she followed a path laid out by an ancient Mandrigelian map scribed on papyrus centuries ago. She had told her daughter once that she had been to Argos but, in truth, she wasn't sure if she had landed on Argos or another isle.

Only when she had come upon the ruins of a white marble temple did she figure that, perhaps, she had reached Sara's home. For Mycenae was the land of imitation, where it is said the gods had taught man to imitate the structures of their Olympian haven.

She landed by the temple ruins, untied her daughter's body, and laid it gently on the rocky ground. Then she tied Antilus to a stone column.

Clad in her scarlet armor, she searched the beaches and shores for any sign of the gods. Finally, when she heard a girl's giggle among desolation, she figured again she had chosen the right path. She followed the laughter. In a clearing in the woods, further away from the shore, she saw a young girl with messy long blond hair, as yellow as the sun, running through the grass.

"Persephone," cried Harmonia. "Persephone. Cora, I must speak with you."

The girl shook her head, laughing harder.

Harmonia chased the grain goddess through bushes and trees until they finally entered yet another clearing near an olive grove. White columns stood among the green grass. Here, they were not ruins. They were in perfect condition, surrounded by green vines and vibrant multicolored flowers. Cora stood here in her ragged scarlet dress kneeling before the columns, out of breath, trying to contain her laughter.

"Come here to die, nymph?" the little brat said.

"Harmonia," said Sara from behind.

Harmonia whirled around. There, in a flowing, shimmering alabaster peplos, the goddess Demeter glided toward her. Yellow light reflected from Sara's white dress. Her face oddly held a welcoming smile. "We meet again, Amazon Queen, ruler of the nymphs. What brings the butcher of man to my home?"

"My daughter, my lord. I ask that your daughter, Persephone, heal her."

"I know."

"Strike her down, Mother!" Cora snapped, losing her smile. "She's a stupid nymph who attacks Father's people. An enemy of Olympus!"

"Wait, Daughter," Sara said, turning with her honey-sweet

smile. "You must learn to listen before you act. The naiad has traveled far and deserves to be heard."

But the little shaggy blond stuck her tongue out at Harmonia. Then Cora said, "And where is the body of your dear dead daughter?"

Harmonia squinted and touched her scabbard.

"Join us for déjeuner here in my villa, Harmonia. There we may deliberate."

She gestured to the open field, and a dozen more stone columns appeared. The columns seemed to distort the air between them, distortions in the shape of walls. It was a home of see-through walls that beautifully blended in with the flowers, grass, and trees. But a gold couch and chairs with a marble table covered with a feast of delicacies—figs, meat, apples, pears, cheeses, and bread—materialized too. And a glass pitcher of white wine.

"You've traveled far and must be hungry?" Sara said, gesturing to the wooden table.

"Yes, my lord," said Harmonia.

"But ..." Sara abruptly turned as they passed a cloudy wall, "do not say '*lord*.' Let's be honest, wood nymph, shall we? You've spent a lifetime forsaking me. Do not start now when you are desperate. It seems…phony." Her words were sharp, but her tone was still as sweet as honey.

Harmonia sat on a gilded chair across from Cora and Sara. She reached for a fig, but Cora's hand passed before hers and snatched it. Then the little girl took it into her mouth, glaring at her. Cora's eyes flickered red as she bit into the fruit. Harmonia reached again and picked up some red grapes. As she bit into them, she found them to be the best grapes she had ever tasted. Then she grabbed some bread and cheese. Cora reached over Harmonia again, practically shooing her hands away, and took the food from her hands. Then she brushed her long golden-blond hair back and leaned on an elbow, eating while scowling at her.

"I'm happy to have found you," Harmonia said.

"Yes," Sara said, "that is an achievement. Just as your entire life has been quite an achievement. You've done amazing things. Starting in the trees and finishing as a butcher of man."

"I can kill her now, Mother," Cora said with her mouth full. She stared at Harmonia and smiled wickedly again. "If you'd permit me, I can slay this nymph before you. I think even the thought could smash her weak, puny skull."

"I'm sure you can, Persephone," said Sara with a chuckle. "But please, the nymph queen is our guest."

"She is our enemy just as you said Uncle is our enemy. Why break bread with her when you want her as dead as I do."

"You have to forgive my daughter," said Sara with a chuckle. "She's grown up alone. She doesn't hide her feelings well, nor know manners."

"Well, I won't help her," Cora scoffed, folding her arms. "Whatever she offers. I don't want to feel the pain again, Momma."

"Shut your mouth, deisa," snapped Sara. "You're here for me to watch over you, not to partake in this delegation. Stay quiet or leave."

"Humph." Then Cora folded her arms and plopped down on a rug beneath them. She grabbed an old wooden horse and started moving it along the ground.

"You wish my daughter to revive her?" Sara asked.

"No!" cried Cora. "I won't do it!"

Sara closed her eyes tight and rubbed her forehead. She heaved a long sigh and sipped some white wine from a crystal glass as her hand shook. Then she forced another fake smile. "Why should I put Cora through that again?"

Cora glanced up from her wooden horse and squinted at Harmonia. "How's your back?"

Harmonia put her food down on the table. "All I have, all

I am, is my daughter. I will give you anything for Nephratee's life if you return her to me."

"I can't give her to you. But…I may be able to give her to your people. To Azure. How long has she been dead?"

Harmonia was distracted again by the strange girl. Cora was singing while she played with the wooden figure of a horse. Cora lifted the toy over her head, as if the horse were gliding through the air, like an Amazon unicorn. The words the girl sang were morbid. It was an odd dirge about dirt and dust. A funeral dirge. Was the girl mocking her? She was wicked enough.

"Two days," Harmonia replied.

"Two days," Sara said. Then she drank some wine. "That's a long time. The body decays fast. But perhaps not too long. What will you offer me for such an act? What can you give me in return?"

"I will give you whatever you ask of me."

"Whatever I ask? I doubt that."

"Don't know why you don't just strike her down, Mother," quipped Cora, still flying her wooden horse in the air. "We'd be clear of two nymph rulers, instead of one."

"My death would mean the continued conquest of Gaia by the Amazon," Harmonia replied to Cora. Sara squinted, but then her fake smile returned. "I would be a martyr."

"But you witnessed the defeat of your army before your tantrum," Sara replied. "Your people are too few to take on the world now."

"Not with your brother's scepter."

"If I kill you," Sara argued pointedly, "your people will not be strong enough to lead. Particularly, as Cora says, without you *and* your daughter. Perhaps Kore is right. Perhaps I should simply slay you now."

"The scepter belongs to the ruling Ambrosia family. The next Azure queen in line will come across it and wield it. Jaida will simply move south into Atala, then Egypt and Hellena, with a force more bent on revenge than ever if they hear of my death."

"But there will be no Azure queen if you and the princess die."

"If I die, Jaida will rule and will wield the scepter as an Ambrosia. It has already been arranged."

"Listen to you!" Sara snapped with disgust. "*Ambrosia.* What absolute arrogance you and my brother hold. You use the name of a god's sustenance to describe your people!"

"It was given to me by—"

"I know who gave it to you. My brother's an idiot. You are a lowly nymph that I could crush with my fingernail. I tell you what. You've received the grace of being in a god's house and have yet to bow before me. Bow to me now in greeting as is proper. Bow to me now and I might forget your first offense this evening. And then I'll forgive your lapse of—"

"No." Harmonia squinted at Sara and shook her head. "No. No. I will never bow to anyone again."

Cora's eyes bulged. She looked back and forth between her mother and Harmonia. Sara's eyes shone red, so red that they lit Harmonia's face. And then her stupid little daughter, Cora, burst into laughter. "Why she's funny, Mother!"

"I am Aidoneus' inamorata," Harmonia said. "Take me. I offer my life as sacrifice to revive my daughter. The Amazons can retreat to Azurea and Zeus can have peace. Then you may gloat over my dead body and Hades' loss. I offer my life, if you revive my daughter's. That is all."

"Again, what makes you think I can't have both you and your daughter?"

"Aidoneus."

Sara smiled. Not a kind smile, a sinister, wicked grin that sent a shiver down Harmonia's back. "You delegate as if you're a goddess. There's never been one more arrogant than you, Harmonia."

"You don't have a choice," Harmonia said with a nod. "My sacrifice will please Zeus. It should please you."

Sara shook her head slowly. "Not after what you did in Caravia. Perhaps if the nymphs abandon Napea? Will you offer this and give me your Crystal Kingdom as well? If you relinquish control of the Isle of Napea, perhaps then I might yet offer your daughter's life."

Harmonia jumped up. She looked up at the clouds. It was an easy thing to do, for Sara's "villa" had no ceiling. It was a pleasant, cool day. She seemed to stare at the azure sky for a moment in thought. Then she looked down and shook her head.

"No, I can't," she said finally, sitting back down. "I've lived my whole life vowing to make what was wrong right. I can't take away what I've given to my people. That would be equal to Nephrea's death. My kingdom, I can't give to you. Even for my daughter, who I love more than any other."

"Queen indeed," Sara said, sipping more wine. "As much as you're my greatest enemy, I respect you." And then Sara raised a glass in a toast to her. Harmonia had not touched the wine, as if she worried it was poison but, with the goddess's gesture, she couldn't help but toast back.

"I will give you anything, Sara, anything. But never Azurea."

"You refuse to bow. Now you refuse to give me your isle. Really, you don't offer me anything but yourself. Just as you have done your entire life, you focus only on one thing. Yourself."

"No different from you, Thesmophoros."

Sara's eyes bulged, furious. They flickered red.

"May I kill her *now*, Mother?" asked Cora.

"*Shut up, Kore!*" Sara snapped. Then she wagged a finger at Harmonia. "What you did in Caravia, Azure Queen, is inexcusable. It was a direct attack on not only man, but the gods. Using the scepter meant a change in the balance of power that, if not checked, could mean the end of Zeus's most beloved creatures—man. Such a weapon makes your people unstoppable. Luckily for you, in Zeus's glorious kindness, he didn't destroy your palace. Nor did he strike you down with lightning."

"That must have only been due to the will of my god."

"You pompous, imperious idiot! No god cares of your business!"

Harmonia raised a hand. "Sara, forgive me, but that's a lie."

"A lie!"

"You said my attack on Caravia was an attack on the gods. That is a lie too. It was a god who helped me fight and bring the continent to its knees. It is my lover, Hades, who gave me the scepter. I was his instrument. In many ways, my conquest of Caravia was by your brother, not me."

"You cross the line, naiad."

"Your family set me up. Hades has been on my side from the beginning. It was a god who exterminated the Mandrigel as I slept. And now it is a god who helped me decimate the Caravians. It was your brother who propped me up. Your brother, who wouldn't even want me to speak with you now."

"Go on, mortal," Sara said with sudden amusement. "Speak more hubris. You think you have no free will, child?"

"You Olympians have caused my ruin. It was you who held me back for years from taking the Mandrigels' fortress. Then Poseidon who drowned Nephrea. Just as I told you when we first met that I did not cause the battle upon our river. No, I am not to blame for Caravia, Sara. You are."

Sara had been listening to her as if she had been putting on a play. But not after those last words. Her face darkened, her sweetness altered, and her eyes no longer flickered. They shone red like fire, illuminating her whole face.

"*How dare you!*" Sara shouted.

Cora recoiled in terror, losing her infernal smugness. The

little girl ran through an invisible wall out into the adjoining field.

Sara raised her hand over Harmonia's head. Harmonia did not wince; she sat staring up at her, awaiting her death. But she was not struck. Instead, Sara waved her hand over the table. The food and glasses violently flew from the table. "I could take your life so fast, but I believe you need to suffer yet!"

"Wait, I didn't want this," Harmonia said, raising her hand. "I speak my mind. I—"

"You are a stupid lowly wood nymph. You don't *mean* anything in your small, stupid little head. You don't speak to a god unless spoken to. No one is quarreling, for if they were, you would have been struck down to ash!"

"Yes, my lord."

"I do not want to hear *'my lord' from your lips! It is a mockery, nymph!*"

So Harmonia said nothing.

She thought Cora had disappeared, but then she spotted the little girl right outside the columns by a bush. Her whole body was shaking. Harmonia had expected the witch brat to be laughing at her again. Instead, Cora was crouched holding her knees, shaking due to her mother's rage.

Sara glanced over too. Then Sara laughed. Her laughter was far more terrible than her rage. "Ah, Harmony, but you entertain Kore. Good! Well done. Come, look up into my eyes again. Challenge me again, as you've always done since the day you were born. I'll pretend your insult never crossed my ears."

"They crossed mine," Cora quipped.

"*Shut up!*" Sara shouted.

"You can have anything, Demeter," said Harmonia, looking up into the god's eyes. "Anything except Azure."

"And this and that." Sara gesticulated. "And a great many other things I cannot have from you. Very well. So be it. No more negotiation. I shall have you then." She reached over the table. Another pitcher of wine and two crystal glasses appeared on the table. Then she poured more white wine into the glasses. "Give me the one thing you hold dearest. Give me yourself. Give that to me. If you make that supreme sacrifice, your greatest treasure, I shall grant you your request. Your daughter shall be reborn. That, along with, indeed, my brother's suffering over your death, shall satisfy Lord Zeus and Olympus. To uphold the agreement, now swear to me. Swear to me and it shall be done. Raise your hand and repeat the following words: *Demeter, daughter of Cronos and Rhea, I forfeit the shield of Aidoneus, my love, in sacrifice for my daughter, Nephratee Ambrosia. As I die, my daughter shall be reborn.*"

"*Demeter, daughter of…*"

"*NO!*" Cora shouted, running up to her. "*Mother. NO! I won't do it! You can kill her anyway. Forget her daughter. And forget her!*"

"Shut up, Kore! You could learn from this nymph." Sara turned back to Harmonia. "But do you really want this exchange? You've trained your army for a quarter of a century. True, they are in shambles, but you still have the finest warriors in the land. You could still mount an invasion. And with your scepter, you could take everything. Are you willing to give all that away? When you are so close to succeeding? For one daughter? I don't understand."

"This is something a god will never understand."

But as Sara was about to explode once again, Harmonia repeated, "*Demeter, daughter of Cronos and Rhea, I forfeit the shield of Aidoneus, my love, in sacrifice for my daughter, Nephratee Ambrosia. As I die, my daughter shall be reborn.*"

"*No!*" Cora shouted again. "*No. I won't do it, Mother! I won't!*"

"Get out, Cora!" yelled Sara. "By the gods, I can't stand your babble! When shall you finally leave me, cursed child!"

"But you can't do this, Mother! It's my hands, not yours! You banished Uncle from ever seeing us again after the last time I saved this stupid nymph. You took Uncle away from me. Now you want me to do the same to her daughter?"

"It is the will of Imada, Kore," Sara explained. Then she raised her brow and pointed to Harmonia. "Let the nymphs rebuild and Atalans fight among themselves. Then Greece, Zeus's chosen land, can grow without interference from Atlantis."

"Now I see Zeus's plan," said Harmonia, nodding sadly.

"You see too much for any mortal!" cried Sara, whirling around. "Too much for your own good. You nymphs are not gods, any more than the dwarfs by the river or the men defending Caravia. And now, like a man, you shall die, Harmonia *Ambrosia*."

42

ENOUGH

Harmonia returned to her camp by the ruins to see her daughter's body one last time. It was cold and dark now, so she built a fire in the woods. Then she walked over to the wrapped body of her daughter and hoisted her up onto Antilus. She kissed her cold cheeks.

"You're better than me," she said, whispering in her daughter's ear. "Forgive me."

"I shall never forgive you for this," said a man's voice. It was Hades. He had startled her, and yet she didn't know where he was.

She unsheathed her sword and searched around the campfire. She looked everywhere but saw nothing until, finally, someone appeared before her. It was Hades wearing a black cloak with a hood. He looked like a shadow as he removed a silver helmet. Then he looked down on her in anger. He had been angry before, but now he seemed more furious than ever.

"Stupid nymph. What are you doing? Making deals with my sister? The same sister who ordered the death of your family? Have you forgotten what she did? Leave Nephrea. Let her die. That is the way of Imada. Bury her in Napea and stop this nonsense."

Harmonia did not sheathe her sword. Instead, she charged him. The Dark Lord fell back in shock, unsheathing his sword. Then they dueled.

"Put down your sword, woman!" Hades said.

"You destroyed me! You used me! Then when I grew too strong, you struck me down!"

"I did nothing of the sort," Hades said, parrying her strike. As renowned as Harmonia was with the sword, she found this god unbeatable. Legend said that Ares himself had learned to fight from him.

"You tricked me! Now Nephrea died because of you!"

"We already spoke of this," he said between the clashes of metal. "You never cared for her. You left her the moment she was born."

"I asked for her the minute I lost her in Caravia!"

"All you ever cared about was building your kingdom. What's gotten into you? You have my scepter. You have the continent. You can take Atlantis and then return here and take Argos from under my sister's nose. Stop this foolishness! Use what I've given you and claim your empire, Harmonia."

"Take it back!" she said, panting, out of breath. Then she hacked her sword against his again. "You can have everything! I want nothing from you. I only want my daughter!"

"ENOUGH!"

He thrust his arm into her sword. Had he been a man, the blow would have severed his limb. But as a god, and with such might and speed, he split her Mandrigelian sword in two. Then he tossed her across the campfire. She lay winded on the ground beside the flames.

Hades approached slowly.

"This is what you do," she said, looking up. "Destroyer of everything. Now, snake, finish me. Kill me here and be done with me."

"Is this what I do?" He threw his sword down. "I won't slay you. *Yet.* Your agreement is not rendered. Your daughter is not yet reborn." Then he sat leaning on his knees, staring at the fire beside her. "Call me a snake? Is that what I am? Perhaps I am a snake. Indeed, behold a viper, slithering under dirt because of sacrifices made for the only one he ever loved. No, Harmonia, I didn't come to kill you. I came to stop you."

She lowered her head and gazed in the fire too, staring at the flickering flames, ignoring him. She sat and said nothing until her breathing settled. Then she turned to him once more. She had lost her anger. Now she felt only hopelessness. Defeat.

"They say you brought us fire," Harmonia said. "You showed Prometheus. Why? Why show man fire? Why create something that always burns out? That fades to ash? Nothing ever lasts. Nothing. Neither will my kingdom. Neither shall any kingdom. Now neither will I. I did everything for Nephrea. There is no ambrosia. For my people—"

"It wasn't for your people," interrupted Hades gently, shaking his head. "As I told you, it was for you. You didn't make conquests for your people. You did it for yourself. I gave to Prometheus and Pandora so that man could live for himself. You and I are the same, Harmony. All I ever did was seek freedom in thought and action. Freedom in pleasure and freedom from pain. Something my family will never understand. Now you ask for pain, foolishly sacrificing yourself for another."

"My nymphs were created by me. Now they *are* me. But this, this I do for my daughter."

"But why?"

"She's better than us." She turned to him and gazed into his eyes. "I'm afraid, Aidoneus, I die here in your arms tomorrow."

And then Harmony saw something that she had never seen before and, perhaps, no being would ever see afterward. She didn't understand it. Nor did she believe it. It was a tear.

A single tear fell from Hades' eye. One single tear from the brute that may never be beheld again.

"I didn't betray you, Harmonia," he said with sudden red, fiery eyes. "My family did. And for that, I'll never forgive them. I will take my revenge on them, as you've taken your revenge on man."

Harmonia touched the tear on his cheek. She ran her fingers down his beard. More tears fell from her eyes too. Then Hades, the snake and leader of the Underworld, reached over and held her in his arms.

"I'm sorry, Aidoneus," she whispered in his ear. "I'm so sorry."

"I love you."

43

RISE OF THE FALLEN GODDESS

CORA DID IT. THROUGH ALL HER PAIN AND MISERY, THE YOUNG goddess Persephone touched the body of the Amazon princess Nephratee Ambrosia with both hands and healed her. And as she touched the wood nymph, she peered into her mind, just as she had done with all those she had healed.

She found that Nephrea was not broken like her mother. This woman, unlike Harmonia, desired to live. And unlike her mother, this young nymph did not carry the regrets that festered so deeply inside Harmonia.

Then Cora peered into her heart.

Cora screamed as she laid both hands on Nephrea's chest. The nymph's body shook. She placed her mouth over hers, bringing air into her lungs. And as Nephrea breathed, her heart beat again. Cora's torment was a distraction from all thoughts. But then Nephrea's thoughts grew strong once more.

The princess worried so much over her nymph sisters. She wanted to live just to help them retreat to Azure. She wanted to live again so that she could help them. To help her friends Vainya, Ilia, and Jaida. And to help her mother.

She wanted to help her mother.

Why? Such deception. Such evil. As Nephrea was near death, her greatest concern was about the welfare of a witch. Why should Nephrea care about the most despicable, fearsome Ice Queen to ever step foot on Gaia? A crystal witch who slaughtered thousands of Caravians, an army, an entire city—including women and children—with the ice magic of her scepter. A butcher that this girl actually loved. Why? This was the same mother who had abandoned her to Egypt and killed and tortured male prisoners of war. But Nephrea cared for her. Because she loved her.

No…there was something else. Something darker. Nephrea didn't know. She didn't know the terrible things her mother had wrought or the horrible person she had become. Much of it had been hidden from Nephrea through deception. The lie felt so dark in the midst of such a bright soul. Who could do such a thing? What…sort of mother?

Sara was gazing down at Cora, watching her. Cora's red eyes looked up at the grain goddess.

Was her mother full of deception too?

Everything turned dark and then images flooded Cora's mind of the nymph battle with the Mandrigel by the Blue River. The Stratos. These were no longer Nephrea's thoughts, they were buried memories of *Harmonia's* thoughts, terrible memories Harmonia had in her mind when Cora revived her. Cora watched as a stubborn nymph—perhaps the most stubborn of all time—stood up straight and strong before the gods in the face of certain death. Then she saw her mother brandish a curved dagger.

All turned dark. Except she heard screams. Screams from every nymph Harmonia had loved.

Cora let go of the nymph and looked up.

"Is it done, Kore?" Sara asked. "Have you fulfilled our agreement?"

Cora nodded. Then she said, "Shall I tell the princess what you did to her family by the river when she awakens, Mother? Or would you prefer to tell her yourself before you abandon me?"

THE END

PARTING WORDS

What did you think of *Harmonia*? By placing a book review, you can inform others of your thoughts and help spread the word about my book.

Want more? Periodically I like to send news regarding current or new projects. If you'd like to be privy, I encourage you to sign up to my email newsletter. Your information will remain private and you can cancel any time.

Sign up at www.alhawke.com or scan the following QR code:

Cora and the nymphs of Azure continue their Greek mythological mayhem in the epic fantasy "Azure Series":

- CORA: RISE OF THE FALLEN GODDESS
- AZURE BLUE
- CORAL RED
- PRINCESS SOJOURN (Prequel)
- AZURE SERIES BOXED SET

ALSO BY A.L. HAWKE

FANTASY: THE AZURE SERIES TRILOGY

- CORA: RISE OF THE FALLEN GODDESS
- AZURE BLUE
- CORAL RED
- PRINCESS SOJOURN (prequel)

URBAN FANTASY ROMANCE

- MY EVIL EYE
- THE GUARDIAN
- NECTAR OF AMBROSIA
- CORA

PARANORMAL ROMANCE

- ALONDRA
- BROOMSTICK
- WINDSTORM
- THE HAWTHORNE WITCH

- SHADES
- HAUNTING JOY
- PHANTOM MASQUERADE

SCIENCE FICTION

- CANDY SAVANT
- MOTHER SAVANT

Books available at https://alhawke.com/books

ABOUT THE AUTHOR

A.L. Hawke is the author of the bestselling Hawthorne University Witch series. The author lives in Southern California torching the midnight candle over lovers against a backdrop of machines, nymphs, magic, spice and mayhem. A.L. Hawke writes fantasy and romance spanning four thousand years, from pre-civilization to contemporary and beyond.

Visit A.L. Hawke at www.alhawke.com

Email: contact@alhawke.com

ACKNOWLEDGMENTS

Thanks to my beta readers Evan D. and George B. for helping shape this novel and reminding me of inconsistencies from the series. It's always a challenge to write a prequel *after* the creation of a trilogy. And to Stephanie Marshall Ward for another amazing thorough job at line editing my manuscript. Thanks to Alexa B. for her proofread edit. And, finally, thanks to Sean Counley who was able to bring the vision in my head onto canvas.

Believe it or not, Harmonia was once a frame narrative, a story within a story, within my earlier published novel, *CORA*. It was removed, expanded, and rewritten into this complete epic fantasy. I couldn't have published this book without all of your help!